COLD GRANITE

Stuart MacBride has scrubbed toilets offshore, flunked out of university, set up his own graphic design company, got dragged into the heady world of the internet, developed massive applications for the oil industry, drunk heaps of wine and created the perfect recipe for mushroom soup. He lives, just left of the back of beyond, in north-east Scotland with his wife Fiona and enough potatoes to feed an army. *Cold Granite* is his first novel.

Visit Stuart MacBride's website at:
www.stuartmacbride.com

STUART MACBRIDE

COLD GRANITE

HARPER

HarperCollins*Publishers*
77–85 Fulham Palace Road,
Hammersmith, London W6 8JB

www.harpercollins.co.uk

This paperback edition 2005
1

First published in Great Britain by
HarperCollins*Publishers* 2005

A catalogue record for this book
is available from the British Library

ISBN 978-0-00-785559-9

Typeset in Meridien
by Palimpsest Book Production Limited,
Grangemouth, Stirlingshire

Printed and bound in Great Britain by
Clays Limited, St Ives plc

For Fiona

ACKNOWLEDGEMENTS

This book is make-believe. What few facts there are come from people who answered a whole raft of daft questions. So, thanks to: Sgt. Jacky Davidson and Sgt. Matt MacKay of Grampian Police for help on police procedure in Aberdeen; Dr Ishbel Hunter, senior anatomical pathology technician at Aberdeen Royal Infirmary's department of pathology, for her graphic advice on post mortems; Brian Dickson, head of security at the *Press and Journal* for the guided tour.

Special thanks have to go to my agent Philip Patterson for sweet-talking the lovely Jane Johnson and Sarah Hodgson at HarperCollins into publishing this book. And to the magnificent Lucy Vanderbilt, Andrea Joyce and the rest of the team for doing such a spectacular job on the international rights. And to Andrea Best, Kelly Ragland and Saskia van Iperen for taking it on board.

Thanks to James Oswald for early input, and to Mark Hayward, my first agent at Marjacq before he left to become a tax inspector, who suggested I stop writing all that SF rubbish and try a serial killer novel instead.

Most of all, thanks to my naughty wife, Fiona: cups of tea, grammatical pointers, spelling, refusing to read the book in case she didn't like it, and putting up with me all these years.

And finally: Aberdeen's really not as bad as it sounds. Trust me . . .

1

Dead things had always been special to him. Their delicate coldness. The feel of the skin. The ripe, sweet smell as they decayed. As they returned to God.

The thing in his hands hadn't been dead for long.

Just a few hours ago it was full of life.

It was happy.

It was dirty and flawed and filthy . . .

But now it was pure.

With gentle hands he placed it reverently on top of the pile with the others. Everything in here was alive once, was busy and noisy and dirty and flawed and filthy. But now they were with God. Now they were at peace.

He closed his eyes and breathed deeply, bathing in the smells. Some fresh, some corpulent. All lovely. This was what it must smell like to be God, he thought, smiling down at his collection. This was what it must smell like to be in heaven. Surrounded by the dead.

A smile spread across his lips like fire in a burning building. He really should take his medication, but not now. Not yet.

Not when there were so many dead things to enjoy.

2

It was pissing down outside. The rain battered against the blue plastic SOC tent's walls and roof, clattering in the confined space, fighting against the constant drone of the portable generators, making conversation impossible. Not that anyone was feeling particularly chatty at a quarter past midnight on a Monday morning.

Not with David Reid lying there. On the freezing ground.

At one end of the lopsided tent a four foot stretch of ditch was cordoned off with blue police tape. Dark, greasy water glinted in the spotlights. The rest of the tent was taken up by riverbank, the winter-yellow grass beaten flat and muddy underfoot.

It was crowded in here. There were four constables from Aberdeen's Identification Bureau, wearing white paper boiler suits: two covering everything with fingerprint powder and sticky tape; one taking photographs; and the fourth videoing the crime scene for posterity. Add to that one decidedly green-looking PC, the duty doctor, a detective sergeant who'd seen better days, and the guest of honour. Little David Brookline Reid. Three months short of his fourth birthday.

They'd had to drag him out of the cold, water-filled ditch before death could be declared. Not that there was any doubt about it. The poor little sod had been dead for a long time. He was lying on his back on a square of blue plastic, exposed for all the world to see, an X-Men T-shirt pulled up around his shoulders. He wasn't wearing anything else.

The camera flashed again, burning away all detail and colour, leaving an imprint on the retina that refused to go away.

Standing in the corner Detective Sergeant Logan McRae closed his eyes and tried to think what he was going to tell little David Reid's mother. Her son had been missing for three months. Three months of not knowing. Three months of hoping her child would turn up safe and sound. While all the time he'd been lying dead in a ditch.

Logan ran a hand over his tired face, feeling the stubble scritch beneath his fingers. Christ, he could kill for a cigarette. He wasn't even supposed to be here!

He pulled out his watch and groaned, his breath coming out in a plume of white fog. Fourteen hours since he'd reported for duty yesterday morning. So much for easing back into the swing of things.

A frigid gust of wind whipped into the tent, and Logan looked up to see a sodden figure hurry in out of the rain. The pathologist had arrived.

Dr Isobel MacAlister: thirty-three, bobbed hair, brunette, five foot four. Makes little mewing noises when the inside of her thigh is nibbled. She was dressed immaculately in a fitted grey trouser suit and black overcoat, the effect only slightly spoiled by a huge pair of Wellington boots flapping about up to her knees.

She cast a professional glance around the crowded tent, freezing when her eyes locked onto Logan. An uncertain smile flickered onto her face before sliding away. Not surprising considering how much of a state he must look. Unshaven, bags under the eyes, dark brown hair which was wild, unkempt and frizzy from the rain.

Isobel opened her mouth and closed it again.

Rain hammered on the tent's roof, the camera clacked and whined as the flash came back up to speed, the generators growled. But the silence was deafening.

It was the duty doctor who broke the spell. 'Aw shite!' He stood on one leg, shaking a water-logged shoe.

Isobel put on her professional face.

'Has death been declared?' she asked, shouting to be heard over the din.

Logan sighed. The moment had passed.

The duty doctor stifled a yawn and pointed at the small, bloated corpse in the middle of the tent. 'Aye, he's dead all right.' He stuffed his hands deep in his pockets and gave a loud sniff. 'If y'want my opinion: he's been dead for a good wee whilie. Least two months.'

Isobel nodded and placed her medical bag on the groundsheet next to the body. 'You're probably right,' she said, squatting down and peering at the dead child.

The doctor rocked back and forth for a while, squelching in the mud, as Isobel snapped on a pair of latex gloves and started unpacking her instruments. 'Aye, well,' he said, 'give us a shout if you need anything, OK?'

Isobel promised she would and the duty doctor gave a small bow and excused himself, squeezing out past Logan into the rain-soaked night.

Logan looked down on the top of Isobel's head, thinking of all the things he'd planned to say the first time he saw her again. To make it all right again. To fix what fell apart the day Angus Robertson got sent down for thirty to life. But whenever Logan pictured this moment there wasn't a murdered three-year-old lying on the ground between them. It kind of put a damper on things.

So instead he said, 'Can you give me a time of death?'

She looked up from the decaying body and blushed slightly. 'Doc Wilson wasn't far off,' she said, not meeting his eyes. 'Two, maybe three months. I'll know better when I do the post mortem. You got an ID?'

'David Reid. He's three.' Logan sighed. 'Been on the Misper list since August.'

'Poor wee sod.' Isobel pulled a slim headset out of her bag, slipped it over her hair and checked that the microphone was working. She inserted a fresh tape into her dictaphone and began her examination of little David Reid.

Half past one in the morning and there was still no sign of the rain letting up. DS Logan McRae stood in the lee of a twisted oak, using the tree as a windbreak, and watched as the photographer's flash filled the SOC tent with staccato lightning. Every time the flash went off, the figures within hurled silhouettes against the blue plastic like a grizzly shadow play.

Four high-powered spotlights sizzled in the torrential downpour, bathing the area around the tent with harsh white light while the generators chugged away in a haze of blue diesel smoke. Cold rain hissing on the hot metal. Outside that circle of light it was pitch black.

Two of the spotlights were trained on the ditch where it emerged from beneath the SOC tent. The late November rains had filled the ditch to overflowing and grim-faced police divers, dressed in dark-blue neoprene dry-suits, groped around in the waist-high water. A pair of bodies from the

Identification Bureau were trying to swear a second tent into place over the divers, fighting a losing battle against the wind and rain as they tried to preserve any forensic evidence from the storm.

Less than eight feet away, the River Don surged past, silent, swollen and dark. Flecks of light danced across its surface: the spotlights reflecting back off the black water, their shapes shattering and reforming beneath the torrential rain. If there was one thing Aberdeen did properly, it was rain.

The river had already broken its banks in a dozen places upstream, flooding the surrounding countryside, turning fields into lakes. Down here it was less than a mile to the North Sea and the water was moving fast.

On the other side of the river the tower blocks of Hayton rose behind a screen of bare trees. Five featureless rectangles punctuated with cold-yellow lights, sheets of rain making them swim in and out of view. It was a horrible night.

A hastily cobbled-together search team was picking its way carefully along the riverbank by torchlight, working out in both directions, even though it was far too dark to find anything. It would look good on the morning news.

Sniffing, Logan dug his hands deeper into his pockets and turned to look up the hill, towards the blistering white television camera lights. They'd gathered not long after Logan had arrived, hungry for a glimpse of dead meat. To begin with it had just been the local press, shouting questions at anyone in a police uniform; then the big boys had arrived. The BBC and ITV, with their cameras and serious-faced presenters.

Grampian Police had issued the standard holding statement, which had been completely devoid of any detail whatsoever. So God only knew what they were finding to talk about up there.

Logan turned his back on them and watched the bobbing torches of the search party as they struggled along in the dark.

This shouldn't have been his case. Not on his first day back. But the rest of Aberdeen's CID were either off on a training course or off getting pissed at someone's retirement bash. There wasn't even a detective inspector on the scene! DI McPherson, who was supposed to be easing Logan back into the swing of things, was busy getting his head stitched back together after someone had tried to take it off with a kitchen knife. So here was Detective Sergeant Logan McRae, heading up a major murder enquiry and praying to God he didn't screw it up before he could hand it over to someone else. Welcome back.

The green-faced PC lurched out of the SOC tent and joined Logan under the twisted tree, squelching all the way. He looked like Logan felt. Only worse.

'Jesus.' The PC shivered and jammed a cigarette in his face as if it was the only thing keeping his head from unravelling. After a moment's thought he offered one to the DS standing next to him, but Logan declined.

The PC shrugged and fumbled a lighter out of the breast pocket of his uniform, setting the cigarette glowing like a hot coal in the darkness. 'Some fuckin' sight for your first day back, eh, sir?'

A plume of white smoke blossomed into the night and Logan took a deep breath, dragging it into his scarred lungs before the wind could whip it away.

'What's Iso . . .' He stopped himself. 'What's Dr MacAlister saying?'

The SOC tent flashed again, the shadow puppets caught in frozen motion.

'No much more than the duty doc, sir. Poor wee bastard was strangled with somethin'. She says the other stuff probably happened later.'

Logan closed his eyes and tried not to picture the child's swollen body.

'Aye.' The PC nodded wisely, the red-hot tip of his fag bobbing up and down in the darkness. 'At least he was dead when it happened. That's something to be grateful for.'

Fifteen Concraig Circle was in one of the newer sections of Kingswells, a suburb just five minutes outside Aberdeen proper, and creeping closer every year. The houses here were billed as 'individually-crafted executive villas', but they looked as if they'd been thrown together by someone with a job lot of yellow brick and no imagination.

Number fifteen was near the start of a winding cul-de-sac, the gardens still too new to be much more than rectangles of grass with stumpy bushes round the edges. Many of the plants still sported tags from the garden centre. The downstairs lights were on, shining through the closed Venetian blinds, even though it was nearly two in the morning.

DS Logan McRae sat in the passenger seat of the CID pool car and sighed. Like it or not, he was currently the senior investigating officer and that meant he had to tell David Reid's mother that her son was dead. But he'd brought along a Family Liaison Officer and a spare WPC to help shoulder the load. At least he wouldn't have to do this on his own.

'Come on then,' he said at last. 'No point putting it off any longer.'

The front door was opened by a heavy-set man in his mid-fifties with a brick-red face, moustache and hostile, bloodshot, eyes. He took one look at WPC Watson's uniform and said, ''Bout bloody time you bastards showed up!' Arms crossed, not moving.

Logan closed his mouth. This wasn't what he'd been expecting. 'I need to speak to Miss Reid.'

'Aye? Well you're too bloody late! The bloody papers were on fifteen minutes ago looking for a bloody quote!' His voice rose with each word

11

until he was bellowing in Logan's face. 'You should have told us first!' He slammed a fist against his own chest. 'We're his bloody family!'

Logan winced. How the hell had the media found out that David Reid's body had been discovered? As if the family wasn't in enough pain.

'I'm sorry, Mr . . . ?'

'Reid. Charles Reid.' The man re-crossed his arms and inflated himself even further. 'Her dad.'

'Mr Reid, I don't know how the press found out about this. But I promise you: whoever's responsible is going to get their backside kicked from here to Stonehaven.' Logan paused. 'And I know that doesn't make everything OK, but right now I need to speak to David's mother.'

Her father glowered down at Logan from the top step. Finally he stepped aside and Logan could see through a glazed door into a small lounge, painted a cheerful yellow. In the middle of a bright-red sofa were two women: one looking like a floral-print battleship, the other like a zombie.

The younger woman didn't look up as the police walked into the living room. Just sat staring blankly at the television, watching Dumbo being tormented by the clowns. Logan looked expectantly at the Family Liaison Officer, but she was doing her damnedest not to make any sort of eye-contact with him.

Logan took a deep breath. 'Miss Reid?'

No reaction.

Logan sank down on his haunches in front of the sofa, blocking her view of the television. She stared right through him as if he wasn't even there.

'Miss Reid? Alice?'

She didn't move, but the older woman scowled and bared her teeth. Her eyes were puffy and red, tears glistening on her round cheeks and jowls. 'How dare you!' she snarled. 'You useless bunch of sh—'

'Sheila!' The older man stepped forward and she shut up.

Logan turned his attention back to the comatose figure on the couch. 'Alice,' he said, 'we've found David.'

At the sound of her son's name there was a flicker of life in her eyes. 'David?' Her mouth barely moved, the word more breathed than spoken.

'I'm sorry, Alice. He's dead.'

'David . . .'

'He was murdered.'

There was a moment's silence and then her father exploded. 'Fuckin' bastard! Fuckin', fuckin' bastard! He was three!'

'I'm sorry.' It was all Logan could think of to say.

'You're sorry? You're *sorry*?' Mr Reid rounded on him, his face scarlet. 'If you bunch of useless bastards had got your fingers out of your arses and found him when he went missing, he'd no be dead! Three months!'

The Family Liaison Officer made flapping, placatory gestures, but Mr Reid ignored her. He was trembling with rage, tears sparking in his eyes. 'Three! Bloody! Months!'

Logan raised his hands.

'Look, Mr Reid, calm down, OK? I know you're upset—'

The punch shouldn't have caught Logan by surprise, but it did. A fist like a breezeblock slammed into his stomach, tearing at the scar tissue, making fire rip through his innards. He opened his mouth to scream, but there was no breath left in his lungs.

Logan's knees buckled. A rough hand grabbed the front of his jacket, pulling him forward, keeping him on his feet as another fist was drawn back, ready to turn him into a bloody pulp.

WPC Watson shouted something, but Logan wasn't listening. There was a crashing sound and the hand holding him let go. Logan collapsed onto the carpet, curling into a ball around his burning stomach. An angry shout, followed by WPC Watson yelling that she was going to break Mr Reid's arm if he didn't calm down.

Mr Reid cried out in pain.

The floral battleship screamed, 'Charlie! Stop it for God's sake!'

WPC Watson said something highly unprofessional and after that everyone was silent.

The patrol car flashed across Anderson Drive, siren blaring. Logan sat in the passenger seat, his face

14

grey and clammy, hands wrapped around his stomach, teeth gritted at every bump and pot-hole.

Mr Charles Reid was strapped in the back, seat-belt done up over his handcuffed wrists. He looked scared.

'Oh God, I'm sorry! Oh God, I'm so sorry!'

WPC Watson screeched the car to a halt in front of Accident and Emergency. In one of the spots marked 'AMBULANCES ONLY'. She helped Logan out of the car as if he was made of glass, pausing only to tell Mr Reid, 'Keep your damn arse in that car till I come back or I'll have your guts for garters!' Just to be safe she plipped on the alarm, locking him in the car.

They made it all the way to the reception area before Logan passed out.

3

Grampian Police Headquarters. The building was grey concrete and glass, a seven-storey tower block, topped by emergency broadcast systems and radio antennas, tucked out of the way at the end of Queen Street, right next door to the Sheriff Court, opposite the grey, granite wedding cake of Marischal College and just around the corner from the Arts Centre, a mock-Roman temple thrown up by the Victorians. Force HQ was a testament to the developer's love of ugly buildings. But it was a stone's throw from the Town House, council chambers and about a dozen pubs.

Pubs, churches and rain. Three things Aberdeen had in abundance.

The sky above was dark and low, the sodium glow of the streetlights giving the early morning a jaundiced feel, as if the streets were unwell. Last night's torrential downpour hadn't let up at all, the heavy raindrops bouncing back off the slick pavements. The drains were already overflowing.

Buses grumbled their way along the road, sending up fountains of spray for anyone daft enough to be out on a day like this.

Cursing, Logan gripped his overcoat closed with one hand and wished a fiery death on all bus-driving bastards. He'd had a bloody awful night: a punch in the guts followed by three hours being prodded and poked by doctors at Accident and Emergency. They'd finally turfed him out into the cold, driving rain at quarter past five this morning with a bottle of painkillers and an elasticated bandage.

He'd managed a whole hour's sleep.

Logan squelched into the Queen Street lobby, and stood dripping at the curved reception desk. His flat was less than two minutes' walk away, but he was still soaking.

'Good morning, sir,' said a pointy-faced desk sergeant Logan didn't recognize, from behind the glass partition. 'Can I help?' He put on his polite smile and Logan sighed.

'Morning, Sergeant,' he said. 'I was supposed to be working with DI McPherson—'

The polite smile vanished as soon as the desk sergeant realized Logan wasn't a member of the public.

'You'll have a hard job: knife in the head.' He made stabbing motions and Logan tried not to flinch. 'Are you . . .' He consulted a pad on the desk, flipping the pages back and forward until he found what he was looking for. 'Detective Sergeant McRae?'

Logan admitted that he was, flashing his warrant card to prove it.

'Aye,' said the desk sergeant, his face not moving a muscle. 'Very pretty. You're to report to DI Insch. He's giving a briefing . . .' He glanced up at the clock. 'Five minutes ago.' The smile flashed again. 'He doesn't like it when people are late.'

Logan was twelve minutes late for the seven-thirty briefing. The room was filled with serious-looking police men and women, and all of them snapped around to look at him as he crept around the door, closing it gently behind him. At the front of the room DI Insch – a large, bald man in a brand new suit – stopped in mid-sentence and scowled as Logan limped his way across to an empty seat in the front row.

'As I was saying,' the inspector glowered at Logan, 'the preliminary pathologist's report puts the time of death around three months ago. Three months is a long time for forensic evidence to hang around a crime scene, especially in the pissing rain. But that doesn't mean we're not going to look for it. Fingertip search: half-mile radius from where the body was found.'

A groan went up from the inspector's audience. It was a lot of ground to cover and there was no chance of them finding anything. Not after three months. And it was still chucking it down outside. This was going to be a long, wet, shitty job.

'I know it's a pain in the arse,' said DI Insch, digging in his pocket for a jelly baby. He examined it, blew the fluff off, and popped it in his mouth. 'But I don't care. This is a three-year-old boy we're talking about. We will catch the bastard that did it. No fuck-ups. Understand?'

He paused, challenging the room to say anything to the contrary.

'Good. And while we're on the subject of fucking up: someone tipped off the *Press and Journal* last night that we'd found David Reid's body.' He held up a copy of that morning's paper. The headline screamed: 'MURDERED TODDLER FOUND!'. The front page was split between a photograph of David Reid's smiling face and one of the SOC tent, lit up from within by the police photographer's flash. The tent's occupants were silhouetted against the plastic walls.

'They called the mother for a quote—' his voice rose and his expression darkened '—before we could tell the poor cow her son was dead!'

Insch slammed the paper down on top of the desk. Angry murmurs came from the crowd.

'You can all expect a visit from Professional Standards over the next couple of days. But believe me,' said DI Insch, slowly and deliberately, 'their witch-hunt is going to look like a teddy bears' picnic compared to mine. When I find out who did this I will screw them to the ceiling by their testicles!'

He took a moment to scowl at everyone.

'Right, today's assignments.' The inspector perched a buttock on the edge of the desk and read out the names: who was going door-to-door, who was searching the riverbank, who was staying behind to answer the phones. The only name he didn't read out was that of Detective Sergeant Logan McRae.

'And before you go,' said Insch, raising his arms as if he was about to bless his congregation, 'I would like to remind you that tickets for this year's pantomime are now on sale at the front desk. Make sure you buy one!'

The troops shuffled out, those on telephone-answering duty lording it over the poor sods who'd spend the rest of the day trudging through the rain. Logan hovered at the back of the queue, hoping to recognize someone. A year off on the sick and there wasn't a single face he could put a name to.

The inspector spotted him loitering and called him over.

'What happened last night?' he asked as the last PC departed, leaving them alone in the briefing room.

Logan pulled out his notebook and began to read: 'The body was discovered at ten-fifteen p.m., by one Duncan Nicholson—'

'Not what I meant.' DI Insch settled on the edge of the desk and crossed his arms. With his large build, bald head and new suit, he looked like a well-dressed Buddha. Only not so friendly.

'WPC Watson dropped you off at Accident and Emergency back of two this morning. Less than twenty-four hours on the job and you've already spent a night in hospital. We've got David Reid's grandfather in a holding cell on an assault charge. And then, to cap it all off, you limp into my briefing. Late.'

Logan shifted uncomfortably. 'Well, sir, Mr Reid was agitated. It wasn't really his fault, if the *Journal* hadn't called he—'

DI Insch cut him off. 'You're supposed to be working for DI McPherson.'

'Err . . . Yes.'

Insch nodded sagely and dragged another jelly baby out of his pocket, popping it in his mouth, fluff and all, chewing around the words. 'Not any more. While McPherson's getting his head stitched back together, you're mine.'

Logan tried not to let his disappointment show. McPherson had been his boss for two years, before Angus Robertson had made a pincushion out of Logan's innards with a six-inch hunting knife. Logan liked McPherson. Everyone he knew worked for McPherson.

All he knew about DI Insch was that he didn't suffer idiots gladly. And the inspector thought everyone was an idiot.

Insch settled back on his haunches and looked Logan up and down. 'Are you going to drop down dead on me, Sergeant?'

'Not if I can help it, sir.'

21

Insch nodded, his large face closed and distant. An uncomfortable silence grew between them. It was one of DI Insch's trademarks. Leave a large enough gap in an interrogation and sooner or later the suspect was going to say something, anything, to fill it. It was amazing the things people let fall out of their mouths. Things they never meant to say. Things they really, really didn't want DI Insch to know.

This time Logan kept his mouth shut.

Eventually the inspector nodded. 'I've read your file. McPherson thinks you're not an arse-hole, so I'm going to give you the benefit of the doubt. But if you end up in A&E like that again, you're out. Understood?'

'Yes, sir. Thank you, sir.'

'Right. Your acclimatization period is hereby cancelled. I can't be arsed with all that pussy-footing-around bollocks. You're either up to the job, or you're not. Post mortem's in fifteen minutes. Be there.'

He levered himself off the desk and patted his pockets, looking for more jelly babies.

'I've got a command meeting from eight fifteen till eleven-thirty, so you'll have to give me the details when I get back.'

Logan looked at the door and then back again.

'Something on your mind, Sergeant?'

Logan lied and said no.

'Good. Given your little trip to A&E last night, I'm making WPC Watson your guardian angel.

She'll be coming back in at ten. Do not let me catch you without her. This is not negotiable.'

'Yes, sir.' Great, he was getting a babysitter.

'Now get going.'

Logan was almost out the door before Insch added: 'And try not to piss Watson off. They don't call her "Ball Breaker" for nothing.'

Grampian Police HQ was big enough to boast its own morgue, situated in the basement, just far enough from the staff canteen not to put people off their soup. It was a large, white, spotless room, with chiller cabinets for bodies along one wall, the floor tiles squeaky under Logan's shoes as he pushed through the double doors. An antiseptic reek filled the cold room, almost masking the odour of death. It was a strange mix of smells. A fragrance Logan had grown to associate with the woman standing on her own by a dissecting table.

Dr Isobel MacAlister was dressed in her cutting gear: pastel-green surgeon's robes and a red rubber apron over the top, her short hair hidden beneath a surgical cap. She wasn't wearing a scrap of make-up, in case it contaminated the body, and as she looked up to see who was squeaking across her nice clean morgue Logan saw her eyes widen.

He stopped and tried a smile. 'Hi.'

She raised a hand and almost waved. 'Hello . . .' Her eyes darted back to the little naked body

23

stretched out on the dissecting table. Three-year-old David Reid. 'We've not started yet. Are you attending?'

Logan nodded and cleared his throat. 'I meant to ask you last night,' he said. 'How have you been?'

She didn't meet his eyes, just re-ordered the gleaming row of surgical instruments on their tray. The stainless steel flashing in the overhead lights. 'Oh . . .' she sighed and shrugged. 'You know.' Her hands came to rest on a scalpel, the shiny metal contrasting with her matt latex gloves. 'How about you?'

Logan shrugged too. 'Much the same.'

The silence was excruciating.

'Isobel, I . . .'

The double doors opened again and in rushed Isobel's assistant Brian, trailing the deputy pathologist and Procurator Fiscal behind him. 'Sorry we're late. You know what these fatal accident enquiries are like, *so* much paperwork!' said Brian, brushing his floppy hair out of his eyes. He flashed an ingratiating smile at Logan. 'Hello, Sergeant, nice to see you again!' He stopped and shook Logan's hand before scurrying off to strap on a red rubber apron of his own. The deputy pathologist and the PF acknowledged Logan with a nod, apologized to Isobel and settled down to watch her work. Isobel would be the one doing all the cutting; the other pathologist, an overweight man in his early fifties with a bald head and hairy ears, was only here to make sure Isobel's findings were correct, as required by Scottish law. Not that he would have dared say anything to her face. And anyway, she was always right.

'Well,' said Isobel, 'we'd better get started.' She pulled on her headset, checked the microphone and whisked through the preliminaries.

As Logan watched, she slowly picked her way over David Reid's remains. Three months in a ditch, covered with an old sheet of chipboard, had turned his skin almost black. His whole body was swollen like a balloon as decomposition worked its corpulent magic. Little patches of white speckled the bloated skin like freckles where fungal growths had taken hold. The smell was bad, but Logan knew it was going to get a lot worse.

A small stainless steel tray sat next to the tiny body and Isobel dropped any debris she found into it. Blades of grass, bits of moss, scraps of paper. Anything the corpse had picked up since death. Maybe something that would help them identify David Reid's killer.

'Oh ho . . .' said Isobel, peering into the dead child's frozen scream. 'Looks like we have an insect guest.' Gently, she delved between David's teeth with a pair of tweezers and for a horrible moment Logan thought she was going to pull out a Death's Head Moth. But the tweezers emerged clutching a wriggling woodlouse.

Isobel held the slate-grey bug up to the light, watching its legs thrashing in the air.

'Probably crawled in there looking for a bite to eat,' she said. 'Don't suppose it'll tell us anything, but better safe than sorry.' She dropped the insect into a small phial of preserving fluid.

Logan stood in silence, watching the woodlouse slowly drown.

An hour and a half later they were standing at the coffee machine on the ground floor, while Isobel's floppy-haired assistant stitched David Reid back together.

Logan was feeling distinctly unwell. Watching an ex-girlfriend turn a three-year-old child inside out on a dissecting table wasn't something he'd ever done before. The thought of those hands, so calm and efficient, cutting, extracting and measuring . . . Handing Brian little plastic phials with chunks and slices of internal organs to bag and tag . . . He shuddered and Isobel stopped talking to ask if he was all right.

'Just a bit of a cold.' He forced a smile. 'You were saying?'

'Death was caused by ligature strangulation. Something thin and smooth, like an electrical cable. There's extensive bruising to the back, between the shoulders, and lacerations to the forehead, nose and cheeks. I'd say your attacker forced the child to the ground and knelt on his back while he strangled him.' Her voice was businesslike, as if cutting up children was something she did every day. For the first time, Logan realized that it probably was. 'There wasn't any evidence of seminal fluid, but after all this time . . .' she shrugged. 'However, the tearing of the anus is indicative of penetration.'

Logan grimaced and poured his plastic cup of hot brown liquid into the bin.

She frowned at him. 'If it's any consolation the damage was post mortem. The child was dead when it happened.'

'Any chance of DNA?'

'Unlikely. The internal damage isn't consistent with something flexible. I'd say it's more likely to be a foreign object than the attacker's penis. Maybe a broom handle?'

Logan closed his eyes and swore. Isobel just shrugged.

'Sorry,' she said. 'David's genitals were removed by what looks like a pair of secateurs, curved blade, some time after death. Long enough for the blood to have clotted. Probably long enough for rigor mortis to have set in.'

They stood in silence for a moment, not looking at each other.

Isobel twisted her empty plastic cup round in her hands. 'I . . . I'm sorry . . .' She stopped and twisted the cup back the other way.

Logan nodded. 'Me too,' he said and walked away.

4

WPC Watson was waiting for him at the front desk. She was muffled up to the ears in a heavy black police-issue jacket, the waterproof fabric slick and glistening with raindrops. Her hair was tucked into a tight bun under her peaked cap; her nose was Belisha-beacon red.

She smiled at him as he approached, hands in pockets, mind on the post mortem.

'Morning, sir. How's the stomach?'

Logan forced a smile, his nostrils still full of dead child. 'Not bad. You?'

She shrugged. 'Glad to be back on days again.' She looked around the empty reception area. 'So what's the plan?'

Logan checked his watch. It was going on for ten. An hour and a half to kill before Insch got out of his meeting.

'Fancy a trip?'

They signed for a CID pool car. WPC Watson drove the rusty blue Vauxhall while Logan sat in the passenger seat, looking out at the downpour. They had just enough time to nip across town to the Bridge of Don, where the search teams would be trudging through the rain and mud, looking for evidence that probably wasn't even there.

A bendy bus rumbled across the road in front of them, sending up a flurry of spray, adverts for Christmas shopping in the west end of town splattered all over it.

Watson had the wipers going full tilt, the wheek-whonk of rubber on the windscreen sounding over the roar of the blowers. Neither of them had said a word since they'd left Force HQ.

'I told the desk sergeant to let Charles Reid off with a warning,' Logan said at last.

WPC Watson nodded. 'Thought you would.' She slid the car out into the junction behind an expensive-looking four-by-four.

'It wasn't really his fault.'

Watson shrugged. 'Not my call, sir. You're the one he nearly killed.'

The four-wheel-drive, all-terrain vehicle – which probably never had to deal with anything more off road than the potholes in Holburn Street – suddenly decided to indicate right, stopping dead in the middle of the junction. Watson swore and tried to find a space in the stream of traffic flowing past on the inside.

'Bloody male drivers,' she muttered before remembering Logan was in the car. 'Sorry sir.'

'Don't worry about it . . .' He drifted back into

silence, thinking about Charles Reid and the trip to Aberdeen Royal Infirmary last night. It hadn't really been Charles Reid's fault. Someone phones your daughter up and asks how she feels about her three-year-old son's murdered body turning up in a ditch. Not surprising he took a swing at the first target that presented itself. Whoever sold the story to the P&J: they were to blame.

'Change of plan,' he said. 'Let's see if we can't find ourselves a slimy journalist.'

'THE PRESS AND JOURNAL. LOCAL NEWS SINCE 1748'. That's what it said at the top of every edition. But the building the paper shared with its sister publication, the *Evening Express*, looked a lot less venerable. It was a low, two-storey concrete-and-glass monstrosity just off the Lang Stracht, squatting behind a high, chainlink fence like a sulking Rottweiler. There being no access from the main road, WPC Watson drove them in through a tatty-looking industrial estate consisting of crowded car showrooms and double parking. The security guard took one look at Watson's uniform and raised the barrier, smiling a gap-toothed smile as he waved them through.

'ABERDEEN JOURNALS LTD' was written in gold lettering on polished granite next to the reception's revolving door, right above a brass plaque proclaiming the paper's history. 'FOUNDED BY JAMES CHALMERS IN 1748 . . .' blah blah blah. Logan didn't bother to read the rest.

The pale lilac walls of the reception area were bare. Only a carved wooden plaque, commemorating the paper's employees lost in World War Two, broke the monotony. Logan had been expecting something a bit more newspaper-ish: framed front pages, awards, photographs of the journalists. Instead it looked as if the paper had only just moved in and hadn't got around to decorating yet.

Weedy pot plants sat on the violently-coloured floor: big linoleum squares of bright blue fake marble, set in a gold-and-pink grid.

The receptionist didn't look much better: pink eyes, lank blonde hair. She reeked of mentholated cough sweets. Peering blearily up at them, she honked her nose on a scabby hanky.

'Welcome to Aberdeen Journals,' she said with zero enthusiasm. 'How can I be of assistance?'

Logan dragged out his warrant card and held it under her runny nose. 'Detective Sergeant McRae. I'd like to speak to whoever phoned the home of Alice Reid last night.'

The receptionist looked at his identification, looked at him, looked at WPC Watson and sighed. 'No idea.' She paused for a sniff. 'I'm only here Mondays and Wednesdays.'

'Well, who would know?'

The receptionist just shrugged and sniffed again.

WPC Watson dug a copy of the morning's paper out of a display rack and slapped it down on the reception desk. 'MURDERED TODDLER FOUND!' She

31

stabbed her finger at the words: 'BY COLIN MILLER'.

'How about him?' she asked.

The receptionist took the paper and squinted her puffy eyes at the by-line. Her face suddenly turned down at the edges. 'Oh . . . him.'

Scowling, she jabbed at the switchboard. A woman's voice boomed out of her speakerphone: '*Aye?*' and she grabbed the phone from its cradle. Her accent suddenly switched from bunged-up polite to bunged-up broad Aberdonian.

'Lesley? Aye, it's Sharon . . . Lesley, is God's Gift in?' Pause. 'Aye, it's the police . . . I dinna ken, hang oan.'

She stuck a hand over the mouthpiece and looked up, hopefully, at Logan. 'Are you going to arrest him?' she asked, all polite again.

Logan opened his mouth and shut it again. 'We just want to ask him a couple of questions,' he said at last.

'Oh.' Sharon looked crestfallen. 'No,' she said into the phone again. 'The wee shite's no gettin' banged up.' She nodded a couple of times then grinned broadly. 'I'll ask.' She fluttered her eyelashes and pouted at Logan, doing her best to look seductive. It was an uphill struggle with a flaky red nose, but she did her best. 'If you're not going to arrest him, any chance of a little police brutality?'

WPC Watson winked conspiratorially. 'See what we can do. Where is he?'

The receptionist pointed at a security door off

32

to the left. 'Don't be afraid to cripple him.' She grinned and buzzed them through.

The newsroom was like a carpeted warehouse, all open plan and suspended ceiling tiles. There must have been a couple of hundred desks in here, all clumped together in little cliques: News Desk, Features, Editorial, Page Layout . . . The walls were the same pale lilac as reception and just as bare. There weren't any partitions and the desktops spilled into one another. Piles of paper, yellow Post-its and scribbled notes oozing from one desk to the next like a slow-motion avalanche.

Computer monitors flickered beneath the overhead lighting, their owners hunched over keyboards, turning out tomorrow's news. Apart from the ever-present hum of the computers and the whirr of the photocopier it was eerily quiet.

Logan grabbed the first person he could find: an older man in saggy brown corduroy trousers and a stained cream shirt. He was wearing a tie that sported at least three of the things he'd had for breakfast. The top of his head had said goodbye to his hair long ago, but a trapdoor of thin strands was stretched over the shiny expanse. He wasn't kidding anyone but himself.

'We're looking for Colin Miller,' said Logan, flipping out his warrant card.

The man raised an eyebrow. 'Oh aye?' he said. 'You goin' to arrest him?'

Logan slipped his identification back in his

pocket. 'Wasn't intending to, but I'm starting to think about it. Why?'

The old reporter hitched up his trousers and beamed innocently at Logan. 'No reason.'

Pause, two, three, four . . .

'OK,' said Logan, 'so where is he?'

The old man winked at him, jerking his head towards the toilets. 'I have no idea where he is, officer,' he said slowly, one innuendo-laden word after another. He finished off with another couple of significant glances towards the gents and a grin.

Logan nodded. 'Thanks, you've been a great help.'

'No I haven't,' said the reporter. 'I've been "vague and rambling" like the "senile old fart" I am.'

As he ambled off back to his desk, Logan and WPC Watson made a beeline for the toilets. To Logan's surprise Watson stormed straight into the gents. Shaking his head, he followed her into the black-and-white-tiled interior.

Her shout of 'Colin Miller?' produced assorted journalistic shrieks as full-grown men scrabbled at their flies and scurried out of the toilets. Finally only one man was left: short, heavily-built, wearing an expensive-looking dark-grey suit. Broad-shouldered, with a pristine haircut, he whistled tunelessly at the urinals, rocking back and forth.

Watson looked him up and down. 'Colin Miller?' she asked.

He glanced over his shoulder, a nonchalant smile on his lips. 'You want tae help me shake this?' he asked with a wink, Glaswegian accent ringing out loud and proud. 'Ma doctor says I'm no to lift anythin' heavy . . .'

She scowled and told him exactly what he could do with his offer.

Logan stepped between them before Watson could demonstrate why she was called 'Ball Breaker'.

The reporter winked, shoogled about a little, then turned from the urinal, zipping himself up, gold signet rings sparkling on almost every finger. A gold chain hung around his neck, lying over the silk shirt and tie.

'Mr Miller?' asked Logan.

'Aye, you wantin' an autograph?' He strutted his way to the sink, hitching up his sleeves slightly as he did so, exposing something chunky and gold on his right wrist and a watch big enough to sleep four on the left. It wasn't surprising the man was well-muscled: he had to be to cart about all that jewellery.

'We want to talk to you about David Reid, the three-year-old who—'

'I know who he is,' said Miller, turning on the taps. 'I did a front page spread on the poor wee sod.' He grinned and pumped soap into his hands. 'Three thousand words of pure journalistic gold. Tell ya, kiddie murders: pure gold, so they are. Sick bastard kills some poor kid and suddenly everyone's dyin' tae read about the wee dead body over their cornflakes. Fuckin' unbelievable.'

Logan resisted the urge to grab Miller by the scruff of the neck and smash his face into a urinal. 'You called the family last night,' he said instead, fists jammed deep in his pockets. 'Who told you we'd found him?'

Miller smiled at Logan's reflection in the mirror above the sink. 'Didn't take a genius, Inspector . . . ?'

'Sergeant,' said Logan. 'Detective Sergeant McRae.'

The journalist shrugged and wriggled his hands under the hand-drier. 'Only a DS, eh?' he had to shout over the roar of warm air. 'Never mind. You help me catch this sick bastard and I'll see you make DI.'

'Help "you" catch . . .' Logan screwed his eyes shut and was assailed by visions of Miller's broken nose bleeding into urinal cakes. 'Who told you we'd found David Reid?' he asked through gritted teeth.

Click. The drier fell silent.

'Told you: didn't take a genius. You found a wee dead kiddie, who else could it have been?'

'We didn't tell anyone the body was a child!'

'No? Ah well, must've been a coincidence then.'

Logan scowled. 'Who told you?'

Miller smiled and shot his cuffs, making sure there was a fashionable inch of starched white visible at the end of both sleeves.

'You never heard of journalistic immunity? I don't have tae reveal my sources. And you can't make me!' He paused. 'Mind you, if the tasty WPC wants tae do a Mata Hari I might be persuaded . . . Gotta love a woman in uniform!'

Watson snarled and pulled out her collapsible truncheon.

The door to the gents burst open, breaking the moment. A large woman with lots of curly dark-brown hair stormed into the toilets, hands on hips and fire in her eyes. 'What the hell is going on here?' she said, glowering at Logan and Watson. 'I've got half the news desk out there with piss all down the front of their trousers.' She rounded on Miller before anyone could respond. 'And what the hell do you think you're still doing here? They're giving a press conference on the dead kid in half an hour! The tabloids are going to be all over the damn thing. This is our bloody story and I want it to stay that way!'

'Mr Miller is assisting us with our enquiries,' said Logan. 'I want to know who told him we'd found—'

'You arresting him?'

Logan only paused for a second, but it was long enough.

'Didn't think so.' She stabbed a finger at Miller. 'You! Get your arse in gear. I'm not paying you to chat up WPCs in the bogs!'

Miller smiled and saluted the glowering woman.

'You got it, chief!' he said and winked at Logan. 'Gotta go. Duty calls and all that.'

He took a step towards the door, but WPC Watson barred his path. 'Sir?' She fingered her truncheon, desperate for an excuse to use it on Miller's head.

Logan looked from the smug journalist to Watson and back again. 'Let him go,' he said at last. 'We'll talk later, Mr Miller.'

The journalist grinned. 'Count on it.' He made his right hand into a gun and fired it at WPC Watson. 'Catch ya later, investigator.'

Thankfully she didn't reply.

Back in the car park, WPC Watson stomped through the rain to their Vauxhall, wrenched the car's door open, hurled her hat in the back seat, thudded in behind the steering wheel, slammed the door shut again, and swore.

Logan had to admit she had a point. There was no way Miller was going to volunteer his source. And his editor, the curly-haired harridan, had made it perfectly clear, in a ten-minute tirade, that there was no way in hell she was going to order him to do so. There was about as much chance of that happening as Aberdeen Football Club winning the Premier League.

A knock on the passenger window made Logan jump and a large, smiling face beamed in at him from the rain, a copy of the *Evening Express* held over his head to keep his thin comb-over dry. It was the reporter who 'hadn't' told them the repulsive Mr Miller was hiding in the men's toilets.

'You're Logan McRae!' said the man. 'See? I knew I recognized you!'

'Oh aye?' Logan shrank back in his seat.

The man in the saggy, faded-brown corduroys nodded happily. 'I did a story, what wis it: a year ago? "Police Hero Stabbed in Showdown with Mastrick Monster!"' He grinned. 'Shite, that wis a damn good story. Nice headline too. Shame "Police Hero" didn't alliterate . . .' A shrug. Then he stuck his hand in through the open car window. 'Martin Leslie, Features Desk.'

Logan shook it, feeling more and more uncomfortable with every second.

'Jesus, Logan McRae . . .' said the reporter. 'You a DI yet?'

Logan said no, he was still a DS, and the older man looked outraged. 'You're kidding! Bastards! You deserved it! That Angus Robertson was one sick bastard . . . You hear he got himself a DIY appendectomy in Peterhead?' He lowered his voice. 'Sharpened screwdriver, right in the stomach. Has to crap in a wee bag now . . .'

Logan didn't say anything, and the reporter leaned on the open window, poking his head in out of the rain.

'So what you workin' on now?' he asked.

Logan stared straight ahead, through the windscreen at the dismal grey length of the Lang Stracht. 'Er . . .' he said. 'I, ehmmm . . .'

'If you're interested in Colin the Cunt,' the older man started in a near-whisper. He stopped, slapped a hand over his mouth and mumbled to WPC Watson, 'Sorry love, no offence.'

Watson shrugged: after all, she'd been calling Miller much worse just minutes ago.

Leslie gave her an embarrassed smile. 'Aye, well, the wee shite swans up here from the *Scottish Sun* thinkin' he's God's fuckin' gift . . . Got kicked off the paper from what I hear.' His face darkened. 'Some of us still believe in the rules! You don't screw your colleagues. You don't phone up a dead kid's mum until you know the police have broken the news. But the little bastard thinks he can get away with murder, just as long as there's a story at the end of it.' There was a bitter pause. 'And his spellin's bollocks.'

Logan gave him a thoughtful look. 'You have any idea who told him we'd found David Reid?'

The old reporter shook his head. 'No idea, but if I find out you'll be the first to know! Be a pleasure to screw him over for a change.'

Logan nodded. 'Right, that's great . . .' he forced a smile. 'Well, we're going to have to get going . . .'

WPC Watson pulled the car out of the space, leaving the old reporter standing on his own in the rain.

'They should make you a DI!' he shouted after the car. 'A DI!'

As they drove out past the security gate Logan could feel his face going red.

'Aye, sir,' said WPC Watson, watching him turn a lovely shade of beetroot. 'You're an inspiration to us all.'

5

Logan was starting to get over his embarrassment by the time they were fighting their way across Anderson Drive, heading back to Force Headquarters. The road had started life as a bypass, but the city had suffered from middle-aged spread and oozed out to fill in the gaps with cold grey granite buildings so that it was more of a belt, stretched across the city and groaning at the seams. It was a nightmare during rush hour.

The rain was still hammering down and the people of Aberdeen had reacted in their usual way. A minority trudged along, wrapped up in waterproof jackets, hoods up, umbrellas clutched tight against the icy wind. The rest just stomped along getting soaked to the skin.

Everyone looked murderous and inbred. When the sun shone they would cast off their thick woollens, unscrew their faces, and smile. But in winter the whole city looked like a casting call for *Deliverance*.

Logan sat staring morosely out of the window, watching the people trudge by. Housewife. Housewife with kids. Bloke in a duffle coat and stupid-looking hat. Roadkill with his shovel and council-issue wheelie-cart full of dead animals. Child with plastic bag. Housewife with pushchair. Man in a mini-kilt . . .

'What the hell goes through his mind of a morning?' Logan asked as Watson slipped the car into gear and inched forward.

'What, Roadkill?' she said. 'Get up, scrape dead things off the road, have lunch, scrape more dead things—'

'No not him.' Logan's finger jabbed at the car window. 'Him. Do you think he gets up and thinks: "I know, I'll dress so everyone can see my backside in a light breeze"?'

As if by magic the wind took hold of the mini-kilt and whipped it up, exposing an expanse of white cotton.

Watson raised an eyebrow. 'Aye, well,' she said, nipping past a shiny blue Volvo. 'At least his pants are clean. His mum won't have to worry about him getting knocked down by a bus.'

'True.'

Logan leaned forward and clicked on the car radio, fiddling with the buttons until Northsound, Aberdeen's commercial radio station, blared out of the speakers.

WPC Watson winced as an advert for double-glazing was rattled out in broad Aberdonian.

They'd somehow managed to cram about seven thousand words and a cheesy tune into less than six seconds. 'Jesus,' she said, her face creased in disbelief. 'How can you listen to that crap?'

Logan shrugged. 'It's local. I like it.'

'Teuchter bollocks.' Watson accelerated through the lights before they could turn red. 'Radio One. That's what you want. Northsound, my arse. Anyway, you're not supposed to have the radio on: what if a call comes in?'

Logan tapped his watch. 'Eleven o'clock: time for the news. Local news for local people. Never hurts to find out what's going on in your patch.'

The advert for double-glazing was followed by one for a car firm in Inverurie done in Doric, Aberdeen's almost indecipherable dialect, then one for the Yugoslavian Ballet and another for the new chip shop in Inverbervie. Then came the news. Mostly it was the usual rubbish, but one piece caught Logan's attention. He sat forward and cranked up the volume.

'. . . earlier today. And the trial of Gerald Cleaver continues at Aberdeen Sheriff Court. The fifty-six-year-old, originally from Manchester, is accused of sexually abusing over twenty children while serving as a male nurse at Aberdeen Children's Hospital. Hostile crowds lined the road outside the courthouse, hurling abuse as Cleaver arrived under heavy police escort . . .'

'Hope they throw the book at him,' Watson said, cutting across a box junction and speeding off down a little side road.

'*. . . The parents of murdered toddler David Reid have been flooded with messages of support today, following the discovery of their three-year-old son's body near the River Don late last night . . .*'

Logan poked a finger at the radio, switching it off in mid-sentence. 'Gerald Cleaver is a dirty little shite,' he said, watching as a cyclist wobbled out into the middle of the road, stuck two fingers up and swore at a taxi driver. 'I interviewed him for the rape murders in Mastrick. Wasn't really a suspect, but he was on the "dodgy bastards" list, so we pulled him in anyway. Had hands like a toad, all cold and clammy. Pawing himself the whole time . . .' Logan shuddered at the memory. 'Not going to beat this one, though. Fourteen years to life: Peterhead.'

'Serve him right.'

Peterhead Prison. That was where they sent the sex offenders. The rapists, paedophiles, sadists, serial killers . . . People like Angus Robertson. People who had to be protected from normal, respectable criminals. The ones that liked to insert makeshift knives into sex offenders. Ta-da. Colostomy bag time for poor old Angus Robertson. Somehow Logan couldn't feel too sorry for him.

WPC Watson said something, but Logan was too busy thinking about the Mastrick Monster to pick anything up. From her expression, he got the feeling he'd just been asked a question. 'Hmmm . . .' he said, stalling for time. 'In what way?' It was a standard fall-back.

WPC Watson frowned. 'Well, I mean, what did the doctor say last night? At A&E?'

Logan grunted and dug a plastic bottle out of his inside jacket pocket, rattling it. 'One every four hours, preferably after meals. Not to be taken with alcohol.' He'd already had three that morning.

She raised an eyebrow, but didn't say anything.

Two minutes later they were pulling into the multi-storey car park at the back of Force Headquarters, making for the section reserved for patrol and CID pool cars. Command officers and senior staff got to use the car park. Everyone else had to make do with what they could get, usually abandoning their cars on the Beach Boulevard, a five-minute walk from the station. It paid to be an Assistant Chief Constable when it was pissing with rain.

They found Detective Inspector Insch perched on the edge of a desk in the incident room, swinging one large leg back and forth, listening to a PC carrying a clipboard. The news from the search teams wasn't good. It was too long since the body had been dumped. The weather conditions were terrible. If, by some miracle, any forensic evidence had managed to survive the last three months it would have washed away in the last six hours. DI Insch didn't say a word as the constable went through his list of negative results, just sat there, munching his way through a packet of fizzy cola bottles.

The PC finished his report and waited expectantly for DI Insch to stop chewing and say something.

'Tell the teams to keep going for another hour. If we've not found anything by then we're calling it a day.' The inspector proffered the almost-empty bag of sweets and the PC took one, popping it into his mouth with obvious delight. 'No one can say we've not taken the search seriously.'

'Yes, sir,' he mumbled, still eating.

DI Insch dismissed the munching constable and beckoned Logan and WPC Watson over. 'Post mortem,' he said without preamble, listening to Logan's account of the desecration of David Reid's body in the exact same way he'd listened to the search team progress reports. Silent. Impassive. Stuffing his face. He finished off the cola bottles and brought out a packet of wine gums.

'Wonderful,' he said when Logan had finished. 'So we've got a paedophile serial killer running around Aberdeen.'

'Not necessarily,' said Watson, accepting a little orange lozenge with 'SHERRY' embossed on the top. 'There's only one body, not a series, and the killer may not even be local . . .'

Insch merely shook his head.

Logan took a 'PORT'. 'The body lay undisturbed for three months. The killer even went back, long after rigor mortis had set in, and took a souvenir. He had to know his hiding place was safe. That screams "local". The fact that he came back and took a bit of the body means this is something special to him. Your man's not done this on a whim: he's been thinking about it for a long time. This is some sort of ritual fantasy he's acting out. He's going to do it again. If he hasn't already.'

Insch agreed. 'I want all missing child reports for the last year pulled. Get the list up on the wall over there. Chances are some of them may have crossed this sick bastard's path.'

'Yes, sir.'

'Oh and, Logan,' said the DI, carefully folding the wine gum packet shut and stuffing it back in his pocket. 'I had a call from the *Journal*. They tell me you've been up there leaning on their new golden boy.'

Logan nodded. 'Colin Miller: used to work on the *Scottish Sun*. He's the one that—'

'Did I ask you to go antagonizing the newspapers, Sergeant?'

Logan's mouth snapped shut. Pause. 'No, sir. We were in the neighbourhood and I thought—'

'Sergeant,' said DI Insch, slowly and deliberately. 'I'm glad you're thinking. That's a good sign. Something I encourage in my officers.' There was a big 'but' coming: Logan could feel it. 'But I don't expect them to go off and annoy the local press without permission. We're going to have to put out appeals to the public. We're going to have to do damage limitation if someone screws something up in the investigation. We're going to need these people on our side.'

'This morning you said—'

'This morning I said I'd nail whoever spoke to the press. And I will. This is our screw-up, not the paper's. Understand?'

He'd screwed up. WPC Watson suddenly took a great deal of interest in her shoes as Logan said, 'Yes, sir. Sorry, sir.'

'OK.' Insch picked a sheet of paper off the desk and handed it to a suitably chastised Detective Sergeant McRae. 'The search teams haven't found a thing. Surprise, surprise. There's an underwater search unit doing the river, but the rain's made it almost impossible. The damn thing's already broken its banks in about a million places. We're lucky the body was found at all. Another couple of days and the river would've swamped the ditch and whoosh . . .' He swept his hand past, the fingertips sparkling with little grains of sugar from the cola bottles. 'David Reid's body would've been washed right out into the North Sea. Next stop Norway. We'd never have found it.'

Logan tapped the post mortem report against his teeth, his eyes focused on a spot just above DI Insch's bald head. 'Maybe it's too much of a coincidence?' he said, frowning. 'David Reid's been lying there for three months, but if no one finds him before the river bursts its banks, he's never going to be found.' His eyes drifted back to the inspector. 'He gets swept out to sea and the story never hits the papers. No publicity. The killer can't read about his achievements. There's no feedback.'

Insch nodded. 'Good thinking. Get someone to drag the finder . . .' He checked his notes. 'Mr Duncan Nicholson. Get him in here and give him a proper grilling, not the half-arsed one he got last night. If the man's got any skeletons in his closet I want to know about them.'

'I'll get an area car to—' was as far as Logan got before the door to the incident room burst open and a breathless PC screeched to a halt.

'Sir,' he said. 'Another kid's gone missing.'

6

Richard Erskine's mother was overweight, over-wrought and not much more than a child herself. The lounge of her middle terrace house in Torry was packed with photos in little wooden frames, all showing the same thing: a grinning Richard Erskine. Five years old. Blond hair, squint teeth, dimpled cheeks, big glasses. The child's life was mapped out in the claustrophobic room, from birth right through to . . . Logan stopped that thought before it could go any further.

The mother's name was Elisabeth: twenty-one, pretty enough if you ignored the swollen eyes, streaked mascara and bright red nose. Her long black hair was scraped back from her round face and she paced the room with frantic energy, eating her fingernails until the quicks bled.

'He's got him, hasn't he?' she was saying, over and over again, her voice shrill and panicky. 'He's got Richie! He's got him and he's killed him!'

Logan shook his head. 'Now we don't know

that. Your son might just have forgotten the time.' He scanned the photograph-laden walls again, trying to find one in which the child looked genuinely happy. 'How long has he been missing?'

She stopped pacing and stared at him. 'Three hours! I already told her that!' She flapped a chewed hand in WPC Watson's direction. 'He knows I worry about him! He wouldn't be late! He wouldn't.' Her bottom lip trembled and tears started to well up in her eyes again. 'Why aren't you out there finding him?'

'We've got patrol cars and officers out there right now looking for your son, Mrs Erskine. Now I need you to tell me what happened this morning. When he went missing?'

Mrs Erskine wiped her eyes and nose on the back of her sleeve. 'He was supposed . . . supposed to come straight back from the shops. Some milk and a packet of chocolate biscuits . . . He was supposed to come straight back!'

She started to cross the lounge again, back and forth, back and forth.

'Which shops did he go to?'

'The ones on the other side of the school. It's not far! I don't normally let him go on his own, but I had to stay in!' She sniffed. 'The man was coming to fix the washing machine. They wouldn't give me a time! Just some time in the morning. I never would have let him out on his own otherwise!' She bit down on her lip and the sobbing intensified. 'It's all my fault!'

'Have you got a friend or a neighbour who could stay with . . .'

Watson pointed at the kitchen. A used-looking older woman emerged carrying a tray of tea things: two mugs only. The police weren't expected to stay for tea, they were expected to get out there and start looking for the missing five-year-old.

'It's a disgrace, so it is,' said the older woman, putting the tea tray down on top of a pile of *Cosmopolitan*s on the coffee table. 'Letting perverts like that run around! They should a' be in prison! It's no as if there's no one handy!' She was talking about Craiginches, the walled prison just around the corner from the house.

Elisabeth Erskine accepted a mug of milky tea from her friend, shaking so much that the hot liquid slopped over the edge. She watched the drops seep into the pale blue carpet.

'You, eh . . .' She stopped and sniffed. 'You don't have a cigarette on you, do you? I . . . I gave up when I got pregnant with Richie . . .'

'Sorry,' said Logan. 'I had to give up too.' He turned and picked the most recent-looking photo off the mantelpiece. A serious little boy, staring at the camera. 'Can we take this with us?'

She nodded and Logan handed it over to WPC Watson.

Five minutes later they were standing in the small back garden, sheltering beneath a ridiculously little porch bolted on above the back door. The tiny square of grass was disappearing under a spreading network of puddles. About a dozen child's toys were scattered about the place, the bright plastic shapes washed clean by the downpour. On the other side of the fence more houses stared back at him, grey and damp.

Torry wasn't the worst bit of the city, but was in the top ten. This was where Aberdeen's fish processing factories were. Tons of white fish landed every week, all to be gutted and filleted by hand. Good money if you could handle the cold and the smell. Huge blue plastic bins of discarded fish guts and bones squatted on the roadside, the rain doing nothing to dissuade fat seagulls from swooping in to snatch a fish head or a beakful of innards.

'What you think?' asked Watson, sticking her hands deep in her pockets, trying to keep warm.

Logan shrugged, watching water overflowing the seat of a bright yellow digger. 'The house been searched?'

Watson pulled out her notebook. 'We got the call at eleven oh five. Mother was hysterical. Control sent round a couple of uniforms from the local Torry stationhouse. First thing they did was go through the place with a fine-toothed comb. He's not hiding in the linen cupboard and his body's not been stashed in the fridge freezer.'

'I see.' That digger was way too small for a five-year-old. In fact a lot of the toys looked as if they belonged in the age three-and-up bracket. Maybe Mrs Erskine didn't want her little baby growing up?

'You think she killed him?' asked Watson,

watching him stare out at the drenched garden.

'No, not really. But if it turns out she has and we didn't look . . . the press would crucify us. What about the father?'

''Cording to the neighbour he's been dead since before the kid was born.'

Logan nodded. That would explain why the woman was so overprotective. Didn't want her son going the same way as his father. 'So what's the state of the search?' he asked.

'We've phoned his friends: no one's seen him since Sunday afternoon.'

'What about his clothes, favourite teddy bear, that kind of thing?'

'All present and accounted for. So he's probably not run away.'

Logan gave the discarded toys one last look and went back into the house. The inspector would be here soon, looking for an update. 'Er . . .' He looked at Watson out of the corner of his eye as they walked through the kitchen and down the hallway towards the front door. 'You've worked with DI Insch before, right?'

WPC Watson admitted that she had.

'So what's with the—' Logan mimed stuffing his face with fizzy cola bottles. 'He trying to give up smoking?'

Watson shrugged. 'Dunno, sir. Maybe it's some sort of obsessive compulsive disorder?' She paused, brow furrowed in thought. 'Or maybe he's just a big fat bastard.'

Logan didn't know whether to laugh or look shocked.

'Tell you one thing though, sir, he's a damn good policeman. And you don't fuck with him twice.'

Somehow Logan had already come to that conclusion all on his own.

'Right.' He stopped at the front door. The hallway was festooned with photographs, just like the lounge. 'Get that picture down to the nearest newsagents. We'll need about a hundred photocopies and—'

'The local boys have already done it, sir. They've got four officers going door to door all along the route Richard would have taken to the shops, handing them out.'

Logan was impressed. 'They don't hang about.'

'No, sir.'

'OK, let's get half a dozen uniform down here to give them a hand.' He pulled out his mobile phone and started dialling, his finger freezing over the last number. 'Oh, ho . . .'

'Sir?'

A flash-looking motor had pulled up at the kerb and out bustled a familiar, short figure, all wrapped up in a black overcoat, wrestling with a matching umbrella.

'Looks like the vultures are circling already.'

Logan grabbed a brolly from the hallway and stepped out into the rain. The icy water thrummed off the umbrella as he stood and waited for Colin Miller to climb the stairs.

'Sergeant!' said Miller, smiling. 'Long time no see! You still carting that tasty . . .' The smile became even broader as he saw WPC Watson scowling from the doorway. 'Constable! We was just talking about you!'

'What do you want?' Her voice was even colder than the grey afternoon.

'Business before pleasure, eh?' Miller dug a fancy dictaphone out of his pocket and pointed it at them. 'You've got another missing kid. Are you—'

Logan frowned. 'How did you know another child's gone missing?'

Miller pointed out at the rain-soaked road. 'You've got patrol cars out broadcastin' the kid's description! How do you think I found out?'

Logan tried not to look as embarrassed as he felt.

Miller winked. 'Ah, don't worry about it. I make an arse of myself all the time, but.' He held the dictaphone up again. 'Now, is this disappearance connected to the recent discovery of—'

'We have no comment to make at this time.'

'Oh, come on!'

Behind Miller another car had pulled up, this one with the BBC Scotland logo emblazoned down the side. The media were going to have a field day. Yesterday a little boy turned up dead, today another one had gone missing. They'd all be jumping to the same conclusion as Miller. He could see the headlines now: 'HAS PAEDOPHILE KILLER

Struck Again?' The Chief Constable would have a fit.

Miller turned to see what Logan was staring at and froze. 'How about if—'

'I'm sorry, Mr Miller. I can't give you any further details at this time. You'll just have to wait for the official statement.'

He didn't have to wait long. Five minutes later DI Insch's mud-splattered Range Rover pulled up. By then a little cordon of newspaper and television people had appeared, forming a wall of microphones and lenses at the foot of the steps, huddling beneath large black umbrellas. Just like a funeral.

Insch didn't bother getting out of his car, just wound down his window and waved Logan over. The cameras turned to watch Logan cross the road and stand in the rain beneath his borrowed umbrella by DI Insch's window, trying not to wince at the smell of wet spaniel that oozed out of the car's interior.

'Aye, aye,' said the inspector, nodding towards the ring of cameras. 'Looks like we're going to be on the telly tonight.' He ran a hand over his bald head. 'Good job I remembered to wash my hair.'

Logan forced a smile. The scars crisscrossing his stomach were starting to bother him as last night's punch in the guts made its presence felt.

'Right,' said Insch. 'I've been authorized to release a statement to the media. Before I do, is there anything I need to know that's going to make me look like an arse here?'

Logan shrugged. 'Far as we can tell the mother's being straight with us.'

'But?'

'Don't know. The mother treats the kid like he's made of glass. Doesn't get out on his own. All his toys are for a kid two years younger than he is. I get the feeling she's smothering the life out of him.'

Insch raised an eyebrow, causing the pink, hairless skin of his head to wrinkle. He didn't speak.

'I'm not saying he hasn't been snatched.' Logan shrugged. 'But still . . .'

'Point taken,' said Insch, smoothing himself down. Unlike the filthy, smelly Range Rover he was immaculately turned out in his best suit and tie. 'But if we play this down, and he turns up all strangled with his willy cut off, we'll be up to our ears in shite.'

Logan's phone went off in an explosion of beeps and whistles. It was the Queen Street station. They'd picked up Duncan Nicholson.

'What . . . ? No.' Logan smiled, the phone clamped to his ear. 'No, stick him in a detention room. Leave him there to sweat till I get there.'

By the time Logan and WPC Watson got back to Force Headquarters a full-blown search was underway. DI Insch had more than trebled the six uniforms Logan had drafted in to help and now more than forty police men and women, four dog-handlers and their alsatians, were out in the freezing rain, searching every garden, public building, shed, bush and ditch between Richard Erskine's home and the shops on Victoria Road.

The desk sergeant told them that Duncan Nicholson had been stuck in the mankiest detention room in the place. He'd been there for nearly an hour.

Just to be on the safe side, Logan and WPC Watson stopped off at the canteen for a cup of tea and a bowl of soup. Lingering over the pea and ham while Nicholson sat in a room, all alone, and worried.

'Right,' said Logan, when they'd finished. 'How'd you like to drag Mr Nicholson into an interview room? Give him the silent glower routine? I'll check up on the search and pop along in about, fifteen, twenty minutes. He should be bricking it by then.'

Watson stood, cast one last longing look at the thick slices of sponge pudding and steaming yellow custard, and headed off to make Duncan Nicholson's life even more miserable.

Logan got an update from the admin officer in the incident room: the search teams hadn't turned up anything and neither had the door-to-door interviews. So Logan grabbed a cup of tea from the machine in the hallway and drank it slowly, filling in the time. Then took another painkiller. When twenty minutes had elapsed he headed down to interview room two.

It was small and utilitarian, done up in a nasty shade of beige. Duncan Nicholson sat at the table, opposite a silent, scowling, WPC Watson. He was looking very uncomfortable.

The room was no smoking and Nicholson obviously had a problem with that. There was a pile of shredded paper on the table in front of him and as Logan entered Nicholson jumped, sending little scraps of white fluttering to the scuffed blue carpet.

'Mr Nicholson,' said Logan, sinking down into the brown plastic chair next to Watson. 'Sorry to keep you waiting.'

Nicholson shifted in his chair, little beads of sweat sparkling on his upper lip. He wasn't a day over thirty-two, but looked closer to forty-five. The hair on top of his head was shaved down to the bone, blue-grey stubble showing between shiny patches of pink scalp. Each of his ears had been pierced in at least three places. The rest of him looked as if it had been thrown together on a Monday morning before the factory was properly awake.

'I've been here for hours!' he said, mustering up as much indignity as he could. 'Hours! There was nae bog! I wis burstin'!'

Logan frowned. 'Dear, dear, dear. There's obviously been some mistake, Mr Nicholson. You came forward of your own free will, didn't you? No toilet? I'll have a word with the duty sergeant. Make sure it doesn't happen again.' He smiled a disarming, friendly smile. 'But we're all here now, so shall we get started?'

Nicholson nodded, smiling a little, feeling reassured. Feeling better.

'Constable, would you do the honours?' Logan passed Watson two brand new audiotapes and she unwrapped them, sticking one in each side of the recorder bolted to the wall before doing the same with a pair of videotapes. The machine clicked and bleeped as she pressed 'RECORD'.

'Interview with Mr Duncan Nicholson,' she said, going through the standard names, date and time.

Logan smiled again. 'Now then, Mr Nicholson, or can I call you Duncan?'

The man on the other side of the table cast a nervous glance at the camera in the corner of the room, over Logan's shoulder. At last he nodded his shaved head.

'So, Duncan, you found the body of David Reid last night?'

Nicholson nodded again.

'You have to say something, Duncan,' said Logan, his smile getting wider by the minute. 'The tape can't hear you if you nod.'

Nicholson's eyes darted back to the staring glass eye of the video camera. 'Er . . . Oh, sorry. Yeah. Yeah, I did. I found him last night.'

'What were you doing down there in the middle of the night, Duncan?'

He shrugged. 'I wis . . . takin' a walk. You

know, had a row with the wife and went for a walk.'

'Down the riverbank? In the dead of night?'

The smile started to fade. 'Er, yeah. I go down there sometimes to, you know, think an' stuff.'

Logan crossed his arms, mirroring the PC sitting next to him. 'So you went down there to think. And just happened to fall over the murdered body of a three-year-old boy?'

'Er, yeah . . . I just . . . Look, I . . .'

'Just happened to fall over the murdered body of a three-year-old boy. In a waterlogged ditch. Hidden beneath a sheet of chipboard. In the dark. In the pouring rain.'

Nicholson opened his mouth once or twice, but nothing came out.

Logan left him sitting in silence for almost two minutes. The man was getting more and more fidgety by the second, his shaved head now as sweaty as his upper lip, the smell of second-hand garlic oozing out of him in nervous waves.

'I'd been . . . drinking, OK? I fell down, nearly killed myself goin' down that bloody bank.'

'You fell down the bank, in the pouring rain, and yet when the police arrived there wasn't a speck of mud on you! You were clean as a whistle, Duncan. That doesn't sound like someone who's just fallen down a muddy bank and into a ditch, now does it?'

Nicholson ran a hand over the top of his head, the stubble making a faint scritching noise in the oppressive interview room. Dark blue stains marked his armpits.

'I . . . I went home to call you. I got changed.'

'I see.' Logan switched the smile back on again. 'Where were you on the thirteenth of August this year, between half past two and three in the afternoon?'

'I . . . I don't know.'

'Then where were you between the hours of ten and eleven this morning?'

Nicholson's eyes snapped open wide. 'This mornin'? What's goin' on? I didnae kill anyone!'

'Who said you did?' Logan turned in his seat. 'Constable Watson, did you hear me accuse Mr Nicholson of murder?'

'No, sir.'

Nicholson squirmed.

Logan produced a list of all the children registered missing in the last three years and placed it on the table between them.

'Where were you this morning, Duncan?'

'I was watching the telly.'

'And where were you on,' Logan leant forward and read off the list, 'the fifteenth of March between six and seven? No? How about the twenty-seventh of May, half-four to eight?'

They went through every date on the list, Nicholson sweating and murmuring his answers. He wasn't anywhere he said. He was at home. He was watching television. The only people who could vouch for his whereabouts were Jerry

Springer and Oprah Winfrey. And they were mostly repeats.

'Well, Duncan,' said Logan when they'd got to the end of the list, 'doesn't look too good, does it?'

'I didn't touch those kids!'

Logan sat back and tried DI Insch's silent treatment again.

'I didn't! I fuckin' came to you lot when I found that kid, didn't I? Why the hell would I do that if I killed him? I wouldn't kill a kid: I love kids!'

WPC Watson raised an eyebrow and Nicholson scowled.

'Not like that! I've got nephews and nieces, OK? I wouldn't fuckin' do something like that.'

'Then let's go back to the start.' Logan shoogled his chair in closer to the table. 'What were you doing wandering about on the banks of the Don in the middle of the night in the pouring rain?'

'I told you I was pissed . . .'

'Why don't I believe you, Duncan? Why do I get the feeling that when the report comes back from Forensics there's going to be evidence linking you to the dead boy?'

'I didn't do anything!' Nicholson slammed his hand down on the tabletop, making the little pile of shredded paper scatter and fall like snow.

'We've got you, Mr Nicholson. You're only kidding yourself if you think you're going to talk your way out of it. I think a little time in the cells is going to do you the world of good. We'll talk again when you're ready to start telling the truth. Interview terminated at thirteen twenty-six.'

He got WPC Watson to escort Nicholson down to the cellblock, hanging on in the interview room until she returned.

'What do you think?' he asked.

'I don't think he did it. He's not the right type. Not smart enough to lie convincingly.'

'True.' Logan nodded. 'But he's lying all the same. No way he was down there having a bit of a late night stagger. You get plastered, you don't go stomping about down the riverbank in the pissing rain for a laugh. He was down there for a reason, we just don't know what it is yet.'

Aberdeen harbour slid by the car window, grey and miserable. A handful of offshore supply vessels were tied up along the docks, their cheery yellow-and-orange paintwork dulled by the pouring rain. Lights glinted in the semi-darkness of the afternoon as containers were winched off lorries and onto the waiting boats.

Logan and WPC Watson were heading back to Richard Erskine's house in Torry. Someone had actually remembered seeing the missing boy. A Mrs Brady had seen a small blond boy wearing a red anorak and blue jeans crossing the waste ground behind her house. It was the only break they'd had.

The half past two news was about to come on

and Logan turned the car radio on, catching the end of an old Beatles track. Not surprisingly Richard Erskine's disappearance was given top billing. DI Insch's voice boomed out of the speakers asking members of the public to come forward with information about the child's whereabouts. He had a natural flair for the dramatic, as everyone who'd seen him in the annual Christmas panto knew, but he managed to keep it in check as the newsreader asked the obvious question:

'Do you think Richard has been taken by the same paedophile who killed David Reid?'

'At this moment we're just looking to find Richard safe and sound. If anyone has any information please call our hotline on oh eight hundred, five, five, five, nine, nine, nine.'

'Thank you, Inspector. In other news: the trial of Gerald Cleaver, the fifty-six-year-old former male nurse from Manchester, continues today under tight security following death threats made to the accused's solicitor, Sandy Moir-Farquharson. Mr Moir-Farquharson spoke to Northsound News . . .'

'Here's hoping it's not just an idle threat.' Logan reached out and snapped the radio off before the lawyer's voice could come through the speakers. Sandy Moir-Farquharson deserved to get death threats. He was the weasely little shite who'd argued leniency for Angus Robertson. Who'd tried to claim that the Mastrick Monster wasn't entirely to blame. That he'd only killed those women because they'd reacted violently against his advances. That they'd dressed provocatively. That they'd been, basically, asking for it.

The media presence outside the door of little Richard Erskine's house had almost doubled by the time they got there. The whole road was packed with cars. There were even a couple of outside broadcast vans. WPC Watson had to park miles away, so they trudged back through the rain, both sheltering under her umbrella.

BBC Scotland had been joined by Grampian, ITN and Sky News. The harsh white television lights bleached colour from the pale granite buildings. No one seemed to take much notice of the winter rain, even though it was battering down from the sky in sheets of frigid water.

The blonde woman with the big boobs from Channel Four News was doing a piece to camera, standing far enough down the street to get the house and the rest of the pack in the background.

'. . . have to ask: does the media's attention on a family's pain, at a time like this, really serve the public interest? When—'

Watson marched right through the shot, her blue and white umbrella completely obscuring the woman from camera.

Someone yelled: 'Cut!'

'You did that on purpose,' whispered Logan as the sounds of a swearing television journalist erupted. WPC Watson just smiled and barged her way through the crowd gathered at the foot of the stairs. Logan hurried after her, trying not to hear the howls of complaint mixed in with the shouted questions and demands for comment.

A Family Liaison Officer was through in the living room with Richard Erskine's mother and the bitter old woman from next door. There was no sign of DI Insch.

Logan left Watson in the lounge and tried the kitchen, helping himself to an open packet of Jaffa Cakes lying on the worktop next to the kettle. A half-glazed door led from the kitchen out into the back garden, the light blocked by a large figure standing outside.

But it wasn't Insch. It was a sad-looking, overweight detective constable with half-past-two o'clock shadow, chain-smoking under the tiny porch.

'Afternoon, sir,' said the DC, not bothering to straighten up, or put his cigarette out. 'Shitty weather, eh?' He wasn't a local lad: his accent was pure Newcastle.

'You get used to it.' Logan stepped out onto the back step next to the DC to do as much passive smoking as he could.

The constable took the cigarette out of his mouth and stuck a finger in, working a nail up and down between his back teeth. 'Don't see how. I mean I'm used to rain like, but Jesus this place takes the fucking biscuit.' He found whatever it was he was digging for and flicked it away into the downpour. 'Think it's going to keep up till the weekend?'

Logan looked out at the low, dark-grey clouds. 'The weekend?' He shook his head and took in another scarred lungful of second-hand smoke. 'This is Aberdeen: it won't stop raining till March.'

'Bollocks!' The voice was deep, authoritative and coming from directly behind them.

Logan twisted his head round to see DI Insch standing in the doorway with his hands in his pockets.

'Don't you listen to DS McRae, he's pulling your leg.' Insch stepped out onto the already crowded top step, forcing Logan and the DC to shuffle precariously sideways.

'Won't stop raining till March?' Insch popped a fruit sherbet into his mouth. '*March*? Don't lie to the poor constable: this is Aberdeen.' He sighed and stuck his hands back in his pockets. 'It never stops fuckin' raining.'

They stood in silence, watching the rain do what rain does.

'Well, I've got a bit of good news for you, sir,' said Logan at last. 'Mr Moir-Farquharson is receiving death threats.'

Insch grinned. 'Hope so. I've written enough of them.'

'He's representing Gerald Cleaver.'

Insch sighed again. 'Why doesn't that surprise me? Still that's DI Steel's problem. Mine is: where's Richard Erskine?'

7

They found the body in the council tip at Nigg, just south of the city. A two-minute drive from Richard Erskine's house. A party of school children had been out on a field trip: 'Recycling and Green Issues'. They arrived by minibus at three twenty-six and proceeded to don little white breathing masks, the kind with the elastic band holding them on, and heavy-duty rubber gloves. Everyone wore waterproofed jackets and Wellington boots. They signed in at the Portacabin office next to the skips at three thirty-seven, before squelching their way into the tip. Walking through a landscape of discarded nappies, broken bottles, kitchen waste and everything else chucked out by hundreds of thousands of Aberdonians every day.

It was Rebecca Johnston, eight, who spotted it. A left foot, sticking up out of a pile of shredded black plastic bags. The sky was full of seagulls – huge, fat bloated things that swooped and screamed at each other in a jagged ballet. One was tugging away at a bloodstained toe. This was what first grabbed Rebecca's attention.

And at four o'clock, on the dot, they called the police.

The smell was unbelievable, even on a wet and windy day like today. Up here on Doonies Hill the rain was bitterly cold. It hammered against the car, gusts of wind rocking the rusty Vauxhall, making Logan shiver even though the heater was going full pelt.

Both he and WPC Watson were soaked to the skin. The rain had paid no attention to their police-issue 'waterproof' jackets, saturated their trousers and seeped into their shoes. Along with Christ knew what else. The car windows were opaque, the blowers making little headway.

The Identification Bureau hadn't turned up yet, so Logan and Watson had built a makeshift tent of fresh bin-bags and wheelie-bins over the body. It looked as if it was going to fly apart at any moment, torn to pieces by the howling wind, but it kept the worst of the rain off.

'Where the hell are they?' Logan cleared a porthole in the fogged-up windscreen. His mood had swiftly deteriorated as they'd struggled with whipping black plastic bags and unco-operative bins. The painkiller he'd taken at lunchtime was wearing off, leaving him sore every time he moved. Grumbling, he pulled out the bottle and shook one into his hand, swallowing it down dry.

At long last an almost-white, unmarked van slithered its way slowly along the rubbish road, its headlights blazing. The Identification Bureau had arrived.

'About bloody time!' said WPC Watson.

They clambered out of the car and stood in the driving rain.

Behind the approaching van the North Sea raged, grey and huge, the frigid wind making its first landfall since the Norwegian fjords.

The van slid to a halt and a nervous-looking man peered out through the windshield at the driving rain and festering rubbish.

'You're not going to bloody melt!' shouted Logan. He was sore, cold, damp and in no mood for dicking about.

A troop of four IB men and women grudged their way out of the van into the downpour and swore the SOC tent up over Logan's makeshift fort. The wheelie-bins and black plastic bags were turfed out into the rain and the portable generators set up. With a roar they burst into life, flooding the area with sizzling white light.

No sooner was the crime scene waterproof than 'Doc' Wilson, the duty doctor, turned up.

'Evenin' all,' he said, turning up the collar of his coat with one hand and grabbing his medical bag with the other. He took one look at the mine-field of crap that lay between the dirt road and the blue plastic marquee and sighed. 'I just bought these bloody shoes. Ah well . . .'

He stomped off towards the tent with Logan and WPC Watson in tow.

An acne-ridden IB officer with a clipboard stopped them at the threshold, keeping them all out in the driving rain until they'd signed in, and then watched them suspiciously until they'd all clambered into white paper boiler suits.

Inside the tent a single human leg rose out of the sea of refuse sacks, from the knee down, like the Lady of the Lake's arm. The only thing missing was Excalibur. The IB video operator was sweeping his way slowly around the remains, filming as the rest of the team carefully collected rubbish from the bags surrounding the one with the leg in it and stuffed the debris into clear plastic evidence pouches.

'Dees a favour?' said the doctor, handing his medical bag to Watson.

She stood silently while he popped the case open and dug out a pair of latex gloves, snapping them on as if he was a surgeon.

'Give us a bittie room then,' he told the bustling IB people.

They stood back and let him get at the body.

Doc Wilson took hold of the ankle with his fingertips, just below the joint. 'No pulse. Either this is yer genuine severed limb, or the victim's dead.' He gave the leg an experimental tug, causing the rubbish in the bag to shift and the IB team to hiss

74

in pain. This was their crime scene! 'Nope. I'd say that leg's weil an' truly attached. Consider death declared.'

'Thanks, Doc,' said Logan as the old man straightened himself up and wiped his latex gloves on his trousers.

'Nae problem. You want us tae hang around till the pathologist and the Fiscal get here?'

Logan shook his head. 'No sense in us all freezing our backsides off. Thanks anyway.'

Ten minutes later an Identification Bureau photographer stuck his head round the entrance to the tent. 'Sorry I'm late, some idiot went for a swim in the harbour and forgot to take his kneecaps with him. Jesus, it's bloody freezing out there.'

It wasn't much warmer inside, but at least it was out of the rain.

'Afternoon, Billy,' said Logan as the bearded photographer unwrapped himself.

The long, red-and-white-striped scarf was stuffed into a jacket pocket, followed by a red bobble hat with 'Up the Dons' stitched into it. He was bald underneath.

Logan was stunned. 'What happened to your hair?'

Billy scowled as he clambered into his white paper rompersuit. 'Don't you bloody start. Anyway I thought you were dead.'

Logan smiled. 'Aye, but I got better.'

The photographer polished his glasses with a

grey handkerchief, and then did the same with the lens of his camera. 'Anybody touched anything?' he asked, spooling a fresh reel of film into place.

'Doc Wilson gave the leg a tug, but other than that it's fresh.'

Billy snapped a huge flashgun onto the top of the camera, smacking it with the side of his hand until it emitted a high-pitched whine. 'OK, back up ladies and gentlemen . . .'

Hard, blue-white light crackled in the confined space, followed by the clatter-whirr of the camera and the whine of the flash. Again and again and again . . .

Billy was almost finished when Logan's phone went off. Cursing, he dragged it out of his pocket. It was Insch, looking for an update.

'Sorry, sir.' Logan had to raise his voice over the battering rain on the tent's roof. 'The pathologist isn't here yet. I can't get a formal identification without moving the body.'

Insch swore, but Logan could barely hear him.

'We've just had an anonymous call. Someone saw a child matching Richard Erskine's description getting into a dark red hatchback this morning.'

Logan looked down at the pale blue, naked leg sticking up out of the garbage. The information had come too late to save the five-year-old.

'Let me know as soon as the pathologist gets there.'

'Yes, sir.'

*

Isobel MacAlister turned up looking as if she'd just stepped off a catwalk: long Burberry raincoat, dark-green trouser suit, cream high-collared blouse, delicate pearl earrings, her short hair artistically tousled. Wellington boots three sizes too big for her . . . She looked so good it hurt.

Isobel froze as soon as she was inside, her eyes fixed on Logan dripping away in the corner. She almost smiled. Placing her medical case down on top of a bin-bag, she got straight to business. 'Has death been declared?'

Logan nodded, trying not to let his voice show how much the sight of her disturbed him. 'Doc Wilson did it half an hour ago.'

Her mouth turned down at the edges. 'I got here as soon as I could. I do have other duties to perform.'

Logan winced. 'I wasn't implying anything,' he said, hands up. 'I was just letting you know when death was declared. That's all.' His heart was hammering in his ears, drowning out the pounding rain.

She stood her ground, staring at him, her face cold and unreadable. 'I see . . .' she said at last.

She turned her back on him, covered her immaculate suit with the standard white boiler suit, pulled on her tiny microphone, recited the standard who, when and where, and got down to work.

'We have a human leg: left, protruding from a refuse sack from the knee down. Big toe has been subject to some form of laceration, probably post mortem—'

'A seagull was eating it,' said Watson, getting a cold smile for her pains.

'Thank you, Constable.' Isobel turned back to the stiff leg. 'Big toe shows signs of predation by a large sea bird.' She reached forward and touched the pale, dead flesh with her fingertips. With pursed lips she started pressing her thumb into the ball of the foot, feeling the toes with her other hand. 'I'll need to get the remains out of the bag before I can give you any estimated time of death.' She motioned for one of the IB team to come over and made him spread a fresh plastic sheet on top of the shifting floor of rubbish. They dragged the bag with the leg sticking out of it from the pile and onto the sheet. All the time Billy flashed and whirred away.

Isobel hunkered down in front of the bin-bag and slit it open with one smooth pass of a scalpel. Rubbish spilled out of the sack, caught by the plastic sheeting. The naked body was curled in a ball, held in the foetal position with brown packing tape. Logan caught a glimpse of pale-blond hair and shivered. Dead children looked smaller than he'd remembered.

The skin was a delicate shade of milk-bottle white between the swathes of brown sticky tape, faint patches of purple forming over the shoulders. The poor little sod had been upside-down in the bag and the blood had pooled in the lowest parts.

'Do you have an ID?' Isobel asked, peering at the small corpse.

'Richard Erskine,' said Logan. 'He's five.'

Isobel looked up at him, a scalpel in one hand an evidence bag in the other. '"He's" not anything,' she said, straightening up. 'This is a girl. Three to four years old.'

Logan looked down at the bundled-up body. 'You sure?'

Isobel slipped her scalpel back into its case, straightened up slowly and looked at him as if he was an idiot. 'Medical degrees from Edinburgh University might not be all they're cracked up to be, but one of the few things they did teach us was the difference between little boys and little girls. The whole absence-of-a-penis thing is kind of a giveaway.'

Logan went to ask the obvious question, but Isobel cut him off.

'And no, I don't mean it's been removed like the Reid boy: it was never there in the first place.' She picked her medical case up off the bin-bag floor. 'If you want a time of death, or anything else, you'll have to wait until I've done the post mortem.' She waved a hand at the IB officer who'd rolled out the plastic carpet for her. 'You: get all this crated up and back to the morgue. I'll continue there.'

There was a quiet 'Yes, ma'am' and she was gone, taking her bag with her. But leaving a chill behind.

The IB officer waited until she was well out of earshot before muttering, 'Frigid bitch.'

Logan hurried out after her, catching up as she clumped back to her car. 'Isobel? Isobel, wait.'

She pointed her keyring at the car: the indicators flashed and the boot popped open. 'I can't tell you anything more till I get the body back to the morgue.' Hopping on one foot, she pulled off a Wellington and dropped it into a plastic-lined box, replacing it with a suede boot.

'What was that all about?'

'All what about?' She went to work on the other Wellington, trying not to get too much garbage on her nice new shoes.

'Look we're going to have to work together, OK?'

'I am well aware of that,' she said, tearing off the boiler suit, flinging it in with the wellies, and slamming the boot shut. 'I'm not the one with the problem!'

'Isobel—'

Her voice dropped twenty degrees. 'Were you purposely trying to humiliate me back there? How dare you question my professionalism!' She wrenched open the car door and climbed in, slamming it in his face.

'Isobel—'

The window slid down and she looked up at him, standing in the pouring rain. 'What?'

But Logan couldn't think of anything to say.

She glowered at him and started the car, doing

a three-point turn on the slippery road, before roaring off into the darkness.

Logan watched the car's tail-lights disappear, cursed under his breath, and trudged back into the tent.

The little girl was lying where Isobel had left her, the IB team too busy bitching about the pathologist's departure to carry out her orders. Logan sighed and hunched down in front of the pathetic, taped-up bundle.

The child's face was almost completely hidden: the packing tape wrapped tightly around her head. The hands were taped together against her chest, and so were the knees. But it looked as if her killer had run out of tape before they could get the legs secured. That was why the left one had been poking out of the bag for a lucky seagull to nibble on.

He pulled out his phone and called in, asking if they'd had any reports of a missing girl, about three or four years old. They hadn't.

Swearing softly, he punched DI Insch's number in to give him the bad news. 'Hello, sir? Yeah, it's DS McRae . . . No, sir.' He took a deep breath. 'It's not Richard Erskine.'

There was a stunned silence at the other end of the line, and then, *'You sure?'*

Logan nodded, even though Insch couldn't see him. 'Definitely. Victim's a little girl, three, maybe four, years old, but she's not been reported missing.'

Foul language erupted from the earpiece.

'That's what I said, sir.'

The Identification Bureau team mimed picking up the body and buggering off to the morgue with it. Logan nodded. The one who'd called Isobel a frigid bitch took out a mobile and called for the duty undertakers. It wouldn't do to cart a dead child about in the back of a grubby van.

'You think the deaths are connected?' There was a hopeful edge to DI Insch's voice.

'Doubtful.' Logan watched as the tiny corpse was gently rolled into a body-bag far too big for it. 'Victim's female, not male. Disposal's different: the kid's been wrapped up in a mile and a half of packing tape. No sign of strangulation. She might have been abused, but we won't know until the post mortem.'

Insch swore again. *'You tell them I want that kid done today, OK? I don't want to spend the night twiddling my thumbs while the media make up horror stories! Today!'*

Logan winced, not looking forward to breaking the news to Isobel. In her current mood she was more likely to do a post mortem on him. 'Yes, sir.'

'Get her cleaned up and photographed. I want posters run off: have you seen this girl?'

'Yes, sir.'

The blue body-bag was picked up by two of the IB team, and carefully placed in the corner of the tent, out of the way. Then they started collecting the rubbish from the bag she'd been dumped in, making sure it was all properly bagged and labelled. Banana skins, empty bottles of wine, broken eggshells . . . The poor little kid hadn't even been worth the effort of a shallow grave. She'd been thrown out with the garbage.

Logan was promising to call the inspector back as soon as they'd heard anything when WPC Watson shouted: 'Hold it!' She darted forward, grabbing a crumpled-up piece of paper from the rubbish that had spilled out onto the plastic sheeting.

It was a till receipt.

Logan asked Insch to wait while Watson unfolded the grimy scrap. It was from the big Tesco in Danestone. Someone had bought half a dozen free-range eggs, a carton of crème fraîche, two bottles of cabernet sauvignon, and a pack of avocadoes. And paid for it with cash.

Watson groaned. 'Damn.' She handed the receipt to Logan. 'I thought he'd've paid by credit card, or Switch.'

'No way we could be that lucky.' He turned the scrap of paper over in his hands. Eggs, wine, posh cream and avocadoes . . . The line under the last item caught Logan's eye and a smile began to blossom.

'What?' Watson looked annoyed. 'What's so funny?'

Logan held the receipt aloft and beamed at her. 'Sir,' he said into the phone, 'WPC Watson's found a supermarket receipt in the bag with the body . . . No, sir, he paid cash.' If Logan's smile were any wider the top of his head would have fallen off. 'But he did collect his Clubcard points.'

South Anderson Drive was a bastard at this time of day, but North Anderson Drive was even worse. The traffic was nose to tail all the way across the city. Rush hour.

The Procurator Fiscal had finally turned up, bustled about the crime scene, demanded an update on the investigation, complained that this was the second dead child to be discovered in as many days, implied that it was all Logan's fault, and sodded off again.

Logan waited until he and WPC Watson were safely cocooned within the fogged-up car before expressing what he'd like to do to the Fiscal with a cactus and a tube of Ralgex.

It took them well over an hour to get from the tip at Nigg to the huge Tesco at Danestone. The store was situated in a prime spot: not far from the swollen River Don, within spitting distance of the old sewage works, the Grove Cemetery and the Grampian Country Chickens slaughterhouse; and close to where they'd found little David Reid's bloated corpse.

The store was busy, all the office workers from the nearby Science and Technology Park picking up booze and ready-meals for another night at home in front of the telly.

There was a customer service desk just inside the entrance, manned by a young-looking man with a long blond ponytail. Logan asked him to get the manager.

Two minutes later a small, balding man with a pair of half-moon glasses arrived. He was wearing the same uniform-blue sweater as the rest of the staff, but his name badge said: 'COLIN BRANAGAN, MANAGER'.

'Can I help you?'

Logan pulled out his warrant card and handed it over for inspection. 'Mr Branagan, we need to get some information on someone who was shopping here last Wednesday.' He pulled out the receipt, now safely encased in a clear-plastic evidence wallet. 'He paid cash, but he used his Clubcard. Can you give me his name and address from the card number?'

The manager took the see-through envelope and bit his lip. 'Ah, well I don't know about that,' he said. 'You see we've got to abide by the Data Protection Act. I can't just go giving out our shoppers' personal details. We'd be liable.' He shrugged. 'Sorry.'

Logan dropped his voice to a near-whisper. 'It's important, Mr Branagan: we're investigating an extremely serious crime.'

The manager ran a hand over the shiny top of his head. 'I don't know . . . I'll have to ask Head Office . . .'

'Fine. Let's go do that.'

Head Office said sorry, but no: if he wanted access to their customers' records he'd have to make a formal request in writing or get a court order. They had to abide by the Data Protection Act. There could be no exceptions.

Logan told them about the little girl's body in the bin-bag.

Head Office changed their minds.

Five minutes later Logan was outside clutching an A4 sheet of paper on which was printed a name, address and total number of Clubcard points earned since September.

8

Norman Chalmers lived in a tightly-packed, three-storey tenement off Rosemount Place. The long one-way street curved away to the right, the dirty grey buildings looming over the crowded road cutting the sky until it was nothing more than a thin strip of angry clouds, tainted orange by the streetlights. Cars were parked along the kerb, jammed in nose to tail, the only break formed by the massive, communal wheelie-bins, chained together in pairs, each one big enough to hold a week's rubbish for six households.

The endless rain drummed off the roof of the CID pool car as WPC Watson cursed her way around the block, yet again, looking for a parking spot.

Logan watched as the building slid by for the third time, ignoring WPC Watson's murmured swearing. Number seventeen looked no different to the rest of the tenement block. Three storeys of unadorned granite blocks, streaked with rust from the decaying drainpipes. Light seeped out through the curtained windows, the muffled sound of after-work television just audible under the downpour.

On the fourth time around Logan told her to give up and double park in front of Chalmers's flat.

Watson jumped out into the wet night, splashing between two parked cars to the pavement, the rain bouncing off her peaked cap. Logan followed, cursing as a puddle engulfed his shoe. He squelched his way to the tenement door: a dark-brown, featureless slab of wood set back behind an elaborate architrave, though the carved woodwork was so heavily coated in years of paint that little detail remained. A steady stream of water splattered off the pavement to their left, the downpipe from the guttering cracked halfway up.

Watson squeezed the transmit button on her radio, producing a faint hiss of static and a click. 'Ready to go?' she said, her voice low.

'Roger that. Exit from the street is secure.'

Logan looked up to see Bravo Seven One idling at the far end of the curving street. Bravo Eight One confirmed that they were ready too, watching the Rosemount Place end, making sure no one was going to do a runner. Bucksburn station had loaned Logan two patrol cars and a handful of uniforms with local knowledge. The officers in the cars were doing a lot better than the ones on foot.

'Check.'

The new voice sounded cold and miserable. It would be either PC Milligan or Barnett. They'd drawn the short straw. The road backed onto another curved avenue of tenements, the back gardens sharing a high dividing wall. So the poor sods had to clamber over the back wall from the adjoining street. In the dark and the mud. In the pouring rain.

'We're in position.'

Watson looked at Logan expectantly.

The building didn't have an intercom, but there was a row of three bells on either side of the doorway, the buttons clarted round the edges with more brown paint. Little labels sulked beneath them, each one giving the name of the occupant. 'NORMAN CHALMERS' was written in blue biro on a square of bloated cardboard sellotaped over the name of the previous owner. Top floor right. Logan stepped back and looked up at the building. The lights were on.

'OK.' He leaned forward and rang the middle buzzer, the one marked 'ANDERSON'. Two minutes later the door was opened by a nervous man in his mid to late twenties, big hair and heavy features, with a large bruise riding high on his cheekbone. He was still dressed from work: a cheap grey suit, the trousers all shiny at the knee, and a rumpled yellow shirt. In fact most of him looked rumpled. His face went pale when he saw WPC Watson's uniform.

'Mr Anderson?' said Logan, stepping forward and sticking his foot in the door. Just in case.

'Er . . . yes?' The man had a strong Edinburgh accent, the vowels going up and down in the middle. 'Is there a problem, officer?' He backed off into the airlock, his scuffed shoes clicking on the brown-and-cream tiles.

Logan smiled reassuringly. 'Nothing for you to worry about, sir,' he said, following the nervous young man into the building. 'We need to speak to one of your neighbours, but his bell doesn't seem to be working.' Which was a lie.

A weak smile spread across Mr Anderson's face. 'Oh . . . OK. Yeah.'

Logan paused. 'If you don't mind my saying so, that's a nasty bruise you've got there.'

Anderson's hand fluttered up to the swollen, purple-and-green skin.

'I . . . I walked into a door.' But he couldn't look Logan in the eye as he said it.

They followed Mr Anderson up the stairs, thanking him for his help as he disappeared inside his first floor flat.

'He was hell of a nervous,' said Watson when the door latch clicked shut, the deadbolt was driven home, and the chain rattled into position. 'Think he's up to something?'

Logan nodded. 'Everyone's up to something,' he said. 'And did you see that bruise? Walked into a door, my foot. Someone's belted him one.'

She stared at the door. 'Too scared to report it?'

'Probably. But, it's not our problem.'

The faded stair-carpet gave out at the middle floor; from here on up it was bare wooden boards that creaked and groaned as they climbed. There were three doors on the top landing. One would lead up to the communal attic, one to the other top floor flat; but the third belonged to Norman Chalmers.

It was painted dark blue and a brass number six had been fixed just below the peephole. WPC Watson flattened herself against the door, keeping herself and her uniform out of the line of sight.

Logan knocked lightly, just as a nervous downstairs neighbour might if he wanted to borrow a cupful of crème fraîche, or an avocado.

There was a creak, the roar of a television set, and then the sound of a deadbolt being drawn back. A key being turned in the lock.

The door was opened by a man in his early thirties with long hair, a squint nose and neatly trimmed beard. 'Hello . . .' was as far as he got.

WPC Watson lunged for him, grabbed his arm and showed him a way nature never intended it to bend.

'What the . . . hey!'

She forced him back into the flat.

'Aaaaaaaaaaaaaaaaaaa! You're breaking my arm!'

Watson pulled out a pair of handcuffs. 'Norman

Chalmers?' she asked, slapping the cold metal bracelets into place.

'I haven't done anything!'

Logan stepped into the small entrance hall, squeezing past WPC Watson and her wriggling captive so that he could get the door closed. The tiny triangular entrance hall offered three panelled-pine doors and an open doorway leading to a galley kitchen looking more like a rubber dinghy than a galley.

Everything was painted in eye-wateringly bright colours.

'Now then, Mr Chalmers,' said Logan, opening a door at random and discovering a compact bathroom in luminous green. 'Why don't we go sit down and have a nice little chat?' He tried another door, this time revealing a large orange lounge with a brown corduroy couch, a fake gas-fire, home cinema system and a computer. The walls were covered with film posters and a huge rack of DVDs.

'What a lovely home you have, Mr Chalmers; or can I call you Norman?'

Logan settled himself down on the nasty brown couch before realizing it was clarted in cat hair.

Chalmers bristled, his hands cuffed behind his back, WPC Watson still holding on to him, stopping him from going anywhere. 'What the hell is this all about?'

Logan smiled like a shark. 'All in good time, sir. WPC Watson, would you be so kind as to read this gentleman his rights?'

'You're arresting me? What for? I haven't done anything!'

'No need to shout, sir. Constable, if you please . . .'

'Norman Chalmers,' she said, 'I am detaining you on suspicion of the murder of an unidentified four-year-old girl.'

'What?' He struggled against the handcuffs as Watson went through the remainder of the speech, shouting over and over again that he hadn't done anything. He hadn't killed anyone. This was all a mistake.

Logan let him run out of steam before holding up a set of duly signed and notarized papers. 'I have here a warrant to search these premises. You were careless, Norman. We found her body.'

'I didn't do anything!'

'You should have used a fresh bin-bag, Norman. You killed her, and just threw her out with all your other rubbish. But you didn't check for incriminating evidence, did you?' He held up the clear plastic wallet with the supermarket till receipt in it. 'Avocadoes, cabernet sauvignon, crème fraîche and a dozen free-range eggs. Do you have a Tesco Clubcard, sir?'

'This is insane! I didn't kill anyone!'

WPC Watson looked down to see a bulge in Chalmers's back pocket. It was a wallet. And there, nestling between a Visa card and membership of the local video shop was a Clubcard. The number on the card matched the one on the receipt.

'Get your coat, Mr Chalmers, you're going for a little ride.'

Interview room three was oppressively hot. The radiator pumped heat into the little beige space and Logan couldn't get it to stop. It wasn't even as if they could open a window. So instead they suffered the heat and the stale air.

Present: DS Logan McRae, WPC Watson, Norman Chalmers and DI Insch.

The inspector hadn't said a word since entering the room, just stood at the back, leaning against the wall, working his way through a family-sized bag of liquorice allsorts. Sweating.

Mr Chalmers had decided not to help the police with their enquiries. 'I told you I'm not saying a bloody thing till you get my lawyer in here.'

Logan sighed. They'd been over this time and time again. 'You're not getting a lawyer until we've finished the interview, Norman.'

'I want a bloody lawyer now!'

Gritting his teeth, Logan closed his eyes and counted to ten. 'Norman,' he said at last, tapping the investigation file against the tabletop. 'We've got Forensics going through your house right now. They're going to find traces of the girl. You know that. If you talk to us now it'll look a damn sight better for you when you get to court.'

Norman Chalmers just stared straight ahead.

'Look, Norman, help us to help you! A wee girl is dead—'

'Are you deaf? I want my fucking lawyer!' He folded his arms and sat back in his chair. 'I know my rights.'

'Your rights?'

'I have a legal right to legal council. You can't interview me without a lawyer present!' A self-righteous smile spread over Chalmers's face.

DI Insch snorted, but Logan almost laughed. 'No you don't! This is Scotland. You get to see your lawyer after we've finished with you. Not before.'

'I want my lawyer!'

'Oh for God's sake!' Logan hurled the file down on the tabletop, causing the contents to spill out onto the Formica. A photo of a little dead body wrapped up in parcel tape. Norman Chalmers didn't even look at it.

At last DI Insch spoke, his voice a low bass rumble in the crowded room.

'Get him his lawyer.'

'Sir?' Logan sounded as surprised as he looked.

'You heard me. Get him his lawyer.'

Forty-five minutes later they were still waiting.

DI Insch stuffed another multicoloured square in his mouth and chewed noisily. 'He's doing this on purpose. The slimy little git's doing it just to piss us off.'

The door opened, just in time to catch the inspector's complaint.

'I beg your pardon?' said a voice from the door, with obvious disapproval.

Norman Chalmers's legal representative had arrived.

Logan took one look at the lawyer and suppressed a groan. He was a tall, thin man wearing a luxurious overcoat, expensive black suit, white shirt, blue silk tie and an earnest expression. His hair had more grey in it than the last time Logan had seen it, but the man's smile was every bit as annoying as he remembered. When the lawyer had cross-examined him, trying to make out that he'd fabricated the whole case. That Angus Robertson, AKA the 'Mastrick Monster', was the real victim.

'Don't worry, Mr Moir-Farquharson.' Insch pronounced it as it was spelt – 'Far-Quar-Son' rather than the traditional 'Facherson', because he knew it annoyed him. 'I was speaking about some other slimy git. How nice of you to join us.'

The lawyer sighed and draped his overcoat over the back of the last spare seat at the interview table. 'Please tell me we don't have to go through all this again, Inspector,' he said, pulling a slender, silver laptop from his briefcase. The soft purr of it powering up was almost inaudible in the crowded little room.

'All what, Mr Far-Quar-Son?'

The lawyer scowled at him. 'You know very well what. I am here to represent my client, not listen to your insults. I don't want to have to make yet another complaint to the Chief Constable about your behaviour.'

Insch's features darkened, but he didn't say anything.

'Now,' said the lawyer, picking away at the laptop's keyboard, 'I have a copy of the charges against my client. I would like to confer with him in private before we make a formal statement.'

'Aye?' Insch left his perch against the wall and leaned his huge fists against the tabletop, looming over Chalmers. 'Well, we'd like to ask your "client" why he murdered a four-year-old girl and threw her body out with the garbage!'

Chalmers jumped out of his seat.

'I didn't! Will you bastards bloody listen? I didn't do anything!'

Sandy Moir-Farquharson laid a hand on Chalmers's arm. 'It's all right. You don't have to say anything. Just sit back down and let me do the talking, OK?'

Chalmers looked down at his lawyer, nodded, and slowly sank back into his seat.

Insch hadn't moved.

'So, Inspector,' said Moir-Farquharson, 'as I said: I'd like to speak to my client in private. After that we will help you with your enquiries.'

'That's no how this works.' Insch scowled at the lawyer. 'You have no legal right of access to this wee shite whatsoever. You are here as a courtesy only.' He leaned in so close there was barely a breath between them. 'I'm running this show, not you.'

Moir-Farquharson smiled calmly up at him.

'Inspector,' he said in his most reasonable voice, 'I am well aware of the vagaries of Scottish law. However, as a sign of good faith, I'm asking you to let me speak to my client in private.'

'And if I don't?'

'Then we sit here till the cows come home. Or your six hours' holding time run out. It's up to you.'

Insch glowered, stuffed the liquorice allsorts back in his pocket and left the room, trailing Logan and WPC Watson behind him. Out in the corridor it was a lot cooler, but the air contained a lot of swearing.

When he had finished cursing the lawyer to the four winds, Insch told Watson to keep an eye on the door. He didn't want either of them doing a runner.

She didn't look too impressed. It wasn't a glamorous task, but that's what you got when you were a lowly WPC. One day she'd make CID, then she'd be the one telling uniforms to guard doorways.

'And, Constable,' Insch leaned in closer, his voice becoming a conspiratorial whisper. 'that was a damn fine bit of police work today: the supermarket receipt. I'll be putting in a good word for you on that one.'

She grinned. 'Thank you, sir.'

Logan and the inspector left her to it, working their way back to the incident room.

'Why did it have to be him?' asked Insch,

parking himself on the edge of a desk. 'I'm supposed to be at the dress rehearsal in twenty minutes!' He sighed: there was no chance he'd make it now. 'We're going to get bugger all out of Chalmers now. God save us from crusading lawyers!'

Sandy Moir-Farquharson was notorious. There wasn't a single criminal defence lawyer in the whole city who could hold a candle to him. Aberdeen's best solicitor advocate, qualified to stand up and defend the guilty in open court. For years the Crown Prosecution Service had been trying to get him to come over to their side, act as a public prosecutor, help put people away, instead of getting them off. But the slippery wee sod wasn't having any of it. He was on a mission to prevent miscarriages of justice! To protect the innocent! And get his face on the telly at every available opportunity. The man was a menace.

But secretly Logan knew if he ever got into trouble himself, he'd want Slippery Sandy representing him.

'So how come you let Hissing Sid suspend the interview?'

Insch shrugged. 'Because we were never going to get anything out of Chalmers anyway. At least whatever the Snake comes up with will be entertaining.'

'I thought he was busy representing our favourite child molester, Gerald Cleaver.'

Insch shrugged and dug the bag of sweets out

of his pocket. 'You know Hissing Sid. That case's got about a week, week and a half left to run. After that he's going to need something else to get his face in front of the cameras.' The inspector offered the open bag to Logan who helped himself to a coconut wheel with a liquorice centre.

'Forensics are going to find something,' Logan said, chewing. 'The girl had to be in his flat. There were food scraps and empty wine bottles in that bag. There's no way he could have got her into that bin-bag anywhere else . . . Unless he's got another property he eats and drinks at.'

Insch grunted, rummaging in the bag. 'Get onto the council in the morning. See if he's got a second property registered anywhere. Just in case.' He found what he was looking for: one of the aniseed disks with blue bobbles on it. 'Listen,' he said, popping the sweet into his mouth, 'the post mortem's been scheduled for quarter to eight this evening.' He paused, his eyes fixed on the floor at his feet. 'I was wondering if you would mind . . .'

'You want me to go?'

'As senior investigating officer I should be there, but . . . well . . .'

The inspector had a little girl about the same age as the victim. Watching a four-year-old being filleted like a side of meat would be rough for him. All the same it wasn't a job Logan was looking forward to. Especially if Dr Isobel MacAlister was going to be the one doing the filleting. 'I'll go,' he said at last, trying not to sigh. 'You should probably be interviewing Chalmers anyway . . . as senior investigating officer.'

'Thank you.' As a token of his esteem he gave Logan the last liquorice allsort.

Logan took the lift down to the morgue, hoping it would be Isobel's night off. Maybe he'd be lucky and get one of her deputies instead? But the way his luck was running he doubted it.

The morgue was unnaturally bright and airy for this time of night, the overhead lights sparkling off the dissecting tables and chiller cabinets. It was nearly as cold in there as it was outside. A heavy layer of disinfectant almost managed to hide the stench of corruption from this morning's post mortem. The smell of David Reid.

He arrived just in time to see the little girl being unloaded from her oversized body-bag. She was still wrapped in the packing tape, only now the shiny brown strips were dusted with white fingerprint powder.

Logan's heart sagged. It was Isobel, not one of her deputies, who stood on the far side of the stainless steel table, directing the little body into place. She was dressed in her cutting gear, the red rubber apron still clean and free from gore. The Procurator Fiscal and the corroborating pathologist were already there, dressed in coveralls, discussing the body with Isobel as she described the rubbish tip where it had been discovered.

She looked up as Logan approached, annoyance shining out from behind her safety goggles, and pulled down her surgical mask. 'I thought DI Insch was SIO on this case,' she said. 'Where is he this time?'

'He's interviewing the suspect.'

She snapped the mask back into place and muttered her displeasure. 'First he skips the David Reid post mortem and now he can't even be bothered to attend this one. I don't know why I bloody bother . . .' Her complaints trailed off into silence as she prepared her microphone and then went through the opening preliminaries. The Procurator Fiscal cast a disapproving glance at Logan. Clearly he agreed with Isobel's reading of the situation.

The shrill bleeping of Logan's mobile phone cut across her listing of those present and she hurled a furious scowl at him. 'I do not allow mobile phones to be used during my post mortems!'

Apologizing profusely, Logan dug the offending article out of his pocket and switched it off. If it was anything important they'd call back.

Still seething, Isobel finished off the introductory procedure, selected a pair of gleaming stainless steel scissors from the tray of instruments and began to snip away at the packing tape, documenting the state of the body as it was uncovered.

Underneath the tape, the little girl was naked.

A big chunk of hair threatened to come away as Isobel tried to unwrap the child's head. She loosened it with acetone, the sharp chemical smell cutting through the room's antiseptic tang and underlying perfume of decay. But at least this body hadn't been lying in a ditch for three months.

Isobel replaced the scissors on the tray and her assistant started packing the tape into labelled evidence bags. The body was still curled up in a foetal position. Gently Isobel worked the rigor out of the joints, flexing them back and forward until she could lay the little girl out flat on her back. As if she was just sleeping.

A blonde four-year-old girl, slightly overweight, with numerous bruises on her shoulders and thighs, the contusions dark on her waxy skin.

A photographer Logan didn't recognize was snapping away as Isobel worked.

'I'll need a good head and shoulders shot,' Logan told him.

The man nodded and perched over the cold, dead face.

Flash, whirr, flash whirr.

'There's a deep incision between the left shoulder and upper arm. It looks like . . .' Isobel pulled at the arm, opening up the deep gash. 'Yes: it goes all the way down to the bone.' She prodded the cut surfaces with a gloved finger. 'It was inflicted some time after death. A single blow from a sharp, flat blade. Possibly a meat cleaver.' She moved in so close to the incision that her nose was almost touching the dark-red flesh. She sniffed. 'There is a distinct smell of vomit in the region of the cut . . .' She stuck out a hand. 'Pass me those tweezers.'

Her assistant did as he was told and Isobel ferreted around in the wound, finally emerging with something grey and gristly.

'There are signs of partially-digested food in the wound.'

Logan tried not to picture the scene. Failed. 'He was trying to cut her up,' he sighed. 'Trying to get rid of the body.'

'And what makes you think that?' Isobel asked, one hand resting lightly on the little girl's chest.

'God knows there's enough talk of dismembered bodies in the papers. He wants to get rid of the evidence, so he tries to hack it up. Only it's not as easy as it sounds. Just trying it makes him sick.' Logan's voice was hollow. 'So he wraps her up in packing tape, stuffs her in a bin-bag and puts her out for the scaffies to take away.' In London they might be refuse disposal operatives, but in Aberdeen they were scaffies.

The Procurator Fiscal actually looked impressed. 'Very good,' he said. 'You may well be correct.' He turned to Isobel's assistant, Brian, who was busy popping the bits of gristle into a little plastic tube. 'Make sure that gets sent off for DNA analysis.'

Ignoring them, Isobel opened the child's mouth, peered in with a tongue depressor and recoiled. 'She appears to have ingested some form of household cleaner. Quite a lot of it from the state of her mouth. The teeth and skin all show signs of corrosive bleaching. We'll get a better idea when we get to the stomach contents.' Isobel closed the child's mouth with one hand, the other supporting the back of the blonde head. 'Hello . . .' She beckoned the photographer closer. 'Take one of this. The back of the head has suffered a severe concussive blow.' Her fingers moved, probing the hair just above the spot where the skull met the neck. 'This wasn't a blunt object, but something wide that tapered to a point.'

'Like the corner of a table?' asked Logan, not liking where this was going.

'No, it would have to be sharp, solid, like the edge of a fireplace, or a brick.'

'Was it the cause of death?'

'If drinking bleach didn't kill her . . . I won't be able to say until I've opened up the skull.'

There was a bone-saw lying on the trolley by the table. Logan didn't want to watch what was going to happen next.

Damn Detective Inspector Insch and his little bloody daughter. He should have been the one standing here watching a four-year-old getting cut up into little chunks, not Logan.

Isobel ran the scalpel blade from behind one ear, all the way across the top of the head to the other, slicing through the skin. Without even flinching, she dug her fingers into the wound and pulled, peeling the scalp forward like a sock. Logan closed his eyes, trying not to hear the sounds as the skin separated from the underlying muscle structure: like breaking up a head of lettuce. Exposing the skull.

The teeth-rattling shriek of the bone-saw echoed around the tiled room and Logan's stomach lurched.

And all the way through it Isobel kept up her detached, emotionless narrative. For once he was glad they weren't seeing each other any more. There was no way he could have her touch him tonight. Not after this.

9

Logan stood outside the front door of Force Headquarters under the concrete canopy, looking out at the dreary buildings. The rain looked as if it was settling in for another night and this end of the town was virtually deserted, enjoying the post-nine o'clock lull. The shoppers had gone home hours ago, the drinkers were all in the pubs, where they'd stay till closing time. The crowds outside the Sheriff Court dispersed for another day.

Force HQ was pretty quiet too. The day shift were long gone: off enjoying a pint, or the arms of a loved one. Or, in DI Steel's case, someone else's loved one. The back shift were drowsy and bloated after a heavy lunch, coasting the last three hours towards midnight and home-time. The night shift still another hour away.

The air was clean and cold, with just the slightest hint of traffic fumes: which was a damn sight better than the smell of burning bone. He never wanted to see the inside of a child's skull again. Grimacing, he clicked the top off the painkillers and swallowed another one. Last night's punch was still making his stomach ache.

Taking one last breath of fresh air, Logan shivered and made his way back into the tiny reception area.

The man behind the glass frowned at him, then recognition dawned and he beamed a welcoming smile. 'It *is* you!' he said. 'Logan McRae! We heard you was coming back.'

Logan did his best to place the middle-aged man with the rapidly receding hairline and wide moustache, and failed.

The man turned and shouted over his shoulder, 'Gary, Gary, come see who it is!'

An overweight man in an ill-fitting uniform stuck his head round from behind the mirrored partition. 'What?' He had a big mug of tea in one hand and a Tunnocks Tasty Caramel Wafer in the other.

'Look!' The moustached one pointed at Logan. 'It's himself.'

Logan smiled uncertainly. Who the hell were they? And then it clicked . . . 'Eric! I didn't recognize you.' Logan peered at all the scalp on display above the desk sergeant's glasses. 'What's happened to everyone's hair? I saw Billy this afternoon: he's bald as a coot!'

Eric ran a hand through his thinning locks and shrugged. 'It's a sign of virility. Anyway, look at you!'

Big Gary grinned at Logan, little flakes of chocolate falling from his caramel wafer down the front of his black uniform like dirty dandruff. 'DS Logan McRae, back from the dead!'

Eric nodded. 'Back from the dead.'

Big Gary took a slurp of his tea. 'You're like that bloke that comes back from the dead. Whatsisname, you know, the one from the bible?'

'What,' said Eric, 'Jesus?'

Big Gary smacked him lightly on the back of the head. 'No not bloody Jesus. I think I can remember Jesus' bloody name. The other one: leper or something. Comes back from the dead. You know.'

'Lazarus?' said Logan, starting to inch away.

'Lazarus! That's right!' Big Gary beamed. Bits of chocolate biscuit were stuck to his teeth. 'Lazarus McRae, that's what we'll call you.'

DI Insch wasn't in his office, or the incident room, so Logan tried the next logical place: interview room three. The inspector was still closeted with Watson, Slippery Sandy and Norman Chalmers. There was a look of utter disgust on Insch's face. Things obviously weren't going well.

Logan politely asked if he could have a word and waited outside until the inspector suspended the interview. When he came out, Insch's shirt was almost transparent with sweat. 'God, it's boiling in there,' he said, wiping his face with his hands. 'Post mortem?'

'Post mortem.' Logan held up the thin manila folder Isobel had given him. 'Preliminary results. We won't get the bloodwork back till later this week.'

Insch grabbed the folder and started flicking through it.

'The results are pretty conclusive,' said Logan. 'Someone else killed David Reid. The MO's different, the method of disposal's different, and the victim was female rather than male—'

'Fuck.' It was more of a grunt than a word. Insch had reached the part of the form marked 'PROBABLE CAUSE OF DEATH'.

'And they can't rule out a fall at this stage,' said Logan.

Insch said fuck again and stomped off down the corridor, heading for the coffee machine by the lifts. He punched in the numbers and handed Logan a plastic cup of pungent, brown, watery liquid with a faint scumming of white froth on the top. 'OK,' he said. 'So Chalmers is out of the frame for the Reid kid.'

Logan nodded. 'We've still got a killer out there, preying on little boys.'

Insch slumped against the coffee machine, making it rock alarmingly. He rubbed a hand across his face again. 'What about the bleach?'

'Applied after death: there wasn't any in her stomach or lungs. Possibly trying to get rid of DNA evidence.'

'Successful?'

Logan shrugged. 'Isobel didn't find any seminal fluid.'

The inspector's shoulders sagged. He stared blankly at the file in his hand. 'How could he do something like that? A wee girl . . .'

Logan didn't say anything. He knew Insch was thinking about his own daughter, trying not to put the two images together.

At last DI Insch straightened his shoulders, his eyes sparkling dark in his round face. 'We're going to nail this bastard to the wall by his balls.'

'But the head injury? If she fell, if it was an accident—'

'We've still got him on concealing a death, getting rid of the body, attempting to pervert the course of justice, maybe even murder. If we can persuade a jury that he pushed her.'

'Think they'll go for it?'

Insch shrugged, sipping suspiciously at his white coffee with extra sugar. 'No. But it's worth a crack. Only fly in the ointment is forensics. So far there's no sign of the girl having ever been in Chalmers's flat. And it's not like the place had been recently cleaned either, the bedroom was your proverbial pigsty. Chalmers says he's got no idea who the girl is. Never seen her before.'

'That's a shock. What's Sandy the Snake saying?'

Insch glowered in the direction of the interview room. 'Same thing the dirty wee shite always says,' he said, mopping the sweat off his head. 'We've got no evidence.'

'What about the receipt?'

'Circumstantial at best. Says the kid could have been stuffed into that bag after it left Chalmers's property.' He sighed. 'And the little sod's right. If we can't find some solid evidence linking Chalmers to the dead girl, we're screwed. Hissing Sid will tear us to pieces. And that's assuming the Procurator Fiscal wants to risk going to trial. Which isn't likely, unless we get something concrete . . .' He looked up from his coffee. 'Don't suppose his prints were all over the packing tape she was wrapped in?'

'Sorry, sir: wiped clean.'

It was all wrong. Why would someone go to all the trouble of making sure there were no fingerprints on the tape and then just chuck the body in a bag full of his own rubbish?

'Well,' said Insch, straightening up, and staring back down the corridor towards interview room number three, 'I suppose we shall just have to ignore the complete lack of hard evidence and keep Mr Chalmers banged up. But I gotta admit, I'm getting a bad feeling about this one. I don't think we're going to make it stick . . .' He stopped and shrugged. 'On the bright side: it'll ruin Sandy the Serpent's day. He won't get to strut his stuff in front of a jury.'

'Maybe another death threat would take his mind off his disappointment?'

Insch smiled. 'I'll see what I can do.'

*

Norman Chalmers was formally arrested and sent back to his cell to appear in court on the next lawful day; Sandy Moir-Farquharson went back to his office; DI Insch went to his dress rehearsal. Logan and WPC Watson went to the pub.

Archibald Simpson's had started life as a bank, the large banking floor transformed into the main bar. The ornate ceiling roses and high cornices were blurred above a fug of cigarette smoke, but the crowd were more interested in the cheap drinks than the architectural details.

As the bar was a two-minute walk from Force HQ it was a popular hangout for off-duty police. Most of the search team were in here. They'd been out in the pouring rain all day, some hunting for forensic evidence on the muddy banks of the River Don, the rest looking for Richard Erskine. Today they'd been searching for a missing child. Tomorrow they'd be looking for a dead body. Everyone knew the statistics: if you didn't find an abducted child within six hours, they were probably dead. Just like three-year-old David Reid, or the unknown girl lying on a slab in the morgue, a big Y-shaped scar running the length of her torso where all her insides had been taken out, examined, weighed, slithered into jars, bagged, tagged and handed into evidence.

They'd spent the first third of the evening talking in serious tones about the dead and missing children. The second third had been spent bitching about the Professional Standards investigation into the leaking of information to the press. Changing their name from Complaints and Discipline hadn't made them any more popular.

And the last third getting seriously drunk.

One of the PCs – Logan couldn't remember his name – lurched back to the table with another round of beers. The constable was entering that stage of drunkenness where everything seemed very funny, giggling as half a pint of lager went all over the table and down the leg of a bearded CID man.

Logan had no intention of being the responsible adult tonight, so he grabbed his pint and walked, a little unsteadily, across to the bandits.

There was a small knot of off-duty officers gathered round a quiz machine, shouting and cheering, but Logan walked right past them.

WPC Watson was standing on her own, jabbing away at a bandit. Flashing lights spiralled round and round the machine's face, glittering and bleeping and dinging away. A half-drunk bottle of Budweiser was clutched in her other hand as she stabbed the flickering buttons, sending the tumblers whizzing round again.

'You look happy,' said Logan as two lemons and a castle appeared on the display.

She didn't even look round. 'Not enough bloody evidence!' Watson hammered the nudge button, getting an anchor for her troubles.

'Have to keep looking,' said Logan, taking a swig, enjoying the warm fuzzy feeling spreading out from the middle of his head. 'Forensics didn't find anything at the flat—'

'Forensics couldn't find shite in a septic tank. What about the bloody receipt?' She stuffed another couple of pounds in the slot and smacked her fist down on the Go button.

Logan shrugged and Watson snarled at the pictures: anchor, lemon, bar of gold.

'We all know he's guilty!' she said, sending the tumblers spinning again.

'And now we've got to prove it. But we wouldn't even have him in custody if it wasn't for you.' Logan had a bit of difficulty with the word 'custody', but WPC Watson didn't seem to notice. He leaned forward and poked her gently in the shoulder. 'That receipt was a damn clever catch.'

He could have sworn she almost smiled as she fed another pound into the machine.

'I didn't spot the Clubcard points. You did that.' She didn't take her eyes off the flashing lights.

'And I wouldn't have if you hadn't found the receipt in the first place.' He beamed at her and took another drink.

She took her eyes off the machine's flashing lights to watch him sway slightly, almost in time with the music. 'What happened to "one four times a day, not to be taken with alcohol"?'

Logan winked. 'I won't tell anyone if you don't.'

She smiled at him. 'Babysitting you is going to be a full time job, isn't it?'

Logan clinked his pint glass against her bottle of beer. 'I'll drink to that!'

10

Six o'clock and the alarm's insistent bleeping
dragged Logan out of his bed and into a blistering
hangover. He slumped at the side of the bed,
holding his head in his hands, feeling the contents swell and throb. His stomach was gurgling
and churning with lurching certainty. He was
going to be sick. With a grunt he staggered to the
bedroom door and out into the hall, making for
the toilet.

Why did he have so much to drink? The pills
said quite clearly they were not to be taken with
alcohol . . .

Afterwards, he leant on the edge of the sink
and let his head droop forward to touch the cool
surface of the tiles, the acid tang of bile still
burning his nostrils.

He slid one eye open, just far enough to make
out the pint glass sitting on top of the cistern.
There was still half a bottle of the painkillers he'd
been given the first time he'd come out of the

hospital, when the scars were still fresh. Logan pulled them out with a trembling hand, struggling with the childproof lid. He filled the glass with water, knocked back a couple of the pebble-sized capsules, and slouched into the shower.

He wasn't feeling that much better by the time he was finished, but at least he didn't smell like a cross between a brewery and an ashtray any more. He was halfway across the hall, rubbing a towel through his hair, when he heard a polite cough.

Logan spun around, heart suddenly racing, his hands balling into fists.

WPC Watson was standing in the kitchen doorway, wearing one of his old T-shirts and waggling a plastic fish slice at him. Her hair, released from its tight regulation bun, fell over her shoulders in dark brown curls. A pair of bare legs stuck out of the bottom of the T-shirt and they were very nice legs indeed.

'Cold, is it?' asked Watson with a smile and Logan suddenly realized he was standing there in the nip, with everything on show.

He clutched the towel swiftly over his exposed nether regions and a furnacelike blush worked its way from the soles of his feet all the way up to the top of his head.

Her smile slipped a bit and WPC Watson frowned, a small crease forming between her neat, brown eyebrows. She was staring at his stomach, where the scars covered the skin with little puckered trails.

'Was it bad?'

Logan cleared his throat and nodded. 'I wouldn't recommend it,' he said. 'Er . . . I . . .'

'Do you want a bacon buttie? There weren't any eggs. Or much of anything else come to that.'

He stood, clutching his towel over his embarrassment, feeling the uncomfortable tingle of an approaching erection.

'Well?' she asked again: 'Bacon buttie?'

'Er, yeah . . . Thanks, that'd be great.'

She turned back into the kitchen and Logan ran for the bedroom, slamming the door behind him. God, how drunk did they get last night? *Not to be taken with alcohol!* He couldn't remember a thing. He didn't even know her first name. How could he sleep with someone when he didn't even know her first name?

He scrubbed himself with the towel, threw it in the corner and fought his still-damp feet into a pair of black socks.

How the hell could he let this happen? He was a DS and she was a WPC. They worked together. He was her superior officer! DI Insch would have a fit if he started seeing a WPC on his team!

Hopping on one leg, he got his trousers on before realizing he'd forgotten to put on any pants. So off came the trousers again.

'What the hell have you done, you idiot?' he asked the panicking reflection in the mirror. 'She works for you!' The reflection looked back at him, the consternation slowly slipping into a knowing smile. 'Aye, but she's not bad is she?'

Logan had to admit that the reflection had a point. WPC Watson was smart, attractive . . . And she could beat the shit out of anyone who used her as a one night stand. She wasn't called 'Ball Breaker' for nothing: that's what DI Insch had said!

'Oh God . . .' A fresh white shirt came out of the wardrobe and he almost strangled himself with a paisley patterned tie before charging back out into the hall. Logan stopped before he got to the kitchen. What the hell was he going to do? Should he come clean and admit he couldn't remember anything? He grimaced. That would go down well: 'Hi, I'm sorry, but I don't remember having sex with you. Was it good?' Yeah, and oh, by the way: 'What's your name?'

There was nothing else for it: he'd have to keep his mouth shut and let her make the first move. Logan took a deep breath and stepped into the kitchen.

The room smelled of frying bacon and stale beer. WPC Watson and her lovely legs were standing in front of the cooker, poking about in the frying pan, making the bacon hiss and crackle. Logan was about to say something complimentary to break the ice when someone spoke behind him, making him jump out of his skin.

'Urrrrrrghhhh . . . Shift over, I don't think I can stand up much longer.'

Logan turned to find a rumpled young man

with a rough growth of stubble and bleary eyes, dressed in casual clothes and scratching his arse, waiting for Logan to clear the way to the kitchen.

'Sorry,' Logan mumbled, letting the youth slouch past and collapse into a chair.

'Gnnnnnnnn, my head,' said the newcomer, burying the offending article in his hands and letting it sink to the tabletop.

Watson looked over her shoulder and saw Logan standing there, all done up in his work suit. 'Sit yourself down,' she told him, grabbing a couple of slices of white bread from a new loaf and slapping about half a pack of fried bacon between them. She thumped it down on the tabletop, and chucked more bacon into the pan.

'Er . . . thanks,' said Logan.

The hungover young man sitting on the other side of the table looked vaguely familiar. Was it one of the search team? The one who spilled lager over that bearded bloke from CID? Watson slammed another bacon buttie onto the table, this time in front of the groaning PC.

'You didn't have to make breakfast,' said Logan, smiling at Watson as she tipped the last of the smoked streaky into the frying pan. A big cloud of hissing steam rose from the pan and she waved it away with the fish slice, little droplets of fat falling from the plastic utensil to splatter on the work surface.

'What, you'd rather he did it?' she asked, pointing at the PC. He didn't look as if he'd make it as far as the toilet if the bacon buttie decided to give him any trouble. 'Don't know about you, but I like my breakfast chunk free.'

Another face Logan only partially recognized appeared around the kitchen door. 'God, Steve,' it said, 'look at the state of ye! If Insch catches you like that he'll have a fit . . .' He stopped when he saw Logan sitting there in his nice clean suit. 'Mornin', sir. Good party last night. Thanks for putting us up.'

'Er . . . Don't mention it.' *Party?*

The face smiled. 'Ooooooh! Nice legs, Jackie! God, bacon butties. Any chance—'

'Bugger all,' said Watson, grabbing another two slices of white and stuffing them with the last of the bacon. 'MacNeil only got four packs and they're all gone. Anyway, I gotta get ready.' She grabbed the tomato sauce off the counter top and squeezed an indecent amount of thick red into the buttie. 'You should have got out your pit earlier.'

The new face creased up with unconcealed envy as WPC Jackie Watson ripped a huge bite out of her buttie. She chewed away contentedly with a large tomato sauce smile plastered across her face.

Not one to give up easily, the man Logan still couldn't place sat himself down on the last remaining chair and lent his elbows on the tabletop. 'God, Steve,' he said, his voice dripping with concern, 'you really look rough. Are you sure you're OK to eat that?' He pointed at the bacon buttie sitting on the tabletop. 'It looks really, really greasy.'

Watson's mouth was full of food, but she still managed to mumble round the edges, 'Don't you listen to him, Steve. Do you the world of good that will.'

'Yeah,' said the PC with no name. 'You get that down you, Steve. Nice hunks of sliced dead pig. Fried in its own grease. Dripping with fat. Just the thing you need to settle a queasy, heaving stomach.'

Steve was starting to go grey.

'Nothing like a bit of lard to settle the old . . .'

The newcomer didn't have to go any further. Steve lurched up from the table, slapped a hand over his mouth and sprinted for the toilet. As the sounds of retching and splattering echoed out of the bathroom the newcomer grinned, snatched up Steve's forgotten buttie and rammed it into his gob. 'God that's good!' he declared, grease running down his chin.

'You're an utter and complete bastard, Simon Rennie!'

The bastard Simon Rennie winked at WPC Jackie Watson. 'Survival of the fittest.'

Logan sat back from the table, chewing on his bacon buttie, trying to remember what the hell happened last night. He couldn't remember any party. Everything was pretty much a blank after the pub. And some of the stuff before that was none too clear either. But apparently he'd had a party and some of the search team had crashed at his place. That made sense. His flat was on Marischal Street: two minutes' walk from Queen Street and Grampian Police Headquarters. But he still couldn't remember anything after they were chucked out of the pub. The PC currently throwing up in his toilet – Steve – had stuck Queen's 'A Kinda Magic' on the jukebox and promptly taken off all his clothes. It couldn't be called a striptease. There was no teasing and too much staggering round like a drunken lunatic.

The bar staff had kindly asked them to leave.

Which explained why half of Aberdeen's constabulary were either in his kitchen wolfing bacon, or in his bathroom chucking their guts up. But it didn't shed any light on WPC Jackie Watson and her lovely legs.

'So,' he said, watching as Watson tore another huge mouthful out of her buttie. 'How come you ended up with cooking duty?' It was a neutral subject. No one would be able to discern the subtext: *did we sleep together last night*?

She wiped her mouth with the back of her hand and shrugged. 'My turn. If it's your first time on a sleepover you have to make the butties. But it's your flat, so it goes to the next one in line.'

Logan nodded as if that made perfect sense. It was too early in the morning and he wasn't up to thinking speed yet. He just smiled in a way that he hoped didn't say anything negative about whatever had happened last night.

'Well,' he stood, dropping his crusts in the bin. 'I've got to go. The briefing's at half-seven, sharp, and I've got some pre-work to do.' Nice and businesslike. No one said anything, or even looked up. 'OK, well, if you can make sure and lock up I'll see you all there . . .' He stopped, expecting some sort of signal from WPC Watson. Jackie! Not WPC Watson: Jackie. He didn't get one. She was too busy eating. 'Yeah. Right,' he said, backing towards the door. 'See you later.'

Outside it was still dark. This time of the morning wasn't going to see the sun for another five months at least. The city was starting up as he climbed Marischal Street to the Castlegate. The streetlights were still on, and so were the Christmas lights. The twelve days of Christmas: Aberdeen's favourite, strung all the way from here to the far end of Union Street.

Logan stopped for a moment, breathing in the cold morning air. The torrential downpour was gone, replaced by a misting drizzle that made the Christmas lights hazy and blurred. Ivory-white light sculpted into lords a-leaping and swans a-swimming against the gunmetal-grey sky. The streets were slowly filling up with cars. The Union Street shop windows offered a riot of Christmas cheer and cheap tat. Above these, grey granite reached up for three or more storeys, the windows dark where offices were yet to open, people yet to wake. The whole scene was washed with amber and sparkling-white from the festive lights. It was almost beautiful. Sometimes the city reminded him why he still lived here.

He grabbed a pint of orange juice and a couple of butteries at the nearest newsagents before pushing his way through the back door of police headquarters and into the dry. The desk sergeant looked up at him as Logan shook himself on the way to the lifts.

'Morning, Lazarus.'

Logan pretended not to hear him.

The briefing room smelled of strong coffee, stale beer and hangovers. The turn-out was one hundred percent, which surprised Logan. Even the vomiting, stripping Constable Steve was sitting up at the back, looking decidedly unwell.

Logan, clutching a stack of photocopied posters of the dead girl, found a seat as close to the front as he could and sat waiting for DI Insch to start things off. The Inspector had asked him to stand up this morning and tell everyone exactly how little they knew about the four-year-old child discovered at the Nigg tip yesterday.

He looked up from his photocopies to see WPC Watson – Jackie – smiling at him. He smiled back. Now that he'd had a bit of time to work the panic out of his system he was beginning to like the idea. It had been four months since he and Isobel had gone their separate ways. It would be nice to start seeing someone again. Soon as the briefing was over he was going to ask DI Insch to assign him a different bodyguard. Surely no one could complain about him seeing her if they weren't working together.

He smiled over at WPC Jackie Watson, her lovely legs hidden beneath a pair of regulation black trousers. She smiled back. All was well with the world.

Logan suddenly became aware that everyone was smiling at him, not just WPC Jackie Watson.

'In your own time, Sergeant.'

He snapped his head around to see DI Insch staring at him. 'Er, yes. Thank you, sir.' He pulled himself out of his seat and over to the desk Insch was sitting on, hoping he didn't look as embarrassed as he felt.

'Yesterday at four p.m. one Andrea Murray, head of Social Studies at Kincorth Academy, called 999 to report the discovery of a human foot sticking out of a bin-bag at the Nigg tip. The foot belongs to an unidentified four-year-old girl: Caucasian, long blonde hair, blue eyes.' He handed a wad of photocopied sheets to the nearest person and told them to take one and pass it on. Each sheet was the same: a photograph from the morgue, full face, eyes closed, her cheeks lined where the packing tape had been. 'Our killer tried to hack up the body for disposal, but didn't have the stomach to go through with it.'

There were rumblings of disgust from the men and women filling the briefing room.

'That means . . .' Logan had to raise his voice. 'That means this was probably his first time. If he'd killed before it wouldn't have been a problem.'

Silence settled back in and Insch nodded approvingly.

Logan handed out a second set of copies. 'This is the statement of Norman Chalmers. We arrested him last night on suspicion of murder after WPC Watson found evidence linking him to the bin-bag the body was dumped in.'

Someone slapped her on the shoulder and WPC Jackie Watson smiled.

'However,' continued Logan, 'we have a problem. Forensics found no sign of the girl ever having been in Chalmers's house. If he didn't take her there, where did he take her?

'I want one team to go through Mr Chalmers's dealings with a fine-tooth comb. Does he rent a garage? Is he housesitting for anyone? Does he have any relatives, recently taken into care, who've left him in charge of the family home? Does he work somewhere he could stash a body without arousing attention?'

There were nods all round the room.

'Next team: door-to-door all over Rosemount. Who was she? How did Chalmers get hold of her?' A hand was raised and Logan pointed at its owner. 'Yes?'

'How come the kid's no been reported missing yet?'

Logan nodded. 'Good question. A four-year-old girl, missing for at least twenty-four hours, and no one bothers to call the police? That's not right. This,' he said, handing around the last set of photocopied sheets, 'is a list from Social Services of all families on the register in Aberdeen, with a child matching the age and sex of our victim. Team three: this is your job. I want each and every family on this list questioned. Make sure you see the kid. We're not taking anyone's word for anything. OK?'

Silence.

'OK. Teams.' Logan set up three four-man teams and sent them off to get started. The rest of the room shifted in their seats, chatting as the 'volunteers' shuffled out.

'Listen up,' said Insch. He didn't have to raise his voice: as soon as he opened his mouth everyone shut up. 'We've had a sighting of a child matching Richard's description getting into a dark red hatchback. Other witnesses claim to have seen a similar car hanging about the neighbourhood over the last few months. Chances are our pervert was staking out the area.' He stopped to look round the room, making sure he made eye contact with every person there. 'Richard Erskine has now been missing for twenty-two hours. Even if some scumbag hasn't grabbed him, it was pissing down and close to freezing last night. His chances aren't good. That means we have to look harder and faster. We will turn this whole bloody city upside down if we need to, but we will find him.'

You could almost smell the determination in the room, just under the cloying funk of hungover constables.

Insch read out the search team rosters and settled back on the desk as they exited the room. As Logan hung back for his instructions he saw the inspector call Steve the Naked Drunkard over, holding him back until everyone else was gone. Then he began to talk in a voice so low Logan couldn't hear a word of it, but he could guess what was being said. The young constable's face started out flushed and swiftly turned a frightened shade of grey.

'Right,' said Insch at last, nodding his large, bald head at the trembling constable. 'You go wait outside.'

Steve the Stripper trudged out, head down, looking as if he'd been slapped.

When the door closed, Insch beckoned Logan over. 'I've got a Noddy job for you this morning,' he said, pulling a family-sized bag of chocolate-covered raisins out of his suit pocket. He fumbled about trying to open it before giving up and using his teeth. 'Bloody glue these things shut . . .' Insch spat out a corner of plastic and poked a finger into the hole he'd made. 'We've been asked to provide police support for the council's environmental health team.'

Logan tried not to groan. 'You're kidding me?'

'Nope. They need to serve notice and the bloke doing it is a nervous wee shite. He's convinced he's going to get murdered if we're not there to hold his hand. The Chief Constable wants us to be accessible. That means we have to be seen to be giving the council all the support it needs.' He pointed the hole in the top of the chocolate raisins in Logan's direction.

'But, sir,' said Logan, politely refusing – the things looked too much like huge rat droppings for his hungover stomach, 'couldn't uniform do this?'

Insch nodded and Logan could have sworn he saw an evil glint in the older man's eye. 'Yes indeed. In fact a uniform *is* going to do this. You're going along to supervise.' He shook a mound of droppings into the palm of his hand and tossed them back. 'That's one of the privileges of rank: you supervise those further down the tree.'

There was a meaningful pause that completely passed Logan by.

'Well,' said Insch, shooing him towards the door. 'Off you go.'

Still wondering what that had been about, Logan left the briefing room. DI Insch sat on the desk, grinning like a maniac. It wouldn't take long before the penny dropped.

A worried-looking Constable Steve was waiting in the corridor. His face had regained a little bit

131

of its colour and was now an unhealthy reddish-green rather than pale grey; but he still looked dreadful. His eyes were pink with bloodshot veins, his breath reeked of extra strong mints, but it wasn't enough to disguise the alcohol oozing out of his pores.

'Sir,' he said, giving a sickly, nervous smile. 'I don't think I should drive, sir.' He hung his head. 'Sorry, sir.'

Logan raised an eyebrow and opened his mouth. Then shut it again. This must be the uniform he was supposed to supervise.

They were riding the lift down to the ground floor when Constable Steve disintegrated. 'How the hell did he know?' he asked, slumping in the corner with his head in his hands. 'Everything. He knew bloody everything!'

Logan could feel dread stomping down his spine. 'Everything?' Did the inspector know he'd got pissed and slept with WPC Watson?

Constable Steve moaned.

'He knew we'd been thrown out of the pub, he knew all about the getting naked . . .' he looked up at Logan with pitiful pink eyes: like a vivisectioned rabbit. 'He says I'm lucky he didn't just fire me! Oh God . . .'

For a moment it looked as if he was going to burst into tears. Then the lift went: 'ping' and the doors slid open onto the car park where a couple of uniformed officers were wrestling a hairy bloke in jeans and a T-shirt out of the back of a patrol car. The man's T-shirt bore a lovely upside-down Christmas tree of blood. His nose was flattened and smeared.

'Buncha fuckin' bastards!' He lunged towards Logan, but the PC holding him wasn't about to let go. 'Fuckin' bastards wis askin' fer it!' Some of his teeth were missing too.

'Sorry, sir,' said the PC, holding him back.

Logan told him it was OK and led PC Steve away through the car park. They could have gone out through reception, but he didn't want anyone else seeing the pink-eyed constable in his current state. And anyway, the council buildings weren't that far away: a walk in the open air would do Steve the world of good.

Outside, the drizzle was refreshing after the oppressive heat of police headquarters. They both stood on the ramp that wound from the rear of the building down to the street with their faces to the rain and stayed that way until a car horn made them jump.

The patrol car flashed its lights. Logan and the hungover PC waved an apology and walked around the side of Force HQ. Outside the Sheriff Court the protesters were already gathering, clutching their banners and placards, desperate for a glimpse of Gerald Cleaver. And an opportunity to string him up from the nearest lamppost.

The Nervous Wee Shite was waiting for them at the main council buildings, shifting from foot to foot, peering at his watch the whole time as if it was going to run off if left unsupervised for more than thirty seconds at a time. He gave PC Steve a worried look and then extended a hand for Logan to shake. 'Sorry to keep you waiting,' he said, even though he'd been standing there long before they arrived.

They exchanged introductions, but Logan had forgotten the man's name within thirty seconds of hearing it.

'Shall we get going?' The forgettable man stopped, fussed with a large leather folder, checked his watch again, and led them off towards a Ford Fiesta that looked in need of the last rites.

Logan sat in the passenger seat next to Mr Nervous, making PC Steve sit in the back, behind the driver. One: he didn't want the council's environmental health 'Danger Man' getting a good look at the bloody state the constable was in; and two: if PC Steve decided to throw up again, it wouldn't be all over the back of Logan's head.

All the way across town their driver kept up a running commentary on what a terrible thing it was to work for the council, but how he couldn't escape to another job because he'd lose all his benefits. Logan tuned him out, just popping back up to the surface with the odd 'Sounds terrible,' and 'I know how you feel,' to keep the man happy. Instead he sat looking out of the window at the grey streets drifting slowly past.

Rush hour was getting to the point at which everyone who should have left for work half an hour ago suddenly realized they were going to be late. Here and there some daft soul sat behind the wheel, cigarette clenched between their teeth, with the window wound down. Letting the smoke out and the drizzle in. Logan watched them with envy.

He was beginning to get the feeling DI Insch had been telling him something with that whole 'Privilege of Rank' speech. Something unpleasant. He ran a slow hand over his forehead, feeling the swollen lump of his brain through the skin.

It was no surprise that Insch had read Steve the riot act. The drunken PC could have caused the whole force a lot of embarrassment. Logan could see the headlines now: 'NAKED COPPER SHOWED ME HIS TRUNCHEON!' If he were Steve's superior officer he'd have given him a bollocking too.

And that was when the penny dropped. Insch had said it right to his face: 'That's one of the privileges of rank: you supervise those further down the tree.' He was a detective sergeant, Steve a constable. They'd all gone out and got pissed and Logan hadn't done a bloody thing to stop the PC getting blootered and bollock-naked.

Logan groaned.

This assignment was as much a punishment for him as it was for Steve.

Twenty-five minutes later they were climbing out of the Nervous Wee Shite's car in front of a dilapidated farm steading, the first outlying arm of a rambling croft on the outskirts of Cults. What little road there was disappeared into the undergrowth. A rundown farmhouse sulked at the end of the track, its grey stone weeping in the neverending rain. Derelict farm buildings sprawled around it, set in a wasteland of hip-deep grass and weeds. Ragwort and docken stuck up through the vegetation, their stems and leaves rust-brown beneath the winter sky. Two windows poked out of the building's slate roof like an empty, hostile stare. Below, a faded red door bore a big painted number six. Each of the rambling steadings had a number scrawled on them in white paint. Every surface was slick with the misty rain, reflecting back the flat, grey daylight.

'Homely,' said Logan, in an attempt to break the ice. And then he smelled it. 'Oh Jesus!' He slapped a hand over his mouth and nose.

It was the cloying, reeking stink of corruption. Of meat left for too long in the sun.

The smell of death.

11

PC Steve lurched once, twice, and charged into the bushes to be noisily and copiously sick.

'You see?' said the nervous man from the council. 'Didn't I tell you it was terrible? Didn't I?'

Logan nodded and agreed, even though he hadn't paid attention to a single word on the way out.

'The neighbours have been complaining about the smell since last Christmas. We've written letter after letter, but we never get anything back,' said the man, clutching his leather folder to his chest. 'The postman refuses to deliver here any more you know.'

'Really,' said Logan. That explained why they never got a bloody reply. Turning his back on the retching constable, he started wading his way through the jungle. 'Let's go see if there's anyone in.'

Not surprisingly, the man from the council let him go first.

The main farm building had once been well cared for. There were little flecks of white paint on the crumbling stone, twisted rusting brackets where hanging baskets would have been. But those days were long gone. Grass was growing in the gutters, blocking the downpipe, and water dripped over the edge. The door hadn't seen a fresh coat of paint for years. Weather and wasps had stripped the last coat away, leaving bare, bleached wood and a small iron number was screwed in the middle, rendered illegible by rust and dirt. The handle didn't look much better. And over the lot was that big, white, hand-painted number six.

Logan knocked. They stood back and waited. And waited. And waited. And . . .

'Oh for God's sake!' Logan abandoned the door and stomped off through the undergrowth, peering into every window on the way.

Inside, the house was shrouded in darkness. He could just make out mounds of furniture in the gloom: shapeless blobs obscured by the filthy glass.

He finally made it back to the front. A perfectly trampled path in the long grass marked the route he'd taken. Closing his eyes, Logan tried not to swear. 'There's no one here,' he said. 'There hasn't been for months.' If someone was still living here, the grass would have been tramped flat between the road and the door.

The council man looked at the house, then

back at Logan, then at his watch and then fumbled his way into his leather folder and pulled out a clipboard.

'No,' he said, reading off the top sheet of paper, 'this property is the residence of one Mr Bernard Philips.' He stopped and fiddled with the buttons on his coat and checked his watch again. 'He, er . . . he works for the council.'

Logan opened his mouth to say something very, very rude, but shut it again.

'What do you mean "he works for the council"?' he asked, slowly and deliberately. 'If he works for the council, why didn't you just serve notice when he turned up for work this morning?'

The man examined his clipboard again. Doing his best not to meet Logan's eyes. Keeping his mouth shut.

'Oh for God's sake,' said Logan. In the end it didn't really matter. They were here now. They might as well get it over with. 'And is Mr Philips at work right now?' he asked, trying to sound calm.

The nervous man shook his head. 'He's got a day off.'

Logan tried to massage away the headache pulsing behind his eyes. At least that was something. 'OK. So if he does live here—'

'He does!'

'If he does live here, he's not staying in the farmhouse.' Logan turned his back on the dark, neglected building. The rest of the farm buildings were arranged with almost casual abandon, and all had numbers painted on the front.

'Let's try over there,' he said at last, pointing at the ramshackle structure with the number one painted on it. It was as good a place to start as any.

A shaking, white-faced Constable Steve joined them outside the steading, looking even worse than he had first thing this morning. You had to give it to DI Insch: when he punished someone he did it properly.

The door to steading number one had been clarted in cheap green paint. There was paint on the wood, up the walls on either side, on the grass beneath their feet . . . Logan gestured to the shivering constable, but PC Steve just stared back at him in mute horror. The smell here was even worse than before.

'Open the door, Constable,' said Logan, determined not to do it himself. Not when he had some poor sod to do it for him.

It took a while, but in the end PC Steve said, 'Yes, sir,' and took a good hold of the handle. It was a heavy sliding door, the runners buckled and flaky with rust. The constable gritted his teeth and yanked. It creaked open, letting out the most godawful smell Logan had ever encountered in his life.

Everyone staggered back.

A small avalanche of dead bluebottles tumbled out of the open door to lie in the misty drizzle.

Constable Steve hurried off to be sick again.

The building had been a cattle shed at some point: a long, low, traditionally-built farm steading, with bare granite walls and a slate roof. An elevated walkway ran down the centre of the building, bordered by knee-high wooden rails. It was the only empty area in the place. Everything else was filled with the rotting carcases of small animals.

The stiff and twisted bodies were covered with a carpet of wriggling white.

Logan took three steps back and bolted for a corner to be sick in. It was like being punched in the guts all over again, each heave sending ripples of pain through his scarred stomach.

Steadings number one, two and three were full of dead animals. Number three wasn't quite packed yet: there was still a good ten or twelve feet of exposed concrete, free of corpses, but covered with a thick yellow ooze. The bodies of flies were crispy under foot.

Somewhere around steading number two Logan had changed his mind: DI Insch wasn't someone who punished drunken PCs properly. He was an utter bastard.

They opened and checked each of the buildings, and Logan's stomach lurched every time PC Steve dragged open a door. After what seemed like a week of retching and swearing they sat outside on a crumbling wall. Upwind. Clutching their knees and breathing through their mouths.

The farm buildings were full of dead cats and dogs and hedgehogs and seagulls and even a couple of red deer. If it had ever walked, flown or crawled it was here. It was like some sort of necromancer's ark. Only there was a hell of a lot more than two of every animal.

'What are you going to do with them all?' asked Logan, still tasting the bile after half a packet of PC Steve's extra strong mints.

The council man looked up at him, his eyes bright pink from repeated vomiting. 'We'll have to remove them all and incinerate the lot,' he said, running a hand over his wet face. He shuddered. 'It'll take days.'

'Rather you than . . .' Logan stopped: something was moving at the end of the long drive.

It was a man in faded jeans and a bright orange anorak. He tramped along the tarmacked portion of the road with his head down, seeing nothing more than his feet beneath him.

'Shhhhhhhhh!' hissed Logan, grabbing the council man and the bilious PC. 'You go round the back there,' he whispered, pointing PC Steve at the building with the number two scrawled on the front.

He watched the PC scurry off through the sodden undergrowth. When he was in place Logan grabbed a handful of the council man's jacket. 'Time to serve your papers,' he said, and stepped out onto the flattened grass.

The man in the orange anorak was less than six foot away when he finally looked up.

Logan hadn't recognized the name, but he knew the face: it was Roadkill.

They sat on a makeshift bench just inside steading number five. Mr Bernard Duncan Philips, AKA Roadkill, had made something like a home in here. A large bundle of blankets, old coats and plastic sacks were piled in the corner, obviously serving as a bed. There was a rough crucifix on the wall above the nest, a half-naked Action Man taking the place of Christ on the home-made cross.

A mound of empty tin cans and egg cartons sat next to the bed, along with a small Calor Gas cooker. It was one of the little ones Logan's father had taken with them on every summer caravan holiday to Lossiemouth. Right now it was hissing away to itself, boiling a kettle of water for tea.

Roadkill – it was hard to think of him as Bernard – sat on a rickety wooden chair, poking away at a small fire. It was a two bar electric job, as dead as the animals in buildings one through three. But it seemed to give him pleasure. He jabbed at it with an elaborate iron poker, humming a tune to himself that Logan couldn't quite make out.

The man from the council was surprisingly calm now that Roadkill was here. He laid out the situation in small, easy-to-understand words: the mounds of dead animals had to go.

'I'm sure you understand, Bernard,' he said,

poking at his clipboard with a finger, 'that you can't keep dead animals here. There's a considerable risk to human health. How would you feel if people started getting sick because of your dead animals?'

Roadkill just shrugged and poked at the fire again. 'Mother got sick,' he said and Logan was struck by the lack of an accent. He'd always assumed that someone employed by the council to scrape dead animals off the road would sound a lot more 'local'. Some of the people round here were almost unintelligible. But not Roadkill. It was clear that the man sitting on a creaking dining chair, jabbing away at a dead electric fire, had suffered some sort of classical education. 'She got sick and she went away,' Roadkill went on, looking up for the first time. 'Now she's with God.' He was a good-looking man, under all the dirt and grime and beard. Proud nose, intelligent slate-grey eyes, weather-reddened cheeks. Give him a bath and a visit to the barber's and he wouldn't look out of place at the Royal Northern Club, where the city's elite held court over expensive five-course lunches.

'I know, Bernard, I know.' The man from the council smiled reassuringly. 'We're going to send a crew in tomorrow to start clearing out the buildings. OK?'

Roadkill dropped the poker. It hit the concrete floor with a clatter that reverberated off the bare stone walls. 'They're my things,' he said, his face working itself up to tears. 'You can't take away my things! They're mine.'

'They have to be disposed of, Bernard. We have to make sure you're safe, don't we?'

'But they're mine . . .'

The man from the council stood, motioning for Logan and Constable Steve to do the same. 'I'm sorry, Bernard, I really am. The team will be here at half past eight on the dot. You can help them if you like.'

'My things.'

'Bernard? Would you like to help them?'

'My special dead things . . .'

They drove back into town with the windows down, trying to get rid of the smell of Bernard Duncan Philips's farm. It clung to their clothes and their hair, rancid and foul. It didn't matter that the drizzle had given way to heavier rain, seeping in through the open windows: getting wet was a small price to pay.

'You wouldn't think it to look at him,' said the man from the council as they worked their way along Holburn Street, making for the council's main headquarters at St Nicholas House. 'But he used to be a really bright lad. Degree in medieval history from St Andrews University. Or so I'm told.'

Logan nodded. He'd suspected as much. 'What happened?'

'Schizophrenic.' The man shrugged. 'He's on medication.'

'Care in the community?' asked Logan.

'Oh he's perfectly safe,' said the man from the council, but Logan could hear the tremor in his voice. That was why he'd been so insistent on a police escort. Care in the community or not, he was scared of Roadkill. 'And he does a good job, he really does.'

'Scraping up dead animals.'

'Well, we can't just leave them to rot at the side of the road, can we? I mean it's not too bad with rabbits and hedgehogs, the cars sort of smush them into paste and the crows and things take care of what's left. But cats and dogs and things . . . You know . . . People complain if they have to drive past a rotting labrador every morning on the way to work.' He paused as a bus pulled out in front of them. 'I don't know what we'd do without Bernard. Before he was released into the community we couldn't get anyone to do it for love nor money.'

Now he actually stopped to think about it, it had been a long time since Logan had seen a dead animal on an Aberdeen street.

The man from the council dropped them off outside Force HQ, thanking them for their help and apologizing for the smell before driving off into the rain.

Logan and PC Steve sprinted for the main door, their feet sending up fountains of water with every step. They were both soaked by the time they pushed through into reception.

The pointy-faced desk sergeant looked up as they squelched their way across the Grampian Police Crest set into the lino: a thistle topped with a crown, above the words 'SEMPER VIGILO'.

'DS McRae?' he said, stretching himself out of his chair like a curious parrot.

'Yes?' Logan was waiting for some sort of 'Lazarus' comment. Those bastards Big Gary and Eric must have told the whole bloody station about it.

'DI Insch says you're to go straight to the incident room.'

Logan took a look down at his soaking trousers and wringing suit. He was desperate to climb into a shower and a dry set of clothes. 'Can it not wait fifteen, twenty minutes?' he asked.

The sergeant shook his head. 'Nope. The DI was very specific. Soon as you got back: straight to the incident room.'

While PC Steve went off to get dry, Logan grumbled his way through the building to the lifts, mashing the button with an angry finger. Up on the third floor he stomped his way down the corridor. The walls were already punctuated with Christmas cards. They were pinned to the corkboards, in between 'HAVE YOU SEEN THIS WOMAN?' and 'DOMESTIC ABUSE . . . THERE'S NO EXCUSE!' and all the other wanted and information posters the media office put out. Tiny bursts of cheer among all the misery and suffering.

The incident room was crowded and bustling.

PCs, WPCs and DCs charged about clutching sheets of paper, or answered the constantly bleating phones. And in the middle of it all Detective Inspector Insch sat on the edge of a desk, peering over someone's shoulder as they scribbled down notes with a phone clamped between their shoulder and their ear.

Something had happened.

'What's up?' asked Logan after he'd squelched his way through the crowd.

The inspector held up a hand for silence, leaning closer so he could read what was being written. Finally he sighed with disappointment and turned his attention to Logan. An eyebrow shot up as he saw the state of his detective sergeant. 'Go for a swim did you?'

'No, sir,' said Logan, feeling water trickling down the back of his neck into his already sodden collar. 'It's raining.'

Insch shrugged. 'That's Aberdeen for you. Could you not have dried yourself off before coming in here, dripping all over my lovely clean incident room?'

Logan closed his eyes and tried not to rise to the bait. 'The desk sergeant said it was urgent, sir.'

'We've lost another kid.'

The car was steaming up too quickly for the blowers to deal with. Logan had cranked them, and the heating, up to full pelt, but the outside world remained obscured behind misty windows. DI Insch sat in the passenger seat, chewing away thoughtfully as Logan squinted through the windscreen at the dark, rain-soaked streets, trying to get them through town to Hazlehead and the place where the latest child had gone missing.

'You know,' said Insch, 'since you came back to work we've had two abductions, found a dead girl, a dead boy and dragged a corpse with no knees out the harbour. All in the space of three days. That's a record for Aberdeen.' He poked about in his packet of fizzy, jelly shapes, coming out with what looked like an amoeba. 'I'm beginning to think you're some sort of jinx.'

'Thank you, sir.'

'It's playing merry hell with my crime statistics,' said Insch. 'Nearly every bloody officer I've got is either out there searching for missing children or trying to find out who the little girl in the bin-bag was. How am I supposed to get the burglaries and the frauds and the indecent exposures sorted out if I don't have any bloody uniforms left?' He sighed and offered the bag to Logan.

'No thank you, sir.'

'I tell you, rank has fewer privileges than you think.'

Logan looked across at the inspector. Insch was not the sort of officer who normally indulged in self-pity. At least not as far as Logan knew. 'Like supervising uniforms, you mean?' he asked.

At this a smile broke over DI Insch's large features. 'Did you like Roadkill's little collection?'

So he had known all about the steadings full of rotting animal corpses. He had done it on purpose.

'I don't think I've been sick so many times in my life before.'

'How was Constable Jacobs?'

Logan was about to ask who Constable Jacobs was, when he realized the inspector was talking about PC Steve: the naked drunkard. 'I don't think he'll forget this morning in a hurry.'

Insch nodded. 'Good.'

Logan thought the large man was going to say something more, but Insch just stuffed another sweetie in his mouth and smiled evilly to himself.

Hazlehead was right on the edge of city, just a stone's throw from the countryside proper. On the other side of Hazlehead Academy only the crematorium stood between civilization and the rolling fields. The Academy had a reputation for drugs and violent pupils, but it wasn't a patch on places like Powis and Sandilands, so things could have been worse.

Logan pulled the car up in front of one of the tower blocks near the main road. It wasn't as big as the ones in town, being a mere seven storeys, and was surrounded by mature, cadaverous trees. The leaves had come off late this year, coating the ground in slimy black clots that clogged the drains and made them overflow.

'You got an umbrella?' asked the inspector, taking a good long look at the horrible weather.

Logan admitted that he had, in the boot, so Insch made him get out of the car and fetch it, not stepping out into the downpour until Logan had the brolly open and was standing right next to the car door.

'Now that's what I call service,' said Insch with a grin. 'Come on then, let's go see the family.'

Mr and Mrs Lumley had a corner apartment near the top of the tower block. To Logan's surprise the lifts didn't reek of piss, nor were they scrawled all over with badly-spelled graffiti. The lift doors opened onto a well-lit corridor and halfway down they found a uniform rummaging about in his nose.

'Sir!' he said, snapping upright and abandoning his excavations as soon as he saw the inspector.

'How long you been here?' asked Insch, sneaking a peek over the PC's shoulder at the Lumley home.

'Twenty minutes, sir.' There was a tiny station-house less than two hundred yards from the tower blocks. Little more than a couple of rooms really, but it did the job.

'You got someone going door-to-door?'

The PC nodded. 'Two PCs and a WPC, sir. The area car's off broadcasting a description.'

'When did he go missing?'

The constable dragged a notebook out of his pocket, flicking it open at the right page. 'The mother called at ten-thirteen. The child had been playing outside—'

Logan was shocked. 'In this weather?'

'Mother says he likes the rain. Dresses up like Paddington Bear.'

'Aye, well . . .' said Insch, stuffing his hands deep in his pockets. 'Takes all sorts. Friends?'

'All at school.'

'I'm glad someone is. Have you checked with the school, just in case our little friend has decided to go learn something?'

The PC nodded. 'We called them straight after the friends. They've not seen him for almost a week and a half.'

'Lovely,' said Insch with a sigh. 'Right, come on then, out the way. We'd better see the parents.'

Inside, the flat was all done up in bright colours, just like the house at Kingswells, where David Reid used to live before he was taken, strangled, abused and mutilated. There were pictures on the walls, like the Erskine's house in Torry, but the kid was a scruffy-looking boy of about five, with a mop of red hair and a face full of freckles.

'That was taken two months ago, at his birthday party.'

Logan turned his attention from the wall to the woman standing in the lounge doorway. She was quite simply stunning: long, curly red hair hanging loose on her shoulders, a small upturned nose and wide green eyes. She'd been crying. Logan did his best not to stare at her considerable bosom as she showed them into the living room.

'Have you found him?' This from a tattered-looking man in blue overalls and socks.

'Give them time, Jim, they've only just got here,' said the woman, patting him on the arm.

'Are you the father?' asked Insch, perching himself on the edge of a bright blue sofa.

'Stepfather,' said the man, sitting back down again. 'His father was a bastard—'

'Jim!'

'Sorry. His dad and me don't get on.'

Logan started a slow inspection of the cheerful room, making a show of examining the photos and the ornaments, all the time watching Jim the stepfather. It wouldn't be the first time a stepson had fallen foul of mum's new husband. Some people took to their partner's kids as if they were their own, others looked at them as a constant reminder that they weren't first. That someone else had shagged the one they loved. Jealousy was a terrible thing. Especially when vented on a five-year-old child.

OK, every photo on the wall showed the three of them looking as if they were having a great time, but people didn't tend to put up pictures of the bruises, cigarette burns and broken bones in the living room.

Logan was particularly taken with a scene on a beach somewhere hot, in which everyone was in their swimming gear, grinning at the camera. The mother's figure was breathtaking, especially in a bottle-green bikini. Even with the scar where she must have had a Caesarean section.

'Corfu,' said Mrs Lumley. 'Jim takes us away somewhere nice every year. Last year it was Corfu, this year it was Malta. Next year we're taking Peter to Florida to see Mickey Mouse . . .' She bit her bottom lip. 'Peter loves Mickey Mouse . . . he . . . Oh God, please find him!' And with that she dissolved into her husband's arms.

Insch cast Logan a meaningful glance. Logan nodded and said, 'Why don't I make us all a nice cup of tea? Mr Lumley, can you show me where the things are?'

Half an hour later Logan and Inspector Insch were standing at the bottom of the tower block's stairwell, looking out at the driving rain.

'What do you think?' asked Insch, ferreting out his bag of fizzy sweeties.

'The stepfather?'

Insch nodded.

'He seems genuinely fond of the kid. You should have heard him banging on about how Peter's going to play for the Dons when he grows up. I don't see him as the wicked stepdad.'

The inspector nodded again. While Logan had been making the tea and questioning the dad,

Insch had been gently pumping the mother for information.

'Me neither. The kid's not had any history of accidents, or mysterious illnesses, or trips to the doctor.'

'How come he wasn't in school today?' asked Logan, helping himself to one of Insch's sweets.

'Bullying. Some big fat kid's been beating the crap out of him 'cos he's ginger. Mother's keeping him off until the school do something about it. She's not told the stepfather though. She thinks he'd go nuts if he knew someone was picking on Peter.'

Insch stuffed a fizzy thing into his mouth and sighed. 'Two kids missing in two days,' he said, not bothering to disguise the sadness in his voice. 'Christ, I hope he's just run away. I really don't want to see another dead kid in the morgue.' Insch sighed again, his large frame deflating slightly.

'We'll find them,' said Logan with a conviction he didn't feel.

'Aye, we'll find them.' The inspector stepped out into the rain, without waiting for Logan to open the brolly. 'We'll find them, but they'll be dead.'

12

Logan and Insch drove back to Force Headquarters in silence. The sky had darkened overhead, storm clouds spreading from one horizon to the other, blotting out the daylight, turning the city dark at two in the afternoon. As they drove the street-lights flickered on, their yellow light making the day seem even darker.

Insch was right of course: they wouldn't find the missing children alive. Not if it was the same man who'd snatched them. According to Isobel the sexual abuse had all happened post mortem.

Logan slid the car across Anderson Drive on autopilot.

At least Peter Lumley had lived a bit first. Poor bloody Richard Erskine had nothing but an over-protective mother. Somehow Logan couldn't see her taking Richard to Corfu and Malta and Florida. Far too dangerous for her little darling. Peter was lucky he had a nice stepdad to take care of him . . .

'You been seen by the Spanish Inquisition yet?' asked Insch as Logan negotiated the roundabout at the end of Queen Street. A large statue of Queen Victoria sat in the middle on a huge granite plinth. Someone had stuck a traffic cone on her head.

'Professional Standards? No, not yet.' He still had that little treat to look forward to.

Insch sighed. 'I had them in this morning. Some jumped-up prick in a smart new uniform, never done a damned day's policing in his life, telling me how important it is to find out who leaked the story to the press. Like I couldn't work that one out for myself. I tell you, I get whoever—'

A dirty Ford van shot out in front of them, causing Logan to slam on the brakes and swear.

'Let's pull them over!' cried Insch with glee. Making someone else's day miserable might make them both feel better.

They gave the driver a stern talking to and ordered her to turn up at nine the following morning with all her documentation. It wasn't much, but it was something.

Back at Force HQ the incident room was in turmoil. The phones were ringing non-stop, following an announcement on Northsound Radio and the lunchtime TV news. All the major channels were carrying the story. Aberdeen was becoming a media hot-spot. The whole force was under the spotlight. And if Insch didn't get this thing solved soon, he'd get his head to play with.

They spent a while going over the various sightings of the two missing boys. Most of them would be a waste of time, but they all had to be investigated, just in case. One of the force's technical experts was busy collating all the reports into the computer, taking every sighting and interview, location, time and date and sticking it into HOLMES, the Home Office Large Major Enquiry System, setting the massive cross-referencing program running, churning out reams and reams of automatically generated actions. It was a pain in the arse, but you never knew when something might prove to be important.

But Logan knew it was all a waste of time, because Peter Lumley was already dead. Didn't matter how many old ladies saw him wandering the streets of Peterhead or Stonehaven. The kid was lying in a ditch somewhere, half-naked and violated.

The admin officer, a woman far too clever to be that thin, handed a stack of paper to Insch: the actions generated by HOLMES while he and Logan had been out. The inspector took them with good grace and skimmed through them. 'Shite, shite, shite,' he said, throwing unwanted sheets over his shoulder as he came to them.

Every time it came across a person's name in a statement, HOLMES produced an action to have that person interviewed. Even if it was just some old woman saying she'd been feeding her cat Mr

Tibbles at the time the kid went missing: HOLMES wanted Mr Tibbles interviewed.

'Not doing that, or that.' Another couple of sheets went fluttering to the floor. When he'd finished the pile had been reduced to a mere handful. 'Get the rest underway,' he said, handing it back to the admin officer.

She gave him a long-suffering salute and left them to it.

'You know,' said Insch, casting a critical eye over Logan, 'you look worse than I feel.'

'I'm not doing anything here, sir.'

Insch parked himself on the edge of a desk and riffled through a stack of reports. 'Tell you what,' he said and handed over the pile of paper. 'If you want to make yourself useful, go through that lot. It's from the door-to-doors in Rosemount this morning. Norman bloody Chalmers gets his appearance in court this afternoon. See if you can find out who that little girl was before they let the bastard out on bail.'

Logan found himself an empty office as far away from the noise and chaos of the incident room as possible. Uniform had been thorough, the times on the statements making it clear that they'd gone back to some buildings more than once to be sure they spoke to everyone.

No one knew who the dead girl was. No one recognized her face from the photograph taken in the morgue. It was as if she hadn't existed before her leg was spotted sticking out of a bin-bag at the tip.

Logan went out to the supply office and got himself a new map of Aberdeen, sticking it up on the wall of his commandeered office. There was one of these in Insch's incident room already, all covered with pins and lines and little sticky tags. But Logan wanted one of his own. He stuck a red pin in the Nigg tip, and another in Rosemount: 17 Wallhill Crescent.

The bin-bag the girl was stuffed into came from the home of Norman Chalmers. Only there was no forensic evidence to tie him to the victim. Other than the contents of the bag. Maybe that was enough to go to trial, but a good defence lawyer – and Sandy Moir-Farquharson wasn't just good: the little shite was brilliant – would rip the case to shreds.

'Right.' He sat back on the desk, arms folded, staring at the two pins in the map.

That bin-bag bothered him. The flat had been covered in cat hair when they'd arrested Chalmers. Logan had spent most of that night in the pub trying to brush the damned stuff off his trousers. There were still stubborn patches of grey fluff sticking to his suit jacket. If the kid had been in the flat, Isobel would have found traces of cat hair during the post mortem.

So she was never in the flat. That much they knew. That was why Insch had asked for a thorough background search on Chalmers, to see where else he could have taken her. But the research teams had come up empty. If Norman Chalmers had somewhere else to take a four-year-old girl, no one knew about it.

'So what if he didn't do it?' he asked himself aloud.

'What if who didn't do what?'

It was WPC Wat . . . Jackie.

'What if Norman Chalmers didn't kill that little girl?'

Her face hardened. 'He killed her.'

Logan sighed and picked himself off the edge of the desk. He might have known she'd be touchy about this. She was still hoping that finding the receipt would crack the case.

'Look at it this way: if he didn't kill her someone else did. OK?'

She rolled her eyes.

Logan went on quickly. 'OK, so if it was someone else it has to be someone who's got access to Norman Chalmers's rubbish.'

'No one does! Who's going to get into his rubbish?'

Logan poked a finger at the map, making the paper crackle. 'Rosemount has those big communal bin things out in the street. Anyone could dump their crap in one. If the killer wasn't Chalmers, then there's only two places they could get the body into that bin-bag: here—' he poked the map again, '—or here, when it gets to the tip at Nigg. If you're going to hide a body at the tip, you're not going to leave a leg sticking out. What would be the point of that? Much easier to just bury it in the rubbish bags.' Logan pulled the Nigg pin out of the map and tapped the red plastic end against his teeth. 'So, the killer didn't dump the body at the tip. It was taken there in the back of a corporation dustcart and poured out the back along with all the other junk. She was put in that bin-bag while it was still out in the street.'

WPC Watson didn't look convinced. 'Chalmers's flat is still the most logical. If he didn't kill her, why's she in a bin-bag along with his garbage?'

Logan shrugged. That was the problem. 'Why do you put anything in a bag?' he asked. 'To make it easier to carry. Or to hide it. Or . . .' He turned back to the table and began sorting through the statements the door-to-door team had taken. 'You're not going to cart a dead girl round in your car looking for a wheelie-bin to stuff it in,' he said, putting all the statements into piles according to their house number in Wallhill Crescent. 'You've got a car: you take the body away and bury it in a shallow grave out by Garlogoie, or up round New Deer. Somewhere isolated. Somewhere no one's going to find it for years and years. If ever.'

'Maybe they panicked?'

Logan nodded.

'Exactly. You panic: you get rid of the body in the first place you can find. Again, you don't go driving round looking for a wheelie-bin. The fact she wasn't wrapped in anything other than packing tape is weird too. A naked little dead girl, all stuck together with brown packing tape? You're not going to go far carrying that . . . Whoever dumped the body lived nearer this particular bin than any of the others in the street.'

He split the piles of statements into two, those within two doors of number seventeen and those farther away. That still left thirty individual flats.

'Can you do me a favour?' he asked, scribbling down the names from each statement onto a fresh sheet of paper. 'Get these down to Criminal Records. I want to know if any of them have priors for anything. Warnings, arrests, parking violations. Anything.'

WPC Watson told him he was wasting his time. That Norman Chalmers was guilty as sin. But she took the names away with her and promised to get back to him.

When she was gone Logan grabbed a bar of chocolate from the machine and a cup of instant coffee, consuming both while he read through the statements again. Someone here was lying. Someone here knew who the little girl was. Someone here had killed her, tried to cut up her body, and thrown her out with the trash.

Trouble was, who?

Over three thousand people went missing in the north-east of Scotland every year. Three thousand people reported missing every twelve months. And yet here was a four-year-old girl missing for at least two days now, according to the post mortem, and no one had come forward to ask what the police were going to do about it. Why hadn't she been reported missing? Maybe because there was no one to notice she was gone?

The familiar jangling tune blared out from his pocket and Logan swore. 'Logan,' he said.

It was the front desk telling him he had a visitor downstairs.

Logan scowled at the pile of statements sitting on the desk. 'OK,' he said at last. 'I'll be right down.'

He dropped his chocolate wrapper and empty plastic cup into the bin and headed down to the reception area. Someone had cranked the heating up too far and the windows were all fogged up as visitors, drenched in the downpour outside, sat and steamed.

'Over there,' said the pointy-faced desk sergeant.

Colin Miller, the *Press and Journal*'s new golden boy from Glasgow, was standing over by the wanted posters. He wore a long black tailored raincoat that dripped steadily onto the tiled floor while he copied down details into a small palm computer.

Miller turned and grinned as Logan approached. 'Laz!' he said, sticking out a hand. 'Good tae see you again. Love what you've done with the place.' He swept a hand round to indicate the steamy, cramped reception area with its soggy visitors and steamy windows.

'My name's DS McRae. Not "Laz".'

Colin Miller winked. 'Oh, I know. I've done me some diggin' since we met in the bogs yesterday. That wee WPC of yours is a bit tasty, byraway. She can bang me up any time, if you know what I mean.' He gave Logan another wink.

'What do you want, Mr Miller?'

'Me? I wanted tae take my favourite detective sergeant out for lunch.'

'It's three o'clock,' said Logan, suddenly aware that, except for a bar of chocolate and a couple of butteries, he'd not had a thing to eat since WPC Watson's bacon buttie this morning. And he'd left that splattered all over the grass at Roadkill's house of horrors. He was starving.

Miller shrugged. 'So it's a late lunch. High tea . . .' He cast a theatrical eye round the reception and dropped his voice to a conspiratorial whisper. 'We might be able to help each other out. Could be I know somethin' you could use.' Miller stood back and beamed again. 'What d'you say? The paper's buyin'?'

Logan thought about it. There were strict rules about accepting gifts. The modern police force was at great pains to make sure no one could point the finger of corruption in their direction. Colin Miller was the last person he wanted to spend more time with. But then again, if Miller did have information . . . And he was starving.

'You're on,' he said.

*

They'd found a corner booth in a little restaurant down in the Green. While Miller ordered a bottle of chardonnay and the tagliatelle with smoked haddock and peppers, Logan contented himself with a glass of mineral water and the lasagne. And some garlic bread. And a side salad.

'Jesus, Laz,' said Miller, watching him tear into the breadbasket and butter. 'Don't they feed you lot?'

'Logan,' said Logan, round a mouthful of bread. 'Not "Laz". Logan.'

Miller leaned back in his seat and swirled his glass of white wine, watching the colours sparkle. 'I don't know,' he said. 'Like I said: I did some diggin'. Lazarus isn't a bad nickname for someone who's come back from the dead.'

'I didn't come back from the dead.'

'Aye you did. 'Cording to your medical reports you were dead for about five minutes.'

Logan frowned. 'How do you know what's in my medical reports?'

Miller shrugged. 'It's my job to know things, Laz. Like I know you found a dead child in the tip yesterday. Like I know you've got someone banged up for it already. Like I know you and the chief pathologist used to be an item.'

Logan stiffened.

Miller held up a hand. 'Easy, tiger. Like I said: it's ma job to know things.'

The waiter arrived with their pasta and the

mood eased a little. Logan found it difficult to fume and eat at the same time.

'You said you had something for me,' he said, shoving salad into his mouth.

'Aye. Your lot dragged a body out the harbour yesterday wi' his knees hacked off.'

Logan took a look at the mound of quivering lasagne on his fork. The meat sauce glistened back at him, red and dripping, the pale-cream pasta poking through like slivers of bone. But his stomach wasn't about to be put off. 'And?' he asked, chewing.

'And you don't know who he is: Mr No-Knees.'

'And you do?'

Miller picked up his wineglass and did the swirling trick again. 'Oh aye,' he said. 'Like I said: it's ma job.'

Logan waited, but Miller just took a slow sip.

'So who is it?' Logan said at last.

'Well, now, that's where we can start helpin' each other, you know?' Miller smiled at him. 'I know some things and you know other things. You tell me your things and I tell you mine. End of the day we're both better off.'

Logan put his fork down. He had known this was coming from the moment the reporter asked him out to lunch. 'You know that I can't tell you anything.' He pushed his plate away.

'I know you can tell me a lot more than you tell the rest of the media. I know you can give me the inside track. You can do that.'

'I thought you already had someone to feed you titbits.' Now that he wasn't eating any more Logan could concentrate on getting angry.

Miller shrugged and twisted a long ribbon of pasta onto his fork. 'Aye, but you're better placed to help me, Laz. You're the man on the scene, like. And before you go stormin' off all huffy, remember: this is a trade. You tell me things, I tell you things. Them bastards should've made you a DI for catchin' that Angus Robertson. Man kills fifteen women an' you catch him single-handed? Shite, you should'a got a medal, man.' He twirled another piece of tagliatelle, loading it up with slivers of smoked fish. ''Stead of which they give you a pat on the back. You get a reward? Did you bollocks.' Miller leaned forward, pointing his fork at Logan. 'You ever thought of writing a book about it?' he asked. 'You could get yourself a fuckin' huge advance on that: serial-killer rapist stalks the streets, no one can lay a finger on him, then up pops DS McRae!' Miller waved his fork around like a conductor's baton as he got into the spirit, the tagliatelle unravelling as he spoke. 'The DS and the brave pathologist track down the killer, only he grabs her! Rooftop showdown: blood, battle, near-fatal injury. Killer gets sent down for thirty to life. Applause and curtain.' He grinned and stuffed the remaining pasta into his mouth. 'Bloody great story. Have to move quick, but, Joe Public doesnae have a long memory. I've got contacts. I can help. Shite, you deserve it!'

He dropped the fork on his plate and dug about in his jacket pocket, coming out with a small wallet.

'Here,' he said, pulling out a dark blue business card. 'You give Phil a call and tell him I sent you. He'll set you up with a fuckin' good deal, man. Best literary agent in London, I'm tellin' you. Done me proud.' He placed the card in the middle of the table, facing Logan. 'That's free byraway. A token of good will.'

Logan said thank you. But left the card sitting where it was.

'What I want from you,' said Miller, going back to his pasta. 'Is what's goin' on with all these dead kiddies. The fuckin' Press Office are givin' out the usual shite: no details. Nothin' meaty.'

Logan nodded. It was standard practice: if you told the media everything they printed it, or staged reconstructions of it, or debated it on live television. Then all the nutters under the sun would be phoning up, claiming they were the new Mastrick Monster, or whatever trite nickname the press were going to give the man who abducted, killed and mutilated little boys before abusing their corpses. If nothing was kept secret there'd be no way of knowing if a call was genuine.

'Now, I know wee David Reid was strangled,' Miller went on, 'but that much was common knowledge. 'I know he was abused.' Again nothing new there. 'I know the sick bastard hacked off the kid's dick with a pair of scissors.'

Logan sat bolt upright. 'How the hell did you know—'

'I know he stuffed something up the kid's bum. Probably couldn't get his own dick up, so he has to use—'

'Who told you all this?'

Miller did his shrug and wine glass routine again. 'Like I said: it's—'

'—your job,' Logan finished for him. 'Sounds like you don't need any help from me.'

'What I want to know is what's goin' on in the investigation, Laz. I want to know what you lot are doin' to catch the bastard.'

'We are pursuing several lines of enquiry.'

'Dead wee boy on Sunday, dead wee girl on Monday, two wee boys snatched. You got a serial killer on the loose.'

'There's no evidence the cases are connected.'

Miller sat back, sighed and poured himself another glass of chardonnay. 'OK, so you don't trust me yet,' said the reporter. 'I can understand that. So I'll do you a favour, just so's you know I'm a good guy. That bloke you dragged out the harbour, the one with no knees, his name was George Stephenson. Geordie to his friends.'

'Go on.'

'He was an enforcer for Malk the Knife. Heard of him?'

Logan had. Malk the Knife: AKA Malcolm McLennan. Edinburgh's leading importer of guns, drugs and Lithuanian prostitutes. He'd turned himself semi-legitimate about three years ago, if you could call property development that. McLennan Homes had bought up big chunks of land on the outskirts of Edinburgh and covered them with little boxy houses. Recently he'd been sniffing around Aberdeen, looking to get into the property game here before the arse fell out of the market. Going up against the local boys. Only Malk the Knife didn't play the game like the local developers. He played hard and he played for keeps. And no one had ever been able to lay a finger on him. Not Edinburgh CID, not Aberdeen, not anyone.

'Well,' said Miller, 'it seems Geordie was up here making sure Malkie got planning permission for his latest building scheme. Three hundred houses on greenbelt between here and Kingswells. Bit of the old bribery and corruption. Only Geordie has the bad luck to run into a planner that isn't bent.' He sat back and nodded. 'Aye, that came as a bit of a surprise tae me too. Didnae think there was any of the buggers left. Anyway, the planner says, "Get ye behind me Satan" and that's just what Geordie does.' Miller held up his hands and made pushing gestures. 'Right in front of the number two fourteen to Westhill. Splat!'

Logan raised an eyebrow. He'd read about someone from the council falling under a bus, but there was never any suggestion it was anything other than an accident. The poor sod was in intensive care at the hospital. They didn't expect him to see Christmas.

Miller winked. 'It gets better,' he said. 'Word is Geordie's got a bit of a problem with the horses. He's been spreading bets round the local bookies like butter. Big money. Only his luck's for shite. Now your Aberdeen bookie's no as . . . entrepreneurial as the ones down south, but they're no exactly Telly Tubbies. Next thing you know Geordie's floatin' face down in the harbour an' someone's hacked off his kneecaps with a machete.' The reporter sat back and swigged a mouthful of wine, grinning at Logan. 'Now is that no worth something to you?'

Logan had to admit that it was.

'Right then,' said Miller, settling his elbows on the tabletop. 'Your turn.'

Logan walked back into Force Headquarters looking as if someone had shoved the winning lottery ticket into his hand. The rain had even let up, allowing him to walk all the way from the Green to the huge Queen Street station without getting wet.

Insch was still in the incident room, giving orders and taking reports. From the look of things they'd had no joy in locating either Richard Erskine or Peter Lumley. The thought of those two little kids, out there, probably dead, took the edge off Logan's good mood. He had no business grinning like a loon.

He cornered the inspector and asked him who was in charge of the missing kneecaps case.

'Why?' asked Insch, his large face full of suspicion.

'Because I've got a couple of leads for them.'

'Oh aye?'

Logan nodded, the grin seeping back onto his face as he repeated what Colin Miller had told him over lunch. When he'd finished Insch looked impressed.

'Where the hell did you get all this?' he asked.

'Colin Miller. The journalist from the *Press and Journal*. The one you told me not to piss off.'

Insch's expression became unreadable. 'I said don't piss him off. I didn't say anything about climbing into bed with him.'

'What? I didn't—'

'Is this the first little chat you and this Colin Miller have had, Sergeant?'

'I'd never seen him before yesterday.'

Insch scowled at him, keeping silent; waiting for Logan to jump in and fill the uncomfortable pause with something incriminating.

'Look, sir,' said Logan, unable to stop himself. 'He came to me. You can ask the front desk. He told me he had something that would help us.'

'And what did you have to give him in return?'

There was another pause, this one even more uncomfortable.

'He wanted me to tell him about the investigation into the abductions and killings.'

Insch stared at him. 'And did you?'

'I . . . I told him I'd have to run any information past you first, sir.'

At this DI Insch smiled. 'Good lad.' He pulled a bag of wine gums out of his pocket and offered them to Logan. 'But if I find out you're telling me lies I'll break you.'

13

Logan's free lunch had turned into rampant indigestion. He'd lied to DI Insch and hoped to God he wasn't going to get found out. After Colin Miller had told him all about the man with no kneecaps, Logan had reciprocated, detailing the missing child investigations. He'd been convinced he was doing good: establishing a rapport with an informant, building bridges with the local press. But Insch had acted as if he was selling secrets to the enemy. Logan had asked Insch for permission to tell Miller everything he'd already told him. And in the end Insch had agreed. God help him if the inspector ever found out the exchange had happened before he'd given the OK.

Someone else Logan didn't want finding that out was the inspector from Professional Standards, currently sitting on the opposite side of the interview room table, dressed in an immaculate black uniform. All parallel creases and shiny buttons. Inspector Napier: thinning ginger hair and a nose like a bottle opener. Asking lots and lots of questions about Logan's return to the force, his recuperation, his status as police hero, and his lunch with Colin Miller.

Smiling sincerely, Logan lied for all he was worth.

Half an hour later he was back in his commandeered office, looking up at the map on the wall, rubbing at the burning sensation sitting in the middle of his chest. Trying not to think about getting fired.

The blue business card Miller had given him was sitting in his top pocket. Maybe the reporter was right. Maybe he did deserve better than this. Maybe he could write a book about Angus Robertson: *Catching the Mastrick Monster*. It had a kind of ring to it . . .

WPC Watson had been in while he was out having lunch, leaving a fresh stack of printouts next to his witness statements. Criminal and civil records of everyone on his list. Logan sifted through it, not liking what he found. Not one of them had form for kidnapping, killing and disposing of young girls' bodies in a bin-bag.

But Watson had been thorough. For each person she'd provided a break-down by age, telephone number, place of birth, national insurance number, occupation, length of time they'd lived at their current address. He had no idea how she'd managed to get hold of all this stuff. Just a shame none of it was of any use.

Rosemount had always been something of a cultural melting pot and that was reflected in Watson's list: Edinburgh, Glasgow, Aberdeen, Inverness, Newcastle . . . There was even a couple from the Isle of Man. Now that was exotic.

Sighing, he pulled the stack of statements over again, the ones he'd marked as being close enough to number seventeen to share a wheelie-bin. He read the bio WPC Watson had produced and then re-read the corresponding statement, trying to get some picture of them from their words. It wasn't easy: every time uniform took a statement they put it into police-statement-speak, a sort of bizarre, stilted English that was so far removed from the way people really spoke it was almost laughable.

'I proceeded to work that morning,' Logan read aloud, 'having first removed the rubbish bag from my kitchen and placed it into the communal bin outside the building . . .' Who the hell spoke like that? Normal people 'went to work': 'proceeding to work' was something only policemen did.

He turned back to the front page of the statement to see who had been so weirdly misquoted. The name was sort of familiar: someone from Norman Chalmers's building. Anderson . . . Logan smiled. It was the man whose bell they'd rung so that they could get into the building without Chalmers knowing. The one WPC Watson thought was up to something.

According to her write-up Mr Cameron Anderson was in his mid-twenties and hailed from

Edinburgh: which explained why he had a first name like Cameron. He worked for a firm of sub-sea engineers making remote operated vehicles for the oil industry. Somehow Logan could picture the nervous young man fiddling about with little remote-controlled submarines.

The next person on the list wasn't much more help and neither was the one after that, but he worked his way slowly through them anyway. If the killer was here they didn't jump off the page and tell him about it.

Finally Logan put the last statement on top of the pile and stretched, feeling his back pop and crack. A yawn threatened to tear his head in half and he let it rip, ending with a tiny, almost inaudible, burp. It was a quarter to seven and Logan had been poring over these damned statements for most of the day. It was time to go home.

Out in the hallway the building was quiet. The bulk of the administrative work got done during the day and after the admin staff went home the place was a lot less noisy. Logan stopped off at the incident room to see if anything had happened while he'd been cloistered in the office looking at statements.

There was a small contingent of uniform in the room: two of them answering the phone while the remaining two got on with filing the reports generated by the last shift. He wasn't surprised to hear they'd had exactly the same amount of success as him. Bugger all.

Still no sign of Richard Erskine, no sign of Peter Lumley, and no one had come forward to identify the little girl lying on a slab in the morgue.

'You still here, Lazarus?'

Logan turned to find Big Gary standing behind him, a couple of mugs in one hand and a packet of Penguin biscuits in the other. The large policeman nodded in the direction of the lifts. 'We've got someone downstairs looking for whoever's in charge of the missing kid investigation. I thought you was all away.'

'Who is it?' Logan asked.

'Says he's the new kid's stepfather.'

Logan groaned. It wasn't that he didn't want to help, it was just that he wanted to go find WPC Watson and discover whether or not they'd had sex last night. And if they had, was she up for a rematch?

'OK, I'll see him.'

Peter Lumley's stepfather was pacing the pink linoleum floor in reception. He'd changed out of his overalls and into a dirty pair of jeans and a jacket that looked as if it wouldn't stop a sneeze, let alone a howling gale.

'Mr Lumley?'

The man spun around. 'Why have they stopped looking?' His face was pale and rough, blue stubble making the skin look even more sallow. 'He's still out there! Why have they stopped looking?'

Logan took him into one of the small reception

179

rooms. The man was shivering and dripping wet.

'Why have they stopped looking?'

'They've been out looking all day, Mr Lumley. It's too dark to see anything out there . . . You need to go home.'

Lumley shook his head, sending small droplets of water flying from his lank hair. 'I need to find him! He's only five!' He sank slowly down into an orange plastic seat.

Logan's phone started blaring its theme tune and he dug it out, switched it off and stuck it back in his pocket without even looking. 'Sorry about that. How's his mother holding up?' he asked.

'Sheila?' Something almost approaching a smile touched Lumley's mouth. 'The doctor's given her something. Peter means the world to her.'

Logan nodded. 'I know you probably don't want to think about this,' said Logan, working his words carefully, 'but has Peter's father been told he's missing?'

Lumley's face closed up. 'Fuck him.'

'Mr Lumley, the boy's father has a right to know—'

'Fuck him!' He wiped a hand across his face. 'Bastard fucked off to Surrey with some tart from his office. Left Sheila and Peter without a fuckin' penny. You know what he sends Peter for Christmas? For his birthday? Fuck all. Not even a fuckin' card! That's what he sends his son. That's how much he cares. Fuckin' bastard . . .'

'OK, forget the father. I'm sorry.' Logan stood. 'Look, we're going to have all the area cars keeping an eye out for your son. There's nothing more you can do tonight. Go home. Get some rest. First light tomorrow morning we'll be searching again.'

Peter Lumley's stepfather slid his head into his hands.

'It's OK,' said Logan, placing a hand on the man's shoulder, feeling the shivering turn into silent sobs. 'It's OK. Come on, I'll give you a lift home.'

Logan signed for one of the CID pool cars, another battered-looking Vauxhall in need of a wash. Mr Lumley didn't say a word all the way from Queen Street to Hazlehead. Just sat in the passenger seat staring out of the window, searching for a five-year-old child.

No matter how cynical you were, it would be impossible not to see the genuine love the man had for his stepson. Logan couldn't help wondering if Richard Erskine's dad was still out, searching for his missing son in the dark and the rain. Before remembering the poor sod had died before Richard was born.

He frowned, working the dirty pool car round the roundabout that lead into Hazlehead proper. Something was nagging at him.

Now he came to think about it: all the time they'd been in that house no one had mentioned the father. All the photos on the wall were of the missing child and his suffocating mother. You would have thought there would have been at least one of Richard's dear departed dad. He didn't even know the man's name.

Logan dropped Mr Lumley at the front door to his block of flats. It was hard to say, 'Don't worry, Mr Lumley, we'll find him and he'll be fine . . .' when he was one hundred percent sure the child was already dead. So he didn't, just made vague reassuring noises before driving off into the night.

As soon as he was out of sight, Logan pulled out his mobile, turned it back on, and called the incident room. A harassed-sounding WPC answered the phone.

'Yes?'

'It's DS McRae,' said Logan, heading back into town. 'Something wrong?'

There was a pause and then: 'Sorry, sir, the bloody press have been on. You bloody name it I've spoken to them: BBC, ITV, Northsound, the papers . . .'

Logan didn't like the sound of that. 'Why?'

'Bloody Sandy the Snake's been stirring up shite. Seems we're all incompetent and trying to pin all the murders on his client, 'cos we haven't got a bloody clue. Says it's Judith Corbert all over again.'

Logan groaned. They'd only ever found her left ring finger, complete with gold wedding band, and Mr Sandy Moir-Farquharson had ripped the prosecution case to shreds. The husband walked free, even though everyone knew he'd done it; Slippery Sandy got a huge cheque, three chat-

182

show appearances and a BBC Crime Special; and three good police officers were thrown to the wolves. Seven years ago and he was still digging her up to beat them with.

Logan swung the car round onto Anderson Drive, making for the back road to Torry. Where little Richard Erskine had gone missing.

'Yeah, that sounds like Sandy. What did you tell them?'

'Told them to get stuffed and speak to the Press Office.'

Logan nodded. 'Quite right. Listen, I need you to look something up for me, OK? Did we get a name for Richard Erskine's father?'

'Hang on . . .' The sound of someone massacring 'Come On Baby Light My Fire' came on as he was put on hold.

He'd got all the way down to Riverside Drive before the WPC's voice replaced the awful rendition. *'Sorry, sir,'* she said, *'we don't have the father's name on file, but the case notes say he died before the child was born. Why?'*

'Probably nothing,' said Logan. 'Listen: I'll be at the Erskine house soon. Call the Family Liaison Officer . . . She still on site?' Distraught mother with a missing child: they wouldn't have assigned a man to look after her.

'Yes, sir.'

'Good. Call her and get her to meet me out front in about . . .' he took a look at the grey buildings drifting past, the windows shining with yellow light, 'two minutes.'

She was waiting for him, watching him make an arse of parking the CID pool car.

Trying not to look as flustered as he felt, Logan left the thing abandoned, half on the kerb, and buttoned up his coat against the rain.

The Family Liaison Officer was better organized than he was: she had an umbrella.

'Evening, sir,' she said as he squeezed himself in under the brolly. 'What's up?'

'I need to know if you've heard anything of the boy's—'

A harsh white flash broke through the rain, cutting him off.

'What the hell?' he asked, spinning around.

There was a scruffy-looking BMW on the other side of the road, the passenger side window rolled down, letting a trickle of smoke escape into the cold night air.

'I think it's the *Daily Mail*,' said the WPC holding the brolly. 'You turn up: they think something's happening. Flash, bang, wallop. If they can make up some shite to go along with it you'll be on the front page tomorrow.'

Logan turned his back on the car, making sure that if they took any more snaps all they'd get was the back of his head. 'Listen,' he said, 'have you heard anything about the child's father?'

She shrugged. 'Only that he's dead. And a right bastard, according to the next-door neighbour.'

'What, did he beat her up, cheat on her?'

'No idea. But the old witch makes him sound like Hitler, only without the winning personality.'

'Sounds lovely.'

Inside the Erskine household the only thing that had changed was the air quality. The walls were still lined with those freaky mother-and-son snaps, the wallpaper was still revolting, but the air was thick with cigarette smoke.

In the lounge, Mrs Erskine was weaving away on the couch, unable to sit still, or upright. A large cut-glass tumbler of clear spirit was clutched in her hands, a half-smoked fag between her lips. The bottle of vodka on the coffee table was well on its way.

Her friend, the next-door neighbour, the one who didn't make tea for the police, was perched in an armchair, craning her long, wrinkly neck to see who the newcomer was. Her beady eyes sparkled as soon as she recognized him. Probably hoping that this was going to be bad news. Nothing like someone else's suffering to make you feel good about yourself.

Logan plonked himself down on the couch next to Mrs Erskine. She looked around at him blearily, and an inch of fag ash tumbled down the front of her cardigan.

'He's dead isn't he? My little Richard is dead?' Her eyes were bloodshot from too much crying and too much vodka, her face creased and florid. She looked as if she'd aged ten years in the last ten hours.

The neighbour leaned forward eagerly, waiting for the moment of truth.

'We don't know that,' said Logan. 'I just need to ask you a couple more questions, OK?'

Mrs Erskine nodded and dragged in another lungful of nicotine and tar.

'It's about Richard's father.'

She stiffened as if someone had run a thousand volts through her. 'He hasn't got a father!'

'Bastard wouldn't marry her,' said the neighbour with obvious relish. This wasn't as good as the kid being dead, but dragging up the painful past was a reasonable substitute. 'Got her up the stick when she was just fifteen and then wouldn't marry her. He was a shite!'

'Yes.' The unmarried Mrs Erskine waved the rapidly emptying glass of vodka in salute. 'He was a shite!'

'Course,' the neighbour went on, her voice a theatrical whisper, 'he still wants to see the child. Can you imagine that? Doesn't want to make the kid legal, but he still wants to take him to Duthie Park and play bloody football!' She leaned over and sloshed another huge shot of vodka into her friend's glass. 'There ought to be a bloody law.'

Logan's head snapped up. 'What do you mean, "he still wants to see the child"?'

'I don't let him anywhere near my little soldier.' Miss Erskine raised the tumbler unsteadily to her lips and swallowed about half in one go.

'Oh, he sends little presents and cards and letters, but I throw them all straight in the bin.'

'You told us the father was dead.'

Miss Erskine looked at him, puzzled. 'No I didn't.'

'Might as well be bloody dead. The amount of bloody good he is.' The neighbour said with a smug flourish. And suddenly Logan got a much better picture of what had happened. WPC Watson had told him the father was dead because that's what the rancid old bitch of a neighbour had told her.

'I see,' said Logan slowly, trying to keep his voice neutral. 'And has the father been informed that Richard's gone missing?' It was the second time he'd asked that question in the space of an hour. He already knew the answer.

'It's none of his bloody business!' shouted the neighbour, getting as much venom into her voice as she could. 'He gave up all his bloody rights when he wouldn't make his bloody child legal. Imagine leaving that poor boy to go through life as a bastard! Anyway, the little shit must know by now—' she pointed at an open copy of the *Sun* lying on the carpet. The headline screamed: 'PAEDOPHILE SICKO STRIKES AGAIN!'

Logan closed his eyes and took a deep breath. The bitter old battleaxe was getting on his nerves. 'You need to tell me Richard's father's name, Mrs . . . Miss Erskine.'

'I don't see why!' The neighbour leapt to her

feet. Now she was playing the noble defender, protecting the poor pissed cow on the sofa. 'It's none of his bloody business what's going on!'

Logan turned on her. 'Sit down and shut up!'

She stood there, mouth agape. 'You . . . you can't talk to me like that!'

'If you don't sit down and button it, I'm going to have the nice constable here take you down to the station and charge you with giving a false statement. Understand?'

She sat down and buttoned it.

'Miss Erskine: I need to know.'

Richard's mother finished her drink and got unsteadily to her feet. She lurched once to the left and then staggered off in the opposite direction: to the sideboard, where she proceeded to rummage about in a low cupboard shelf, scattering bits of paper and small boxes over the floor.

'Here!' she said triumphantly, holding a deckle-edged cardboard folder with gold ribbons embossed on the side. Just the sort of thing they used to give you when you got your photograph taken at school. She almost threw it at Logan.

Inside was a boy, maybe a little over fourteen. He had a huge pair of eyebrows and a slight squint, but the resemblance to the missing five-year-old was unmistakable. In the corner of the picture, over the mottled blue-and-grey photographer's background, were the words: 'To My Darling Elisabeth, I Will Love You For All Eternity, Darren XXX' written in a child's artificially neat handwriting. Pretty heady sentiments for someone just clearing puberty.

'He was your childhood sweetheart?' asked Logan, turning the brown photo-folder over in his hands. There was a golden sticker with the photographer's name, address and telephone number and another, white paper, spelling out 'Darren Caldwell: Third Year, Ferryhill Academy'.

'He was a bastard!' said the friend again, relishing every syllable.

'Do you know where he lives?'

'Last I heard he'd upped sticks and moved to Dundee of all places! Dundee!' The friend stuck another fag in her mouth and lit it. She sucked air through it, making the tip glow fiery-red before hissing the smoke out of her nose. 'Little bastard can't wait to get away, can he? I mean here's his kid, growing up without a father and he buggers off to Dundee first chance he gets!' She took another deep drag. 'Ought to be a bloody law.'

Logan didn't point out that, since Darren Caldwell wasn't allowed to see his son, it made no difference where he stayed. Instead he asked Miss Erskine if he could keep the photograph.

'Burn it for all I care,' was all she said.

Logan let himself out.

It was still chucking it down outside and the foosty-looking BMW was still parked where it had a good view of the front of the house. Keeping his head covered, Logan sprinted for the pool car.

Cranking the heating up, he set the blowers on full and made his way back to Force Headquarters.

Outside the big concrete-and-glass building there was a knot of television cameras, most of them sporting a serious broadcast journalist looking seriously into the camera and making serious statements about the quality of Grampian Police. The WPC he'd spoken to hadn't been kidding: Sandy the Snake had really whipped up a storm.

Logan tucked the CID car into the car park around the back, steering well clear of the reception area on his way to the incident room.

The room was a flurry of activity again. But this time the whirlwind was centred around a harassed-looking press officer who was standing, clutching a clipboard to her chest, trying to get details out of the four officers on duty while every phone in the place went off. As soon as she clapped eyes on Logan her face lit up. Here was someone to share the stress.

'Sergeant—' she started, but Logan held up a hand and grabbed one of the few silent phones.

'Just a minute,' he said, dialling the records office.

The phone was picked up almost immediately.

'I need to get a vehicle check on one Darren Caldwell,' he said, doing a quick bout of mental arithmetic. Darren had knocked up Miss Erskine when she was fifteen, plus nine months for gestation, plus five years for the kid's age. Presuming they were in the same class when their 'eternal love' turned physical Darren had to be twenty-one – twenty-two by now. Give or take a few months. 'He's in his early twenties and allegedly living in Dundee . . .' He nodded as the officer on the other end of the phone recited the details back to him. 'Yeah, that's right. How quick can you get that for me? OK, OK, I'll hold.'

The press officer was standing in front of him, looking as if someone had dropped a live herring down her pants. 'The press are all over us!' she wailed while Logan held on for his vehicle check. 'That bloody Hissing Sandy Lawyer Bastard is calling us every shade of shite under the sun!' Her face was florid, the beetroot tinge extending from her blonde fringe all the way down her neck like sunburn. 'Do we have anything to tell them? Anything at all? Anything that makes us look like we're getting somewhere?'

Logan put one hand over the mouthpiece and told her they were pursuing several lines of enquiry.

'Don't give me that!' She almost exploded. 'That's the shite I give them when we haven't got a bloody clue! I can't tell them that!'

'Look,' he said, 'I can't just conjure arrests out of thin . . . Hello?'

The voice on the phone was back: *'Aye, I've got fifteen Darren Caldwells in the north-east. Mind, only one of them lives in Dundee and he's in his late thirties.'*

Logan swore.

'*But I've got one Darren Caldwell, twenty-one, livin'
in Portlethen.*'

'Portlethen?' It was a little town about five miles
south of Aberdeen.

'*Aye. Drives a dark red Renault Clio. You want the
registration number?*'

Logan said he did, closed his eyes and thanked
God something was starting to go his way. A witness had seen a child matching Richard Erskine's
description getting into the back of a dark red
hatchback. He copied down the registration
number and address, thanked the man on the
other end of the phone and beamed at the agitated press officer.

'What? What? What have you got?' she
demanded.

'We're hoping an arrest will be imminent.'

'What arrest? Who are you arresting?'

But Logan was already gone.

14

The PC he'd grabbed from the locker room sat behind the wheel of the CID pool car, breaking the speed limit, heading south. Logan sat in the passenger seat, watching the dark countryside whip past the window. Another PC and a WPC sat in the back. Traffic was light at this time of night and it wasn't long before they were drifting slowly past the address Logan had been given for Darren Caldwell.

It was a new-looking bungalow on the south side of Portlethen, part of a winding development of identical, new-looking bungalows. The front garden was little more than a few square feet of grass, bordered with wilted roses. Some limp red petals still clung to the flower heads: the rain had battered off the rest. They lay in a soggy heap at the base of the bushes, turning a sickly shade of brown in the streetlights.

Sitting in the small lock-block drive was a dark red Renault Clio.

Logan got the driver to park around the corner. 'OK,' he told the PCs, unbuckling his seatbelt, 'we're going to take this nice and easy. You two work your way round the back. Let me know when you're in place and we'll ring the doorbell. If he runs: you grab him.' He turned to the WPC in the back, wincing as the movement pulled at the scars on his stomach. 'When we get to the house I need you to keep out of sight. If Caldwell sees police on his doorstep he's going to freak. I don't want this turning into a siege. OK?'

Everyone nodded.

It was freezing cold as Logan climbed out of the car. The rain had changed from thick, heavy drops back into a fine, icy drizzle that leached all the warmth out of his hands and face by the time they reached the front door. The two PCs had disappeared around the back.

A couple of lights were on in the house, the sound of a television seeping out from the lounge. A toilet flushed and Logan reached for the doorbell.

The phone blared in Logan's pocket. He cursed quietly and punched the pickup. 'Logan.'

'What's going on?' It was Insch.

'Can I call you back, sir?' he whispered.

'No you bloody well can't! I just got a call from HQ. They tell me you've commandeered three uniforms and are off arresting someone! What the hell is going on?' There were some muffled noises from the ear-

piece and the sound of a band striking up. *'Shite,'* said Insch. *'I'm on. You better have a damn good explanation when I get off stage, Sergeant, or I'll . . .'* A woman's voice, terse and insistent, just too faint for Logan to make out the words, and then: *'All right, all right. I'm coming.'* And then the line went dead.

The WPC stood on the doorstep looking at him with her eyebrows arched.

'He's about to go on stage,' explained Logan, stuffing the phone back in his pocket. 'Let's get this over and done with. If we're lucky we can meet him in the bar after the show with some good news for a change.'

He rang the bell.

A thin bout of male swearing drifted out of the bathroom window. At least they knew someone was home. Logan leaned on the bell again.

'Hold on! Hold on, I'm coming!'

About a minute and a half later a shadow fell over the part-glazed front door and a key was rattled in the lock. The door swung open and a face popped into the gap.

'Hello?' it said.

'Darren?' asked Logan.

The face frowned, a pair of thick black eyebrows sinking down over eyes that didn't quite look in the same direction. Darren Caldwell might be five and a bit years older than his school photograph, but he hadn't changed that much. His jaw was a little wider and his hair looked styled, rather than cut by his mum, but it was definitely the same man.

'Yes?' said Darren, and Logan gave the door a sudden shove.

The young man staggered backwards, tripped over a little nest of tables and fell full length on the floor. Logan and the WPC stepped inside, closing the door behind them.

'Tsk, tsk.' Logan shook his head. 'You should get a security chain fitted, Mr Caldwell. Makes it harder for people to come in uninvited. You never know who's out there.'

The young man scrabbled to his feet, balling his fists. 'Who are you?'

'You have a lovely home, Mr Caldwell,' said Logan, letting the WPC get between him and the possibility of physical violence. 'You don't mind if we take a look around?'

'You can't do this!'

'Oh yes I can.' Logan pulled the search warrant out and waved it in his face. 'Now where shall we start?'

The house was a lot smaller on the inside than it looked. Two bedrooms, one with a double bed covered in a yellowy-grey crocheted blanket crammed into it, jars of moisturiser cluttering up the vanity unit; the other with a single bed up against one wall opposite a little computer desk. A barely-dressed young woman pouted from a poster above the bed. Very saucy. The bathroom contained the nastiest avocado-coloured suite

Logan had seen in a long time and the kitchen was just big enough for all three of them to stand in, as long as they didn't move about too much. The lounge was taken up by a widescreen television and a huge, lime-green sofa.

There was no sign of the missing five-year-old boy.

'Where is he?' asked Logan, poking about in the cupboards, pulling out tins of beans and soup and tuna.

Darren looked left and right, almost at the same time. 'Where's who?' he said at last.

Logan sighed and slammed the cupboard doors.

'You know bloody well "who", Darren. Where's Richard Erskine. Your son? What have you done with him?'

'I've not done nothing to him. I've not seen him for months.' He hung his head. 'She won't let me.'

'You've been seen, Darren. People reported your car.' Logan tried to peer out through the kitchen window, but all he could see was himself staring back, reflected in the glass.

'I . . .' Darren sniffed. 'I used to drive round there. See if I could get a glimpse of him, you know, out playing or something? But she wouldn't let him out, would she? Wouldn't let him be like the other kids.'

Logan flicked the light-switch off, plunging the kitchen into darkness. Without the light turning the window into a mirror he could see out into

197

the back garden. The pair of policemen he'd dispatched to watch the back were there, shivering away in the cold drizzle. There was a shed in one corner.

Smiling he snapped the lights back on, making everyone squint.

'What?'

'Come on,' he said, grabbing Darren by the collar, 'let's go take a look in the shed.'

But Richard Erskine wasn't in there. Just a Flymo, a couple of trowels, a bag of fertilizer and a pair of secateurs.

'Arse.'

They stood in the lounge, drinking piss-poor tea. The room was crowded with two soggy PCs, the WPC, Darren Caldwell and Logan. The man of the house sat on the sofa, looking more and more unhappy with every minute that passed.

'Where is he?' asked Logan again. 'You're going to have to tell us sooner or later. Might as well be now.'

Darren scowled at them. 'I haven't seen him. I've got no idea what you're talking about.'

'OK then,' said Logan, perching on the arm of the lime-green settee, 'where were you yesterday morning at ten a.m.?'

Darren sighed theatrically. 'I was at work!'

'And you can prove this, can you?'

A nasty grin burst into life on Darren's face. 'Fuckin' right I can. Here—' he snatched the phone off the low coffee table and thrust it at Logan, before dragging a copy of the *Yellow Pages* out from beneath a pile of *Hello!* magazines. 'Broadstane Garage,' he said, pulling the thick, yellow directory open and flicking through it with angry fingers. 'Call them. Go on: speak to Ewan. He's my boss. Ask him where I was. Go on.'

As he took the phone and the *Yellow Pages*, Logan had a nasty thought: what if Darren was telling the truth?

Broadstane Garage had a display ad: something cheesy with a smiling spanner and a happy nut and bolt. The advert said 'OPEN 24 HOURS' so Logan dialled the number. The ringing tone sounded in his ear, over and over and over. He was just about to hang up when a gruff voice shouted: *'Broadstane Garage!'* in his ear.

'Hello?' said Logan, when his hearing had returned. 'Is this Ewan?'

'Who's this?'

'This is Detective Sergeant Logan McRae of Grampian Police. Are you Darren Caldwell's employer?'

The voice on the other end of the phone became instantly suspicious. *'What if I am? What's he done?'*

'Can you tell me where Mr Caldwell was between the hours of nine and eleven yesterday morning?'

Darren sat back on the settee smiling his smug smile and Logan got that sinking feeling again.

'Helping me rewire a Volvo. Why?'

'You're sure?'

There was a small pause and then: *'Course I'm bloody sure. I was there. If he was somewhere else I'd've bloody noticed. Now what's this all about?'*

It took another five minutes to get rid of him.

Logan put the phone down and tried to hide the disappointment in his voice. 'It seems we owe you an apology, Mr Caldwell,'

'Fucking right you do!' Darren stood up and pointed at the front door. 'Now why don't you get off your lazy arses and go look for my son?'

He was good enough to slam the door behind them.

They trailed off through the drizzle to the rusty Vauxhall Logan had signed for. All this way for nothing. And now he had no good news to give DI Insch. He just had to hope the performance had gone well tonight. Perhaps the inspector would be in a good mood and not to take a bite out of his backside.

The PC behind the wheel turned the engine over, the car windows rapidly steaming up. He cranked up the blowers, but it made little difference. Instead he pulled off his clip-on tie and tried to wipe the worst of the fog away. It just moved the fuzzy moisture around.

With a sigh they settled back to wait for the small patches of clear glass to creep up the windscreen.

'You think his alibi's for real?' asked the WPC in the back.

Logan shrugged.

'The garage is open twenty-four hours: we'll check it out on the way back into town.' But Logan already knew the alibi would hold. Darren Caldwell couldn't have snatched his son while the five-year-old went to the shops for milk and chocolate biscuits.

But he'd been so sure!

Eventually the blowers made enough of a dent in the fog to see out. The PC clicked on the head-lights and pulled away from the kerb. They made a three point turn in the cul-de-sac and went back the way they'd come. Logan watched Darren's house slide past the passenger window. He'd been so sure.

As they drove through Portlethen, heading for the dual carriageway back to Aberdeen, Logan saw the lights of the big DIY stores and super-market twinkling up ahead. The supermarket would have alcohol. And right now Logan thought that going home with a bottle of wine was a very good idea. He asked the PC driving to make a short detour.

While the others waited in the car Logan slumped round the shelves, piling crisps and pickled onions into his basket. They'd gone out expecting to find the missing kid alive and well, returning to Force Headquarters as heroes. Instead they were going back empty handed with Logan looking like an idiot.

He threw a bottle of Shiraz in on top of the

crisps, cursing as he realized he'd crushed half of them. Looking sheepish he sneaked back to the snack aisle and swapped the salt-and-vinegar-flavoured crumbs for a fresh packet.

Imagine Darren Caldwell living in that little house, not allowed to see his son, still driving around Torry trying to catch a glimpse of him. Poor sod. Logan had never had children. There had been a sticky moment when a girlfriend was two weeks late, but thankfully nothing ever came of it. He could only imagine what it must be like to have a son and be completely excluded from his life.

There were only two checkouts open, one manned by a girl with more spots than skin, the other by an old man with a gnarled face and shaky hands. Neither of them seemed capable of working at much beyond a slow crawl.

The woman in front of him in the queue had bought about every kind of ready-meal imaginable: curry and chips, pizza and chips, chicken chowmein and chips, burgers and chips, lasagne and chips . . . There wasn't a single piece of fruit or vegetable in her trolley, but there were six two-litre bottles of Diet Coke and a chocolate gateau. So that was all right.

Logan let his attention wander while the ancient man fumbled with the barcode scanner and the pre-packaged dinners. All the little shops – the shoe repair place, the photo-lab, the dry cleaners and the one selling grotesque glass clowns and porcelain figurines – were in darkness, the shutters down. Anyone having a last-minute, life-or-death need for an ornamental Scottie dog playing the bagpipes would just have to come back tomorrow.

He shuffled forward a step as the woman started packing her mound of microwave meals into plastic bags.

A children's television theme blared out from somewhere near the exit and Logan looked up to see an old woman hovering over one of the children's rides – a blue plastic railway engine rocking serenely back and forth making 'chuff-chuff' noises. He watched the old woman smiling and bobbing in time with Thomas the Tank Engine until the theme tune ended and the railway engine ground to a halt. Granny opened her handbag, pulled out her purse and rummaged unsuccessfully inside for enough change to make the ride start up again. A sad-looking little girl emerged from Thomas's innards. She took Granny's hand and walked slowly out the door, all the time looking regretfully back at the engine's grinning face.

'. . . to pack?'

'Hmm?' Logan dragged his attention back to the man working the checkout.

'Ah says, do yous want a hand to pack?' He held up Logan's packet of crisps. 'Yer shopping, do yous want a hand to pack?'

'Oh, no. No thanks.'

Logan stuffed the wine, crisps and pickles into

a plastic bag and headed back out to the car. He probably should have bought a few beers for the cold, damp and disappointed constables he'd dragged all the way out here, but it was too late now.

There was a sound of laughter and Logan turned to see the little girl from the supermarket jumping up and down in a puddle while Granny laughed and clapped.

He stood and stared at the scene, a frown creeping onto his face.

If Richard Erskine's dad wasn't allowed to see him, chances were his grandparents weren't either. Everybody loses . . .

The main bedroom hadn't looked much like the sort of place a twenty-two-year-old man slept in. That crocheted throw and all those jars of moisturiser. The half-naked woman and the computer, that was more like it.

He jumped back in the car, slinging the shopping at his feet.

'How do you fancy paying Mr Caldwell another visit?' he asked with a smile.

The dark red hatchback was still on the drive, but now there was a light blue Volvo estate sitting in front of the house, two wheels up on the kerb. That made Logan's smile widen.

'Pull up in the same place as last time,' he told the driver. 'You two around the back, we'll take the front.'

Logan gave them a minute to get in position and then strode up the front path and mashed the doorbell with his thumb.

Darren Caldwell opened the door. His face went from annoyance to panic and then to flustered anger, all in the space of a heartbeat.

'Hello, Darren,' said Logan, sticking his foot in the door so it couldn't be slammed in his face. 'Mind if we come in again?'

'What the fuck do you want now?'

'Darren?' It was a woman's voice, high and slightly wobbly. 'Darren there's policemen in the back garden!'

Darren's eyes darted to the open kitchen door and then back to Logan.

'Darren!' came the woman's voice again. 'What we going to do?'

The young man's shoulders sagged. 'It's OK, Mum,' he said. 'Why don't you put the kettle on?' He stood back and let Logan and the WPC in.

There was a pile of shopping bags in the middle of the lounge floor. Logan opened one and found brand new clothes for a small child inside.

A woman in her late forties emerged from the kitchen clutching a tea towel to her chest, working it through her fingers like a set of rosary beads. 'Darren?' she asked.

'It's OK, Mum. It's too late.' He slumped down on the horrible green settee. 'You're going to take him away aren't you?'

Logan motioned for the WPC to block the lounge door.

'Where is he?' he asked.

'It's not fair!' Darren's mother shook the tea towel in Logan's face. It had little dancing sheep on it. 'Why can't I see my grandson? Why can't he stay with his father?'

'Mrs Caldwell—' Logan started, but she hadn't finished yet.

'That rotten little cow took him away and won't let us see him! He's my grandson and I'm not allowed to see him! What kind of mother does that? What kind of mother doesn't let a child see his own father? She doesn't deserve to have him!'

'Where is he?' asked Logan.

'Don't you tell him anything, Darren!'

Darren pointed towards the smaller of the two bedrooms, just visible over the WPC's shoulder. 'He's just gone to sleep,' he said so quietly Logan could barely hear him.

The WPC jerked her head in the direction of the bedroom and Logan nodded. She returned with a sleepy-looking little boy in blue and yellow tartan pyjamas. He yawned and stared blearily at all the people in the living room.

'Come on, Richard,' said Logan. 'It's time to go home.'

15

A patrol car sat outside the front door of Darren Caldwell's house, the lights off, the engine slowly ticking over. Inside, one of Logan's commandeered PCs was reading the young man his rights while his mother collapsed in tears on the lime-green sofa. And little Richard Erskine was fast asleep.

Sighing, Logan stepped out into the misty drizzle. It was getting stuffy in there and he was beginning to feel sorry for Darren. He was little more than a kid. All he'd wanted to do was see his son. Maybe have him to stay for a bit. Watch him growing up. Instead he was going to end up with a criminal record, and probably a restraining order too.

Logan's breath curled away in wisps of white fog. It was getting colder. He hadn't decided what to do about the owner of the Broadstane Garage. Supplying a false alibi: perverting the course of justice. Not that it mattered now they had the kid. Alibi or not, Darren had been caught red-handed.

Still, perverting the course of justice was a serious offence . . .

He stuck his hands deep in his pockets and stared out at the street. Silent houses, drawn curtains, the occasional twitch as some nosy neighbour tried to figure out what the police were doing at the Caldwell household.

Warning, or press charges?

He shivered and turned to go back into the house, his eyes sliding over the small garden with its border of dying roses to the pale blue Volvo. He pulled out his mobile phone and dialled Broadstane Garage's number from memory.

Five minutes later he was standing in the small kitchen with Darren Caldwell, the other officers dispatched to the lounge with a cup of tea and puzzled expressions. Darren slumped against the sink, shoulders hunched, staring through his reflection into the dark garden. 'I'm going to go to prison, aren't I?' The question little more than a whisper.

'Are you sure you don't want to change your statement, Darren?'

The face in the darkened glass bit its lip and shook its head. 'No. No, I did it.' He wiped a sleeve over his eyes and sniffed again. 'I took him.'

Logan settled back against the worktop.

'No you didn't.'

'I did!'

'You were at work. The Volvo you were re-wiring

was your mother's. I called the garage back and checked the registration number. You lent her your car. She was the one who grabbed Richard Erskine. Not you.'

'It was me! I told you it was me!'

Logan didn't reply, letting the silence grow. In the lounge someone turned on the television: muffled voices and canned laughter.

'You sure you want to do this, Darren?'

Darren was.

They drove back to Force Headquarters in silence, Darren Caldwell staring out of the window at the shining streets. Logan handed him over to the custody sergeant, watching as the contents of Darren's pockets were stacked in a little blue tray, all signed and accounted for, along with his belt and shoelaces. Nervous sweat sparkled on his face, and his eyes were pink and watery. Logan tried not to feel guilty.

The building was quiet as he made his way up to the main reception area. Big Gary was on the front desk, a phone to his ear and a gleeful expression on his face. 'No, sir, no . . . aye. I'm sure that must have been a terrible shock . . . All over the front of your trousers . . . Yes, yes I'm taking this all down . . .' No he wasn't: he was drawing a picture of a man in a suit being squashed by a smiling man in a police car. The man doing the squashing looked like Big Gary and the squashee bore a striking resemblance to everyone's favourite lawyer.

A grin broke over Logan's face. Settling on the edge of the desk, he lugged into Big Gary's end of the conversation.

'Oh, yes. I agree. Dreadful, dreadful . . . No, I don't think so, sir.' He scrawled the words 'POMPOUS WEE SHITEBAG' across the notepad and then punctuated it with lots of little arrows pointing at the squashed figure.

'Yes, sir, I'll make sure all the area cars are looking for the perpetrator. It'll be our top priority.' He slipped the phone back in its cradle before finishing with, 'Soon as the Lord Provost walks in here and starts giving out free blowjobs.'

Logan picked the doodle-covered pad off the table and examined the happy tableau. 'Didn't know you had an artistic bent, Gary.'

Gary grinned. 'Slippery Sandy: someone threw a bucket of blood all over him. Called him a "rapist lovin' bastard" and fucked off.'

'My heart bleeds.'

'You got some messages by the way: a Mr Lumley. Called about six times in the last two hours. Wanting to know if we've found his son. Poor sod sounds desperate.'

Logan sighed. The search teams had all gone home: there was nothing more they could do until morning. 'Did you get hold of DI Insch?' he asked.

Gary shook his head, sending his jowls wobbling. 'No chance.' He checked his watch. 'Show doesn't finish for . . . 'bout another five minutes.

You know what he's like about people callin' when he's givin' his all for the theatre. Did I ever tell you about the—'

The door at the end of the reception area burst open, banged against the wall and rebounded again. DI Insch stormed through in a flurry of gold and scarlet, his curly-toed boots squishing on the floor tiles. 'McRae!' he bellowed, face furious under a thick layer of make-up. He wore a stick-on goatee beard, complete with handlebar moustache. When he ripped it off it left a patch of angry pink around his mouth. A white tidemark showed where his turban must have sat, the skin of his bald head shiny under the overhead lights.

Logan jumped to attention. He opened his mouth to ask how the night's performance had gone but DI Insch got there first. 'What the blue fucking hell do you think you're playing at, Sergeant?' He snatched off his clip-on earrings and slapped them on the desk. 'You do not—'

'Richard Erskine. We found him.'

Beneath the make-up, all the colour went out of the inspector's face. 'What?'

'He's not dead. We found him.'

'You're kidding me!'

'Nope. We've got a press conference scheduled in twenty minutes. The mother's on her way in to the station.' Logan stepped back and surveyed the deflating DI in his pantomime villain costume. 'That's going to look great on TV.'

*

Wednesday morning started far too early. Quarter to six and the phone was ringing off the hook.

Bleary and confused, Logan fumbled his way out from beneath the duvet and tried to switch off the alarm clock. It just went clunk at him. Logan picked it up, saw what time it was, swore, and sank back into the bed, one hand trying to rub some life into his face.

The phone was still ringing.

'Bugger off!' he told it.

The phone kept on ringing.

Logan dragged himself into the lounge and snatched up the handset. 'What?'

That's a great phone manner you've got there by the way,' said a familiar Glaswegian voice. *'Now are you goin' tae open your front door or what? I'm freezin' my nuts off out here!'*

'What?'

The doorbell bing-bonged and Logan swore again.

'Hold on,' he told the phone before putting it down on the coffee table and staggered out of his flat, down the communal stairs to the building's front door. It was still pitch dark outside, but sometime during the night the rain had stopped. Now everything was coated in a crust of frost, reflecting the yellow streetlights. The reporter – Colin Miller – was standing on the doorstep, holding a mobile phone in one hand and a white plastic bag in the other. He was impeccably dressed in a dark grey suit and black overcoat.

'Jesus, it's fuckin' freezing!' The words came out in a cloud of fog. 'You lettin' me in or what?' He raised the plastic bag up to eye level. 'I brought breakfast.'

Logan squinted out into the dark. 'Do you have any idea what time it is?'

'Aye. Now open up before all this shite gets cold.'

They sat at the kitchen table, Logan slowly coming back to life, Miller helping himself to the contents of Logan's cupboards while the kettle grumbled and rattled to a boil. 'You got any proper coffee?' he asked, slamming one set of doors and moving on to the next.

'No. Instant.'

Miller sighed and shook his head. 'Bloody place is like a third world country. Never mind. I can slum it . . .' The reporter dug out a couple of huge mugs and spooned in dark brown granules and sugar. He suspiciously examined the carton of semi-skimmed milk lurking in the fridge, but after sniffing it once or twice thumped it down on the table along with a tub of spreadable butter.

'I wasnae sure what kind of breakfast you'd like so we've got croissants, sausage rolls, steak pies and Aberdeen rolls. Help yourself.'

Logan dug a couple of rowies out of the bag and slathered one with butter. He took a big bite and sighed happily.

'Don't know how you can eat that shite,' said

Miller, handing Logan a coffee. 'You know what's in them?'

Logan nodded. 'Fat, flour and salt.'

'No, not fat: *lard*. Only a fuckin' Aberdonian could come up with a roll that looks like a cowpat. There's half a ton of saturated animal fat and half a ton of salt in that! No surprising you're all dropping dead of heart attacks.' He pulled the bag over and helped himself to a croissant, tearing off a chunk, spreading it with jam and butter and dipping it in his coffee.

'You can talk!' Logan watched a thin film of sparkling grease float to the surface of the reporter's mug. 'Your lot invented deep-fried pizzas!'

'Aye, touché.'

Logan watched him rip, spread and dip another chunk of croissant, waiting until the reporter's mouth was full of soggy bread before asking him why he'd come round at this ungodly hour.

'Can a friend no pop round tae have breakfast with another friend?' The words came out muffled. 'You know, nice and social . . .'

'And?'

Miller shrugged. 'You did good last night.' He reached into the bag and came out with another croissant and a copy of that morning's *Press and Journal*. The front page held a big photo of the press conference. 'POLICE HERO FINDS MISSING CHILD' said the headline in big, bold letters. 'Found that little kiddie all by your ownsome. How'd you do it?'

Logan dug a steak pie out of the bag, surprised to find it was still warm from the baker's oven. He munched down on flaky pastry, coating the newspaper with crumbs as he read and ate at the same time. He had to admit: it was a good story. There wasn't much in the way of fact, but Miller had managed to weave what there was into something a lot more interesting than it should have been. It looked as if the reporter was the paper's golden boy for a reason. There was even a recap of Logan's capture of the Mastrick Monster, just so everyone would know that DS Logan McRae was worthy of the title 'POLICE HERO'.

'I'm impressed,' Logan said, and Miller smiled. 'All the words are spelled right.'

'Cheeky bastard.'

'So why are you really here?'

Miller settled back in his seat, cradling his mug of coffee close to his chest, but not close enough to stain his nice new suit. 'You know damn fine why: I want the inside story. I want the scoop. This stuff,' he poked the photo on the paper's front page, 'it's no got a long shelf life. Today, tomorrow, an' that's yer lot. Kiddie's turned up safe and well and it was nothin' more than his dad. A domestic. No blood an' guts for the punters to get all shocked an' horrified about. If the kid was dead, it'd run for weeks. As it is, day after tomorrow no one will want to know.'

'Bit cynical.'

Miller shrugged. 'Call it like I see it.'

'That why your colleagues don't like you?'

Miller didn't even flinch, just popped a swollen chunk of coffee-stained bread into his mouth. 'Aye, well . . . No one likes a smart arse, no when it makes them look bad.' He put on a passable Aberdonian accent: '"Yer nae a team player!", "That's no the way we dae things up here!", "You keep this up and you're oot!"' He snorted. 'Aye, they don't like me, but they publish my stuff, don't they? I've had more front pages since I got here than most of them old buggers have had in their whole bloody lives!'

Logan smiled. Touched a nerve there.

'So,' Miller polished off the last of his croissant, sooking the crumbs off his fingertips, 'you goin' to tell me how you found the missing kid or what?'

'No chance! I've already had one visit from Professional Standards, looking for whoever told you we'd found David Reid's body. They'll have my arse in a sling if I go handing out information without official permission.'

'Like you did yesterday?' asked Miller innocently.

Logan just looked at him.

'OK, OK,' said the reporter, collecting up the breakfast debris. 'I get the hint. Quid pro quo: right?'

'You have to tell me who your source is.'

Miller shook his head. 'No goin' to happen. You know that.' He stuffed the milk and butter back in the fridge. 'How'd you do with that info I gave you?'

'Er . . . we're following it up.' Logan lied. The sodding body in the harbour! The one with no knees! After Insch chewed him out for talking to the press he'd not actually spoken to the DI in charge of the investigation. He'd been too busy sulking.

'OK, well you go an have a wee word with your DI and I'll tell you what I've found out about George Stephenson's last known whereabouts. That sound fair?' He pulled a freshly-printed business card out of his wallet and placed it on the table. 'You've got till half-four. "How Did Police Hero Find Missing Kid?" Day after tomorrow: no one cares. You give us a shout when you know.'

16

It was too late to go back to bed, so Logan grumbled his way into the shower and then up the road to Force Headquarters. The street was like a sheet of glass, the council having done its usual sterling job of not gritting the streets and pavements. But at least it wasn't raining any more. Above his head the clouds were purple and dark grey, the rising sun still more than two hours away.

Headquarters was like a grave as he pushed through the main doors. There was no sign of the media army that had been camped there the night before. All that was left was a pile of crumpled fag ends, lying in the gutter like frozen worms.

Big Gary shouted a friendly 'Mornin', Lazarus!' as Logan made for the lifts.

'Morning, Gary,' said Logan, really not in the mood for another barrage of bonhomie.

'Here,' called Gary, after making sure there was no one else about. 'Did you hear? DI Steel's bagged someone else's wife. Again!'

Logan paused, despite himself. 'Whose is it this time?'

'Andy Thompson in Accounts.'

Logan winced. 'Ouch. That's rough.'

Big Gary raised his eyebrows. 'You think so? I always thought his wife was kinda tasty meself.'

A balding head with a wide moustache poked itself out from behind the mirrored partition that separated the front desk from the small admin area around the back, and locked eyes on Logan. 'Sergeant,' said Eric – the other half of the Big Gary and Eric Show – without a great deal of warmth in his voice. 'Could I have a word with you in my office, please?'

Puzzled, Logan followed him around behind the two-way mirror. The admin area was a jumble of filing cabinets, computers and boxes of crap, piled against the walls, opposite a long, chipped Formica table covered with in-trays and piles of paper. Logan got the feeling something nasty was about to happen. 'What's up, Eric?' he asked, parking himself on the edge of the table: just like DI Insch.

'Duncan Nicholson,' said the desk sergeant, folding his arms. 'That's what's up.' Logan looked at him blankly and Eric let out an exasperated sigh. 'You had a couple of uniform bring him in for questioning?' No reaction. 'He found the dead kid down the Bridge of Don!'

'Oh,' said Logan. 'Him.'

'Yes, him. He's been in the holding cells since

Monday afternoon.' Eric checked his watch. 'Forty-three hours! You have to charge him or let him go!'

Logan closed his eyes and swore. He'd forgotten all about the man. 'Forty-three hours?' The legal limit was six!

'Forty-three hours.'

Eric crossed his arms and let Logan stew for a while. Today was turning into an utter bastard.

'I released him Monday evening,' said Eric when he thought Logan had suffered enough. 'We couldn't hold him any longer. As it was we had him far longer than we should have.'

'Monday?' That was two days ago! 'Why didn't you call me?'

'We did! About a dozen times. You turned off your phone. Tried again last night too. If you're going to have people picked up you have to deal with them. You can't just abandon them here and leave us to sort it out. We're not your mother!'

Logan swore again. He'd switched off his mobile while he was in the little girl's post mortem. 'Sorry, Eric.'

The desk sergeant nodded. 'Aye, well. I've made sure there's no sign of anything wrong in the logbook. As far as everyone's concerned: nothing happened. He came in on a voly, he was held for a bit, he was released. Just don't let it happen again, OK?'

Logan nodded. 'Thanks, Eric.'

Logan slouched his way along the corridor to

the small office he'd commandeered the day before, grabbing a plastic cup of coffee on the way. The building was beginning to stir as the early birds drifted into work. Closing the door behind him, Logan sank into the chair behind the desk and stared at the map pinned to the wall, not really seeing the streets and the rivers.

Duncan Nicholson. He'd forgotten all about leaving him in the cells to sweat. He let his head sink forward until it was resting on top of the stack of statements. 'Bastard,' he said into the pile of paper. 'Bastard, bastard, bastard . . .'

There was a knock at the door and he snapped upright. The statement on top of the pile fluttered to the floor. He was wincing down to pick it up when the door opened and WPC Watson peered in.

'Morning, sir,' she said and then caught the expression on his face. 'You OK?'

Logan forced a smile and sat back down. 'Never better,' he lied. 'You're in early.'

WPC Watson nodded. 'Yeah, I've got court this morning: caught a bloke yesterday afternoon playing with himself in the ladies' changing rooms at Hazlehead swimming pool.'

'Sounds classy.'

She smiled and Logan found himself feeling a lot better.

'Can't wait for him to meet my mum,' she said. 'Look, I got to run: he's giving evidence in this Gerald Cleaver sex abuse thing and I'm not to let him out of my sight. But I wanted to tell you we're all dead impressed you found that kid.'

Logan smiled back. 'It was a team effort,' he said.

'Bollocks it was. We're all going out tonight again, not a big sesh, just a quiet drink. If you want to join us . . . ?'

Logan couldn't think of anything he'd like more.

He was feeling a lot better about himself as he walked down the corridor to the incident room and DI Insch's morning briefing. WPC Jackie Watson wanted to go out with him again tonight. Or at least she wanted him to join her and her colleagues for a drink after work. Which was kind of the same thing. Sort of . . . They still hadn't talked about what had happened the night before last.

And she still called him 'sir'.

But then he still called her 'Constable'. Not the most romantic of pet names.

He opened the door to the incident room and was met by a thunderous round of applause. Blushing, Logan made his way to a seat at the front, settling down in the chair as his face went beetroot red.

'OK, OK,' said DI Insch, holding up a hand for silence. Slowly the clapping faded to a halt. 'Ladies and gentlemen,' he went on when it was quiet once more. 'As you all know, last night Detective

Sergeant Logan McRae returned Richard Erskine to his mother, after discovering the child at his grandmother's house.' He stopped and beamed at Logan. 'Come on: stand up.'

Blushing even harder, Logan pulled himself out of his seat and the clapping started again.

'That,' said Insch, pointing at the embarrassed DS, 'is what a real policeman looks like.' He had to call for silence again and Logan sank back into his seat, feeling thrilled, delighted and horrified all at the same time. 'We've found Richard Erskine.' Insch pulled a manila folder from the desktop and pulled out an eight-by-six photograph of a red-haired boy with freckles and a gap-toothed smile. 'But Peter Lumley is still missing. Chances are we're not going to find him kipping at his grandma's: the father can't be arsed with the kid. But I want it checked out anyway.'

Insch took another picture from his folder. This one wasn't so palatable: a blistered, swollen face, black and speckled with mould, the mouth open in a tortured scream. A post mortem photograph of David Reid.

'This is what Peter Lumley is going to end up looking like if we don't get him back soon. I want the search area widened. Three teams: Hazlehead golf course, riding stables, park. Every bush, every bunker, every pile of manure. I want them searched.' He started rattling off names.

When Insch was finished and everyone had gone, Logan brought him up to date on the dead girl they'd found in a rubbish bag. It didn't take long.

'So what do you suggest?' asked Insch, settling back on the desk and rummaging through his suit pockets for something sweet.

Logan did his best not to shrug. 'We can't put on a reconstruction. We've got no idea what she was wearing before she went into the bin-bag and they won't let us re-enact dumping a body. Her picture's gone into all the papers. We might get something out of that.' The only good thing about Aberdeen being the 'dead kiddie capital of Scotland' right now was that the national tabloids and broadsheets were more than happy to parade the dead girl's photo for their readers.

Insch located an old-looking Murray Mint and popped it in his mouth. 'Keep on it. Someone out there must know who the poor wee sod is. Norman Chalmers had his fifteen minutes in court yesterday: remanded without bail. But the Fiscal's no happy. We come up with something solid, or Chalmers walks.'

'We'll find something, sir.'

'Good. The Chief Constable is worried about all these missing kids. It looks bad. Lothian and Borders have been on "offering their assistance". Even sent us up a preliminary psychological pro-file.' He held up four sheets of paper, stapled together, the crest of Lothian and Borders Police clearly visible on the covering page. 'If we don't watch out, Edinburgh are going to take over. And we'll all end up looking like sheep-shagging, small-town halfwits.'

'That's nice,' said Logan. 'What's the profile say?'

'Same thing these bloody things always say.' Insch flipped through the sheets. 'Blah, blah, blah, "crime scene indicators", blah, blah, "pathology of the victim", blah, blah.' He stopped, a wry smile on his face. 'Here we go: "the offender is most likely a Caucasian male, in his early to late twenties, living alone or with his mother. He is most likely intelligent, but does not do well academically. As a result he will have a menial job that brings him into contact with children".'

Logan nodded. It was the standard profile for just about everything.

'You'll like this bit,' said Insch, putting on an academic voice: '"The offender has difficulty forming relationships with women, and may have a history of mental health problems . . . " Mental health problems! Talk about stating the bloody obvious!' The smile vanished from his face. 'Of course he's got mental bloody health problems: he kills children!' He crumpled up the profile and lobbed it, overhand, at the wastebasket by the door. It bounced off the wall and skittered across the blue carpet tiles, coming to rest under the second row of chairs. Insch snorted in disgust. 'Anyway,' he said, 'it looks like DI McPherson's not going to be back for another month at least. Thirty-seven stitches to keep his head together.

Lovely. Nothing like some mad bastard with a kitchen knife to get a couple of weeks with your feet up in front of the telly.' He sighed, not noticing the pained look on Logan's face. 'That means I've got his caseload to carry as well as my own. Four post office break-ins, three armed assaults, two violent rapes and a partridge in a bloody pear tree.' He poked a friendly finger in Logan's chest. 'And that means I'm delegating the Bin-Bag Girl to you.'

'But . . .'

Insch held up his hands. 'Aye, I know it's a big case, but I've got my hands full with David Reid and Peter Lumley. They might not be connected, but the last thing the Chief Constable wants is a paedophile serial killer running loose, picking up little boys whenever he feels the urge. Every other DI we've got is up to their ears, but you found Richard Erskine without adult supervision, and the media think the sun shines out of your arse. So this one's yours.'

'Yes, sir.' Logan's stomach had already started churning.

'OK,' said Insch, hopping down off the desk. 'You get going on that. I'll go see what kind of Muppets I've inherited from McPherson.'

Logan's little office was waiting for him. Expectantly. As if it knew he was carrying the can now. There was a copy of the photo they'd released to the media sitting on his desk. The one they'd taken in the morgue, touched up so she didn't look quite so dead. She must have been pretty when she was alive. A four-year-old girl with shoulder-length blonde hair that curled softly around her pale face. Button nose. Round face. Round cheeks. According to the report her eyes were blue-green, but in the photo her eyes were shut. No one liked looking into the eyes of dead children. He took the picture and fixed it on the wall next to his map.

So far the response to the media appeal had been negligible. No one seemed to know who the little girl was. That would probably change by this evening when her picture went out again on the television. Then there would be a flood of helpful people phoning up to give them a whole heap of useless information.

He spent the next two hours poring over the statements again. He'd read it all before, but Logan knew the answer was in here somewhere. Whoever dumped the body lived within spitting distance of that wheelie-bin.

At last he gave up on the cold mug of coffee he'd been nurturing for the last hour and stretched the knots out of his back. He was getting nowhere. And he still hadn't spoken to anyone about the body in the harbour. Maybe it was time for a break?

DI Steel's office was one floor up, blue scuffed carpet tiles and creaky-looking furniture. There was a sign on the wall with 'No Smoking' written in big red letters, but that didn't deter the inspector. She sat at her desk, the window cracked slightly to let the curling cigarette smoke drift out into the blazing sunshine.

Detective Inspector Steel was Laurel to DI Insch's Hardy. Where Insch was fat, she was thin. Where Insch was bald, Steel looked as if someone had sellotaped a Cairn terrier to her head. Rumour had it she was only forty-two, but she looked a lot older. Years of chain smoking had left her face looking like a holiday home for lines and wrinkles. She was wearing a trouser suit from Markies, in charcoal grey so it wouldn't show the ash that fell constantly from the end of her fag. The burgundy blouse underneath it hadn't fared so well.

It was hard to believe she was the biggest womanizer on the force.

There was a mobile phone rammed between her ear and her shoulder and she talked into it out of one side of her mouth so as not to disturb the cigarette sticking out of the other. 'No. No. No . . .' she said in a hard staccato. 'You get this: I get hold of you, I will rip you a new arsehole. No . . . no, I don't care who the fuck you have to screw around. You don't come across with the goodies before Friday, you and I are going to fall out . . . Fucking right I will . . .' She looked up, saw Logan standing there and waved him towards a tatty-looking chair. 'Yes . . . yes, that's better. I knew we could come to an understanding. Friday.' DI Steel snapped her mobile shut and smiled evilly.

'Fully fucking fitted kitchen, my arse. You give these people an inch they'll piss all over you.' She picked a packet of king-size up off her desk and shook it in Logan's direction. 'Fag?'

Logan declined and she smiled at him again.

'No? Aye, you're right: it's a fucking filthy habit.' She winkled a cigarette out of the pack and lit it from the one she was still smoking, before grinding the stub out on the windowsill. 'So what can I do for you, Mr Police Hero?' she asked, settling back in her chair, her head wreathed in fresh smoke.

'Your floater: Mr No Kneecaps.'

Steel raised an eyebrow. 'Listening.'

'I think it's George "Geordie" Stephenson. He was an enforcer for Malcolm McLennan—'

'Malk the Knife? Fuck. I didn't think he was doing business up here.'

'Word has it Geordie was sent up to cut a deal with the planning department: three hundred houses on greenbelt. The planner said no and Geordie pushed him under a bus.'

'I don't believe you.' She even went so far as to take the cigarette out of her mouth. 'Someone from Planning turned down a bribe?'

Logan shrugged. 'Anyway: it seems that Geordie had a liking for the horses. Only Lady Luck is not Geordie's friend. And he was into some of the local bookies for some serious money.'

DI Steel settled back in her seat, picking at her teeth with a chipped fingernail. 'I'm impressed,' she said at last. 'Where'd you hear this?'

'Colin Miller. He's a reporter on the P&J.'

She took a long draw on her fag, making the end glow hot orange. Smoke trickled down her nose as she examined Logan in silence. The room was shrinking, the walls obscured by curling layers of tobacco fog until only that glowing orange eye remained. 'Inschy tells me you're running the kid-in-the-bin-bag case now.'

'Yes, ma'am.'

'He tells me you're not a complete waste of skin.'

'Thank you, ma'am.' But he wasn't sure if that was really a compliment.

'Don't thank me. If you're not a fuck-up, people notice. They give you things to do.' She smiled at him through the smoke and Logan felt a small chill go down his spine. 'Inschy and me: we've been talking about you.'

'Oh?' There was something unpleasant coming: he could feel it.

'It's your lucky day, Mr Police Hero. You're going to get another chance to shine.'

17

Logan went straight to DI Insch. The inspector sat on the edge of a desk like a large, round vulture and listened calmly as Logan complained about DI Steel slope-shouldering the no-knees investigation onto him. He was just a detective sergeant! He couldn't carry multiple homicide investigations! Insch listened and tutted and commiserated and then told him that things were tough all over and he shouldn't be such a bloody prima donna.

'What have you got going on the bin-bag case?' asked Insch.

Logan shrugged. 'The appeal went out on the telly last night, so there's a pile of sightings to go through. There was this one old lady who said we could call off the search, because little "Tiffany" was playing in the sand pit at the foot of the garden.' He shook his head. 'Silly old bat . . . Anyway, I've got a dozen uniform out working their way through the list.'

'So you're basically twiddling your thumbs till something comes up, then?'

Logan blushed and admitted that yes, he was.

'So what's to stop you digging into the floater?'

'Well, nothing as such, it's just that . . .' He tried not to meet Insch's eyes. 'Well, there's the incident lines—'

'Get a uniform to take the calls.' Insch settled back on his large rump, arms crossed.

'And . . . and . . .' Logan stopped talking and flapped his arms a little. Somehow he couldn't get the words out: *I'm terrified of screwing all this up*.

'And nothing,' said Insch. 'You can have WPC Watson when she's finished in court.' He checked his watch. 'I've not factored her into any of the search teams anyway.'

Logan just slumped slightly.

'Well, what are you waiting for?' The inspector levered himself off the desk and dug out a half-eaten packet of Polo Mints, helping himself to one before winding the tinfoil shut like a silvery fuse. 'Here.' He tossed the little dynamite-shaped package to Logan. 'Call it an early Christmas bonus. Now bugger off and get to work.'

When they heard that Logan had a body in the morgue that might be Geordie Stephenson, Lothian and Borders Police were delighted. But before they threw a full-blown party with cake and balloons, they wanted to make sure Logan's stiff really was Malk the Knife's favourite enforcer. So they emailed up everything they had on the man: fingerprints, criminal record, and a nice big photo that Logan had printed off in colour. Twelve copies. Geordie had a large face with heavy features, bouffant hairstyle and a porn-star moustache. Just the sort of face to go demanding money with menaces with. He looked a lot more battered and pasty now he was dead, but it was definitely the same man they'd dragged out of the harbour with his knees hacked off. And to make matters certain, the fingerprints were an exact match.

Logan phoned Lothian and Borders back to give them the news. Geordie Stephenson was now collecting debts in the great beyond. They promised to send Logan up some cake.

Now that they had a positive ID, the next thing to do was find out who killed him. And Logan was willing to bet it had something to do with Geordie's gambling habit. So that meant doing the rounds of the bookies in Aberdeen. Flash Geordie's face and see who squirmed.

Logan popped into his little incident room on the way out, just to make sure everything was still going OK. On Insch's instructions he'd commandeered an efficient-looking WPC with sandy-brown hair and thick eyebrows to woman the phones and co-ordinate the uniforms going door-to-door. She sat at the cluttered table with a phone headset on, taking down yet another possible identity for the dead girl. Then she brought him up to speed with the latest developments, which took all of three seconds – there weren't any – and promised to call him on his mobile if anything came up.

That done, all he had to do now was pick up WPC Watson from the Sheriff Court and get cracking.

She was still sitting in the main courtroom, watching a huge youth with a pockmarked face giving evidence. WPC Watson looked up and smiled as Logan sat down next to her.

'How's it going?' he whispered.

'Getting there.'

The kid on the stand wasn't much more than twenty-one, and sweat made his flushed, lumpy face shine in the courtroom lights. He was massive. Not fat, just big-boned. Big jaw, big hands, long, bony arms. The grey suit the CPS had lent him to make him look more credible as a witness, was far too small, straining at the seams every time he moved. His dirty-blond hair looked as if it hadn't seen a comb for a long time and his big hands fluttered and fidgeted as he mumbled his way through his encounter with Gerald Cleaver.

An eleven-year-old boy, so badly beaten by his drunken father that he gets to spend three weeks in Aberdeen Children's Hospital. And that's where his luck goes from bad to worse. Gerald Cleaver, in charge of the wards at night, practises his own special 'bedside manner' while the kid's strapped to the bed. Making him do things that would make a porn star blush.

The prosecutor gently drew the details from him, speaking softly and reassuringly even when the tears start to flow.

Logan split his attention between the jury and the accused as the boy spoke. The fifteen men and women looked appalled at what they were hearing. But Gerald Cleaver's face remained as expressionless as a slab of butter.

The prosecutor thanked the witness for his courage and handed him over to counsel for the defence.

'Here we go.' WPC Watson's voice dripped with contempt as Slippery Sandy the Snake stood, patted his client on the shoulder and wandered over to the jury. Casually, he leaned on the rail at the front of the box and smiled at the assembled men and women. 'Martin,' he said, not looking at the trembling young man but at the jury, 'you're not exactly a stranger to this court, are you?'

The prosecutor was on his feet as if someone had run a thousand volts up his bum.

'I object. The witness's past situation has nothing to do with the case being tried.'

'Your honour, I am merely trying to establish the veracity of this witness.'

The judge looked down his nose, through his glasses and said, 'You may proceed.'

'Thank you, your honour,' said the Snake. 'Martin, you've been up before this court thirty-eight times, haven't you? Breaking and entering, criminal assault, numerous charges of possession, one of possession with intent to supply, shoplifting, arson, indecent exposure . . .' He paused. 'When you were fourteen you tried to have sex with a minor and when she refused you beat her so severely she required forty-three stitches to put her face back together again. She can never have children. And just yesterday you were arrested for masturbating in a ladies' changing room—'

'Your honour, I strongly object!'

And that was how it went for the next twenty minutes. Sandy the Snake calmly ripped the witness to shreds and left him a swearing, sobbing, scarlet-faced wreck. Every humiliation Gerald Cleaver had submitted him to was explained away as the disturbed fantasy of a child in desperate need of attention. Until, in the end, Martin had lunged for the lawyer, screaming, 'Fuckin' kill you!'

He was restrained.

Sandy the Snake shook his head sadly, and excused the witness.

Watson swore all the way back to the cells, but she perked up when Logan told her about his new assignment.

'DI Steel wants me to follow up on Geordie Stephenson: that body they dragged out the

236

harbour,' he said as they made their way down the long corridor that linked courtroom number one to the holding cells. 'I said I'd need some help, and Insch volunteered you. Said you'd keep me right.'

Watson smiled, pleased at the compliment, not knowing Logan had made it up himself.

Martin Strichen had been escorted from the court straight to the holding cells. By the time Logan and Watson got down there he was sitting on a thin grey bunk with his head in his hands, moaning softly beneath the flickering overhead lights. The back of his borrowed suit jacket was groaning under the strain, the seam getting more and more visible with every shivering sob.

Looking down at him, Logan didn't know what to think. It was terrible that any child should have to undergo the kind of abuse Cleaver subjected his victims to. Even so, Slippery Sandy's words stayed with him. That list of crimes. Martin Strichen was a dirty wee toerag. But that didn't mean he hadn't suffered at the hands of Gerald Cleaver.

Watson signed for Martin Strichen and they led him, handcuffed and whimpering, up through the building and out the back entrance. It was only a short walk to the pool car Logan had appropriated. As Watson pushed her prisoner's head down so it wouldn't bang on the roof of the car, Strichen said, 'She was fourteen.'

'What?' Watson peered into the car, into Martin Strichen's puffy red eyes.

'The girl. We was both fourteen. She wanted to, but I couldn't. I didn't force her . . . I couldn't do it.' A large, tear-shaped drop suspended from the tip of his nose and as she watched it slowly fell, sparkling in the early afternoon light.

'Arms up.' She buckled the seatbelt around him, making sure that Grampian Police didn't end up in court defending a negligence claim if they crashed the car. As her hair brushed his face she heard him whisper, 'She wouldn't stop laughing . . .'

They dropped their passenger off at Craiginches Prison. Once the rigmarole of signing him back into custody was over and done with, they were ready to start on DI Steel's investigation.

Logan and WPC Watson slogged their way around Aberdeen's less salubrious bookmaking establishments, showing the staff Geordie Stephenson's porn star picture but getting nothing but blank stares for their troubles. There was little point in visiting the majors – William Hill and Ladbrokes – they weren't likely to hack Geordie's kneecaps off with a machete if he failed to settle his debts.

But the Turf 'n Track in Sandilands was exactly that kind of place.

The shop had been a baker's back in the sixties when the neighbourhood was a bit more upmarket. Not *that* much more upmarket, but back in the days when you could walk the streets after dark. The shop was part of a block of four equally tatty and run-down establishments. All were covered in graffiti, all had heavy metal grilles on the window, and all had been broken into and robbed at gunpoint many times. Except the Turf 'n Track, which had been robbed only once in living memory. And that's because the McLeod brothers hunted down the bloke who burst into their father's shop waving a sawn-off shotgun and tortured him to death with a gas lighter and a pair of needle-nosed pliers. Allegedly.

Council-owned housing surrounded the shops – three- and four-storey concrete tenement buildings thrown up in a hurry and left to rot. If you needed a home fast, had no money and weren't fussy, this was where you ended up.

A poster outside the grocer's next door declared: 'MISSING: PETER LUMLEY' beneath a colour picture of the five-year-old's smiling, freckled face. Some wit had drawn on a pair of glasses, a moustache and 'RAZ TAKES IT UP THE ARSE'.

There were no community notices pinned up outside the Turf 'n Track: it offered only blacked-out windows and a green-and-yellow plastic sign. Logan pushed through the door into the gloomy interior where the air was thick with the smell of hand-rolled tobacco and wet dog. The inside was even shabbier than the outside: dirty plastic seats in grimy orange, sticky linoleum with cigarette burns and holes worn all the way through to the concrete floor. Woodwork so thickly impregnated by generations of cigarette smoke that it oozed sticky black. There was a chest-high counter running across the room, keeping the punters away from the paperwork, the tills, and the door to the back room. An old man sat in the corner, a grey-muzzled Alsatian at his feet, a tin of Export in his hand. His attention was fixed on a TV screen with dogs screeching round a track. Logan was surprised to see a pensioner in here. He thought they were all too scared to come out on their own. And then the man took his eyes off the television to examine the newcomers.

There were tattoos all the way up his neck: flames and skulls; his right eye cloudy-white and slack.

Logan felt a tug at his sleeve and WPC Watson hissed in his ear, 'Isn't that—'

But the old man got there first, shouting, 'Mr McLeod! There's some fuckin' police bastards here tae see you!'

'Now, now Dougie, that's not nice,' said Logan, taking a step towards the old man. The Alsatian was on its feet in an instant, teeth bared, its low growl making the hair on Logan's neck stand on end. A string of saliva spiralled down between the animal's broken teeth. It was an old dog, but it was vicious enough to frighten the crap out of him.

Nobody moved. The dog kept on snarling, the

old man kept on glowering, and Logan kept on hoping he wasn't going to have to run for his life. Eventually a round face stuck itself out of the back room.

'Dougie, what have I told you about that fuckin' dog?'

The old man cracked a smile, exposing green-and-brown dentures. 'You said if the pigs come in, let 'im tear their fuckin' throats out.'

The newcomer frowned, then a smile broke his face in two. 'Aye, you're right. So I did.' He was a good thirty years younger than Dougie, but the old man still called him 'Mr' McLeod.

Simon McLeod had inherited his father's coarse features. His left ear was missing a chunk, courtesy of a Rottweiler called Killer whose head now adorned the back office.

'What do you bastards want then?' he asked, settling his massive arms on the counter.

Logan pulled out a colour picture of Geordie and held it out in front of him. 'You recognize this man?'

'Fuck you.' He hadn't even looked at the picture.

'Nice offer, but I'll pass this time.' Logan slapped the photo down on the grimy counter. 'Now: do you recognize him?'

'Never seen him before.'

'He was a loudmouthed git from Edinburgh. Came up here to do a job for Malk the Knife. Made some big bets and didn't settle them.'

Simon McLeod's face closed up. 'We don't have a lot of people who don't settle. It's against management policy.'

'Take another look, Mr McLeod. Sure you don't recognize him? Ended up floating face down in the harbour with his kneecaps missing.'

Simon's eyes opened wide and he slapped a hand over his mouth. 'Oh, *him!* God, now you mention it, I do remember something about hacking his kneecaps off and throwing him in the harbour! Christ, why'd you no say so sooner? Aye: I kilt him and I'm no fuckin' bright enough to lie about it if the police come in here askin' stupid fuckin' questions.'

Logan bit his tongue and counted to five. 'Do you recognize him?'

'Get to fuck and take your bitch with you. The smell's upsettin' Winchester.' He pointed at the snarling Alsatian. 'And even if I did recognize him, I'd sooner eat shite out a whore's arse than tell you.'

'Where's your brother Colin?'

'None of your fuckin' business: that's where he is. Now you goin' to fuck off, or what?'

Logan had to admit that there wasn't a lot more they could do here. He was all the way to the door before a thought struck him and he turned. 'Hacked off,' he said, frowning. 'How did you know the man's kneecaps had been hacked off? I never said anything about that. I just said they were missing!'

McLeod just laughed. 'Aye, well done, Miss Marple. When someone ends up in the harbour with no knees like that it's a message. It's no a very good message if everyone doesnae get it. Every fucker in the city knows you don't do what he did. Now fuck off.'

They stood outside on the top step of the Turf 'n Track, watching clouds scud across the sky. There was just enough fading sunshine to cut through the seasonal chill and Logan watched a pair of plastic bags playing chase around the concrete in front of the boarded-up shops.

WPC Watson leaned on the steel rail that ran along the front of the fortified buildings. 'What now?'

Logan shrugged. 'We were never going to get anything out of the McLeods. We might have pulled in a couple of their punters, but can you see Dougie breaking down and spilling his guts?'

'Not his own guts, no.'

'So now we stick the photo under the noses of the other shopkeepers here. You never know. If we don't mention the McLeods they might actually tell us something.'

The Liverpudlian owner of the Chinese take-away didn't recognize Geordie's face and neither did either of his Aberdonian staff. The video store had shut down years ago though the windows were still full of posters for forgotten blockbusters and 'straight to video' releases just visible through the aerosol scrawl. Last on the row was a combined newsagents, greengrocer and off-licence. The owner took one look at WPC Watson's uniform and got a sudden attack of laryngitis. But he did sell Logan a packet of extra strong mints.

Back outside again, the clouds had darkened the sky, the dying daylight giving up as the first fat drops of rain began to fall. They struck the concrete with a lifeless thud, one at a time, making large dark-grey circles that spread out, joining up as the heavens decided to really let rip. Dragging his suit jacket up over his head Logan ran for their rusty Vauxhall. Watson got there first and cranked on the blowers. They sat and steamed gently as the blowers did their best to clear the windows, sharing a packet of mints, watching hazy figures running for the shop doors to get in out of the rain for a mid-afternoon chicken chowmein, or the latest issue of *Leather and Chains Monthly*.

Simon McLeod was up to something. But then the McLeods were always up to something. The trouble was proving it. They were from the old school: the kind in which lessons were taught with a claw hammer. No one ever saw anything. No one ever squealed.

'So where now?'

Logan shrugged. 'Next bookies on the list I suppose.'

WPC Watson stuck the car into reverse and backed out of the parking space. The headlights clicked on, turning the stair-rod rain into silver daggers. They'd almost reached the main road when a rust-and-green estate car appeared out of nowhere. Watson slammed on the brakes, shouted 'Fuck!' and stalled the engine.

As the estate parked roughly in front of the Turf 'n Track, she wound down the window and hurled a mouthful of abuse out into the rain. Most of which involved the driver of the offending car's rectum and WPC Watson's boot. She stopped in mid-sentence. 'Oh, God. Sorry, sir!'

Logan raised an eyebrow.

She blushed. 'I kinda forgot you were there. I mean he didn't indicate or anything. Sorry.'

Logan took a deep breath and thought about what DI Insch had told him about the privileges of rank. He couldn't just sit there and say nothing. She was in uniform for God's sake! What if it got back to the papers? 'Do you think a policewoman, in full uniform, leaning out of a car window, swearing her head off, does a lot for the Force?'

'I didn't think, sir.'

'Jackie, when you do something like that you make us all look like a bunch of arseholes. You piss off everyone who sees it, or hears about it second-hand. And you put your job on the line.'

Her blush went from strawberry to beetroot. 'I . . . sorry.'

He let her stew in silence for a slow count of ten, silently cursing inside. He'd hoped for a chance to impress her with his witty repartee, or his deductive acumen. Make her see what a great guy he was. The sort of guy you slept with twice. Giving her a dressing down hadn't been part of the plan. An 'undressing' down maybe . . .

Eight. Nine. Ten.

'Come on,' he said, trying out a friendly smile on her. 'I won't say anything about it if you don't.'

Not looking him in the eye, she said, 'Thank you, sir,' and started the car.

18

The atmosphere in the car never got much beyond polite as they made their way through the remaining bookies on Logan's list. WPC Watson called him 'sir' and answered his questions, but she never volunteered anything unless it was directly pertinent to the case.

It was a crappy afternoon.

They slogged their way from the car to one betting shop after another.

'Have you seen this man?'

'No.'

Sometimes the 'no' came with a free 'fuck off' and other times the 'fuck off' was silent. But it was always there. Except for the owner and staff at J Stewart and Son: Bookmakers est. 1974 in Mastrick. Who were surprisingly nice to them. Disturbingly, suspiciously nice.

'Jesus, that was freaky,' said Logan as they clambered back into the car. 'Look, they're still smiling at us.' He pointed through the windscreen at a large woman with ratty grey hair tied into a bun on the top of her head. She waved back.

'Seemed nice enough to me,' said Watson, negotiating the car out of the car park. It was the most she'd said for about an hour.

'You never met Ma Stewart before?' asked Logan as they headed back towards the station. When WPC Watson didn't reply he took that as a no. 'I arrested her once,' he said as they drifted onto the Lang Stracht, the wide road carved up into bus lanes and weird pseudo-box-junctions liberally sprinkled with bollards and pedestrian crossings. 'Pornography. She was peddling it to school kids out the back of an old Ford Anglia. Nothing too heavy – no animals or anything like that. Just good old-fashioned German hard-core. Videos and magazines.' He snorted. 'Half the bloody children in Mastrick knew more about sex than their biology teacher. We got called in when this eight-year-old asked if you could get pregnant from fisting.'

A small smile flickered round the corners of WPC Watson's mouth.

The offices of the *Press and Journal* went by on the left and Logan winced. With all the excitement and panic of being put in charge of the bin-bag case he'd forgotten all about Colin Miller's visit this morning. He still hadn't talked to DI Insch about the reporter's request for an exclusive. And Miller said he had more information on 'Geordie' too. Logan pulled his phone out to call DI Insch, but didn't get any further than punching in the first two numbers.

A crackly voice boomed out of the radio. Someone had beaten up Roadkill.

They hadn't meant it to go this far. That was what the ringleaders said when questioned by the Police and the Press. They just wanted to make sure their children were safe. It wasn't right, was it? A grown man like that hanging around the school gates. And it wasn't the first time he'd done it either. Most afternoons he was there, just when the kids were getting let out. And he wasn't right in the head. Everyone knew he wasn't right in the head. He smelled funny. It wasn't right.

So what if he got roughed up a little bit? It wasn't as if they'd meant it to go that far. But kids were missing! You know: kids. Kids like the ones that went to Garthdee Primary School. Kids like theirs. If the police had come sooner it wouldn't have got out of hand. If they'd come when they were called, none of this would have happened.

So when you really thought about it, it was all the police's fault.

The man sitting on the other side of the inter-view table had seen better days. Yesterday for example. That was the last time Logan had set eyes on Bernard Duncan Philips, AKA Roadkill. He'd been pretty tatty-looking then, but at least his nose hadn't looked as if someone had taken a sledgehammer to it. Bruises were already running rampant across his face and one eye was swollen shut, the skin an angry purple. His beard was clean and spiky on one side where the hospital had washed away the dried blood. His lip was swollen up like a sausage and he winced every time he smiled. Which wasn't often.

The accusations levelled against him by the 'concerned parents' who'd beaten him up were too serious to ignore. So as soon as he was released from Accident and Emergency, he had found himself in police custody. And he fitted the Lothian and Borders profile: white male, mid-twenties, mental health problems, menial job, no girlfriend, lives alone. The only error was the claim that he wouldn't do well academically. Roadkill had a degree in medieval history. But, as Insch said, see how much bloody good that had done him.

It had been a long, difficult and convoluted interview. Every time it looked as if they were about to get some sort of consistent statement out of Roadkill off he'd go on another rambling tangent. All the time gently rocking back and forward in his seat. As Roadkill was mentally ill they'd had to drag in an 'appropriate adult' to make sure everything was above board, so a social worker from Craiginches Prison had to sit next to Roadkill as he rocked and rambled and smelled.

The interview room stank to high heaven. Eau de Rotting Animal and BO Pour Homme. Roadkill really, really needed a bath. DI Insch had grabbed the first opportunity to get the hell out of there, leaving Logan and the social worker to suffer while he went off to check on Roadkill's incoherent statement.

Logan shifted in his seat and wondered for the umpteenth time where the inspector had got to. 'Do you want another cup of tea, Bernard?' he asked.

Bernard didn't say anything, just went on folding a bit of paper in half and in half again. And, when it was folded so tight it was a little solid lump that couldn't be folded any more, he unfolded it carefully and started all over again.

'Tea? Bernard? You want some more tea?'

Fold. Fold. Fold.

Logan slumped in his seat and let his head fall back until he was staring at the ceiling. Off-grey ceiling tiles, the pockmarked kind. The ones that looked like the surface of the moon. God this was dull. And it was going on six! He was supposed to be meeting WPC Jackie Watson for a quiet drink.

Fold. Fold. Fold.

Logan and the social worker complained about Aberdeen Football Club's latest performance for a bit before lapsing into gloom and silence again.

Fold. Fold. Fold.

Six twenty-three and the inspector stuck his head round the interview room door and asked Logan to join him in the corridor.

'You get anything out of him?' asked Insch when they were both outside.

'Only a really nasty smell.'

Insch popped a fruit pastille into his mouth and chewed thoughtfully. 'Well, his statement checks out. The council van drops him off after work in the same place just before four every day. They've been doing it for years. He gets the four twenty-two bus to Peterculter, regular as clockwork. Wasn't hard to find a bus driver who remembered him, the smell's hard to forget.'

'And the bus stop is—'

'Right outside Garthdee Primary School. Apparently he used to go to school there, before he went mental. Probably feels safer with a familiar routine.'

'And did any of our "concerned parents" bother to ask him why he was there every afternoon?'

Insch snorted, and helped himself to another pastille. 'Did they bollocks. They saw a ragged-arsed bloke who smells funny, hanging about outside the school and decided to beat the crap out of him. He's not our killer.'

So it was back into the smelly interview room.

'Are you sure there isn't something you want to tell us, Mr Philips?' asked Insch, settling back down into his chair.

There wasn't.

'Right,' said the inspector. 'Well, you'll be happy to know we've managed to corroborate your version of events. I know you're the one who was attacked, but we had to make sure the accusations against you were groundless, OK?'

Fold. Fold. Fold.

'OK. I've asked the council to make sure that you get dropped off somewhere else after work from now on. Further along the road. Nowhere near the school. The people who attacked you aren't very bright. They might decide to have another go.'

Silence.

'We've got their names.' It hadn't been hard, the silly sods had identified themselves with pride! They'd taken a paedophile off the streets! They'd saved their kids from a fate worse than death! That they'd just committed criminal assault didn't seem to cross their minds. 'I'd like you to make a statement so we can press charges.'

Logan recognized his cue and pulled out a notepad, ready to take down Roadkill's complaint.

Fold. Fold. Fold.

The paper was getting loose along the seams where it'd been folded again and again. A perfect square flapped away from one corner and Roadkill scowled at it.

'Mr Philips? Can you tell me what happened?'

Carefully the battered man pulled the square of paper free and placed it in front of him. It was perfectly lined up with the edges of the desk.

And then he started folding again.

Insch sighed.

'OK. How about the sergeant here writes down

what happened and you can sign it? Would that make things easier?'

'I need my medicine.'

'Sorry?'

'Medicine. It's time for my medicine.'

Insch looked at Logan. He shrugged. 'They probably gave him some painkillers at the hospital.'

Roadkill stopped folding his paper and placed both hands on the desk. 'Not painkillers. Medicine. I need to take my medicine. Or they won't let me go to work tomorrow. They wrote me a letter. I have to take my medicine or I can't go to work.'

'It'll only take a few minutes, Mr Philips. Perhaps—'

'No statement. No minutes. Medicine.'

'But—'

'If you're not going to arrest me, or charge me, I'm free to go. You can't force me to make a complaint.'

It was the most lucid thing Logan had ever heard him say.

Roadkill shivered, hugging himself with his arms. 'Please. I just want to go home and take my medicine.'

Logan looked at the tattered, bruised figure and put down his pen. Roadkill was right: they couldn't force him to make a complaint against the people who blackened his eye, split his lip, loosened three of his teeth, cracked one of his ribs and kicked him repeatedly in the goolies. They were his goolies after all. If he didn't want the people kicking them to be punished, it was his call. But Grampian Police weren't about to just turn him loose on the street either. The stupid people would still be out there. And by now the Press would be too. 'LOCAL MOB CAPTURES KIDDIE FIEND!' No, 'mob' sounded too negative. These violent, stupid people were heroes, after all. 'PARENTS CAPTURE COUNCIL PAEDOPHILE!' Yes, that was much more like it.

'Are you sure about this, Mr Philips?' asked Insch.

Roadkill just nodded.

'OK. Well in that case we'll get your possessions returned and DS McRae here will give you a lift home.'

Logan swore very quietly. The social worker beamed, glad not to have been lumbered with the task. Smiling from ear to ear, he shook Logan's hand and made good his escape.

While Bernard Duncan Philips was signing for the contents of his pockets, Insch tried to make it up to Logan by offering him a fruit pastille. It would be going on half-seven, eight before he got back into town. He'd have to tell Jackie he was going to be late. With any luck she'd wait for him, but after this afternoon's performance that was far from certain.

'So he's definitely not our boy, then?' said Logan, accepting the sweet grudgingly.

'Nope. Just some poor mad smelly bugger.'

They stood and watched the battered and bruised figure as he painfully bent down and rethreaded his shoelaces.

'Anyway,' said Insch, 'got to go. It's curtain up in an hour and a half.' He patted Logan on the shoulder and turned on his heel, whistling the overture.

'Break a leg,' Logan told the inspector's retreating back.

'Thank you, Sergeant.' Insch gave a cheerful wave, without turning round.

'No seriously,' said Logan. 'I hope you fall and break your bloody leg. Or your neck.' But he waited until the door had closed and Insch was well out of earshot.

When Roadkill was finally reunited with his personal possessions Logan forced a smile onto his face and escorted him to the car park at the back of the building. A flustered-looking PC grabbed them just as Logan was signing for yet another car. 'Desk sergeant says you've got another two messages from a Mr Lumley.'

Logan groaned. The Lumley's Family Liaison Officer should have been handling these calls. He had enough on his plate as it was. He felt guilty almost immediately. The poor sod had lost his son. The least he could do was return the man's phone calls. He rubbed at the headache growing behind his eyes.

'Tell him I'll see to it when I get back, OK?'

*

They went out the back way. The front of Force Headquarters was all lit up, television camera spotlights making everything stand out in sharp relief. There were dozens of them. Roadkill's face was going to be all over the country before the end of the day. And it didn't matter if he was innocent or not, by breakfast time tomorrow half the nation would know his name.

'You know, it might be a good idea if you took a couple of weeks off work. Let the idiots forget about it?'

Roadkill had his hands wrapped round the safety belt, tugging it gently every six seconds, making sure it was still working. 'Need to work. Man has no purpose without work. It defines us. Without definition we do not exist.'

Logan raised an eyebrow. 'OK . . .' The man wasn't just schizophrenic: he was crazy.

'You say "OK" too much.'

Logan opened his mouth, thought better of it and closed it again. There was no point arguing with a crazy person. If he wanted to do that he could go home and talk to his mother. So instead he drove them through the fading rain. By the time they'd reached Roadkill's small farm on the outskirts of Cults it had stopped entirely.

He took the car as far up the drive as there was road. The council clear-up crew had been hard at work all day. Two large metal waste containers loomed in the car's headlights. They were each the size of a minibus, their yellow paintwork chipped and scratched, sitting in the weeds next to steading number one. Huge padlocks kept the container doors shut, as if anyone was going to break in to get at the rotting animal corpses inside.

Logan heard a small sob from beside him and realized the padlocks were probably a good idea.

'My beautiful, beautiful dead things . . .' There were tears running down Roadkill's bruised cheek into his beard.

'You didn't help them?' Logan asked, pointing at the containers.

Roadkill shook his head, his long hair swinging back and forth like a funereal curtain. His voice was tortured and low.

'How could I help the Visigoths sack Rome?'

He got out of the car and walked over the trampled weeds and grass to the steading. The door was lying open, letting Logan's headlights fall on the bare concrete floor. The piles of dead animals were gone. One steading down, two more to go.

Logan left him sobbing gently outside the empty farm building.

19

The evening didn't go exactly as Logan had planned. WPC Jackie Watson was still at the pub when he finally got there, but she was also still smarting from his reprimand. Or maybe there was a lingering smell of Roadkill about him, even though he'd had the car windows open all the way back? 'Oh, how the stench of you clings . . .' Whatever it was, she spent most of her time speaking to the Bastard Simon Rennie and a WPC Logan didn't recognize. No one was rude to him, but they didn't exactly fall over themselves to make him feel welcome. This was supposed to be a celebration! He'd found Richard Erskine. Alive!

Logan called it a night after only two pints and sulked his way home, via the nearest chip shop.

He didn't see the dark grey Mercedes lurking under the streetlight outside his flat. Didn't see the heavy-set man get out of the driver's seat and pull on a pair of black leather gloves. Didn't see him crack his knuckles as Logan balanced the cooling fish supper in one hand while the other hunted for his keys.

'You didn't call.'

Logan almost dropped his chips.

He spun around to see Colin Miller standing with his arms crossed, leaning back against a very expensive-looking automobile, his words wreathed in fog. 'You were supposed to call me by half-four. You didn't.'

Logan groaned. He'd meant to speak to DI Insch, but somehow never got around to it. 'Yeah, well,' he said at last. 'I spoke to the DI . . . He didn't feel it was appropriate.' It was a barefaced lie, but Miller wouldn't know that. At least it would sound as if he'd tried.

'No appropriate?'

'He thinks I've had quite enough publicity for one week.' Might as well be hung for a lying bastard as a lamb. 'You know how it is . . .' He shrugged.

'No appropriate?' Miller scowled. 'I'll show him no' a-fuckin'-propriate.' He pulled out a palmtop and scribbled something onto it.

The next morning started with about a dozen road traffic accidents. None of them fatal, but all blamed on the inch of snow that had fallen overnight. By half-eight the skies were gunmetal-grey and low enough to touch. Tiny flakes of white drifted down on the Granite City, melting as soon as they hit the pavements and roads. But the air smelled of snow. It had that metallic tang which meant that a heavy fall wasn't far away.

The morning's *Press and Journal* had hit Logan's doormat like a tombstone. Only this time the funeral wasn't his. Just his fault. Right there on the front page was a big picture of Detective Inspector Insch done up in his pantomime villain outfit. It was one of the show's publicity shots and Insch had on his best evil snarl. 'D.I. PLAYS THE FOOL WHILE OUR CHILDREN DIE' ran the headline.

'Oh God.'

Under the photo it said: 'IS PANTO REALLY MORE IMPORTANT THAN CATCHING THE PAEDOPHILE KILLER STALKING OUR STREETS?'

Colin Miller strikes again.

Standing at the sink, he read how the inspector had been 'prancing around on stage like an idiot, while local police hero Logan McRae was out searching for little Richard Erskine'. And the rest of the article went downhill from there. Miller had done a first-rate hatchet job on DI Insch. He'd made a well-respected senior police officer look like a callous bastard. There was even a quote from the Chief Superintendent saying that this was 'a very serious matter that would be thoroughly investigated'.

'Oh God.'

'COUNCIL WORKER ATTACKED BY CONCERNED PARENTS' barely made it onto page two.

*

Insch was in a foul mood at the morning briefing and everyone did their damnedest to make sure they didn't do or say anything to set him off. Today was not a good day to screw up.

As soon as the briefing was over Logan scurried away to his little incident room, doing his best not to look guilty. He only had one WPC today: the one womanning the phones. Every other available officer was going to spend today looking for little Peter Lumley. Someone had stuck a rocket up Insch's backside and he was determined to share the experience. So it would be just Logan, the WPC, and the list of possible names.

The team he'd had working their way through Social Services' 'at risk' register had turned up exactly nothing. All the little girls were right where they should have been. Some of them had 'walked into the door' and one had 'fallen down the stairs after burning herself on the iron', but they were all still alive. A couple of the parents were now facing charges.

But that wasn't the only thing Logan had to worry about now. Helping DI Steel on the Geordie Stephenson inquiry seemed to consist of DI Steel smoking lots of cigarettes while Logan did all the work.

There was a new map of Aberdeen pinned to the wall, this one covered with little blue-and-green pins marking every bookmaker in town. The blue ones were 'safe' – not the kind of place that took your kneecaps if you failed to pay up. The green ones were kneecap territory. The Turf 'n Track was marked in red. So was the harbour where they dragged the body out of the water. And next to it was a post mortem head-and-shoulders photo of Geordie Stephenson.

He wasn't much to look at. Not now he was dead anyway. The bouffant hairstyle was all flattened to his head and the porn-star moustache stood out, heavy and black, against the waxy skin. It was odd, but seeing the dead man's photograph Logan got the feeling he'd seen him somewhere before.

According to the information Lothian and Borders Police had sent up, Geordie Stephenson had been quite a character in his youth. Assault mostly. A bit of collecting for small loan sharks. Breaking and entering. It wasn't until he started working for Malk the Knife that he stopped getting caught. Malk was very particular about his employees staying out of prison.

'How'd you get on then?' It was DI Steel, hands rammed deep in the pockets of her grey trouser suit. Yesterday's ash-coated blouse was gone, replaced by something shimmery in gold. The bags under her eyes were a deep, saggy purple.

'Not too great,' Logan plonked himself down on the desk and offered the inspector a chair. She sank into it with a sigh and a small fart. Logan pretended not to hear.

'Go on then.'

'OK.' Logan pointed at the map. 'We went through all the bookies marked in green. The only one that looks likely is this one—' he poked the red pin, 'Turf 'n Track—'

'Simon and Colin McLeod. Lovely pair of lads.'

'Not as lovely as their clientele. We got to meet one of their regulars: Dougie MacDuff.'

'Shite! You're fucking kidding me!' She pulled out a battered pack of cigarettes. They looked as if she'd sat on them. 'Dirty Doug, Dougie the Dog . . .' she excavated a slightly flattened fag from the pack. 'What else did they use to call him?'

'Desperate Doug?'

'Right. Desperate Doug. After he choked that guy with a rolled-up copy of the *Dandy*. You'd've still been in nappies.' She shook her head. 'Fuck me. Those were the days. I thought he was dead.'

'Got out of Barlinnie three months ago. Four years for crippling a builder's merchant with a ratchet screwdriver.'

'At his age? Good old Desperate Doug.' She popped the cigarette in her mouth, and was at the point of lighting it when the WPC on the phones gave a meaningful cough and pointed at the 'No Smoking' sign. Steel shrugged and stuffed the offending fag in her top pocket. 'So how's he looking these days?'

'Like a wrinkly old man.'

'Aye? Shame. He was fucking tasty in his day. Quite the lady-killer. But we couldn't prove it.' She drifted off into silence, her eyes focused on the past. Eventually she sighed and came back to the here and now. 'So you think the McLeod brothers are our likely lads?'

Logan nodded. He'd read their files again. Hacking off someone's kneecaps with a machete was right up their street. The McLeods had always been hands-on when it came to debt control. 'Problem's going to be proving it. There's no way in hell either of them's going to admit killing Geordie and dumping him in the harbour. We need a witness, or some forensic evidence.'

Steel dragged herself out of the chair and gave an expansive yawn. 'Up all night shagging, you know,' she said with a conspiratorial wink. 'Get on to Forensics: have them run every bloody test they've got. And it wouldn't hurt to take another look at the body. It's still in the morgue.'

Logan stiffened. That meant having to speak to Isobel again.

DI Steel must have seen him flinch, because she laid a nicotine-stained hand on his shoulder. 'I know it's not going to be easy. Not now she's got herself a bit of rough. But to fuck with her! You've got a job to do.'

Logan opened and closed his mouth. He didn't know she was seeing someone else. Not already. Not when he was still on his own.

The inspector stuffed her hands back in her trouser pockets, clasping the squashed packet of cigarettes. 'Got to go. Fucking bursting for a fag. Oh, and if you see DI Insch: tell him I liked his picture in the papers this morning.' Another wink. 'Very sexy.'

Detective Inspector Insch didn't look very sexy when Logan saw him next. He was riding the elevator down from the top floor. And that meant a meeting with the Chief Constable. Insch's nice new suit was stained darker grey under the arms and down the back.

'Sir,' said Logan. Trying not to make eye contact.

'They want me to give up the pantomime.' His voice was low and flat.

Guilt stampeded up Logan's back until it sat on top of his head, like a big sign saying: 'I DID IT! IT WAS ME!!!'

'The Chief Constable thinks it's not conducive to the image Grampian Police wants to portray. Says they can't afford to have that kind of negative publicity associated with a major murder enquiry . . . Either the panto goes, or I do.' He looked as if someone had pulled the stopper out, leaving him to slowly deflate. This was not the DI Insch Logan knew. And it was all his fault. 'How long have I been doing Christmas panto for? Twelve, thirteen years? Never been a bloody problem before . . .'

'Maybe they'll forget all about it?' tried Logan. 'You know, when it all blows over. This time next year no one will remember a thing.'

Insch nodded, but he didn't sound convinced.

'Perhaps.' He mashed his features round in a circle with his podgy hands. 'God, I'm going to have to tell Annie I can't go on tonight.'

'I'm sorry, sir.'

Insch tried a brave smile. 'Don't be, Logan. It's not your fault. It's that bastard Colin Miller.' The forced smile turned into a scowl. 'Next time you see him you tell him I'm going to rip his bloody head off and crap down his neck.'

The morgue was quiet, just the hum of the air conditioning breaking the silence. All the dead bodies had been tidied away, the dissecting tables lying empty and sparkling beneath the overhead lights. Not only were there no dead people in here, there were no living ones either.

Gingerly, Logan made his way across to the wall of refrigerated drawers. One by one he read the name cards on the drawer doors, looking for George Stephenson. He stopped when he reached the one marked 'UNKNOWN FEMALE CAUCASIAN CHILD: APPROX 4 YEARS OLD', one hand on the cool metal drawer handle. The poor wee sod was lying in there, cold and dead without even a name.

'Sorry.' It was all he could think of to say.

He worked his way along the row. There was no sign of a George Stephenson, but there was an 'UNKNOWN MALE CAUCASIAN: APPROX 35 YEARS'. DI Steel hadn't told the morgue they'd IDed the body yet. Something else for Logan to do. He unlatched the drawer and pulled it open.

Lying on the flat steel surface of the drawer was a large, dead man, in a white plastic body-bag. Gritting his teeth, Logan pulled on the zip.

The head and shoulders that appeared from the bag were the same as the photo pinned up on Logan's incident room wall. Only the real thing had a wrinklier look to it, as if someone had peeled the face down from the top of the head so they could open the skull with a bone-saw and extract the brain. The skin was waxy and pallid, deep purple bruises marking where the blood had pooled and congealed after death. There was another bruise on the left temple. In the photograph Logan always thought it was just a shadow. The main attraction was still hidden.

He pulled the zip all the way down, exposing a naked body that had been past its prime even when it was alive. According to Lothian and Borders Police, Geordie had been a keep-fit fanatic in his younger days. Someone who took a lot of pride in his appearance. The man on the slab had a beer belly, his thick forearms and shoulders more fat than muscle. Even without the pallor of death he would have been pasty white. Milk-bottle skin, with moles and a faint scarlet rash.

And no kneecaps. Both hairy legs had ragged holes in them where a normal person would keep their knees. The flesh was torn and tattered around the joint, yellow bone poking through the mess of hacked-up tissue. Whoever had done this hadn't been bothered about making a tidy job of it. This was unelective surgery by enthusiasm rather than skill.

Logan's eyes moved past the gore. There were distinct ligature marks around both ankles. The wrists too. Angry bruises, torn skin. The signs of a struggle. He winced. From the look of things Geordie had been tied up and awake while one of the McLeod boys took his kneecaps off. Hack after hack. And George Stephenson had been a big lad. He would've put up one hell of a fight. So it was both McLeods: Colin and Simon. One to hold him down, the other to wield the machete.

There were other marks too. Contusions, scrapes, damage from floating about in the harbour all night. What looked like teeth-marks.

Logan hadn't read the post mortem report yet, but he recognized bite-marks when he saw them. He squatted down beside the body and peered at the indentations. Dark purple weals in the pale skin. Slightly irregular, as if a few teeth were missing. He didn't think of the McLeods as being biters. Not Simon anyway. Colin? There always was something not right about that boy, from the moment he'd jammed a live cat onto the railings surrounding Union Terrace Gardens to the time he'd been caught taking a crap on his grandmother's tombstone. Not right. And he didn't have a full set of choppers, due to a bottle fight in a karaoke bar. He'd have to get Forensics to make a cast of the bite. See if they couldn't match it up to Colin McLeod's dental records.

The door banged behind him and he straightened up to see Isobel deep in conversation with her assistant, Brian, who finished saying something and made a big, expansive gesture with his hands. Isobel threw back her head and laughed.

Oh Brian, you're so damn funny with your floppy girl's hair and your massive nose. Was this the bit of rough DI Steel was talking about? Even with his stomach full of stitches Logan could kick the shite out of him in two minutes flat. How was that for rough?

Isobel stopped laughing as soon as she saw him standing there over the naked body of Geordie Stephenson. 'Hello?' she said, flushing slightly.

'I have an ID for this gentleman.' Logan's voice was slightly less warm than the corpse.

'Ah, right . . .' She looked at him, then at the body laid out on the slab. She gestured to her assistant. 'Well . . . Brian will be able to help you.' She flashed a brittle smile, and then she was gone.

Brian took down George Stephenson's details, scribbling them down in a little pad. Logan was finding it very difficult to keep his voice polite and even. Was this little shite of a man screwing Isobel? Did she make those small mewing noises for him?

Brian spiked the last full stop with a flourish and popped the pad back in his jacket. 'Oh, and before you go I've got something for you . . .' he said.

Logan had the sudden feeling he was going to pull a pair of Isobel's panties out of his pocket but

270

instead Brian crossed the room and picked a large manila envelope out of the internal mail tray.

'Bloodwork on your unknown four-year-old girl. Some interesting stuff in there.' He handed the envelope over then busied himself zipping up Geordie's body-bag and tidying the corpse away while Logan flipped through the report.

Brian wasn't kidding. It was very interesting.

In the canteen at lunchtime there was only one topic of conversation: was DI Insch for the chop? Logan ate in silence at a table as far away from everyone else as possible. The lasagne tasted like damp newspaper to him.

A wave of silence went through the room and Logan looked up to see DI Insch walking up to the counter for his usual: scotch broth, macaroni cheese and chips, jam sponge and custard.

'Please God,' said Logan under his breath, 'let him sit somewhere else . . .'

But Insch took one look round the canteen, fixed his eyes on Logan and made a beeline for his table.

'Afternoon, sir.' Logan pushed the half-eaten lasagne away.

To his immense relief DI Insch just grunted a hello and started in on his soup. And when that was all gone he launched himself at the macaroni, drowning the chips in salt and vinegar, smothering the cheesy pasta with black pepper. Munch, munch, munch.

Logan felt daft, just sitting there, watching the inspector eat. So he poked at his lasagne with a fork. Breaking down the layers into a big homogeneous mush. 'Got the bloodwork back on the little dead girl,' he said at last. 'She was pumped full of painkillers. Temazepam mostly.'

Insch's eyebrow shot up.

'It wasn't enough to kill her. Not an overdose or anything, but it looked like she'd been on them for a while. The lab thinks it would have kept her spaced out. Docile.'

The last of the pasta disappeared into Insch and a chip used to mop up the remaining, vinegar-laced, cheese sauce. He chewed thoughtfully. 'Interesting,' he said at last. 'Anything else?'

'She had TB at some point.'

'Now we're getting somewhere.' Insch stacked his empty plate on top of the soup bowl and pulled his dessert to centre stage. 'Not that many places in the UK you can still catch TB. Get onto the health boards. It's a notifiable disease. If our girl had it she'll be on their lists.' He scooped up a spoonful of custard and sponge, a smile on his lips. 'About bloody time we got some good luck.'

Logan didn't say anything.

272

20

Matthew Oswald had worked for the council for six months, straight out of school with fewer qualifications than his mother had been hoping for. His father didn't care that much. He'd never got a qualification in his life and it hadn't done him any harm, had it? So Matthew picked up his lunchbox and went to work for Aberdeen City Council's sanitation department.

The life of a scaffy wasn't as bad as a lot of people thought. You got out in the fresh air, the guys were a laugh, the pay wasn't that bad, and if you screwed up nobody died. And, since the invention of the wheelie-bin, there wasn't much heavy lifting. Not like in the old days, as Jamey, the driver of their wagon, liked to say.

So, all in all, life was OK. A bit of money in the bank, mates at work and a new girlfriend who wasn't shy about letting him get his hand up her jumper.

And then came the offer of overtime. He should

have said no, but more cash meant a season ticket to the football. Matthew lived for Aberdeen Football Club. Which was why he was now dressed in a blue plastic boiler suit, black Wellington boots, thick black rubber gloves, safety goggles and a breathing mask. The only skin showing was where his forehead didn't quite fit under the boiler suit's elasticated hood. He looked like something out of the X-Files and was sweating like a bastard.

The sleet pounding down out of the dark grey sky didn't make any difference to the sweat running down his back and into his boxers. But there was no way in hell he was taking the damn rubber rompersuit off!

Grunting, he lifted the shovel up to shoulder height and stuffed another load of rotting carcasses into the huge waste container. Everything stank of death. Even through the breathing mask he could smell it. Rotting meat. Vomit. He'd lost his breakfast and lunch yesterday. Not today though. Today he'd kept his Weetabix where they were supposed to be.

All bloody day yesterday and all bloody day today. And from the look of it all bloody day tomorrow. Shovelling up dead animals.

The filthy bastard who owned the place was standing in the doorway to one of the steadings, the one they'd cleared out yesterday. He didn't seem to notice the sleet either, just stood there in a ratty jumper looking miserable as his sicko collection was carted away.

Matthew had seen his dad's paper this morning. Some parents in Garthdee had beaten the shite out of the bloke for hanging round their kids' school. The man's face was a patchwork of purple-and-green bruises. Served him fucking right, thought Matthew as he trudged back through the sleet for another shovelful of rotting corpses.

They were almost halfway through the pile in this building. One-and-a-half down, one-and-a-half to go. Then it would be a long shower, a season ticket and drinking till he puked. He was going to get so wasted when this was over!

Thinking such happy thoughts, Matthew rammed his shovel into the mound of festering meat and fur. The pile slithered and slipped as he worked. Cats and dogs and seagulls and crows and fuck knows what else. Gritting his teeth, he hefted the mound of dead things on the end of his shovel. And then he saw it.

Matthew opened his mouth to say something – to call over the nervous bloke from the council who was supposed to be running things here, tell him what he'd found. But what came out was a high-pitched scream.

He dropped his shovelful of dead things and raced outside, slipping, slithering, falling to his knees; ripping off his breathing mask, throwing up his Weetabix into the snow.

Logan was parked on the other side of the road from the Turf 'n Track, watching the betting shop through the sleet and a pair of binoculars. The weather was horrendous. The delicate fall of snow he'd seen this morning had let up for a while and then this had started. Thick globs of sleet hammering down out of the filthy sky, cold and wet and treacherous. It was already getting dark.

He'd phoned every health authority in the country, asking them for details of any little girls they'd treated for TB in the last four years. Like DI Insch he was optimistic; this should be a straightforward bit of policing. She'd had TB and now she was better. Which meant that she must have been treated at one of the health authorities. She'd be on their books. And Logan would have a name.

The latest jingly jangly tune finished on the radio and the DJ announced the mid-afternoon news. Logan stuffed an extra strong mint into his mouth and turned it up slightly.

'Closing arguments continue today in the case of Gerald Cleaver, the fifty-six-year-old from Manchester accused of sexual abuse while working as a male nurse at Aberdeen Children's Hospital. With almost three weeks of testimony behind them, most of which has been extremely graphic and disturbing, the jury is expected to retire late tomorrow evening. Police security has been stepped up following a number of threats to Cleaver's life. Cleaver's lawyer, Mr Moir-Farquharson, who has himself been the target of death threats during the trial, was assaulted two nights ago when someone threw a bucket of pig's blood over him.'

Logan gave a small cheer and a one-man Mexican wave in the driver's seat of the rusty pool car.

'I will not be intimidated by the work of a tiny, misdirected, minority.' The new voice was Sandy the Snake's. *'We have to make sure that justice is done here—'*

Logan drowned out the rest with booing and loud raspberries.

There was movement across the road and he sat up straight, peering through his binoculars. The front door to the shop opened and Desperate Doug stuck his head out, took one look at the weather and stuck his head back in again. Thirty seconds later Winchester, the large Alsatian who'd been desperate to take a chunk out of Logan yesterday, was unceremoniously booted out into the sleet. The dog tried to get back in, was belted with Dougie's walking stick, then stood dejected as the door closed in its face. It stayed there for a minute, the sleet soaking into its greying fur, staring at the shop and then loped down the concrete steps into the car park. It circled a few times: sniffing the lampposts, the metal banister, peeing on some, ignoring others. Then at last it bunched its backend in under itself and gingerly coiled a huge turd in the middle of the car park.

That done, it turned and barked its head off at the Turf 'n Track's front door until Desperate Doug got up to let it in again. Two steps inside the betting shop and the Alsatian shook itself dry, sending

277

a flurry of water and melting sleet all over its owner.

Suddenly Logan liked the dog a lot more. He settled back in his seat and let the radio's music wash over him.

A rust-green estate car lurched past his window, turned right into the small collection of shops, and slid to a halt in the newly beturded car park. It was the same car WPC Watson had hurled all that abuse at. Logan sighed. He was back to thinking of her as WPC Watson. Not Jackie of the Lovely Legs any more. And all because he had to tell her off for swearing at the driver of that ruddy car.

The estate car's driver rummaged about for something on the back seat, then hopped out clutching a plastic carrier bag and nearly fell on his backside in the slush. He had the collar of his jacket turned up and a newspaper held over his shaved head, trying to keep the worst of the weather off. He slipped and slid his way up the disabled ramp to the bookies.

Logan frowned and turned the binoculars on the newcomer as he pushed his way through the door into the shop. The man's ears were festooned with piercings and he had a haunted look that was instantly recognizable: Duncan Nicholson. The same Duncan Nicholson who'd just happened to fall over the murdered body of a three-year-old boy. In a waterlogged ditch, hidden beneath a sheet of chipboard in the dark, in the pouring rain.

'What are you doing here, you little toerag?' Logan asked himself quietly.

Mastrick wasn't local for Nicholson. He lived in the Bridge of Don, well across the city. Big journey to make on a shitty day like this.

And then there was that carrier bag. Or what was in it.

'I wonder . . .'

But Logan's trail of thought was shattered as the police radio spluttered into life. They'd found another body.

It was dark by the time Logan reached the farm on the outskirts of Cults. The gate was open, a patrol car parked next to it containing a pair of unhappy-looking constables, just visible through the fogged-up windscreen. They were blocking access to the farm road. Logan pulled up next to them and rolled down his window. The PC in the driver's seat did the same.

'Afternoon, sir,'

'What's the story?'

'DI Insch is here, so's the Fiscal. Duty doctor's just arrived. IB are stuck in traffic. And there's about six blokes from the council in one of the steadings. We had to restrain them from killing the property's owner.'

'Roadkill?'

'Yup. He's holed up in the farmhouse with Insch. The inspector doesn't want him going any-where till death's been declared.'

Logan nodded and started to wind up his window. The sleet was beginning to blow into the car.

'Sir?' asked the PC behind the wheel of the patrol car. 'Is it true we had him in custody last night and let him go?'

Logan felt a sickening lurch in the pit of his stomach. He'd been thinking the same thing ever since he'd heard. Worrying all the way over from Mastrick. They'd released Roadkill without charge and now another child was dead. He'd even given the guy a lift!

The sleet was thickening, turning into flurries of real snow as Logan slithered the pool car up the rutted driveway towards Roadkill's farm. The steadings loomed out of the dark, the car's headlights picking out the open doors.

Blue police tape was stretched across the doorway of steading number two. The one they'd been emptying today.

Logan pulled up behind the duty doctor's car. There was another patrol car here, empty this time. Its occupants would be taking statements from the guys who'd found the body. Stopping them from tearing Roadkill to pieces. The only car not parked next to the snow-shrouded waste containers was DI Insch's Range Rover. The big four-by-four was the only one that could handle the rutted drive in the snow. It was abandoned in front of the farmhouse. A faint yellow light flickered in one of the downstairs windows.

Logan looked from the steading with its warning tape to the farmhouse, fading in and out of view through the growing blizzard. Might as well get the nasty bit over and done with.

It was freezing cold outside and as soon as Logan killed his car lights it was dark as well. He jumped back in the car and dug a flashlight out from under a pile of posters with Peter Lumley's face on them. Please God: let it be him. Don't let it be some other poor little bastard. Not another one.

The torch dispelled just enough darkness for Logan to see where he was putting his feet. The snow was building up in the hollows and pot-holes, hiding them, making it far too easy to slip and fall. Logan stumbled his way through the grass to steading number two, the fat snowflakes sticking to his jacket.

Inside, it smelled terrible. But not as bad as it had on that first day when he'd made PC Steve drag open the heavy wooden door. The wind took away some of the smell, but it was still bad enough to make Logan gag as he crossed the threshold. Coughing, he pulled a handkerchief out of his pocket and held it over his nose and mouth.

Half the carcases were gone and the concrete floor slippery with ooze and decayed body fluids. Doc Wilson, dressed in the regulation white paper boiler suit, was hunched down in front of the pile of corpses, his open medical bag sitting on top of a flattened bin-bag to keep it out of the slime.

Logan pulled on a set of coveralls. 'Evening, Doc,' he said, carefully picking his way across the concrete.

The duty doctor turned. A white mask hid the lower part of his face. 'How come when it's a messy job it's always me gets called, eh?'

'Just lucky I guess,' said Logan. The humour was forced, but the doctor managed a small smile behind his mask.

He pointed at the open bag and Logan helped himself to a pair of latex gloves and a mask. The smell suddenly vanished, replaced by an over-whelming reek of menthol that made his eyes water. 'Vicks VapoRub,' Doc Wilson said. 'Old pathology trick. Covers a multitude of sins.'

'What are we looking at?'

Please God let it be Peter Lumley.

'Difficult to tell. The poor wee sod's nearly rotted all away.'

The Doc lumbered to the side and Logan got his first real look at what had sent Matthew Oswald screaming out into the snow to throw up his Weetabix. A child's head protruded from the mass of animal corpses. There were no real features left, the bone poking out through slimy grey.

'Oh Christ.' Logan's stomach lurched.

'I dinna even know if it's a boy or a girl. We'll no know till we dig the body out and examine it properly.'

Logan looked at the grim head, the empty eye-

sockets, the mouth hanging open, the teeth protruding from the shrunken gums. A matted mess
of hair was almost indistinguishable from the fur
of the animals piled up all around the body. A
pair of small pink clasps were embedded in the
putrid scalp. Barbie hairgrips.

'It's a girl.' Logan stood. He couldn't take any
more of this. 'Come on, Doc. Declare death and
leave this for the pathologist.'

The doctor nodded sadly. 'Aye. Perhaps you're
right. Poor wee sod . . .'

Logan stood outside in the snow, his face turned
into the wind, letting the cold and damp wash
away the stench of decay. It didn't dispel his
nausea though. Shivering, he watched as Doc
Wilson clambered his way through the snow and
into his car. No sooner was the door closed than
out came the cigarettes and the doctor was
wreathed in smoke.

'Lucky bastard.'

He turned his back on the scene and trudged
out into the blizzard, making for the farmhouse,
the torch's beam a bar of white, swirling and
whirling, marking his progress through the long
grass. Ten steps and his trousers were soaked to
the knee, his shoes full of icy water. By the time
he got to the front door his teeth were clattering
in his head, the steady clacka-clacka-clacka running counterpoint to his shivers.

Light flickered from the kitchen window, but

Logan could only make out silhouettes through the filthy glass. He didn't bother knocking, just heaved and shoved at the swollen door. Inside, the house was even more dilapidated than he'd expected. With no one living here for God knows how long, the place had turned into a mausoleum of mould. He ran the torch over the hallway, picking out the remains of wallpaper and furniture. Here and there the plaster was gone from the walls, exposing the lath beneath. Dark fungus clustered round the holes like flies round an open sore. The staircase was missing rungs and one step was broken, the board snapped in the middle and sticking up at the ends. But there were still photos on the walls.

Logan brushed a clearing in the dust-covered glass of one, and a happy-looking woman smiled back at him. He made the clean patch bigger and a little boy appeared, grinning at the camera, wearing a smart new set of clothes, his hair all combed straight. There was a striking family resemblance. Bernard Duncan Philips and his mother in better times. Before he started collecting dead things. Before there was a little girl's corpse in steading number two.

The kitchen was cramped and dark. Piles of cardboard boxes lined the room, the constant damp making them sag at the corners. Mildew covered the walls, lending the place a smell of desolation. And in the middle of the room sat a tatty kitchen table with two treacherous-looking chairs.

Bernard Duncan Philips, AKA Roadkill, was slumped in one of them, DI Insch leaning against the sink opposite. Between them a small candelabrum flickered. Only two of its five sockets had any candles in them, and they were little more than stubs. No one said a word as Logan entered.

Insch's face was like stone, scowling down at the sagging figure. He must have been thinking the same thing as Logan: they'd had him last night and they'd let him go. And now they had another dead child on their hands.

'I've sent the duty doctor home.' Logan's voice was swallowed by the gloom.

'What did he say?' asked Insch, not taking his eyes off Roadkill.

'It's probably a little girl. We don't know how old. She's been dead for a long time. Maybe years.'

Insch nodded and Logan knew he was feeling relieved. If the kid had been dead for years then it didn't matter that they'd let Roadkill go last night. No one had died because of that.

'Mr Philips here has declined to comment. Haven't you, Mr Philips? You won't tell me who she is, or when you killed her. Funny how we've now got two dead girls on our books, isn't it? Even funnier how we've got some sick bastard running round killing little boys and sticking things up their arses. Cutting off their dicks.'

Logan frowned. David Reid had turned up dead

and mutilated in a ditch on the other side of the city. Roadkill liked to keep his dead things. He wouldn't leave a prize like that lying out in the open.

'You know,' said Logan, trying to play good cop. 'We could make this a lot easier for you, Bernard. You tell us what happened. In your own words, OK? I'm sure you didn't mean for all this to happen, did you?'

Roadkill slumped forward until his head rested on the scarred tabletop.

'Was it an accident, Bernard? Did it just happen?'

'They're taking them all away. All my beautiful dead things.'

Insch slammed his huge fist down on top of the table, making the candelabrum and Roadkill jump. Hot wax spattered onto the wood. Bernard Duncan Philips slowly sank back down to the tabletop, covering his head with his arms.

'You're going to jail. You hear that? You're going to Peterhead Prison, with all the other sick bastards. The paedophiles, rapists, murderers. You going to be someone's bitch up there? Going to find the love of your life in some hairy-arsed Weegie bastard? 'Cos if you don't start talking to us I'm going to make sure you get shacked up with the skankiest arse-raping bastard they've got up there!'

It was designed to get a response. But it failed. In the uneasy silence Logan could hear a quiet tune. Roadkill was humming something to himself. It sounded like 'Abide with me'.

The kitchen window filled with light and Logan cleared a hole in the grubby glass. The Identification Bureau van was struggling its way up the track. It stopped outside steading number two. There was another car behind it. Something sleek and expensive which was having trouble with the snow-covered drive. By the time it drew level with the farm buildings, the technicians had started humping their equipment from the warmth and safety of the van into the charnel house.

The car's driver clambered out into the snow. It was Isobel.

Logan sighed. 'That's IB and the pathologist.' He watched her turn her collar up and slither around to the boot of her car. She was wearing a long camel-coloured coat over her tan suit. She struggled out of her Italian leather boots and into a pair of wellies before clumping her way into the steading.

Thirty seconds later she was out in the snow again, bent double, breathing hard. Trying not to be sick. A grim smile spread itself over Logan's face. It wouldn't do to appear human in front of the lower ranks.

Insch pushed himself away from the sink and produced a pair of handcuffs. 'Come on, Philips. On your feet.'

Logan watched as the bedraggled figure was

read his rights and the cuffs were snapped into place, hands behind his back. Then Insch dragged Roadkill out of the kitchen and off into the snow.

Alone in the house, Logan blew out the candles and followed.

21

This time Roadkill's 'appropriate adult' was a run-down man in his early fifties, thinning on top and sporting a ridiculous little moustache. Lloyd Turner: an ex-schoolteacher at Hazlehead Academy who'd recently lost his wife and wanted something to take his mind off being alone all the time. He sat at the table next to Bernard Duncan Philips, facing the combined scowls of Detective Inspector Insch and DS Logan McRae.

The small room smelled. Not just the usual, inexplicable whiff of cheesy feet, but the stale sweat and rotting animal odour that Roadkill exuded. The bruises Logan had seen last night had blossomed. Dark purple and green spread over the prisoner's face, disappearing into his matted beard. His hands fluttered on the tabletop, the skin dirty, the nails black. The only clean thing about him was the white paper boiler suit the Identification Bureau had given him when they'd taken his clothes away for forensic examination.

Logan and Insch had spent three hours getting exactly nowhere. The only thing they could get out of Roadkill was that someone was stealing all his precious dead things. They'd tried being nice; they'd tried being nasty. They'd tried getting the ex-teacher with the moustache to talk to him, to explain the seriousness of the situation. Nothing.

DI Insch rocked back in his seat, making the plastic creak. 'Right,' he said with a sigh. 'Let's try this again shall we?'

Everyone round the table grimaced, except for Roadkill. He just went on humming. Abide with bloody me. It was beginning to drive Logan mad.

The teacher put up his hand. 'I'm sorry, Inspector. I think it's quite clear Bernard is not in any fit state to be interrogated.' He cast a sideways glance at the smelly man sitting next to him. 'His mental state is a matter of record. He needs help, not incarceration.'

Insch slammed his chair forward. 'And the kiddies lying dead in the morgue need to be safe and sound at home, not killed by a twisted weirdo!' He crossed his arms, straining the seams on his shirt, making himself look even bigger. 'I want to know where Peter Lumley is, and how many other little kiddies he's killed.'

'Inspector, I understand that you're only doing your job, but Bernard isn't in any fit state to answer questions. Look at him!'

They did. His hands were like wounded birds, flapping away on top of the table. His gaze was

290

far and distant. He wasn't even in the same room as them.

Logan glanced at the clock on the wall. Seven-twenty. Past the time when Roadkill started asking for his medicine yesterday. 'Sir,' he said to Insch, 'can I have a word with you outside?'

They walked to the coffee machine, passing an array of interested faces. The word was all round the station, on the radio, and probably the evening news. The Aberdeen Child-killer was behind bars. Now all they had to do was get him to talk.

'What's on your mind, Sergeant?' asked Insch, punching in the number for white coffee, extra sugar.

'We're going to get nothing out of Roadkill tonight, sir. He's schizophrenic. He needs to take his medication. Even if we got a confession out of him it'd get ripped to shreds in court. Mentally ill suspect, denied medication, confesses after a three-hour interrogation? What would you do?'

Insch blew across the top of his plastic cup of coffee and sipped experimentally at the liquid. When he spoke at last it was with the voice of a very tired man. 'You're right of course.' He sat the coffee down on the nearest table and hunted through his pockets for something sweet. In the end Logan had to offer him one of his extra strong mints.

'Thanks. I've been thinking the same thing for the last hour. Just didn't want to let it go. Just in case.' He sighed. 'Just in case Peter Lumley's still alive somewhere.'

It was wishful thinking and they both knew it. Peter Lumley was dead. They just hadn't found his body yet.

'What about the crime scene?' asked Logan.

'What about it?'

'The dead girl we found might not be the only one in the pile.' The next bit was what had been causing him trouble since the farmhouse. 'And then there's David Reid. He was abandoned. The MO just doesn't fit. Roadkill's a collector. He wouldn't just leave the body lying out like that.'

'Maybe he likes them rotted before he hoards them.'

'If it is him, he cut the genitals off David Reid. They'll be at the farm somewhere.'

Insch screwed up his face. 'Shite. We're going to have to go through every last carcase he's got out there looking for it. Talk about your proverbial needle in a haystack.' He mashed his features with a pair of tired hands. 'Right.' He took a deep breath and straightened his back. The authority had returned to his voice. 'We're going to have to do this the hard way. If we can't get a confession out of Philips we'll tie him to the bodies. The little girl we found at his home; no problem there. And there must be something linking him to David Reid and Peter Lumley. I want you to get a dozen uniform question everyone where the children were last seen. Get me a witness. We're not letting the bastard get away again.'

*

That night Logan's dreams were full of rotting children. They ran through the flat, wanting to play. One sat on the living room floor, little chunks of skin falling onto the polished floorboards, bashing away at a xylophone Logan had been given for his fourth birthday. Clank and clink and boing, a cacophony that was more like a phone ringing than music.

And that's when he woke up.

Logan staggered through to the lounge and grabbed the ringing phone from its cradle. 'What?' he demanded.

'An' a merry Christmas to you too.' Colin Miller.

'Oh God . . .' Logan tried to rub some life into his face. 'It's half-six! What is it with you and mornings?'

'You found another body.'

Logan shuffled to the window and looked for Miller's expensive automobile in the darkened street. There was no sign of it. At least that meant he was to be spared a visit from the cheerful fairy this morning.

'And?'

There was a pause on the other end of the phone. *'And you arrested Bernard Philips. Roadkill.'*

Stunned, Logan let the curtain fall back. 'How the hell did you know that?' There was nothing in the press pack to identify who'd been arrested, just the normal: 'a suspect has been taken into custody and a report sent to the Procurator Fiscal'.

'You know how: it's ma job. Poor wee thing, rottin'

away in that pile of crap … I want the inside track, Laz. I've still got stuff on Geordie Stephenson you don't know. Everybody wins.'

Logan couldn't believe his ears. 'You've got a bloody cheek after what you did to DI Insch yesterday!'

'Laz, that's just business. He screwed you over and I took him down a couple of pegs. Did I write one bad word about you? Did I?'

'That's not the point.'

'Ah, loyalty. Like it. Good quality in an officer of the law.'

'You made him look like an idiot.'

'Tell you what: I lay off the pantomime dame and you and me has a chat over breakfast?'

'I can't do that. I need to get Insch to clear anything I say, OK?'

There was another pause.

'You gotta be careful what you do with your loyalty, Laz. Sometimes it can do you more harm than good.'

'What? What the hell is that supposed to mean?'

'Take a look at the morning's paper, Laz. See whether or not you need a friend in the press.'

Logan settled the phone back in its cradle and stood in the darkness of the lounge, shivering. There was no way he could just go back to bed now. Not until he knew what Miller had done. What the morning paper contained.

Half past six. His own copy wouldn't be delivered for another hour and a bit. So he dressed quickly and slid his way through the ankle-deep snow up to the Castlegate and the nearest newsagent.

It was a small shop, the kind that tried anything once. The walls were festooned with shelves: books, pots, pans, light bulbs, tins of kidney beans . . . Logan found what he was looking for on the floor by the counter – a thick bundle of fresh papers, still wrapped in protective plastic to keep the snow from soaking into the newsprint.

The proprietor, a stocky man with three fingers missing on his left hand, a greying beard and a gold tooth grunted a good morning as he slit the plastic open. 'Jeezuz,' he said, picking a paper off the top of the pile, holding it up so Logan could see the front page. 'They had the bastard an' they let him go! Can you fuckin' believe that?'

There were four photographs, slap bang in the middle of the page: David Reid, Peter Lumley, DI Insch and Bernard Duncan Philips. Roadkill was out of focus, bent over a shovel full of squashed rabbit, his wheelie-bin sitting next to him on the road. The two boys smiled out from school photographs. Insch was in full panto get-up.

Above the lot the headline screamed 'House Of Horror: Dead Girl Found In Pile Of Rotting Animals!' and underneath that 'Killer Released From Police Custody Only Hours Earlier'. Colin Miller strikes again.

'Buncha fuckin' clowns: that's what they are. Tell

you: five minutes alone with this sick bastard. That'll do me. Got fuckin' grandchildren that age.'

Logan paid for his paper and left without saying a word.

It had started to snow again. Thick white flakes drifted down from the dark sky, the clouds lit dark-orange, reflecting back the streetlights. All the way up Union Street the twelve days of Christmas glittered and sparkled, but Logan didn't see any of it. He stood outside the newsagent, reading by the light of the shop window.

There was an in-depth exposé of Roadkill's life – the schizophrenia, the two-year stay in Cornhill, the dead mother, the collection of dead bodies. Miller had even managed to get hold of some of the crowd that attacked Roadkill outside the primary school gates. The quotes were full of bravado and righteous indignation. The police had treated them like criminals for attacking that sicko, when all the time there was a dead girl lying in that pile of filth!

Logan winced as he read how the police had Roadkill in custody, but DI Insch, recently seen strutting about on stage while children were being abducted, murdered and violated, had ordered his release. Against the advice of local police hero DS Logan 'Lazarus' McRae.

Logan groaned. Bloody Colin Miller! Probably thought he was doing him a favour, making him look like the voice of reason, but Insch would blow a gasket. It would look as if Logan had gone to the *Press and Journal* with the story. As if he was stabbing the inspector in the back.

Peter Lumley's stepfather was waiting for him when he pushed through the front doors to Force Headquarters. The man looked as if he hadn't slept for a month and his breath would have made wallpaper curdle: stale beer and whisky. He'd seen the papers. He knew they'd arrested someone.

Logan took him into an interview room and listened as he'd ranted and raved. Roadkill knew where his son was. The police had to make him talk! If they couldn't, he would! They had to find Peter!

Slowly Logan calmed him down, explained that the man they had in custody might not have anything to do with Peter going missing. That the police were doing everything they could to find his son. That he should go home and get some sleep. In the end it was fatigue that made him consent to a lift home in a patrol car.

By the time the working day had begun Logan was feeling terrible. There was a knot in his stomach, and not just the scar tissue. Half past eight and there was still no sign of Insch. There was a shit-storm brewing and Logan was going to be right in the middle of it.

The morning briefing came and went, Logan handing out the assignments, getting the teams together. One lot to go question every house-holder within a mile of the children's last known position, both pre- and post mortem. Had they seen this man – Roadkill – hanging around? Another lot to go through the records for anything and everything relating to Bernard Duncan Philips. And last, by far the largest team, would get the nastiest job of all: digging through a ton of rotting animal corpses, looking for a severed penis. This wasn't a job for the council's sanitation department any more. This was a murder enquiry.

No one asked where DI Insch was, or said a single word about the front page spread in this morning's P&J. But Logan knew they'd all read it. There was an undercurrent of hostility in the room. They'd jumped to the conclusion Logan knew they would: that he'd gone to the press and screwed over Insch.

WPC Watson wouldn't even meet his eyes.

When the briefing was over and everyone had shuffled out, Logan tracked down DI Steel. She was sitting in her office, feet up on the desk, smoking a fag and drinking coffee, a copy of the morning paper spread over the clutter on her desk. She looked up as Logan knocked and entered, saluting him with her mug.

'Morning, Lazarus,' she said. 'You looking for your next victim?'

'I didn't do it! I know what it looks like, but I didn't do it!'

'Aye, aye. Shut the door and park your arse.' She pointed at the rickety chair on the other side of her desk.

Logan did as he was told, politely refusing the offer of a cigarette.

'If you did go to the press with this,' she poked the paper, 'you're either so fucking stupid you can't breathe unsupervised, or you've got some serious political ambitions. You ambitious, Mr Local Police Hero?'

'What?'

'I know you're not stupid, Lazarus,' she said, waving her fag in the air. 'Speaking to the press would always come back and bite you on the arse. But this could kill DI Insch's career. With him out the way, and the press on your side, you're a shoe-in for his job. The rank and file will hate you, but if you can live with that, you keep going up the tree. Next stop Chief Inspector.' She even gave him a salute.

'I swear I didn't speak to anyone! I wanted to let Roadkill go too; there was no evidence against him. I even gave him a lift home!'

'So how come this reporter's polishing your arse with one hand and spanking Insch with the other?'

'I . . . I don't know.' Liar. 'He thinks we're friends. I've only spoken to him half a dozen times. And DI Insch cleared every word.' Big fat liar. 'I don't think he likes the inspector.' At least that bit was true.

'I can relate to that. Lots of people don't like Inschy. Me? I like him. He's big. You see an arse like that: you've got something to sink your teeth into.'

Logan tried not to form a mental picture.

DI Steel took a deep drag on her cigarette, letting the smoke hiss out through a happy smile. 'You spoken to him yet?'

'What, DI Insch?' Logan hung his head. 'No. Not yet.'

'Hmm . . . Well he was in early. I saw his four-wheel-drive girl-mobile in the car park this morning. Probably hatching a plot with the upper brass: getting you transferred to the Gorbals.' She sat and smiled and for the life of him Logan couldn't tell if she was joking.

'I was hoping that maybe you could speak to him—'

The smile turned into a laugh.

'Want me to ask him if he fancies you?'

Logan could feel the colour running up his neck to his cheeks. He knew what DI Steel was like. Had he actually come in here expecting her to be sympathetic and supportive? Maybe he really was too stupid to breathe unsupervised. 'I'm sorry,' he said, picking himself out of his seat. 'I should get back to work.'

She stopped him only when the door was swinging closed. 'He's going to be fucking pissed off. Maybe not at you, maybe at this Miller bloke, but he's going to be pissed off. Be prepared to be shouted at. And if he won't listen to you, maybe have to think omelettes and eggs. Just because you didn't start this doesn't mean you can't play it out.'

Logan stopped. 'Play it out?'

'Ambition, Mr Hero. Like it or not you could still end up sitting in his seat. You don't have to like the way it came about, but you might make DI because of this.' She lit another cigarette from the smouldering remains of the last one, before flipping the dogend into her coffee. It gave a short hiss as she winked at him. 'Think about it.'

Logan did. All the way down to his mini incident room. The WPC was back on the phone, taking names and statements. With Roadkill's arrest all over the papers and the television news, everyone and their maiden aunt was coming forward with information. Murdered kiddie, officer? No problem: I saw her getting into a Corporation dustcart. Bold as brass with this bloke from the papers . . .

The health authorities had started responding to his request for information on little girls with TB in the last four years as well. The list of possibles was small, but it would get bigger as the day wore on.

Logan scanned the names, most of which had already been scored out by his WPC. They weren't interested in any child that wouldn't be between three and a half and five by now. They'd know who she was by the end of the day.

He was expecting the call, but it still made his innards clench: report to the superintendent's office. Time to get his arse chewed out for something he didn't do. Other than lie to Colin Miller. And DI Insch.

'I'm just going out for a walk,' he told the WPC on the phones. 'I may be some time.'

The super's office was like a furnace. Logan stood to attention in front of the wide oak desk with both hands clasped behind his back. DI Insch was sitting in a mock-leather, mock-comfortable visitor's chair. He didn't look at Logan as he entered and took up his position. But Inspector Napier, from Professional Standards, stared at him as if he was a science experiment gone wrong.

Behind the desk sat a serious-looking man with a bullet head and not a lot of hair. He was wearing his dress uniform. All buttoned up. Not a good sign.

'Sergeant McRae.' The voice was larger than the man, filling the room with portent. 'You know why you're here.' It wasn't a question; there was a copy of that morning's *Press and Journal* on the desk. Neatly lined up with the blotter and the keyboard.

'Yes, sir.'

'Do you have anything to say?'

They were going to fire him. Six days back on the job and they were going to throw him out on his scarred backside. He should have kept his head down and stayed off on the sick. Goodbye pension. 'Yes, sir. I want it known that DI Insch has always had my complete support. I didn't give this story to Colin Miller and I didn't tell anyone that I disagreed with DI Insch's decision to release Road . . . Mr Philips. Because it was the right decision, at the time.'

The superintendent settled back in his chair, fingers steepled in front of his round face. 'You have been speaking to Miller though, haven't you, Sergeant?'

'Yes, sir. He called me at half-six this morning wanting details of Mr Philips's arrest.'

DI Insch scrunched in his seat. 'How the hell did he know we'd arrested Roadkill? It wasn't public bloody knowledge! I'll tell you this—'

The superintendent held up his hand and Insch fell silent. 'When I challenged him he said it was his job to know,' said Logan, falling into policeman-giving-evidence mode. 'This isn't the first time he's had knowledge he shouldn't have. He knew when we found David Reid's body. He knew the killer had mutilated and violated the corpse. He knew the girl's body we found was decomposed. He has someone on the inside.'

On the other side of the desk an eyebrow was raised, but not a word was spoken. The DI-Insch-patented-interview-technique. Only Logan wasn't in any mood to play.

'And it's not me! There's no way I would tell a reporter I disagreed with my superior's decision to release a suspect! Miller wants a friend in here and he thinks he can get that if he "helps" me. This is all about selling papers!'

The superintendent let the silence stretch.

'If you want my resignation, sir—'

'This isn't a disciplinary hearing, Sergeant. If it was you'd have a federation representative with you.' He paused and glanced at Insch and Napier before turning back to Logan. 'You can wait in the reception area outside while we discuss this matter further. We'll call you back when we have reached our decision.'

Someone had poured freezing-cold concrete into Logan's innards. 'Yes, sir.' He marched out of the room, shoulders back, head up, and closed the door behind him. They were going to fire him. That or transfer him out of Aberdeen. Find some crappy backwater in Teuchter-land and make him serve out his days pounding the beat, or worse: school-liaison work.

Finally he was summoned back into the room by the hook-nosed, ginger-haired inspector from Professional Standards. Logan stood to attention in front of the super's desk and waited for the axe to fall.

'Sergeant,' said the superintendent, picking up the newspaper off his desk, folding it in half and dropping it neatly into the bin. 'You will be pleased to hear that we believe you.'

Logan couldn't help noticing the sour expression on Inspector Napier's face. Not everyone appeared to agree with the verdict.

The superintendent settled back in his seat and examined Logan. 'DI Insch tells me you're a good officer. And so does DI Steel. Not someone who would go to the media with this kind of thing. I have respect for my senior officers. If they tell me you're not a . . .' He paused and offered a practised smile. 'If they tell me you wouldn't go to the papers without authorization, I'm prepared to believe them. However . . .'

Logan straightened his back and waited for a transfer out to the sticks.

'However, we can't let something like this go unanswered. I can tell the world we're standing behind DI Insch one hundred percent. Which we are. But that's not going to make this all go away. These stories: the pantomime, releasing Philips less than a day before a dead girl is discovered at his home . . .' He raised a hand before DI Insch could do more than open his mouth. 'I am not, personally, of the opinion that the inspector has done anything wrong. But these stories are highly damaging to the Force's reputation. Every second edition in the country has got some rehashed version of Miller's story. The *Sun*, *Daily Mail*, *Mirror*, *Independent*, *Guardian*, *Scotsman*: hell, even *The Times*! Telling the world that Grampian Police are incompetent idiots.' He shifted uncomfortably in his chair and straightened out his uniform. 'Lothian and Borders have been on the phone to the Chief Constable again. They say they have resources experienced in this kind of investigation. That they would welcome the opportunity to "assist" us.' He scowled. 'We have to be seen to be doing something. The public are baying for blood; but I am not prepared to give them DI Insch.' He took a deep breath. 'There is one other approach we can take. And that's to engage this Colin Miller. He seems to have developed a rapport with you, Sergeant. I want you to speak to him. Get him back on board.'

Logan risked a look at DI Insch. His face was like thunder. Napier looked as if his head was about to explode.

'Sir?'

'If this trouble with the press continues, if the bad publicity keeps coming, we will have no alternative: DI Insch will be suspended on full pay, pending an examination of his conduct. We will be forced to hand the child murder investigations over to Lothian and Borders Police.'

'But . . . but, sir: that's not right!' Logan's eyes darted between the superintendent and the inspector. 'DI Insch is the best person for this job! This isn't his fault!'

The man behind the desk nodded his head and smiled at DI Insch. 'You were right. Loyalty. Let's make sure it doesn't come to that then, Sergeant. I want this leak found. Whoever's been feeding Miller information, I want it stopped.'

Insch growled. 'Oh don't you worry, sir. When I find the guilty party I will make sure they never speak to anyone ever again.'

Napier stiffened in his seat. 'Just make sure you stay within the rules, Inspector,' he said, clearly annoyed that Insch had usurped his responsibility for finding the mole. 'I want a formal disciplinary hearing and a dismissal from the force. No comeback. No shortcuts. Understood?'

Insch nodded, but his eyes were like coals in his angry pink face.

The superintendent smiled. 'Excellent. We can make this all go away. We just need a conviction. Philips is in custody. We know he's the killer. All we have to do is get forensic evidence and witnesses. You've got that in hand.' He stood up behind his desk.

'You'll see. Two weeks from now this will all be over and we'll be all back to normal. Everything will be fine.'

Wrong.

22

DI Insch walked Logan back to the main incident room, grumbling and swearing under his breath the whole way. He wasn't happy. Logan knew the superintendent's idea to butter Colin Miller up didn't sit well with Insch's view of the world. The reporter had the whole country calling him incompetent. Insch wanted revenge, not his DS off playing patty cake.

'Honestly, I didn't talk to Miller,' said Logan.

'No?'

'No. I think that's why he did it. The thing with the panto and now this. I wouldn't give him anything without going through you. He didn't like that.'

Insch didn't say anything, just pulled out a packet of jelly babies and started biting their heads off. He didn't offer the bag to Logan.

'Look, sir. Can't we just issue a statement? I mean: the body had been there for years. Letting him go after he was beaten up couldn't change that.'

They'd reached the incident room door and Insch stopped. 'That's not the way it works, Sergeant. They've sunk their teeth into my arse; they won't let go that easily. You heard the super: if this goes on much longer, I'm off the case. Lothian and Borders will be running the show.'

'I didn't mean for this to happen, sir.'

Something like a smile flickered onto Insch's face. 'I know you didn't.' He offered the open bag of jelly babies and Logan took a green one. It tasted like five pieces of silver. Insch sighed. 'Don't worry: I'll have a word with the troops. Let them know you're not a rat.'

But Logan still felt like one.

'Listen up!' said DI Insch, addressing the uniforms sitting at desks, answering phones, taking statements. They went quiet as soon as they saw him. 'You've all seen my picture in the paper this morning. I let Roadkill go on Wednesday night, and the next day a girl's body turns up in his collection of dead things. Turns out I'm an incompetent arse with a penchant for dressing up in funny clothes when I should be out fighting crime. And you'll also have read that DS McRae told me not to let Roadkill go. But being an idiot I did it anyway.'

Angry murmurs started, all directed at Logan. Insch held up a hand and there was instant silence. But the glaring continued.

'Now I know you think DS McRae's a shitebag right now, but you can forget it. DS McRae did not go to the papers. Understood? If he tells me any of you have been giving him grief . . .' Insch made a throat-cutting gesture. 'Now get your arses back to work and tell the rest of the shift. This investigation will continue and we *will* get our man.'

Half past ten and the post mortem was well underway. It was a nasty, rancid affair and Logan stood as far from the dissecting table as he could. But it wasn't far enough; even with the morgue's extractor fan going full belt the smell was over-powering.

The body had burst when the IB tried to lift it out of the pile at the farm. They'd had to scrape what was left of the internal organs off the steading floor.

Everyone in the room was wearing protective gear: white paper boiler suits, plastic shoe-covers, latex gloves and breathing masks. Only this time Logan's mask wasn't full of menthol chest rub. Isobel paced slowly up and down the table, prod-ding the corpulent flesh with a double-gloved finger, making detailed and methodical notes into her dictaphone. The bit of rough – Brian – trailed along after her like some sort of demented puppy. Floppy-haired wanker. DI Insch was again con-spicuous by his absence, having used Logan's guilty conscience to get out of it, but the PF and the back-up pathologist were there. Keeping as far away from the rotting corpse as possible without being somewhere else.

It was impossible to tell if the child had been strangled like David Reid. The skin was too heavily rotted around the throat. And something had been nibbling away at the flesh. Not just little wriggly white things either, and God knew there were enough of those, but a rat or a fox or something. A cold sweat beaded Isobel's forehead as her running commentary faltered. Carefully, she lifted the internal organs out of the plastic bag they'd been shovelled into, trying to identify what it was she held in her hands.

Logan was convinced he'd never get the smell out of his nostrils. Little David Reid had been bad, but this one was a hundred times worse.

'Preliminary findings,' said Isobel when it was finally over, scrubbing and scrubbing at her hands. 'Four cracked ribs and signs of blunt trauma to the skull. Broken hip. One broken leg. She was five. Blonde. There's a couple of fillings in her rear molars.' More soap, more scrubbing. It looked as if Isobel was trying to get clean all the way down to the bone. Logan had never seen her so shaken up by work before. 'I'd estimate the time of death between twelve and eighteen months ago. It's hard to be sure with so much decomposition . . .' She shivered. 'I'll need to run some laboratory tests on the tissue samples to be sure.'

Logan placed a gentle hand on her shoulder. 'I'm sorry.' He wasn't sure what for. That their relationship had fallen apart? That once Angus Robertson was put away, they had nothing in common? That she'd had to suffer what she suffered on that tower block rooftop? That he hadn't got to her sooner . . . That she'd just had to carve up a badly decomposed child like a turkey?

She smiled sadly at him, but tears sparkled at the edges of her eyes. For a moment there was a connection between them. A shared moment of tenderness.

And then Brian, her assistant, ruined it all. 'Excuse me, Doctor, you have a phone call on line three. I've put it through to the office.'

The moment was gone and so was Isobel.

Roadkill was undergoing psychiatric evaluation by the time Logan was heading across town to the steadings and their gruesome contents. He didn't hold out any hopes of Bernard Duncan Philips being found fit to stand trial. Roadkill was a nutjob and everyone knew it. The fact he kept three farm buildings full of dead animals he'd scraped off the road was a bit of a giveaway. Not to mention the dead child. The smell was still clinging to him.

Logan wound the car's windows down as far as he dared, wisps of snow flickering in to melt in the heat of the blowers. That post mortem was going to stay with him for a long, long time. Shuddering, he turned the heat up again.

The city was grinding to a halt in the heavy snowfall. Cars slithered and stalled all the way down South Anderson Drive, some up on the kerb, others just churning away in the middle of the four-lane road. At least his police-issue, rust-acned Vauxhall wasn't having too much difficulty.

Up ahead he could see the yellow on-off flash of a gritter spraying salt and sand across two lanes. The cars behind were hanging back, trying to avoid getting their paintwork scratched.

'Better late than never.'

'Sorry, sir?'

The PC doing the driving wasn't someone Logan had recognized straight away. He would have preferred WPC Watson, but DI Insch wasn't having any of it. He'd picked the new PC to accompany Logan because he was less likely to give Logan a hard time for the story in the morning paper. Besides, WPC Jackie Watson was in court again today with her changing-room wanker. Last time he was giving evidence against Gerald Cleaver, this time he was there to be tried. Not that it was going to take long. He'd been caught red-handed. Literally. Grimacing away in the ladies' changing room, dick in hand, banging away for all he was worth. It'd be in, plead guilty, mitigating circumstances, community service order and out again in time for tea. Maybe she'd be more inclined to speak to him with a successful prosecution under her belt?

It took them twice as long as it should have done to get across the Drive and out to Roadkill's farm on the outskirts of Cults. Visibility was so bad they couldn't see more than fifty yards in front of the car. The snow took everything away.

A crowd of reporters and television cameras was huddled outside the entrance to Roadkill's farm, shivering and sneezing in the snow. Two PCs, dressed up in the warmest gear they could get under their luminous yellow coats, guarded the gate, keeping the Press out. Snow had piled up on their peaked caps making them look slightly festive. The expression on their faces spoiled the image. They were cold, they were miserable and they were fed up with the army of journalists poking microphones in their faces. Asking them questions. Keeping them out of their nice warm patrol car.

The small lane was clogged with cars and vans. BBC, Sky News, ITN, CNN – they were all here, the television lights making the snow leap out in sharp contrast to the dark grey sky. Earnest pieces to camera stopped as soon as Logan's car pulled into view; then they descended like piranhas. Logan, stuck at the centre of the feeding frenzy, did just what DI Insch had told him: kept his bloody mouth shut as microphones and cameras were pushed through the open windows.

'Sergeant, is it true you've been given control of this case?'

'DS McRae! Over here! Has Inspector Insch been suspended?'

'Has Bernard Philips killed before?'

'Did you know he was mentally unstable before the body was discovered?'

There was more, but it was lost in the cacophonous barrage of noise.

The PC drove gently through the crowd, all the way to the locked gate. Then came the voice Logan was waiting for: 'Laz, 'bout time, man. I'm freezin' ma nuts off out here!' Colin Miller, rosy cheeks and red nose, dressed up in a thick black overcoat, thick padded boots, and furry hat. Very Russian.

'Get in.'

The reporter clambered into the back seat, and another heavily wrapped-up man joined him.

Logan turned sharply, wincing as his stomach reminded him of the staples holding it together.

'Laz, this is Jerry. He's ma photographer.'

The photographer peeled a hand out of a thick snow glove and extended it for shaking.

Logan didn't take it. 'Sorry, Jerry, but this is a one-man-only deal. There will be official police photographs available for the story, but we can't have unauthorized photos doing the rounds. You have to stay here.'

The reporter tried his friendliest smile. 'Come on, Laz, Jerry's a good lad. He'll no take any gore shots, will you, Jerry?'

Jerry looked momentarily confused and Logan knew that was exactly what he'd been told to take.

'Sorry. You and you only.'

'Shite.' Miller pulled off his furry cap, shaking the snow into the footwell of the back seat. 'Sorry, Jerry. You go wait in the car. There's some coffee in a thermos under the driver's seat. Don't eat all the gingersnaps.'

315

Swearing under his breath, the photographer clambered out of the car, into the crowd of journalists and the steadily falling snow.

'Right,' said Logan as they drove slowly through the blizzard. 'Let's make sure we're clear on the rules here: we get editorial rights over any story. We supply the photographs. If there's something we don't want you to print because it jeopardizes the investigation, you don't print it.'

'An' I get full exclusive rights. You don't do this for anyone else.' Miller's smile was positively obscene.

Logan nodded. 'And if you say one bad word about DI Insch I will personally kill you.'

Miller laughed, holding up his hands in mock surrender. 'Whoa there, Tiger. No taking the piss out the Pantomime Dame. It's a deal.'

'The constables on duty have been told to answer your questions. As long as they're appropriate.'

'Is that fit-looking WPC of yours going to be here?'

'No.'

Miller shook his head sadly. 'Shame. I had an inappropriate question for her.'

They started by getting into full biohazard boiler suits, complete with gas masks. Then Logan began the tour. Steading number one: empty but for the residue of slime and ooze. Steading number two was where Miller got the first real lungful of the

316

stench. He went surprisingly quiet as they stepped in amongst the decaying, furry corpses.

The scale of the pile was truly staggering. Even with half the dead animals removed to the waste containers outside, there were still hundreds of them in here. Badgers, dogs, cats, rabbits, seagulls, crows, pigeons, the occasional deer. If it had died on Aberdeen's roads, it was here. Decaying slowly.

A hole in the pile was cordoned off. This was where they'd found the little girl.

'Christ, Laz,' said Miller, his voice muffled by the breathing mask. 'This is fuckin' grim!'

'Tell me about it.'

They found the search team in steading number three. They were dressed in the same blue protective suits, working their way through the mound of decaying carcases by hand.

Corpse by corpse they picked them up, placed them on a table for examination and then piled them for disposal in the waste containers.

'Why this one?' asked Miller. 'How come they're not emptying the one where the girl was?'

'Philips kept the steadings sequentially numbered.' Logan pointed out through the door. 'One through five. Six is the farmhouse. His plan must've been to fill them all. One by one.'

A pair of constables pulled a mangy-looking spaniel/labrador cross from the pile and carried it between them to the table.

'This is the building he was in the middle of

filling. If he took Peter Lumley, this is where he'll be.'

Logan could see Miller frowning behind his safety goggles. 'If you're looking for another kid, how come you're doing it like this? Why examine all the things one by one? Why no just turf the shite out till you find him?'

'Because we might not be looking for all of him. There's still a bit of David Reid missing.'

Miller looked at the pile of dead things and the police men and women going through the lot by hand. 'Jesus. You're looking for his dick? In this? Fuck me, but you bastards deserve a medal! Or your heads examined.' Another rabbit was added to the table, given a brief inspection, and then thrown in the pile for disposal. 'Fuck . . .'

Outside, snow was slowly consuming the waste containers. A thick coating lay on top, drifts climbed the sides. Logan had a nasty thought as he watched a shovelful of examined remains being stuffed into one of the containers.

It wasn't easy running in Wellington boots and heavy snow, but Logan managed to get there just as the last seagull was tipped in. 'Hold it,' he said, grabbing the man with the shovel. No not a man, a woman. It was difficult to tell in the shapeless protective gear.

'Where did you put the original contents?'

She looked at him as if he were mad, snow swirling down all around them. 'What?'

'The original contents: the council were filling

these things. Where did you put the bodies they'd already put in there? Have you gone through them already?'

A look of unhappy comprehension appeared on the WPC's face. 'Shit!' She threw her shovel down into the snow. 'Shit, shit, shit!' Three deep breaths and then, 'Sorry, sir. We've been at this all day. We've just been throwing the bodies in. No one thought about checking the stuff already in there.' Her shoulders slumped and Logan knew how she felt.

'Come on. We'll empty this thing into steading number one and check the contents as we go. One group keeps going where they are, the other goes through this lot.' Fun, fun, fun. 'I'll break the good news to the team.' Why not? he thought to himself, they already hate me. Might as well give them good reason for it.

The news went down every bit as badly as Logan had anticipated. The only thing that made them feel any better was that he was prepared to pitch in and help. At least for a while.

And that was how Logan spent his afternoon. Miller, bless his cotton socks, swallowed his pride and picked up a shovel. The spaniel/labrador was near the top of the pile this time. Last in, first out. But slowly they worked their way through the contents of the waste container.

Logan was sure he'd examined the same burst-open rabbit about thirty times when the screaming started.

Someone came running out of steading number three clutching his hand to his chest. He slipped on the snow and went flat on his back. The screaming stopped for a moment as all the wind was knocked out of him.

The team abandoned their carcases and charged towards the fallen figure. Logan got there just as the screaming started up again.

Blood was oozing out of the constable's thick rubber glove through a neat puncture mark in the palm. The victim tore off his mask and goggles. It was PC Steve. Ignoring the calls to calm down, he carried on screaming as he dragged the bloody glove off his injured hand. There was a ragged hole in it: right in the meaty bit between his thumb and forefinger. It pulsed dark-red blood, running down the blue plastic boiler suit and into the snow.

'What did you do?'

PC Steve went on screaming so someone slapped him one. Logan couldn't be sure, but it looked like the Bastard Simon Rennie.

'Steve!' Rennie said, preparing to haul off and smack him again, 'What happened?'

PC Steve's eyes were wild, darting between the steading and his bleeding hand. 'Rat!'

Someone dragged their belt out from underneath their boiler suit and wrapped it around Steve's wrist, pulling hard.

'Jesus, Steve,' said the Bastard Simon Rennie, peering at the hole in his friend's hand. 'That must've been one big rat!'

'Fucking thing was like a Rottweiler! Ah, bastard that hurts!'

They stuffed a plastic bag with snow and stuck Steve's bleeding hand into it, trying not to notice as the snow inside slowly turned from white to pink and then to red. Logan wrapped the whole lot in a spare boiler suit and told PC Rennie to take him to the hospital, lights and music all the way.

Miller and Logan stood side by side as the lights flickered into life on top of the patrol car. It did a messy three point turn on the slippery road before creeping off into the blizzard, siren blazing.

'So,' said Logan as the flashing lights were swallowed by the snow. 'How are you enjoying your first day on the Force?'

23

Logan stayed at the farm as long as he could, examining animal carcases with the rest of the team. Even with all that protective gear on he felt dirty. And everyone was on pins and needles after the rat attack. No one wanted to join PC Steve in A&E waiting for a tetanus and rabies shot.

In the end, he had to call it a day: he still had work to do back at Force HQ. They dropped an ashen-faced Colin Miller off at the gate to the farm track. He was knackered, going straight home to drink a bottle of wine. Then he was going to climb into the shower and exfoliate until he bled.

The gaggle of reporters and television cameras outside the farm had thinned out. Now only the hardcore remained, sitting in their cars with the engines running and heaters going full blast. They leapt from the warm safety of their vehicles as soon as Logan's car appeared.

No comment was all they got.

DI Insch wasn't in the incident room when Logan got back to FHQ. Getting an update from the team manning the phones was an uncomfortable experience. Even after the inspector's speech they obviously still thought Logan was shite in a suit. No one actually said anything, but their reports were curt and to the point.

Team one: door-to-door – 'Have you seen this man?' – had generated the usual raft of contradictory statements. Yes, Roadkill had been seen talking to the boys, no he hadn't, yes he had. The Hazlehead station had even set up a roadblock to ask drivers if they'd seen something on their way into and out of town. A long shot, but worth a try.

Team two: Bernard Duncan Philips's life story. They'd been the most successful. There was a large manila folder sitting on the inspector's desk containing everything anyone knew about Roadkill. Logan perched himself on the edge of the desk and flicked through the collection of photocopies, faxes and printouts. He stopped when he got to the report on the death of Bernard's mother.

She'd been diagnosed with bowel cancer five years ago. She'd been ill for a long time, unable to cope. Bernard had come home from St Andrews, leaving a PHD behind, in order to look after his sick mother. Her GP had insisted she get help, but she refused. Bernard was on mummy's side and chased the man off the family farm with a pickaxe. Which was when they spotted the mental problems.

Then her brother, who'd found her face down on the kitchen floor, made her go to the hospital. Exploratory surgery and bingo: cancer. They tried treating it, but the cancer had spread to her bones by February. And in May she was dead. Not in the hospital, but in her own bed.

Bernard shared the house with her for two months after she died. A social worker had gone to check on Bernard. The smell had met her at the farmhouse door.

So Bernard Duncan Philips got a two-year spell in Cornhill, Aberdeen's only 'special needs' hospital. He responded well to the drugs so out he had gone into the care of the community. Which roughly translated meant they wanted the bed freed up for some other poor sod. Bernard buried himself in his work: scraping dead animals off the road for Aberdeen City Council.

Which explained a lot.

Logan didn't need an update on team three: he'd seen enough at first hand to know they weren't getting anywhere fast. Making them go through all that stuff in the waste containers hadn't helped, but at least now they knew they hadn't missed anything. At the rate they were going it'd be Monday at the earliest before they'd worked their way through all three steadings-worth of animal corpses. Providing the superintendent authorized the overtime.

Logan's mini incident room was empty by the time he got there. The lab results had come back on the vomit Isobel had found in the deep cut in the little girl's body. The DNA didn't match the sample from Norman Chalmers. And Forensics still hadn't come up with anything else. The only thing tying him to the girl was the supermarket till receipt. Circumstantial. So they'd had to let Norman Chalmers go. At least he'd had the good sense to go quietly, rather than in a barrage of media attention. His lawyer must have been gutted.

There was a neatly typed note sitting on Logan's desk, summarizing the day's sightings. He scanned through them sceptically. Most looked like utter fantasy.

Next to it was the list of every female TB sufferer under the age of four in the whole country. It wasn't a big list; just five names, complete with addresses.

Logan pulled over the phone and started dialling.

It was gone six when DI Insch stuck his head round the door and asked if Logan had a moment. The inspector had a strange look on his face and Logan got the feeling this wasn't going to be good news. He put one hand over the phone's mouthpiece and told the inspector he'd just be a minute.

The other end of the phone was connected to a PC in Birmingham who was, at that moment, sitting with the last girl on Logan's list. Yes she was still alive and was Logan aware that she was Afro-Caribbean? So probably not the dead white girl lying on a slab in the morgue then.

'Thanks for your time, Constable.' Logan put the phone down with a weary sigh and scored off the final name. 'No luck,' he said as Insch settled on the edge of the desk and started rummaging nosily through Logan's files. 'All children in the right age group treated for TB are alive and well.'

'You know what that means,' said Insch. He had hold of the statements Logan had picked out as being nearest to Norman Chalmers and his wheelie-bin. 'If she's had TB and been treated, it wasn't in this country. She's—'

'—not a British national,' Logan finished for him before burying his head in his hands. There were hundreds of places in the world still regularly suffering from TB: most of the former Soviet Union, Lithuania, every African nation, the Far East, America . . . A lot of the worst places didn't even keep national records. The haystack had just got an awful lot bigger.

'You want some good news?' asked Insch, his voice flat and unhappy.

'Go on then.'

'We've got an ID on the girl we found at Roadkill's farm.'

'Already?'

Insch nodded and placed all of Logan's statements back in the wrong order. 'We looked through the missing persons list for the last two years and ran a match on the dental records. Lorna Henderson. Four and a half. Her mother reported her missing. They were driving home from Banchory, along the South Deeside road. They'd had a row. She wouldn't shut up about getting a pony. So the mother says: "If you don't shut up about that damn pony you can walk home".'

Logan nodded. Everybody's mum had done that at one time or another. Logan's mother had even done it to his dad once.

'Only Lorna really, really wants a pony.' Insch pulled out a crumpled bag of fruit sherbets. But instead of popping one in his mouth, he just sat there and stared morosely into the bag. 'So the mother makes good on the threat. Pulls the car over and makes the kid get out. Drives off. Doesn't go far, just around the next bend. Less than half a mile. Parks the car and waits for Lorna. Only she never shows up.'

'How the hell could she put a four-year-old girl out of the car?'

Insch laughed, but it was humourless. 'There speaks someone who's never had kids. Soon as the little buggers learn to talk they don't stop till their hormones kick in and they become teenagers. Then you can't get a bloody word out of them. But a four-year-old will moan all day and all night if it really wants something. So in the end the mother snaps and that's it. Never sees her daughter ever again.'

And there was no way she was ever going to now. When the body was finally released for burial it would be a closed casket affair. They wouldn't let anyone see what was inside that box.

'Does she know? That we've found her?'

Insch grunted and stuffed the untouched sherbets back in his pocket. 'Not yet. That's where I'm off to now. Tell her that she let her kid get caught by a sick bastard. That he battered her to death and stuffed her body in a pile of animal carcasses.'

Welcome to hell.

'I'm taking WPC Watson with me,' said Insch. 'You want to come?' The words were flippant, but the voice wasn't. The inspector sounded low. Not surprising given the week they'd just had. Insch thought he could bribe Logan into coming by dangling WPC Watson in front of him. Like a carrot in a police uniform.

Logan would have gone without the bribe. Telling a mother her child was dead wasn't something he was looking forward to, but Insch looked as if he needed the support. 'Only if we go for a drink afterwards.'

They pulled up at the kerb in DI Insch's Range Rover, the massive car towering over all the little Renaults and Fiats that lined the street on either side with their white hats of pristine snow. No one had said much on the trip out. Except for the Family Liaison Officer, who'd spent the whole trip making 'Who's a pretty girl?' noises at the smelly black-and-white spaniel in the back of Insch's car.

The area was nice enough: some trees, a bit of grass. You could still see fields if you climbed on the roof. The house was at the end of a two-up, two-down terrace, all done out in white harling, the little white chips of stone and quartz sparkling in the streetlights, mimicking the snow.

The blizzard had turned into the occasional lazy flake, drifting slowly through the bitter night. They tramped through the ankle-deep snow to the front door together. Insch taking the lead. He pressed the doorbell and 'Greensleeves' binged and bonged from somewhere inside. Two minutes later the door was opened by a displeased, damp woman in her mid-forties, wearing a fluffy pink bathrobe. She wore no make-up, the faint remains of mascara smearing outwards from her eyes towards her ears. Her hair was wet, hanging over her face like damp string. The look of irritation on her face vanished as she saw WPC Watson's uniform standing at the back.

'Mrs Henderson?'

'Oh God.' She clutched at the front of the robe, twisting the neck tightly shut. All the colour went from her face. 'It's Kevin isn't it? Oh God . . . he's dead!'

'Kevin?' Insch looked flustered.

'Kevin, my husband.' She stepped back into

the tiny hall, her hands all a flutter. 'Oh God.'

'Mrs Henderson: your husband's not dead. We—'

'Oh, thank the Lord for that.' Instantly relieved, she ushered them through the hall into a pink, candy-striped living room. 'Excuse the mess. Sunday's usually my day for the housework, but I had a double shift at the hospital.' She stopped and surveyed the room, moving a discarded nurse's uniform off the sofa and onto the ironing board. The half-empty bottle of gin was swiftly tidied away to the sideboard. Above the fireplace was a framed fake oil painting, one of the ones photographers churn out. A man, a woman and a fair-haired little girl. A husband, a wife and a murdered child.

'Of course Kevin doesn't live here right now . . . He's having a break . . .' There was a pause. 'It was after our daughter went missing.'

'Ah. That's why we're here, Mrs Henderson.'

She waved them towards a lumpy brown sofa, the leather covered up with pink-and-yellow throws. 'Because Kevin doesn't live here? It's only temporary!'

Insch pulled a clear plastic envelope from his pocket. There were two pink hairclips in it. 'Do you recognize these, Mrs Henderson?'

She took the envelope, peered in at the contents and then back at Insch and went pale for the second time. 'Oh God, these were Lorna's! Her favourite Barbie hair things. She wouldn't go

330

out of the house without them! Where did you get them?'

'We found Lorna, Mrs Henderson.'

'Found? Oh God . . .'

'I'm sorry, Mrs Henderson. She's dead.'

She seemed to turn in on herself and then: 'Tea. That's what we need. Hot sweet tea.' She turned her back and scurried away into the kitchen, her towelling bathrobe flapping as she went.

They found her sobbing into the kitchen sink.

Ten minutes later they were back in the lounge, Insch and Logan on the lumpy settee, WPC Watson and Mrs Henderson on matching lumpy brown armchairs, the Family Liaison Officer standing behind her making consoling noises, one hand on Mrs Henderson's shoulder. Logan had made a big pot of tea and it sat steaming away on top of a coffee table festooned with *Cosmopolitan* magazines. Everyone had a cup, but no one was drinking.

'It's all my fault.' Mrs Henderson seemed to have shrunk two sizes since their arrival. The pink bathrobe was draped around her like a cloak. 'If we'd only bought her that damn pony . . .'

DI Insch shifted forward on the settee slightly. 'I'm sorry to have to ask you this, Mrs Henderson, but I need you to tell us about the night Lorna went missing.'

'I never really believed it. You know: that she wasn't coming back. She'd just run away. One day she'd just walk back through that door and everything would be right again.' She looked down into her teacup. 'Kevin couldn't take it. He kept blaming me. Every day. "It's your bloody fault she's gone!" he'd say. He was right. It was my bloody fault. He . . . he met this woman at the supermarket where he works.' She sighed. 'But he doesn't really love her! He's just punishing me . . . I mean, she's got no breasts. How can a man love a woman with no breasts? He's only doing it to punish me. He'll come back. You'll see. One day he'll walk right back in that door and everything will be all right again.' She fell back into silence, chewing away at the inside of her cheek.

'About the night Lorna went missing, Mrs Henderson, did you see anyone on the road? Any vehicles?'

Her eyes came up from her cup, glistening and far away. 'What? I don't remember . . . It was a long time ago and I was so angry with her. Why didn't we buy her that bloody pony?'

'How about vans, or trucks?'

'No. I don't remember. We went over all this at the time!'

'A man with a cart?'

She froze in place. 'What are you trying to say?'

DI Insch kept his mouth shut. Mrs Henderson stared at him for a moment and then jumped to her feet. 'I want to see her!'

DI Insch, put his cup carefully down on the carpet. 'I'm sorry, Mrs Henderson. That's not going to be possible.'

'She's my daughter, damn it, and I want to see her!'

'Lorna's been dead for a long time. She's . . . you don't want to see her, Mrs Henderson. Please trust me. You want to remember her how she was.'

Standing in the middle of the lounge, Mrs Henderson scowled down at DI Insch's bald head. 'When did you find her? When did you find Lorna?'

'Yesterday.'

'Oh God . . .' she slapped a hand over her mouth. 'It's him isn't it? The man in the papers! He killed her and buried her in that filth!'

'Calm down, Mrs Henderson. We have him in custody. He's not going anywhere.'

'That filthy bastard!' She hurled her teacup against the wall. It exploded, raining shards of china, staining the wallpaper with lukewarm, milky tea. 'He took my baby!'

No one said much on the way back either. The Family Liaison Officer called in a neighbour to look after Mrs Henderson, who collapsed into tears as soon as the large, concerned woman arrived. They left the pair of them weeping on the sofa and let themselves out.

The roads were quiet as the grave as they

headed back towards the centre of town: the snow was keeping everyone but the gritters inside.

Eight o'clock. A familiar figure slipped past as Insch swung the car round the Hazlehead roundabout. Peter Lumley's stepfather, trudging through the falling snow, shouting his son's name. Logan stared glumly at the soaking, cold figure until they'd left him far behind. He still had that dreadful visit from the police to look forward to. When they finally told him that his son's body had been found.

Insch checked in with Control and got an address for Mr Henderson. He shared an apartment with his flat-chested supermarket woman in the less salubrious end of Rosemount.

They went through the same painful scene again. Only this time there was no self-blame. This time it was all directed at his stupid bitch ex-wife. His girlfriend sat on the couch in tears as he raged and swore. This wasn't like him, she said. He was usually such a gentle man.

And then back to Force Headquarters.

'Christ, that was a fun day.' Insch sounded completely drained as he shambled across to the lifts. He mashed the up button with a fat thumb. Surprisingly the doors slid open immediately. 'Look,' he said getting in, leaving Logan and WPC Watson standing in the corridor. 'Why don't you two get changed and meet me back here in five. I've got two forms to fill in and then I'll buy you both a drink.'

WPC Watson looked at Logan and then back at the inspector. She looked as if she was searching for a good excuse to be somewhere else. But before she could find it, the lift doors slid shut, taking DI Insch away.

Logan took a deep breath.

'If you'd rather not,' he said to her 'I understand. I can tell the inspector you had a prior engagement.'

'You that keen to get rid of me?'

Logan raised an eyebrow. 'No. Not at all. I thought . . . Well, after all that crap in the papers . . . you know,' he pointed at himself, 'Mr Shitebag.'

She smiled. 'With all due respect, sir: you can be a right arse at times. I met Miller, remember? I know he's a wanker.' The smile slipped. 'I just didn't know if you'd want me there. After that outburst. Swearing at the car?'

Logan beamed. 'No! It's OK. Honestly. OK, the swearing wasn't OK—' Her smile slipped and Logan charged on, afraid he'd screwed it all up again, '—but that's got nothing to do with anything. I'd like you to come. Especially if Inspector Insch is buying.' He stopped. 'Not that I wouldn't want you to come if I was paying . . . It's . . .' He clamped his mouth shut to keep any more babble from falling out.

She looked at him for a moment. 'Right,' she said at last. 'I'll go get changed then. See you out front.'

335

As she disappeared Logan was sure she was laughing at him. He stood alone in the corridor, blushing furiously.

At the front desk, Big Gary was settling down to another night shift. He smiled and waved Logan over.

'Hey, Lazarus, nice to see you getting the recognition you deserve!'

Logan frowned and Gary whipped out a copy of the day's *Evening Express*, the *Press and Journal*'s sister paper. There on the front page was a photograph of figures in blue rubber suits, picking through blurry animal carcasses by hand.

'HOUSE OF HORROR: BRAVE POLICE HUNT FOR EVIDENCE'

'Let me guess,' Logan sighed, 'Colin Miller again?' He must have worked fast.

Gary smacked the side of his nose with a finger. 'Got it in one, Mr Local Police Hero.'

'Gary, as soon as I outrank you I'm going to have you out there,' he pointed out into the snow, 'pounding the beat again.'

Gary winked. 'And until then you'll just have to put up with it. Biscuit?' He held up a packet of Kit Kats and despite himself Logan smiled. And took one.

'So what else is Mr Miller saying?'

Gary puffed out his chest, flipped the paper over and read aloud, in his best Shakespearean voice: 'Blah, blah, blah, snow and ice, blah, blah. Flowery shite about how brave all the police are

for digging through "a gruesome mine of death".
Blah, blah, searching for "the vital evidence that
will make our children safe from this beast". Oh,
you'll like this bit. "Local Police Hero Logan
'Lazarus' McRae was not above helping his team
sort through the carcases by hand". Apparently
you also saved Constable Steve Jacobs' life when
a huge rat attacked him. God bless you, sir!' Gary
cracked a salute.

'PC Rennie did all the work. All I did was tell
someone to get him to hospital!'

'Ah, but without your firm leadership no one
else might have thought of it!' He wiped an imaginary tear from his eye. 'You're an inspiration to
us all, so you are.'

'I hate you.' But Logan was smiling when he
said it.

WPC Watson was easier to think of as 'Jackie'
when she was out of uniform. The austere black
had been replaced by a pair of jeans and a red
sweatshirt, her curly brown hair falling down
over her shoulders. She cursed and tugged at it
as she struggled into a thick padded jacket.

At least one of them would be dressed for the
snow. Logan was still in his working suit. He
never got changed at the station. With his house
only two minutes' walk away there never seemed
any point.

She joined them at the desk, begged a Kit Kat
off Big Gary and consumed it with delight.

Logan waited until she had a good mouthful

before asking, 'How'd your prisoner get on this morning?'

She munched and crunched and eventually mumbled that he'd been given forty-two hours' community service with the council's Parks Department, as usual, and put on the sex offenders' register.

'As usual?'

Watson shrugged. 'Turns out he always gets the Parks Department,' she said, producing a small shower of chocolate crumbs. 'Planting, weeding, fixing stuff. You know.' She swallowed and shrugged. 'Judge took pity on him, what with giving evidence in the Gerald Cleaver case and all. Went through the whole thing again, only without Sandy the Snake making out it's all some weird, twisted fantasy. Got to confess I kinda feel sorry for the kid. Can you imagine getting treated like that? Abusive father, drunkard mother and when you go to hospital you get Gerald bloody Cleaver fiddling about with you under the sheets.'

Silence settled in as they considered the flabby male nurse with a thing for little boys.

'You know,' said Big Gary, 'if it wasn't for Roadkill, I'd've put money on Cleaver for the dead kiddies.'

'How? He was in custody when Peter Lumley went missing.'

Gary flustered. 'Might have had an accomplice.'

'And he was a fiddler, not a killer,' chipped in Jackie. 'He liked them alive.'

Logan winced. It wasn't a nice image, but she was right.

But Big Gary wasn't going to let go of it that easily. 'Maybe he can't get it up any more? Maybe that's why he kills them!'

'It doesn't change the fact that he's been locked up for the last six months. It's not him.'

'I'm not saying it was him. I'm just saying it could have been.' Gary scowled. 'And to think I let you buggers eat my biscuits! Ungrateful sods.'

24

One drink turned into two. Two turned into three. Three turned into a curry and four more. By the time Logan said goodnight to DI Insch and WPC Watson, all was right with the world again. OK, with the inspector there he and Jackie couldn't get up to anything, but Logan got the feeling they might have. If Insch hadn't been there.

None of which mattered at four-thirty in the morning when he staggered out of bed to drink his own bodyweight in water before falling queasily back to sleep.

Lorna Henderson's post mortem report was sitting on DI Insch's desk when Logan got in to work. Seven o'clock on the dot, even if it was a Saturday morning. The inspector was already there, sitting behind his desk looking slightly more pink than usual.

Lorna Henderson had died from blunt trauma. The cracked ribs would have crushed her left lung, the impact to the left temple shattering her skull, the one to the back of her head finishing off the job. The leg break was jagged, just above the knee. A four-year-old girl, beaten to death. Roadkill had really gone to town.

'You think we're going to get anything out of him?' asked Logan, turning the pathology photographs face down so that he wouldn't have to look at them any more.

Insch snorted. 'Doubt it. Doesn't matter though. We've got so much forensic evidence there's no way he's going to beat this one. Not even Slippery Sandy can get him off. Mr Philips is going to spend the rest of his life in Peterhead Prison with all the other sick bastards.' He pulled a packet of sherbet fruits from his pocket and offered them round the incident room. That done he settled down to working his way through the remainder. 'You taking Miller back up to the farm today?' The reporter's name came out as if Insch was describing a foul smell.

'No,' Logan grinned. 'For some reason he's not too keen. Can't think why.'

Friday's little expedition had been quite enough for the reporter. Today's *Press and Journal* had nothing but nice words for the police. It was much the same as the *Evening Express* story, only with more editorializing. At least DI Insch was out of the spotlight.

'What about you?' he asked. 'How's your floater going?'

'Getting there.'

'DI Steel tells me you're keen on the McLeod brothers?'

Logan nodded. 'It's their kind of gig. Hands on. Brutal.'

Insch almost smiled. 'Take after their dad, that pair. Going to get them for it?'

Logan tried not to shrug, but he knew it wasn't a foregone conclusion. 'Doing my damnedest. I've got Forensics crawling all over the clothes they found the body in. Might get something out of it. If not, maybe one of their punters will cough . . .' He stopped, remembering Duncan Nicholson running into the shop, out of the rain.

Insch popped something green and fizzy into his mouth. 'Not likely. Can you imagine anyone stupid enough to rat on the McLeod brothers? They'd tear him apart.'

'What?' Logan was dragged back from Nicholson: that plastic bag. 'Oh, yeah. Probably. Simon McLeod said the whole thing was a warning. A message. That everyone in the city knew what it meant.'

'Everyone in the city, eh?' Insch crunched as he chewed. 'How come I've no heard anything about it then?'

'No idea. I'm hoping Miller can shed some light on that one.'

Twelve o'clock and Logan was sitting down to a big plate of steak-and-ale pie, chips and beans.

The Prince of Wales was an old-fashioned place: all wood panelling and real ale, the low ceiling yellowed by generations of cigarette smokers. It was busy, full of men press-ganged into Saturday morning shopping by their wives and girlfriends. This was their reward: a pint of cold beer and a packet of prawn cocktail crisps.

The pub was made up of little rooms stitched together by short corridors. Logan and Miller sat in one at the front, next to the window. Not that the view was up to much, just the other side of a tall alley, the granite grey and dull and wet from the freezing-cold rain.

'So,' said Miller spearing a mangetout. 'Have you got the bastard tae confess yet?'

Logan munched his way through a mouthful of beef and crispy pastry, wishing he'd gone for a pint of beer to wash it down and take the final edge off his hangover. But drinking on duty was tantamount to raping sheep in the Chief Constable's eyes, so Logan was stuck with a pint of fresh orange and lemonade. 'We're pursuing our enquiries.' The words came out muffled.

'Nail his bloody arse to the wall. Sick wee shite that he is.' Miller wasn't on duty, so he could drink. Only he didn't have a nice pint of Dark Island, but a large glass of chilled Sémillon Chardonnay with his salmon en croûte.

Logan watched the reporter take a delicate sip at his wine and smiled. Miller was a weird fish and to be honest, Logan was starting to like him.

Even if he had come within a whisker of getting DI Insch fired. The clothes and the wine and the croissants and the chunky gold jewellery just added to the pantomime.

Logan waited until the reporter had a mouthful of salmon before asking, 'What about George Stephenson then?'

'Mmmph . . .' Small flakes of pastry fell down the front of Miller's delicate ivory shirt. 'What about him?'

'You said you still had information. Stuff I didn't know?'

Miller smiled, letting even more pastry fall free. 'How 'bout the last place he was seen alive?'

Logan took a guess: 'Turf 'n Track?'

Miller's smile became impressed. 'Aye: spot on. Turf 'n Track.'

Logan knew it would be. Now all they had to do was prove it. 'One of the McLeod brothers told me, "everyone knows you don't do what Geordie did", that it was a warning. Want to fill me in?'

Miller played with his wine glass, letting the light filter through it onto the wooden tabletop, making a little golden spotlight that danced across the grain.

'You know he was into the local bookies for a fair chunk of money?'

'You said that. How much?'

'Two hundred and fifty thousand, six hundred and forty-two pounds.'

It was Logan's turn to be impressed. That was

a hell of a lot of money. 'So how come they killed him? Why not just cripple him a little? He can't pay up if he's dead. Not to mention they're killing off one of Malk the Knife's boys. I hear Malkie doesn't take kindly to that kind of thing.'

'Aye, risky. If you do in one of Malkie's boys without his permission he's going tae come down on you like a ton of shite.'

Logan's heart sank: the last thing Aberdeen needed was a spate of tit-for-tat killings. Gang warfare in the Granite City. Wouldn't that be fun? 'So why did they kill him then?'

Miller sighed and put his knife down. 'They kilt him because everyone knows that you don't do what he did.'

'What the hell does that mean?'

'It means . . .' Miller looked around the little room. A small corridor led off towards where they'd picked up lunch and another, out of sight in the opposite corner, led back through into the bar. Everyone else was chatting away, eating, drinking, enjoying being out of the horrible weather. No one was paying them the slightest bit of attention.

'Listen, you know who Geordie worked for. You don't piss him off twice, OK? Maybe you can get away with it once, but you do it twice and you're no in for a good time, know what I mean?'

'We've been over that!'

'Aye, we have.'

Miller was looking increasingly uncomfortable.

345

'You know how come I ended up in sunny Aberdeen?' He waved his fork at the dreich weather on the other side of the window. 'How come I gave up a post on the *Sun* tae come to this shite-hole?' But he dropped his voice, so no one would hear him call Aberdeen a shite-hole. 'Drugs. Drugs and whores.'

Logan raised an eyebrow.

Miller scowled. 'No me, you dirty bastard. I was doin' a story about all this crack comin' intae Glasgow from Edinburgh. They wis smugglin' it over from Eastern Europe inside prossies. You know: the old plastic-bag-up-the-fanny routine. Do it when they're on the blob and the sniffer dogs don't smell it. An' even if they do smell somethin' everyone's too fuckin' embarrassed to say anything.' He took another sip of his wine. 'And you'd be surprised how much crack cocaine you can stuff up a Lithuanian tart's minge. Fuckin' heaps of the stuff.'

'What's this got to do with Geordie?'

'I'm comin' to that. So anyways, I'm doin' my Clark Kent routine: diggin' up the dirt, really fuckin' great stories. I mean I'm gettin' nominated for awards left right and centre. Investigative Journalist of the Year, book deals, the whole works. Only I find out who's runnin' the scam, don't I? I come up with a name. The big man in charge of flyin' all these tarts, packed full of drugs, into the country.'

'Let me guess: Malcolm McLennan.'

'These two great big fuckers grabbed me on Sauchiehall Street. In broad daylight, but! Bundles me into a big black car. I am politely requested to drop the story like a radioactive tattie. If I'm fond of my fingers. And my legs.'

'And did you?'

'Course I fuckin' did!' Miller emptied half his wine glass in a single gulp. 'No bastard's hackin' off my fingers with a butcher's knife.' He shivered. 'Malk the Knife put the word about and next thing I know I'm out of a job. No paper in the central belt'd touch me with a bargepole.' He sighed. 'So here I am. Don't get me wrong: it's no that bad a place to wind up. Good job, lots of front page inches, nice car, flat, met a nice woman . . . Money's no what I'm used to, but still . . . An' I'm still alive.'

Logan settled back in his seat and examined the man sitting opposite him: the tailored suit, the gold baubles, the silk tie, even on a pissing-down Saturday in Aberdeen.

'So that's why I've not seen anything in the papers about Geordie's body turning up in the harbour with no knees? You're scared to publish anything in case Malk the Knife finds out about it?'

'I go putting his business on the front page again and it's goodbye to all ten little piggies.' The reporter waved his fingers at Logan, the rings sparkling in the pub's overhead lights. 'No, I'm keepin' my mouth shut on this one.'

'Then why are you talking to me?'

Miller shrugged. 'Just 'cos I'm a journalist, it don't mean I'm an amoral, parasitic wanker. I mean it's no like I'm a lawyer or anything. I got a social conscience. I'm givin' you information so you can catch the killer. I'm keepin' my head down so it doesn't cost me my fingers. Come time for court you're on your own: I'm off to the Dordogne. Two weeks of French wine and haute cuisine. I'm no tellin' any bugger anythin'.'

'You know who did it, don't you?'

The reporter finished off his wine and smiled lopsidedly. 'No. But if I find out you'll be the first to know. No that I'm lookin' any longer. Got safer fish to fry.'

'Like what?'

But Miller just smiled. 'You'll read about it soon enough. Anyway, gotta dash.' He stood and shrugged his way into his thick black overcoat. 'I've got a meetin' with this bloke from the *Telegraph*. Lookin' for a four-page spread in tomorrow's Sunday supplement. "In Search Of The Dead: Catching The Aberdeen Child-Killer." Very classy.'

Danestone had started out as farmland, like most of the outer regions of Aberdeen, but it had held out against the developers longer than the rest. So, by the time its green fields fell beneath the bulldozer, the mantra was build 'em quick and build 'em close together. The traditional grey granite blocks and gunmetal roof slates were nowhere to be seen: here it was all oatmeal harling and pantiles, winding cul-de-sacs and dead-end roads. Just like every other anonymous suburb.

But unlike the middle of Aberdeen, where the tenements and tall granite buildings cut the daylight down by an hour, the sun shone in abundance, the whole development sitting on a south-facing hill along the banks of the River Don. The only drawback was the proximity of the chicken factory, paper mills and sewage treatment plant. But you couldn't have everything. As long as the wind didn't blow from the west you were fine.

The wind wasn't blowing from the west today. It was howling in from the east, straight off the North Sea, and full of icy horizontal rain.

Shivering, Logan wound the car window back up again. He'd parked a little down the road from a compact two-up two-down, the small garden looking half-dead in the battering rain. They'd been there for an hour, him and a bald DC in a parka jacket and there was still no sign of their target.

'So where is he then?' asked the DC, wriggling deeper into his insulated coat. All he'd done since they'd left the station was bitch about the weather. About the fact they were working on a Saturday. That it was raining. That it was cold. That he was hungry. That the rain was making his bladder twitchy.

Logan tried not to sigh. If Nicholson didn't turn up soon there was going to be another murder in the papers tomorrow. 'WHINGING POLICE BASTARD THROTTLED WITH OWN GENITALS IN PARKED CAR!' He was just deciding whether it should be an OBE or a knighthood he'd get for killing the moaning wee sod when a familiar, battered, rust-encrusted, green Volvo growled its way past. The driver mounted the kerb in his enthusiasm to park, before scrambling about in the back seat of the car for something.

'Show time.' Logan opened his door and hurried out into the freezing rain. Grumbling, the DC followed.

They got to the Volvo just as Nicholson clambered out, clutching a pair of plastic bags. His face went white when he saw Logan.

'Afternoon, Mr Nicholson.' Logan forced a smile, even though there was icy water streaming down his neck, soaking into his shirt collar. 'Mind if we look in the bags?'

'Bags?' The rain glittered on Duncan Nicholson's shaven head, running off him like nervous sweat. He shoved the bags behind his back. 'What bags?'

The unhappy DC stepped forward and growled from within his parka's fur-lined hood. 'I'll give you what fucking bags!'

'Oh these!' They were produced again. 'Shopping. Been to Tesco, haven't I? Something for lunch. Now if you'll excuse me—'

Logan didn't move. 'They're Asda carrier bags, Mr Nicholson. Not Tesco's.'

Nicholson looked from Logan to the grumpy DC. 'I . . . I . . . er . . . recycling. I recycle my plastic bags. Gotta do our bit for the environment.'

The DC took another step. 'I'll fucking do for your environment—'

'That's enough, Constable,' said Logan. 'I'm sure Mr Nicholson is as keen as we are to get out of the rain. Shall we go inside, Mr Nicholson? Mind, it's nice and dry down at the station. We could give you a lift.'

Two minutes later they were sitting in a small green kitchen, listening to the kettle boil. It was a nice enough house on the inside, if you didn't mind concussing your cat. The walls were covered with patterned wallpaper, borders and friezes, expensive olive carpeting, big, framed, mass-produced oil paintings. Not a book in sight.

'What a *lovely* home you have,' said Logan, looking at Nicholson. Shaved head, tattoos and enough metalwork in his ears to set off every metal detector from here to Dundee. 'Decorate it yourself, did you?'

Nicholson mumbled something about his wife being keen on those makeover shows. Everything was co-ordinated: kettle, toaster, blender, tiles and oven. All of it green. Even the linoleum was green. It was like sitting inside a huge bogey.

The two carrier bags were sitting on the tabletop.

'Shall we take a look inside then, Mr Nicholson?'
Logan pulled one of them open and was surprised
to see a packet of bacon and a tin of beans staring
back at him. The other one had crisps and chocolate biscuits. Frowning, he tipped them out onto
the table. Chocolate and crisps, beans and bacon
. . . And right at the very bottom a pair of thick
manila envelopes. Logan's frown turned into a
smile.

'What have we here?'

'Never seen them before in my life!'

It wasn't rain dripping down Nicholson's face
now: it really was nervous sweat.

Logan snapped on a pair of latex gloves and
picked up one of the envelopes. It stank of cigarette smoke. 'Anything you'd like to say before I
open these?'

'I just carry them. I don't know what's in them
. . . They're not mine!'

Logan tipped the contents out onto the table.
Photographs. Women hanging out the washing;
women getting ready for bed. But mostly it was
children. At school. Playing in the garden. One
in the back seat of a car, looking scared. Whatever
Logan had been expecting, it wasn't this. Each of
the pictures had a different name written on the
back. No address, just a name. 'What the hell is
this?'

'I told you: I don't know nothing about what's
in them!' His voice was getting higher, panicky.
'I just carry them.'

The grumpy DC grabbed hold of Duncan Nicholson's shoulders, shoving him back into his seat with a crash.

'You filthy wee shite!' He grabbed a photo of a small boy, sitting in a sandpit with a stuffed rabbit. 'Was this how you found him? Is it? Did you photograph David Reid? Decide you wanted him? You filthy fuck!'

'It isn't like that! It's nothing like that!'

'Mr Duncan Nicholson, I'm detaining you on suspicion of murder.' Logan stood, looking down at the spread of children's faces, feeling sick. 'Read him his rights, Constable.'

There wasn't really room in the small house for four IB technicians, the video operator, photographer, Logan, the grumpy DC and two uniformed officers, but they squeezed in anyway. No one wanted to wait outside in the driving rain.

The contents of the two envelopes were now all bagged and tagged. Envelope number two wasn't full of pictures; it was full of money and little pieces of jewellery.

Upstairs there was a cupboard, opposite the bathroom. Three foot long, four foot wide, just big enough to hold a computer, fancy-looking colour printer, and a barstool. And a bolt that only fastened from the inside.

There were shelves of CDs on the wall, the kind you burn at home, all labelled and dated, and boxes of high-quality, glossy printouts under the bench the computer sat on. Women and children; mostly children. They found a top-of-the-range digital camera in the bedroom.

There was a rattling sound from downstairs and everyone suddenly went quiet.

Creak. And the front door opened.

'Dunky? Can you give me a . . . Who the hell are you?'

Logan poked his head down the stairs to see a heavily pregnant woman dressed in a black leather coat and carrying a stack of shopping bags staring in disbelief at the crowd of policemen filling her house.

'Where's Duncan? What have you bastards done with my husband?'

25

The news came over the police radio at three o'clock, just as Logan was getting back to Force Headquarters. The Gerald Cleaver trial had finally come to its verdict after four weeks in the media spotlight.

'Not guilty? How the hell could they find him not guilty?' asked Logan, as the grumpy DC stuffed their rusty pool car into the parking lot.

'Hissing Bloody Sid,' came the reply. Sandy Moir-Farquharson had struck again.

They hurried out of the car and up through to the briefing area. The room was full of uniform, most of whom looked soaked to the skin.

'Listen up!' It was the Chief Constable himself, looking sharp as a pin in his neatly pressed dress uniform. 'We are going to have a lot of angry people out there.' That was an understatement: the crowd of protesters had been an almost permanent fixture outside the courthouse. They wanted to see Gerald Cleaver sentenced to life in

Peterhead Prison. Letting him go free was like lighting the blue touch paper and stuffing the firework down your trousers.

The police presence outside the court buildings had been minimal, just enough to keep everything under control; but that was about to change. The Chief Constable wasn't taking any chances.

'The eyes of the world are on Aberdeen,' he said, striking an inspiring pose. 'With every day that passes, the anti-paedophile movement grows. And quite rightly. But we cannot let a few, misguided, individuals turn the protection of our children into an excuse for violence. I want this to go peacefully. There will be no riot shields. This is a community policing initiative. Understood?'

There were a few nods.

'You will be out there representing the best of this proud city. Make sure everyone knows that Aberdeen takes law and order very seriously!'

He paused for a second, as if expecting a round of applause, before yielding the floor to DI Steel who gave everyone their assignments. She looked stressed. She'd been responsible for the Gerald Cleaver case.

Logan wasn't uniform, so his name was left off the list, along with the rest of CID, but he shuffled along after the last team anyway, pausing at the front door to look out at the freezing rain and the angry mob outside the Sheriff Court building.

The crowd was bigger than Logan had anticipated: about five hundred people, filling the space in front of the court, spilling down the stairs and into the 'official business only' car park. Television crews were visible as tiny islands of calm in the unhappy sea of faces and placards:

'DOWN WITH EVIL CLEAVER!'

'GIVE CLEAVER THE CHOP!'

'PERVERT BASTARD!'

'LIFE MEANS LIFE!'

'DEATH TO PEDIPHILE SCUM!!!'

Logan winced as he read that last one. Nothing like stupid people with righteous fury and a mob on their side. Last time there had been this kind of fervour three paediatricians had their surgery windows smashed. Now it looked like they were after the foot fetishists.

Things were already beginning to get ugly.

They chanted and shouted abuse at the court building: men, women, parents and grandparents, all gathered together, baying for blood. The only things missing were the pitchforks and burning torches.

And then the crowd went quiet.

The large glass doors swung open and out into the rain came Sandy Moir-Farquharson. Gerald Cleaver wasn't with him: there was no way Grampian Police were going to turn Cleaver out into that mob, no matter how guilty they thought he was.

Sandy the Snake smiled at the crowd as if they were old friends. This was his moment in the sun. Television cameras from around the world were here. Today he would shine on the global stage.

A forest of microphones leapt up all around him.

Logan stepped out into the rain, morbid curiosity dragging him on until he was close enough to hear the lawyer's words.

'Ladies and gentlemen,' said Moir-Farquharson, pulling folded sheets of paper from his jacket pocket, 'my client will not be available for comment at this time but he has asked me to read the following statement.' He cleared his throat and stuck his chest out. '"I wish to thank everyone for their kind words of support during this ordeal. I have always maintained my innocence and today the good people of Aberdeen have vindicated me."'

At this the silence became punctuated with angry noises.

'Oh Christ,' muttered a uniform standing next to Logan, 'could they no have got him to keep his mouth shut?'

'"Now that" . . .' Sandy the Snake had to raise his voice to be heard, ' . . . "Now that my good name has been cleared I will"—' He didn't get any further.

A huge scruffy young man lunged out of the crowd, shoved his way through the ring of reporters and clobbered the lawyer one. Right on the nose. Sandy the Snake staggered back, tripped, and went down. The crowd roared in approval.

A ring of black uniforms appeared out of

nowhere, grabbing the scruffy man before he could really put the boot into the fallen lawyer. They picked up a bleeding Sandy Moir-Farquharson and helped him back into the court building, frogmarching his attacker in behind him.

Nothing else happened for half an hour. Nothing but the freezing rain. Most of the crowd gave up and dispersed to the bars and their homes until there were only a handful of protesters left to see an unmarked minibus with tinted windows pull out onto the road and head away towards the centre of town.

Gerald Cleaver was free.

Back at Force Headquarters Logan joined a long queue of dripping, sniffing, police men and women. Up at the head of the line the canteen staff ladled out steaming bowls of Scotch broth. Standing next to the cutlery, the Chief Constable shook everyone's hand and told them what a great job they'd done of preventing trouble.

Logan accepted the soup and the handshake with equal magnanimity, then squelched down over to a table by the fogged-up window. The soup was hot and tasty and a damn sight more use than the handshake. But at least the soup was free.

A delighted Detective Inspector Insch plonked himself down on the other side of the table, between a couple of drenched PCs. He sat beaming at everyone and everything. 'Right on the nose!'

he said at last. 'Bang! Right on the nose.' He grinned and dug a spoon into his soup. 'Whap!' He put the spoon back down. 'Did you see it? Slippery little sod stands there and spouts his drivel and someone gets up and twats him one. Bang!' He slammed a huge fist into a huge hand, making the PC sitting next to him jump and miss his mouth with the spoon, sending a cascade of soup down the front of his tie. 'Sorry, son.' Insch offered the spluttering PC a napkin. 'Right on the bloody nose!' He stopped and the grin got even wider. 'It'll be on the news tonight! I'm going to record it and whenever I feel like a laugh—' he mimed pointing a remote control, stabbing his finger down on a pretend button. 'BANG! Right on the nose.' He sighed happily. 'Days like this I remember why I joined the force.'

'How's DI Steel taking it?' asked Logan.

'Hmm? Oh . . .' Insch's smile faded. 'Well she's happy about the nose-punching but well pissed off they let that slimy little pervert go free.' He shook his head. 'She spent ages getting the victims to testify. Poor buggers had to stand there and tell everyone what that pervert did to them. Hissing Sid humiliates them. Cleaver goes free, and all that pain was for nothing.'

Silence settled over the table, everyone concentrating on their soup.

'You want to go see him?' asked Insch when the last of Logan's soup was gone.

'What, Cleaver?'

'No, the hero of the hour!' He raised his hands in the classic fisticuffs pose. 'He who floats like a butterfly and stings like a fist to the nose.'

Logan smiled. 'Why not?'

There was a small crowd outside the holding cells. All happy and chattering. With a growl, DI Insch sent them packing. Didn't they know this was highly unprofessional? Did they want people to think it was OK to go committing assault? Shamefaced, the uniformed onlookers dispersed, leaving just Logan, Insch and the custody sergeant outside the blue-painted door. The sergeant was scribbling a name on the board next to the cell and Logan frowned. It looked familiar, but he couldn't work out why.

'Mind if we pay your boy a visit?' asked Insch when the scribbling was done.

'What? No, sir, you go ahead. Are you in charge of the investigation?'

Insch beamed again. 'I bloody well hope so!'

The room was small without being cosy: brown lino floor, cream walls and a hard wooden bench-seat running along the wall. The only natural light came from two small frosted panes of heavy-duty glass set into the top of the outside wall. The whole place smelled of armpits.

The cell's occupant was curled up on the wooden bench, lying on his side in the foetal position. Moaning quietly.

'Thank you, Sergeant,' said Insch. 'We can take it from here.'

'OK.' The custody sergeant backed out of the cell and winked at Logan. 'Let me know if Mohammed Ali here gives you any trouble.'

The cell door shut with a dull clang and Insch settled down on the bench next to the curled up figure. 'Mr Strichen? Or can I call you Martin?'

The figure shifted slightly.

'Martin? Do you know why you're here?' Insch's voice was soft and friendly, completely unlike any tone Logan had ever heard him use on a suspect.

Slowly, Martin Strichen levered himself up until his legs were hanging over the edge of the bench, his socks making damp footprints on the lino. They'd confiscated his shoelaces and his belt and anything else dangerous. He was huge – not fat – but large everywhere, arms, legs, hands, jaw . . . Logan stopped when he got to the pock-marked face. Now he knew where he recognized the name from: Martin Strichen was WPC Watson's changing-room wanker, the one he'd given a lift back to Craiginches Prison. The one who'd been giving evidence in the Gerald Cleaver case.

No wonder he'd smacked Slippery Sandy on the nose.

'They let him go.' His voice was little more than a whisper.

'I know they did, Martin. I know. They shouldn't have, but they did.'

'They let him go because of him.'

362

Insch nodded. 'And that's why you hit Mr Moir-Farquharson?'

A muffled mumble.

'Martin, I'm going to write up a little statement and then I'm going to ask you to sign it, OK?'

'They let him go.'

Gently, Insch took Martin Strichen through the events of the afternoon, taking special delight in the moment of impact, getting Logan to write it all down in tortured police-speak. It was an admission of guilt, but Insch had taken great pains to make it sound as if it was all Sandy the Snake's fault. Which it was anyway. Martin signed it and Insch released him from custody.

'Do you have anywhere to go?' asked Logan as they walked him through reception to the door.

'Staying with my mother. The court said I have to, while I do my community service.' His shoulders sagged even further.

Insch patted him on the back. 'It's still raining; I can get a patrol car to give you a lift if you like?'

Martin Strichen shuddered. 'Said she'd kill me if she saw another police car outside the house.'

'OK. If you're sure.' Insch extended his hand and Strichen shook it, his huge paw engulfing the inspector's. 'And, Martin,' he looked into the lad's troubled hazel eyes, 'thank you.'

Logan and Insch stood at the window, watching Martin Strichen disappear into the rainy afternoon. Only four o'clock and it was already dark outside.

'When he was on the stand,' said Logan, 'he swore he'd kill Moir-Farquharson.'

'Really?' Insch sounded thoughtful.

'You think he'll try something?'

A smile broke across the inspector's face. 'Let's hope so.'

There were no smiles in interview room number three. It was packed to the gunwales with DI Insch, DS McRae, a damp WPC, and Duncan Nicholson. The tapes in the recording unit whirred away to themselves, the red light on the video camera winking away in the corner of the room.

Insch leaned forward and smiled the kind of smile crocodiles reserve for sick wildebeest. 'Sure you don't just want to come clean, Mr Nicholson?' he asked. 'Save us all a lot of trouble. You just cough to it all and tell us what you've done with Peter Lumley's body.'

But Nicholson just ran a hand across his shaved head, making scratching noises as he wiped the sweat away. He looked awful– shaking, sweating, arms wrapped around himself, eyes darting from Logan to Insch to the door.

Insch popped open a clear plastic wallet and pulled out a photo of a little boy on a tricycle. The child was in what looked like a back garden, the strut of a whirly washing line visible between an out-of-focus towel and a pair of jeans. Insch held up the photo with the image facing away from him so he could read the name in biro on the back. 'So tell me, Mr Nicholson, who's Luke Geddes?'

Nicholson licked his lips and darted a nervous glance at the door, the wet WPC, everywhere but the child on the bike.

'Is he one of your little victims, Nicholson? Next on your list for picking up, killing and screwing? No? What about this one—' Insch dug another photo out of the wallet, a little blond boy in his school uniform, walking down a street alone. 'Stir any memories? Stir anything else? Get you hard, does it?' He pulled out another photo. 'What about this one?' Little boy sitting on the back seat of a car, looking scared. 'This your car? Looks like a Volvo to me.'

'I didn't do anything!'

'Bollocks you didn't. You're a lying wee scumbag and I am going to send your arse to jail till you die.'

Nicholson swallowed hard.

'We have some other photographs,' said Logan. 'Would you like to see them, Mr Nicholson?' He turned over a manila folder and took out the pictures of David Reid's post mortem.

'Oh God . . .' Nicholson went grey.

'You remember little David Reid, don't you, Mr Nicholson? The three-year-old you kidnapped, strangled and raped?'

'No!'

'Surely you remember him? You went back for bits of him didn't you? With a pair of secateurs?'

'No! God, no! I didn't do it! I only found him! I didn't touch him!' He grabbed at the table as if he were about to fall off the floor and slam into the ceiling. 'I didn't do anything!'

'I don't believe you, Duncan.' Insch gave his crocodile smile again. 'You are a filthy wee shite and I am going to put you away. And when you're up in Peterhead Prison you're going to find out what happens to people like you. People who fiddle with kids.'

'I didn't do anything!' Tears streamed down Nicholson's face. 'I swear I didn't do anything!'

A half hour later DI Insch suspended the interview, using the excuse of a 'comfort break'. They left Duncan Nicholson in the interview room with the soggy WPC and strolled back to the main incident room. Nicholson was a wreck, sobbing, wailing, trembling. Insch had put the fear of God into the man and now wanted him to stew in his own juices.

Logan and Insch passed the time drinking coffee, eating fizzy jelly shapes and talking about the dead girl they'd dug out of Roadkill's steading. The teams had been back up there all day, working their way through the piles of dead things, finding nothing.

Logan opened his folder again, taking out a school photograph of David Reid – a happy-looking lad with slightly squint teeth and a mop of hair that no amount of combing would tame.

Nothing like the swollen, dark, rotting face in his post mortem photos. 'You still think he did it?' he asked.

'Roadkill?' Insch shrugged and chewed. 'Doesn't look likely any more, does it? Not with laughing boy up there, with his collection of kiddie pics. Mind you, maybe they've got some sort of paedophile ring thing going.' He scowled. 'That'd be great, wouldn't it? A whole bunch of the sick bastards out there.'

'None of the kids in Nicholson's photos are naked, though. Nothing smutty.'

Insch raised an eyebrow. 'What, you think they're just artistic?'

'No. You know what I mean. It's not kiddie porn, is it? It's bloody sinister and creepy, but it's not porn.'

'Maybe Nicholson doesn't like to look at them that way. Maybe this is just his selection process. Follow some kids, take some pictures, pick a lucky winner for the paedophile sweepstakes.' He made a gun with his fingers and picked off an imaginary child. 'Gets his kiddie porn first hand, in the flesh. Real and immediate.'

Logan wasn't convinced, but he kept his mouth shut.

At last a PC stuck his head round the door and told them a Mr Moir-Farquharson wanted to see them. And was going to make himself a pain in everyone's backside until he had. Insch pursed his lips, thought about it, and finally asked the

PC to show Sandy the Snake into a detention room.

'What do you think Hissing Sid wants?' asked Logan as the PC left.

Insch grinned. 'A whinge, a moan . . . Who cares? We get to poke fun at the wee shite while he's in pain.' He rubbed his hands together. 'Sometimes, Logan my lad, God smiles on us.'

Sandy Moir-Farquharson was waiting for them in a ground-floor detention room. He didn't look very happy. There was a thin white plaster crossing the, now squint, bridge of his nose and there were dark circles beneath his eyes. If they were lucky those bags would settle into a pair of beautiful black eyes.

His briefcase was sat in the middle of the table in front of him and he drummed his fingers impatiently on the leather surface, glowering at Insch and Logan as they entered.

'Mr "Far-Quar-Son",' said the inspector. 'How nice to see you up and about again.'

Sandy the Snake scowled at him. 'You let him go,' he said in a low, threatening voice.

'That's right. He made a statement and has been bailed to return here on Monday at four.'

'He broke my nose!' The words were punctuated with a fist, slammed down on the tabletop, making the briefcase jump.

'Oh, it's not that bad Mr Far-Quar-Son. In fact it lends you a rugged, manly air. Doesn't it, Sergeant?'

Logan kept his face straight and said that it did.

Sandy frowned, but couldn't tell if they were taking the piss or not. 'Really?' he said at last.

'Yes,' said Insch, poker-faced. 'Someone should have broken your nose a long time ago.'

The lawyer's frown became a scowl. 'You do know that someone's been sending me death threats? That someone threw a bucket of blood over me?'

'Yes.'

'And that this Martin Strichen has form for violence?'

'Now, now Mr Far-Quar-Son, Mr Strichen was in police custody when you were attacked with that blood. And we've analysed your death threats. There are at least four people sending the letters and none of them were postmarked Craiginches Prison. So it's probably not Mr Strichen.' He smiled. 'But if you like we could take you into protective custody? I have a number of lovely cells downstairs. A couple of throw cushions, some flowers, it'll be just like home!'

A silent scowl was the only reply he got.

Insch beamed. 'Well, if you'll excuse us, Mr Far-Quar-Son, we have real police business to attend to.' He stood and motioned for Logan to do the same. 'But if anyone makes good on any of those death threats, you make sure and give me a call. DS McRae will show you out.' His smile widened. 'Try and keep him from stealing the silverware, Logan: you know what these lawyers are like.'

Logan walked the lawyer all the way to the front door.

'You know,' said Sandy, scowling at the rain hammering down out of the ash-coloured sky. 'I have children too. The way that fat bastard goes on, you'd think I lived to put perverts back on the streets.'

Logan raised an eyebrow. 'You got Gerald Cleaver off.'

The lawyer buttoned his coat. 'No I didn't.'

'Yes you did! You picked the bloody case to pieces!'

Moir-Farquharson turned and looked Logan in the eye. 'If the case had been solid I couldn't have picked it apart. I didn't let Cleaver off: you did.'

'But—'

'Now if you'll excuse me, officer, I have other matters to attend to.'

Back in the interview room Duncan Nicholson was fidgeting as if someone had stuck a mains cable up his bum. His shirt was drenched with sweat and his eyes roamed the room in perpetual motion, never settling on one thing for more than a moment.

Logan went back to the seat nearest the tape machine and got the thing ready to start recording again.

'I . . . I want protective custody!' said Nicholson,

before Logan had managed to press the record buttons.

'Craiginches secure enough for you?' asked Insch. 'Just till you go to Peterhead of course.'

'No! Like on the films: protective custody. Somewhere safe . . .' He scrubbed at his sweat-drenched face. 'They'll kill me if they find out I've talked!' His bottom lip trembled and for a moment Logan thought he was going to dissolve into tears again.

Insch dug his packet of fizzy shapes out and stuffed a couple into his mouth. 'No promises,' he said around a mouthful of orange-and-straw-berry dinosaurs. 'Start the tape, Sergeant.'

Nicholson hung his head, staring fixedly at his hands, trembling away on the tabletop in front of him. 'I . . . I've been working for some bookies, moneylenders, you know . . .' His voice cracked and he had to take a deep breath before he could go on. 'Kinda like a debt control researcher, you know: I follow people who won't pay up. Take photographs of them and their families. I . . . I print them out at home and give the pictures to the people they owe money to.' He drooped even further in his seat. 'The bookies use the pictures to threaten them. Encourage them to pay up.'

Insch curled his lip. 'Your mum and dad must be so proud!'

A tear ran down Nicholson's cheek and he wiped it away with the back of his sleeve. 'It's no illegal to take photos of people! That's all I did. Nothing else! I didn't touch any kids!'

DI Insch snorted. 'What a load of bollocks!' He leaned forward in his chair, planting his huge fists on the table. 'I want to know what you were doing in a ditch in the Bridge of Don with the mutilated body of a three-year-old boy. I want to know why you had an envelope full of cash and jewellery.' He stood. 'You're a dirty wee shite, Nicholson. You deserve to go down for the rest of your miserable little life. You can stay here and lie all you want; I'm going to speak to the Procurator Fiscal. Get him all fired up to nail your arse to the wall. Interview suspended at—'

'I slipped.' Nicholson was in floods of tears, the panic clear in his eyes. 'Please! I slipped!'

Logan sighed. 'You told us that already. What were you doing there?'

'I . . . I was on a job.' Nicholson stared into Logan's eyes, and Logan knew they'd broken him.

'Go on.'

'I was on a job. Little old lady. Widow. Keeps a bit of cash in the house. Some silver. Bit of jewellery?'

'So you ripped her off?'

Nicholson shook his head, teardrops falling like diamonds to explode against the dirty Formica tabletop. 'Didn't get that far. I was out of my face. Way too stoned to do a house. Been keeping the stuff I nicked under a tree on the bank above the river. You know. Keeping it out of the way in case you lot come round and search the house.' He shrugged, his voice becoming more and more of a mumble. 'I was rat-arsed. Wanted to count it before I did the old lady's house. It was pissing with rain. Slipped and fell all the way down the bank. What, twenty foot? In the dark, in the bloody rain. Ripped my jacket, jeans, nearly cracked my head open on a big fuckin' rock. Ended up in the ditch. Tried to pull myself out with this big dod of chipboard, only it's loose. It moves and there's this thing bobbing about in the water.' He started to sob. 'First I'm thinking it's a dog, you know, a bull terrier, or something . . . 'Cos . . . 'cos it's all black. So I'm about to get the hell out of there when I see this shiny thing, sparkling in the rain. You know, like a silver chain or something . . .' He shuddered. 'I think it's one of mine. I'm so fuckin' wrecked I think it's part of my stash. So I go to pick it up and the thing rolls over. And it's a dead kid. And I scream and I scream and I scream . . .'

Logan leaned forward. 'What happened then?'

'I got the fuck out of there quick as I could. Straight home. Into the shower, try to wash that filthy dead water off me. Called the police.'

And that's where I came in, thought Logan. 'What about the thing?' he asked.

'Eh?'

'The shiny thing you found on the body. What was it? Where is it?'

'Tin foil. It was just a bloody bit of tin foil.'

Insch glowered at him. 'I want the names of all the poor sods you've robbed. I want the loot. All of it!' He looked down at the pile of photographs in their clear plastic wallet. 'And I want the names of all the bookies you take photos for. And if anyone in these photographs has been hurt, and I don't care if it's just falling off their bicycle, I'm going to charge you with conspiracy to commit assault. Understand?'

Nicholson buried his head in his hands.

'Well,' said Insch with a generous smile, 'thank you for assisting us with our enquiries, Mr Nicholson. Logan, be a good lad and escort our guest here to his cell. Something south-facing with a view and a balcony.'

Nicholson cried all the way.

26

The preliminary forensic report came in just after six. It wasn't good. There was nothing tying Duncan Nicholson to David Reid other than the fact that he'd found the body. And he had a cast iron alibi for the time Peter Lumley went missing. Insch had dispatched two PCs to where Nicholson claimed to be hiding his stash. They came back with their patrol car's boot full of stolen property. It was beginning to look as if Nicholson was telling the truth.

So that meant all bets were back on Roadkill. That still didn't sit well with Logan. He couldn't see the man as a paedophile killer, even if he did keep a dead girl in one of his outbuildings.

In the end DI Insch called a halt to proceedings. 'It's time to go home,' he said. 'We've got everyone banged up, they'll all still be there come Monday morning.'

'Monday?'

Insch nodded. 'Yes, Monday. Logan, you have

my permission to take Sunday off. Observe the Sabbath. Go watch the footie, drink beer, eat crisps, have some fun.' He stopped and gave a sly smile. 'Maybe take a nice WPC to dinner?'

Logan blushed and kept his gob shut.

'Whatever. I don't want to see you back here till Monday morning.'

The rain had stopped by the time Logan left Force Headquarters. The desk sergeant had cornered him with another three messages from Peter Lumley's stepfather who was still convinced they could find his child. Logan tried to lie to him, tell him it was all going to be all right, but he couldn't. So he promised to call as soon as he heard anything. There was nothing else he could do.

The night had turned from chilly to bitterly cold, a thin dusting of frost glittering on the pavements. As Logan stepped out onto Union Street his breath hung about him in a cloud. It was Baltic.

For a Saturday night the streets were strangely silent. Logan didn't fancy going back to his empty flat. Not yet. So he went to Archibald Simpson's instead.

The pub was crowded with noisy groups of youngsters wrapping themselves around pitchers of cocktails, keeping out the cold by getting as pissed as possible as quickly as possible. Come chucking out time there would be vomiting, a bit of fighting and, for some, a trip to the cells. Or maybe A&E.

'Oh to be young and stupid again,' he muttered,

squeezing his way through the throng to the long, wooden bar.

The snatches of conversation he heard on the way were predictable enough. A bit of boasting about how wrecked someone was last night and how much more wrecked they were going to get tonight. But underneath it all there was another theme. The topics of alcohol and sexual prowess were being challenged by Gerald Cleaver getting off scot-free.

Logan stood at the bar, waiting for one of the frayed-looking Australians to serve him, listening to a fat man in a bright yellow shirt holding forth to a lanky, bearded bloke in T-shirt and waistcoat. Cleaver was scum. How could the police have screwed up so badly the sicko got away with it? It was obvious Cleaver was guilty, what with all these children turning up dead. And there they were letting a known paedophile back on the streets!

Little and Large weren't the only ones on the 'stupid police' rant. Logan could hear at least half a dozen others banging on about the same topic. Didn't they know this was where most of Aberdeen's off-duty policemen drank? A lot of the dayshift would be in here, having a pint after work. Bemoaning Cleaver's release. Spending some of that overtime they were all getting.

When he finally managed to get served Logan took his pint of Stella and went for a wander through the other sections of the huge pub, looking for someone he knew well enough to talk to. He smiled and waved at clumps of PCs, only vaguely recognizing them out of uniform. In the far corner he spotted a familiar figure wreathed in cigarette smoke, surrounded by depressed looking detective sergeants and constables. She threw her head back and poured another lungful of smoke into the cloud above her head. As she came back down her eyes locked on Logan and she gave him a lopsided smile.

Logan groaned: she'd seen him. Now he had to go over.

A DC shoogled over, making room for Logan and his pint at the small table. Above their heads a television burbled away quietly to itself, local adverts for garages, chip shops and double-glazing, filling the space between programmes.

'Lazarus,' said DI Steel, the word coming out slightly slurred through a haze of cigarette smoke. 'How you doing, Lazarus? You made Chief Inspector yet?'

He should have never sat down here. He should have grabbed a pizza across the road and gone home. He forced some lightness into his voice and said, 'Not yet. Maybe Monday.'

'Monday?' The inspector laughed like a drain, rocking back and forth with fag ash spilling from her cigarette down the front of the DC who'd shoogled. '"Maybe Monday". Priceless . . .' She cast an eye over the glass-crowded tabletop and frowned. 'Drink!' she said, digging an old leather wallet from an inside pocket and handing it to the ash-covered DC. 'Constable, I want you to get another round. People are dying of thirst here!'

'Yes, ma'am.'

'Whiskies all round!' DI Steel slapped the tabletop. 'And make them doubles!'

The detective constable headed off to the bar, taking the inspector's wallet with him.

Steel leaned closer to Logan, dropping her voice into a conspiratorial whisper. 'Between you and me, I think he's a bit drunk.' She sat back and beamed at him. 'You know, with Inschy getting kicked for the Roadkill pantomime thing and Cleaver going free, there's bound to be at least one inspector's job coming up!'

Logan didn't have anything to say to that, but DI Steel's face fell.

'Sorry, Lazarus.' She dropped the cigarette and ground it into the wooden floor. 'It's been a shitty day.'

'It's not your fault they let Cleaver go. If anyone's to blame, it's Hissing Bloody Sid.'

'I'll drink to that!' she said, and did, downing a large whisky in a single gulp.

A familiar-looking DC on the opposite side of the table was staring up at the television above their heads. He grabbed the inspector by the arm. 'It's coming on!'

Logan and DI Steel twisted round in their seats as the opening titles of the local news flickered across the screen and the noise level in the pub took a sudden dip, as every off-duty police man and woman in the place turned to face the nearest television.

Someone a lot less attractive than she could have been was speaking seriously into the camera from behind her news desk. The volume wasn't loud enough to pick out any real words, but a photo of Gerald Cleaver's face appeared over her left shoulder. Then the scene changed to an exterior shot of Aberdeen Sheriff Court. The crowd were thrusting their placards in the air and suddenly a woman in her mid-forties filled the screen, clutching her 'DEATH TO PEDIPHILE SCUM!!!' placard with pride. She banged her gums with righteous fury for all of fifteen seconds, not one word of it audible in the crowded pub, before being replaced by another shot of the courthouse through the crowd. The big glass doors were opening.

'Here we go!' said DI Steel with glee.

Sandy Moir-Farquharson appeared through the doors and proceeded to read his client's statement. The camera zoomed in, just in time to see a figure lunge from the crowd and smack his fist into Sandy the Snake's face.

A huge cheer went up from the pub.

The newsreader's concerned and serious face reappeared, said something, and then the punch was shown again.

Another huge cheer.

And then it was something about traffic on the

Dyce to Newmacher road and everyone went happily back to their drinks.

DI Steel had a misty-eyed smile on her face as she gulped another large whisky. 'Wasn't that the most beautiful thing you've ever seen?'

Logan agreed that it was pretty damn good.

'You know,' said Steel, lighting up another cigarette, 'I would love to shake that kid's hand. Hell, I'd even be tempted to go straight for a night. What a star!'

Logan tried not to form a mental picture of DI Steel and Martin Strichen going at it like knives, but failed. To take his mind off it he glanced back up at the television. Now it was showing a full-screen photo of Peter Lumley, missing since last Tuesday. Ginger hair, freckles and smile. Cut to an exterior of Roadkill's farm. Then to a press conference with the Chief Constable looking stern and committed.

The good mood slowly ebbed out of Logan as the pictures flickered in front of him. Peter was lying dead somewhere and Logan had the nasty feeling they still hadn't got the man responsible. No matter what DI Insch thought.

And then it was adverts. A garage in Bieldside, a dress shop in Rosemount and a government road safety thing. Logan watched in silence as the car screeched to a halt, but not before striking the boy crossing the road. The kid was small, the grille and bumper catching him in the side, making his legs flail out as he pin-wheeled into the bonnet, cracking his head against the metal before sailing off to smack into the tarmac. It was in slow motion, every impact horribly clear and choreographed. The legend 'KILL YOUR SPEED, NOT A CHILD' blazed across the screen.

Logan stared up at the screen with a growing look of pain on his face. 'Son of a bitch.'

They'd got it wrong.

It took till eight o'clock to get everyone gathered in the morgue. DI Insch, Logan and Dr Isobel MacAlister, who looked even less happy at being dragged back into work than the inspector, being dressed up to the nines in a long black dress, cut low at the front. Not that Logan was afforded much in the way of gratuitous skin to ogle. Isobel had pulled a luminous orange fleece over the evening dress, hands stuffed deep in the pockets, trying to keep warm in the cold, antiseptic morgue.

She'd been at the theatre. 'I hope this is important,' she said, giving Logan a look which made it clear that nothing could be more important than an evening with her bit of rough at Scottish National Opera's new production of La Bohème.

Insch was dressed in jeans and a tatty blue sweatshirt. It was the first time Logan had ever seen him out of his work suit, not counting his pantomime villain outfit. He scowled as Logan apologized for dragging them all down here at this time on a Saturday night. Again.

'OK,' said Logan, selecting the refrigerated drawer that held the remains of the little girl they'd found at Roadkill's steading. Gritting his teeth, he pulled it open, staggering back as the putrid smell fought against the room's antiseptic tang. 'Right,' he said, his face creased up, trying hard to breathe exclusively through his mouth. 'We know the girl died from blunt trauma—'

'Of course she did!' snapped Isobel. 'I told you that in my post mortem report. The fractures to the front and back of her skull would have caused massive brain damage and death.'

'I know,' said Logan, pulling the X-rays out from the case file and holding them up to the light. 'You see this?' he asked, pointing at the ribs.

'Broken ribs.' Isobel glared. 'Did you drag me out of the theatre to show me things I bloody well told you in the first place, Sergeant?' The last word came out dripping in venom.

Logan sighed. 'Look, we all thought the injuries were caused by Roadkill beating the girl—'

'The damage is consistent with a beating. I said so in the post mortem! How much more time do we have to spend going over this? You said you had new evidence!'

Logan took a deep breath and stacked the X-rays end on end so they formed the skeleton of a complete child. Broken hip, leg, ribs, fractured skull. The image was less than four feet tall. Dropping down onto his knees, Logan held the skeleton image so that its feet were touching the floor. 'Look at the ribs,' he said, 'look how far they are off the ground.'

DI Insch and Isobel did. Neither of them looked impressed.

'And?'

'What if the damage isn't down to a beating?'

'Oh come off it!' Isobel said. 'This is pathetic! She was beaten to death!'

'Look how far the broken ribs are off the ground,' Logan said again.

Nothing.

'Car,' said Logan, moving the X-rays like a macabre shadow puppet. 'The first point of impact is the hip.' He twisted the image around the waist, lifting it as he turned the top half clockwise. 'The ribs hit the top edge of the radiator.' He moved the X-ray girl again, bending the head hard right. 'Left hand side of the skull smacks into the bonnet. Car slams on the brakes.' He pulled the X-ray upright and rotated it back towards the morgue's floor. 'She hits the tarmac, the right leg snaps. Back of her head caves in as it hits the deck.' He laid the X-rays on the floor at his feet.

His audience looked on in silence for a full minute before Insch said, 'So how come she ends up in Roadkill's house of horrors then?'

'Bernard Duncan Philips, AKA Roadkill, comes along with his shovel and his wheelie-cart and does what he always does.'

Insch looked at him as if he'd just plucked the dead child's rotting corpse from its refrigerated drawer and proceeded to do the Dashing White Sergeant round the room with it. 'It's a dead girl! Not a bloody rabbit!'

'It's all the same to him.' Logan looked down at the contents of the drawer, feeling a heavy weight pressing down between his ribs. 'Just another dead thing scraped off the road. She was in steading number two. He'd already filled one building.'

Insch opened his mouth. Looked at Logan. Looked at Isobel. And back to the X-rays lying on the floor. 'Bastard,' he said at last.

Isobel stood in silence, her hands thrust deep into the pockets of her bright orange fleece, an unhappy expression on her face.

'Well?' Logan asked.

She drew herself up to her full height and, with a voice like frozen bleach, agreed that the injuries were consistent with the scenario described. That it was impossible to tell what order the injuries occurred in, because of the state of decay. That the injuries had looked consistent with a severe beating. That she'd made the best call she could, based on the state of the body. That she couldn't be expected to be clairvoyant.

'Bastard,' said Insch again.

'He didn't kill her.' Logan slid the refrigerated door shut, the dull clang echoing off the cold, white tiles. 'We're back to square one.'

Bernard Duncan Philips' 'appropriate adult' turned up after an hour and a half of frantic telephone calls, looking like something the cat dragged in. It was the ex-schoolteacher, Lloyd Turner, again, smelling strongly of mint, as if he'd been drinking alone and didn't want anyone to know about it. Ten o'clock shadow blurring the edges of his thin moustache. He fussed with his papers as Logan went through the standard details for the tape.

'We want you,' said DI Insch, now dressed in his spare suit, 'to tell us about the dead girl, Bernard.'

Roadkill's eyes darted round the room and the ex-teacher gave a long-suffering sigh.

'We have been over this already, Inspector.' His voice was old and tired. 'Bernard's not well. He needs help, not incarceration.'

Insch screwed his face up. 'Bernard,' said Insch with careful deliberation, 'you found her, didn't you?'

Lloyd Turner's eyebrows shot up his head. 'Found her?' he asked, looking at the stinking, tatty figure sitting next to him with barely concealed surprise. 'Did you find her, Bernard?'

Roadkill shifted in his seat and stared down at his hands. Small, burgundy clots covered his fingers like parasites. The skin was raw around the fingernails where he'd been picking and chewing his hands into submission. He didn't even look up, and his voice was small and broken. 'Road. Found her on the road. Three hedgehogs, two crows, one seagull, one tabby cat, two long-haired cats, black-and-white, one girl, nine rabbits, one roe deer . . .' His eyes misted up, his voice becoming rough, 'My beautiful dead things . . .' A sparkling tear escaped his eye, clearing the long eyelashes, to run down the weathered skin of his cheek and into his beard.

Insch folded his arms and settled back in his seat. 'So you took the little girl back to your "collection".'

'Always take them home. Always.' Sniff. 'Can't just throw them out like garbage. Not dead things. Not things that used to be alive inside.'

And with that Logan was forced to remember a single leg sticking out of a bin-bag in the middle of the council tip. 'Did you see anything else?' he asked. 'When you picked her up. Did you see anything: a car, or a lorry or anything like that?'

Roadkill shook his head. 'Nothing. Just the dead girl, lying at the side of the road. All broken and bleeding and still warm.'

The hairs went up on the back of Logan's neck. 'Was she alive? Bernard, was she still alive when you found her?'

The ratty figure sank down against the table, resting his head in his arms on the chipped Formica top. 'Sometimes the things get hit and they don't die right away. Sometimes they wait for me to come and watch over them.'

'Oh Christ.'

They put Roadkill back in his cell and reconvened in the interview room: Logan, Insch and Roadkill's appropriate adult.

'You do know you're going to have to release him, don't you?' said Mr Turner.

Logan raised an eyebrow, but Insch said: 'Your arse I will.'

The ex-schoolteacher sighed and settled back into one of the uncomfortable plastic seats. 'The most you have on him is failing to report an accident and the illegal disposal of a body.' He rubbed at his face. 'And we all know the Crown Prosecution Service isn't going to take this for criminal trial. One good psychiatric report and the whole thing goes nowhere. He hasn't done anything wrong. Not by his reckoning anyway. The girl was just another dead thing found at the side of the road. He was doing his job.'

Logan tried not to nod his head in agreement. Insch wouldn't have appreciated it.

The inspector ground his teeth and stared at Mr Turner, who shrugged. 'I'm sorry, but he's not guilty. If you don't release him I'm going to go to the press. There are still enough cameras out there to get this all over the morning news.'

'We can't let him go,' said Insch. 'Someone will rip his head off if we do.'

'So you admit that he's done nothing wrong then?' There was something distinctly patronizing about the way Turner said it, as if he was back in the classroom again and DI Insch had just been caught behind the bike sheds.

The inspector scowled. 'Listen, sunshine: I ask the leading questions in here, not you.' He rummaged in his pockets for something sweet and came up empty-handed. 'With Cleaver going free, the great, good and stupid of the community are on the lookout for anyone even slightly dodgy. Your boy had a dead girl in his shed. He's going to be top of their list.'

'Then you'll have to provide him with protective custody. We'll speak to the press: get them to understand that Bernard is innocent. That you've decided to drop all the charges.'

Logan cut in. 'No we haven't! He's still guilty of hiding the body!'

'Sergeant,' said Mr Turner with condescending patience, 'you have to understand how this works. If you try to take any of this to court, you're going to end up losing. The Procurator Fiscal won't stand for another cock-up. He's got enough egg on his face with the Cleaver fiasco. Mr Philips will go free. Question is: how much tax payers' money do you want to waste getting there?'

Logan and DI Insch stood in the empty incident room, looking down at the growing bustle of activity in the car park. Mr Turner had been as good as his word. He was standing in front of the cameras, enjoying his moment in the spotlight. Telling the world that Bernard Duncan Philips had been absolved of all charges, that the system worked.

The ex-teacher had been right: the Procurator Fiscal didn't want to touch the case with a stick.

And the Chief Constable wasn't that happy about it either. So Roadkill was off to stay at a safe house somewhere in Summerhill.

'What do you think?' asked Logan, watching as yet another camera crew joined the throng. It was almost eleven o'clock, but still they came.

Insch glowered down at the assembled press. 'I'm screwed, that's what I think. First the bloody panto thing, then Cleaver gets away with twelve years of systematic child abuse, and now Roadkill's back on the streets. How long did we have him banged up? Forty-eight hours? Maybe sixty at a push. They're going to eat me alive . . .'

'How about we go to the media too? I could have a word with Miller. See if he can put our side across?'

Insch gave a sad laugh. 'Small-town Journalist Saves Police Inspector's Career from the Toilet?' He shook his head. 'Don't see it coming off, do you?'

'Worth a shot though.'

In the end, Insch had to admit he had nothing to lose.

'After all,' said Logan, 'we've just prevented a serious miscarriage of justice. Surely that's got to count for something?'

'Aye. It should.' The inspector's shoulders sagged. 'But if it wasn't Roadkill and it wasn't Nicholson, then we've still got a killer out there, picking off children. And we haven't got a bloody clue who it is.'

27

By the time Logan climbed out of bed and into the shower, Sunday was tearing at the windows of his flat with wintry fingers. Snow, coming down in small icy flakes, whipped back and forth in the gusting wind. It was cold, it was dark, and it was no longer the day of rest he'd been promised.

Struggling into a grey suit, with matching expression, Logan doddered around his warm home, trying to put off the moment when he'd have to step out into the bloody awful weather. And then the phone went: the inimitable Colin Miller looking for his exclusive.

Logan grumbled his way down the communal stairs to the building's front door. Half a ton of flying ice tried to get in as he struggled his way out into the frigid morning. The snow attacked him like frozen razorblades, slashing at his exposed face and hands, making his cheeks and ears sting.

The day was dark as a lawyer's soul.

Miller's flash motor was waiting for him at the

kerb, the interior lights on, something classical blaring out through the glass as the reporter hunched over a broadsheet newspaper. Logan slammed the apartment door shut, not caring if he woke his neighbours. Why the hell should he be the only one up and about on a crappy day like this? He slipped and slithered his way around the car to the passenger seat, bringing a flurry of icy, white flakes with him.

'Watch the leather!' Miller had to shout over the opera blaring from the car's stereo. He cranked down the volume a bit as the thin crust of snow slowly defrosted on Logan's heavy overcoat.

'What, no rowies today?' asked Logan, wiping ice out of his hair before it could turn into a frigid trickle down the back of his neck.

'Think I'm goin' tae let you spill greasy crumbs all over my nice new motor? This interview goes well an' I'll buy yous an Egg McMuffin. OK?'

Logan told him he'd sooner eat a deep-fried turd. 'And how come you can afford a flash car like this? Thought all you reporters lived in penury.'

'Aye, well,' Miller shrugged and pulled away from the kerb. 'I did this bloke a favour once. Didn't publish a story . . .'

Logan raised an eyebrow, but Miller wouldn't say any more.

Traffic was light at this time on a Sunday morning, but the weather slowed what little there was down to a crawl. Miller slotted his car in behind a once-white truck, the top covered with a foot of icy snow, the rest of it covered with three inches of dirt. Some wag had scrawled the usual 'I WISH MY WIFE WAS THIS DIRTY' and 'WASH ME' in the grime. The writing glowed in Miller's headlights as they slowly made their way across town to Summerhill.

The safe house didn't look any different to the others in the street: just another concrete box with a small garden out front, buried under a growing blanket of white. A sagging willow tree stood forlorn in the middle, bent under the weight of snow and ice.

'Right,' said Miller, parking behind a battered Renault. 'Let's go get us an exclusive.' The reporter's attitude towards Roadkill had changed dramatically since Logan told him about the road accident. Bernard Duncan Philips was no longer to be strung up by his balls until they popped. Now he was a victim of society's disposable culture, in which the mentally ill could be thrown out into the community to fend for themselves.

Bernard Duncan Philips was roused from his bed by a large, plainclothes policewoman and prodded downstairs to perform for the reporter. Miller's questioning technique was good, making Roadkill feel relaxed and important, while a snazzy digital recorder whirled silently in the middle of a coffee table that had seen better days. They went over his glittering academic career, ruined by his mother's ill health, then delicately tiptoed around the descent into mental illness and the death of Mrs Roadkill Senior, God rest her soul. There was nothing there Logan hadn't got from the files, so he spent his time drinking over-strong tea, poured from a cracked brown pot. And counting the roses on the wallpaper. And the blue silk bows. Between the pink stripes.

It wasn't until Miller got onto the subject of Lorna Henderson, the dead girl in steading number two, that Logan started paying attention again.

But, good though he was, Miller wasn't getting that much more out of his subject than DI Insch had. The whole topic made Roadkill twitchy. Agitated.

It wasn't right. They were *his* dead things. They were taking them away.

'Come on now, Bernard,' said the plainclothes WPC, womanning the teapot again. 'There's no need to get excited, is there?'

'My things. They're stealing my things!' He jumped to his feet, sending a plate of chocolate digestives clattering to the ground. A pair of wild eyes darted at Logan. 'You're a policeman! They're stealing my things!'

Logan tried not to sigh. 'They have to take them away, Bernard. You remember we came round with the man from the council? They were making people sick. Like your mum. Remember?'

Roadkill screwed up his eyes tight. Teeth gritted. Fists pressed hard against his forehead. 'I want to go home! They're my things!'

The large policewoman put down the teapot and made soothing noises, as if the grubby, ranting man was a small child with a skinned knee. 'Shoosh, shoosh,' she said, stroking Roadkill's arm with a plump hand covered in rings. 'It's all right. Everything will be all right. You'll be safe here with us. We won't let anything happen to you.'

Slowly, uncertainly, Bernard Duncan Philips sat back down on the edge of his seat, his left foot crunching a chocolate digestive to crumbs on the carpet.

But the interview went downhill from there. No matter how clever, or careful, Miller's questions were they still managed to upset Roadkill. And he just kept coming back to the same thing, time and time again: he wanted to go home: they were stealing his things.

Aberdeen beach was desolate and freezing. The North Sea raged, dark grey, between the whipping curtains of snow. The boom of granite-coloured waves smashing into the concrete beachfront punctuated the howling storm, sending spray twenty feet into the air, where the wind threw it against the shopfronts.

Most of the businesses hadn't bothered opening this morning. It wasn't as if there was going to be a lot of passing trade for the tourist shops, amusement arcades and ice-cream parlours. But Miller and Logan were ensconced at a window table in the Inversnecky Café, wolfing down smoky bacon butties and drinking strong coffee.

'Well that was a waste of bloody time,' said Miller, picking a rubber band of bacon fat from his roll. 'You should be buyin' me breakfast after that. No the other way around.'

'You must've got something!'

Miller shrugged and curled the fat into the unused ashtray. 'Aye: he's off his friggin' trolley. I got that loud and bloody clear. Mind you, no exactly news, is it?'

'I'm not looking for much,' said Logan. 'Just something that lets everyone know he didn't kill that little girl. He didn't do it so we had to let him go.'

The reporter wrapped himself around a large bite, chewing thoughtfully. 'Your bosses must be bricking it if they've asked you to come beggin' for a puff piece.'

Logan opened and shut his mouth.

Miller winked at him. 'It's OK, Laz, I can run with this. Give it the patented Colin Miller Midas Touch. We slap a copy of the X-rays on the front cover. Get the graphics department to knock us up some "kiddie gets smacked by Volvo" pictures. Bob's your uncle. But that's no going to come out till Monday. You see the telly this mornin'? They're havin' a field day. Your pantomime dame's going to be out of a job by then. Letting Roadkill go. Twice.'

'He didn't kill that kid.'

'That's no the point, Laz. The public sees all

396

these nasty things happenin': dead boys in ditches, dead lassies in bin-bags, children abducted left, right and centre. Cleaver goes free, even though we all know he did it. And now Roadkill's out too.' He ripped another bite from his buttie. 'As far as they're concerned he's guilty.'

'But he didn't do it!'

'No one gives a toss about the truth any more. You know that, Laz.'

Gloomily Logan had to admit that he did. They sat and ate in silence.

'So how's your other story coming?' he asked at last.

'Which one?'

'When you told me you were backing off Geordie No-Knees you said you had safer fish to fry.'

The reporter took a slurp of coffee. 'Oh aye. That.' Miller paused, gazing out through the window at the snow and the waves and the battling sea. 'No that well.' He lapsed into silence.

Logan let the pause go on for long enough to make sure the details weren't going to come out of their own accord. 'Well? What was it?'

'Hmm?' Miller dragged his attention back into the café. 'Oh right. There's this rumour that there's a bloke in the market for somethin' special. Somethin' no many people sell.'

'Drugs?'

The reporter shook his head. 'Nah. Livestock.'

Well that sounded bloody daft. 'What? Pigs and chickens and cows and things?'

'No that kind of livestock.'

Logan sat back in his seat and examined the taciturn reporter. His face, usually an open book, was closed and lined. 'So what kind of livestock is this buyer after?'

Miller shrugged.

'Difficult to tell. No one's sayin' bugger all. Nothin' that makes sense anyway. Maybe a woman, man, boy, girl . . .'

'You can't just buy people!'

The look Miller gave Logan was a mixture of pity and contempt. 'You sail up the Clyde in a banana skin? Course you can bloody buy people! Take a stroll down the right streets in Edinburgh and you can buy anythin' you like. Guns, drugs. Women too.' He leaned forward and dropped his voice to a whisper. 'Did I no tell you Malk the Knife imports tarts from Lithuania? What you think he does with them?'

'I thought he hired them out . . .'

Miller laughed sourly. 'Aye he does. Hires and sells. You get discount on the shop-soiled ones.'

The disbelieving look on Logan's face made him sigh. 'Look: most of the times it's pimps doin' the buyin'. One of your tarts pops an overdose so off you go to Malkie's Cash & Carry. Get yourself a replacement. One nearly-new Lithuanian whore at bargain basement prices.'

'Jesus!'

'Most of the poor bitches can't even speak English. They get bought, hooked on smack, hired out, used up and chucked back on the street when they're too skanky to turn a decent trick.'

They sat in silence, just the dull hiss of the cappuccino machine and the faint sounds of the storm outside filtering through the double-glazing.

Logan wasn't going back to the office. That's what he told himself when Miller dropped him off at the Castlegate. He was going to nip along to Oddbins, pick up a couple of bottles of wine, some beer, and then settle down in front of the fire in the flat. Book, wine, and a carryout for tea.

But he still found himself standing in the dreary front lobby of Force Headquarters, dripping melting snow onto the linoleum.

As usual there was a pile of messages from Peter Lumley's stepfather. Logan did his best not to think about them. It was Sunday: he wasn't even supposed to be here. And he couldn't face another of those desperate phone calls. So instead he sat at his desk staring at the picture of Geordie Stephenson. Trying to read something in those dead eyes.

Miller's tale of women for sale had set him thinking. Someone in Aberdeen wanted to buy a woman, and here was Geordie, representing one of the biggest importers of flesh in the country, up on business. Maybe not the same business – property not prostitution – but all the same . . .

'You really screwed up, didn't you, Geordie?' he told the morgue photograph. 'Come all the way up from Edinburgh to do a wee job and end up floating face down in the harbour with your knees hacked off. Couldn't even manage to bribe a member of the planning department. I wonder if you told your boss someone was interested in buying himself a woman? Cash. No questions asked.'

Geordie's post mortem report was still sitting on Logan's desk, unread. What with everything that had gone on this week, there just hadn't been time. He picked the manila folder off the tabletop and started to flick through it when his phone blared into life.

'Logan.'

'*Sergeant?*' It was DI Insch. '*Where are you?*'

'FHQ.'

'*Logan, don't you have a home to go to? Didn't I tell you to take a nice WPC out and show her a good time?*'

Logan smiled. 'Yes, sir. Sorry, sir.'

'*Well, it's too late for any of that now.*'

'Sir?'

'*Get your arse over to Seaton Park. I've just got the call: they've found Peter Lumley.*'

Logan's heart sank. 'I see.'

'*I'll be there in about . . . God, it's blowing a blizzard out here. Make it thirty minutes to be safe. Maybe forty. Keep it low profile, Sergeant. No blue lights, no sirens and no fuss. OK?*'

'Yes, sir.'

*

Seaton Park was a pretty place in the summer – wide banks of green grass, tall mature trees, a bandstand. People picnicked on the grass, played an impromptu game of football, made love beneath the bushes. Got mugged after dark. It wasn't a stone's throw away from Aberdeen University's student halls of residence, so there was a steady stream of naïve newcomers with money in their pockets.

Today it was like something out of *Dr Zhivago*. The sky hadn't lightened as day went on but just hung there, throwing snow down over everything.

Logan trudged across the park, trailing a PC wrapped up like an Eskimo behind him. The rotten sod was using Logan as a windbreak as they fought their way through the snow. Their goal was a low concrete building in the middle of the park, the walls on one side coated with a crust of white. The public loos were closed during the winter. Anyone caught short would have to make peecicles behind a bush. They went around the side, glad to get out of the bitter wind, to where the ladies' entrance was hidden behind a small recess.

The door was open, just a crack, the wood splintered and torn where a padlock was meant to keep it shut. Instead the big brass lock hung uselessly from its metal clasp. Logan pushed the door open and stepped into the female toilets.

It actually seemed colder in here than it had outside. A pair of uniform kept an eye on three well-wrapped-up children between the ages of six and ten, their breaths fogging the air. The kids looked excited and bored in turn.

One of the uniforms looked up from his charges. 'Cubicle number three.'

Logan nodded and went to take a look.

Peter Lumley wasn't alive any more. Logan knew it as soon as he opened the black-painted cubicle door. The child was lying on the floor, curled up around the bottom of the toilet, as if he were giving it a cuddle. The fiery red hair was dull and pale in the cold light, the freckles almost indiscernible against the waxy, blue-white skin. The little boy's T-shirt was pulled up, covering his face and arms, leaving the pale skin of his back and stomach exposed. He wasn't wearing any-thing else.

'You poor wee sod . . .'

Logan frowned, peering at the child's exposed body, unable to get any closer in case he contam-inated the crime scene. Peter Lumley wasn't like the little boy they'd found in the ditch. Peter Lumley was still anatomically intact.

The loos were getting a little crowded. Insch had turned up red-faced and swearing just after the duty doctor and the Identification Bureau. The IB lads had turned up, as instructed, in their own clothes, leaving the white van with all its gear in the car park next to St Machar's Cathedral where it wouldn't draw attention to itself.

As Insch stomped the snow off his boots, the

IB team and everyone else struggled into their white overalls, shivering in the frigid air and bitching about how cold it was.

'So what's the score?' asked Insch as the duty doctor peeled off his paper coveralls and tried to wash his hands in one of the sinks.

'The poor little lad's dead. Dunno how long for. He's pretty much frozen solid. Weather like this plays merry hell with the old rigor mortis.'

'Cause of death?'

The doctor wiped his hands dry on the inside of his fleecy jacket. 'You'll have to get confirmation from the Ice Queen, but it looks like ligature strangulation to me.'

'Same as last time.' Insch sighed and dropped his voice so the children who weren't dead couldn't hear him. 'Any sign of sexual assault?'

The doctor nodded and Insch sighed again.

'Righty ho.' The doctor wrapped and tucked and zipped himself into his many-layered thermal insulation. 'If you don't need me any more, I'll bugger off somewhere warmer. Like Siberia.'

With death declared the IB team set about collecting everything they could get their glove-covered hands on. Lifting fibres, dusting for prints. Photographer clicking and whirring away, video operator recording everything and everyone. The only thing they didn't do was move the body. Not one of them wanted to incur the wrath of the pathologist. Isobel had got herself quite a reputation since Logan had returned to the force.

'One week today, isn't it?' asked Insch as they stood against the wall and watched the Identification Bureau work. Logan admitted that it was. Insch dug a packet of jelly babies from his coat pocket and offered them around. 'What a great bloody week it's been too,' he said, chewing. 'You thinking of taking a holiday anytime soon? Let the crime statistics get back to normal again?'

'Ha bloody ha.' Logan stuck his hands in his pockets and tried not to think about how Peter Lumley's stepfather would look when they told him what they'd found.

Insch nodded at the three children, slowly turning blue in the crowded ladies lavatory. 'What about them?'

Logan shrugged. 'They say they were out making snowmen. One of them needed a wee, so they came in here, and that's when they found the body.' He looked over at them: two girls of eight and ten and a boy, the youngest at six. Brother and sisters. They all had the same ski-jump nose and wide brown eyes.

'Poor kids,' said Insch.

'Poor kids, my arse,' said Logan. 'How do you think they got in here? Took an eight-inch screwdriver to the clasp on the door, wrenched the padlock clean off. A passing patrol caught them at it.' He pointed at the two frozen PCs. 'The little sods would have done a runner if these guys hadn't shown up and grabbed them.'

Insch switched his attention from the kids to

the two uniforms. 'A passing patrol? In the middle of Seaton Park? In this weather?' He frowned. 'Sound a bit far-fetched to you?'

Logan shrugged again. 'That's their story and they're sticking to it.'

'Hmmm . . .'

The PCs shifted uncomfortably under Insch's gaze.

'Think anyone saw the body being dumped?' he said at last.

'No. I don't.'

Insch nodded. 'Nah, me neither.'

'Because the body wasn't dumped: it was stored. The kids had to break in. The door was padlocked with the body inside. That means the killer put the padlock on. He thought the body was safely locked away. Ready for him to come back to, whenever he felt the urge. He's not claimed his trophy.'

An evil smile spread across the inspector's face. 'That means he's coming back. We've finally got a way to catch this bastard!'

And that's when Dr Isobel MacAlister arrived, stamping into the toilets in a thick woollen coat, a flurry of snow, and a foul mood. Standing in the entranceway, she took in the scene, her face falling even further into a scowl upon seeing Logan. It looked as if she was bearing a grudge: not only had Logan ruined her evening at the theatre, he'd proved her wrong about the child being beaten to death. And Isobel was *never* wrong.

'Inspector,' she said, completely blanking the man she used to sleep with. 'If we can make this quick?'

Insch pointed at cubicle number three and Isobel swept off to examine the body, her Wellington boots flapping and slapping as she walked.

'Is it just me,' whispered Insch, 'or did it suddenly just get colder in here?'

They broke the news to Peter Lumley's parents that evening. Mr and Mrs Lumley didn't say a word. As soon Logan and the Inspector appeared they knew. They just sat side by side on the sofa in silence, holding each other's hands as DI Insch intoned the fateful words.

Without saying a word Mr Lumley got up, picked his coat off the hook, and walked out.

His wife watched him go, waiting for the door to shut behind him, before finally bursting into tears. The Family Liaison Officer hurried over to offer her a shoulder to cry on.

Logan and Insch let themselves out.

28

The plan was simple. Everyone coming to, or going from, the murder scene would keep a low profile. The number of people visiting the lavatories would be kept to a minimum, the padlock refixed to the door. The body would be taken out in secret and a pair of PCs left behind to watch the loos. This would be done from the safety and warmth of a pool car, parked up out of the way, with a clear sight of the ladies. The relentless snow had wiped clean the morass of footprints around the toilets, making everything a smooth, rounded white, leaving no sign that anyone had ever been there. The three kids who had found the body would not be charged with breaking and entering, just so long as they kept their mouths shut. No one was to know that Peter Lumley's body had been found. The killer would come back with his scissors, looking to take his souvenir, and the PCs would arrest him. What could possibly go wrong?

Miller's puff-piece on the tragic life and times of Bernard Duncan Philips, AKA Roadkill, was relegated to page four, along with a bit on new tractors and a charity jumble sale. It was a good article, no matter how deeply it was buried in the paper. Miller had turned Roadkill into a sympathetic character, his mental health problems caused by the tragic death of his mother. An intelligent man, abandoned by society and making the best sense he could of the confusing world around him. It went a long way towards making Grampian Police look as if they knew what they were doing when they let him go.

And if that had been the only story Miller had written for the P&J that morning, everyone at Force Headquarters would have been a lot happier.

Miller's second story was spread across the front page under the banner headline: 'CHILD-KILLER STRIKES AGAIN! BOY'S BODY FOUND IN TOILET.'

'How the hell did he find out?' Insch slammed his fist down on the tabletop, making cups, papers and everyone in the briefing room jump.

The plan to catch the killer returning for his trophy was officially screwed up beyond repair. Every single gory detail was spread across the front page of the *Press and Journal* in tones of indignant outrage.

'That was the best chance we had of grabbing this bastard before he kills again!' Insch grabbed his copy of the paper, shaking with fury as he shoved the front page spread at them all. 'We could have caught him! Now some other kid is going to wind up dead because some stupid bastard couldn't keep their bloody mouth shut!'

He hurled the paper across the room. It spiralled through the air, exploding into a flurry of pages as it hit the far wall. Behind him, Inspector Napier stood in full dress uniform, looking like a ginger-haired Grim Reaper. He didn't say a word, just glared at them all from under his furrowed eyebrows as DI Insch fumed.

'I'll tell you what I'm going to do,' said Insch, digging in his pocket. He produced a thick, brown leather wallet, opened it and dragged out a handful of cash. 'First person who comes to me with a name, gets it.' He slapped the money down on the table.

There was a moment's silence.

Logan pulled out his own wallet and added all his cash to the inspector's pile.

And that started a stampede: uniform, detectives, sergeants all emptying their pockets and throwing their money down. By the time they'd finished there was a tidy amount sitting on the desk. It wasn't huge as rewards go, but it was heartfelt.

'All very nice,' said Insch with a wry smile, 'but we still don't know who the blabbermouth is.'

They filtered back to their seats and the

inspector watched them go with something approaching pride on his face. Napier's expression was less clear-cut: his eyes sweeping the room's occupants, looking for signs of guilt, focusing on Logan far too often for comfort.

'Right,' said Insch. 'Either there's a lying bastard in here who thinks chipping in lets them off the hook, or Miller's mole works for someone else. I'm hoping it's the latter.' The smile vanished from his face. 'Because if it is one of this team I will personally crucify them.' He plonked himself down on the edge of the desk. 'Sergeant McRae, hand out the assignments.'

Logan read the list of names, sending out search teams to comb through the snow-covered park. Other teams going door-to-door looking for anyone who might have seen the body being hidden. Everyone else was to follow up the numerous telephone calls from concerned citizens. Most of them had come in as soon as they heard Roadkill had been released. Amazing how many people suddenly remembered his wheelie-cart near where the kids went missing.

Finally the morning briefing wound down and everyone filtered out, glancing at the pile of money on the desk as they went, their faces as grim as the weather outside, until only Napier, Logan and DI Insch remained.

The inspector swept the money off the table and into a big brown envelope. Writing, 'BLOOD MONEY' on the front in big black letters.

'Any ideas?'

Logan shrugged. 'Someone in the IB team? They've got access to all the bodies.'

Napier raised a cold eyebrow. 'Just because your team put money in the pot it doesn't mean they're not guilty. It could be anyone here.' He said that last bit looking directly at Logan. 'Anyone.'

Insch thought about it, his face dark and distant. 'We could have got him,' he said at last, sealing the envelope. 'We could have staked the place out and he'd've come back.'

Logan nodded. They could have caught him.

Napier continued to stare at Logan.

'Anyway,' Insch sighed and stuffed the brown envelope full of money into an inside pocket. 'If you'll excuse us, Inspector: post mortem's at nine. We wouldn't want to be late. Logan's old girlfriend would have our guts for garters.'

Down in the basement, Logan and Insch found Dr Isobel MacAlister with an audience. Her floppy-haired bit of rough was flouncing around in his usual effeminate, moronic manner. Three medical students stood with notebooks at the ready, all earnest and keen to learn just how one should go about butchering a murdered four-year-old. She didn't even look at Logan as she said a curt hello to the inspector.

Peter Lumley's naked body was laid out in the middle of the slab, pale and waxy and very, very dead. The students took notes, the bit of rough simpered, and Isobel cut and examined and extracted and weighed. It was exactly the same story as little David Reid, only without the advanced state of decay and genital mutilation. Strangled with a cord of some kind, probably plastic-coated. Something inflexible inserted into the body after death.

Another dead child on the slab.

Logan's little incident room was empty when he returned from the post mortem, feeling sick. Geordie Stephenson's dead face stared blankly down from the wall. Two cases. Both going nowhere.

There was a large padded envelope from Forensics sitting in his in-tray addressed to 'DETECTIVE SERGEANT LAZARUS MCRAE'.

'Bunch of bastards.'

He sank into a chair and ripped the envelope open. It contained a forensics report, with all the easy-to-understand words taken out and replaced with half a ton of indecipherable jargon. The other thing was a set of teeth, cast in cream resin.

Logan pulled the teeth out of their baggie and frowned. Someone must have screwed up. This was supposed to be a cast of the bite-marks on Geordie's body. They were supposed to match Colin McLeod. The only way these were going to match Colin McLeod was if he was a bloody were-wolf. One with a few missing teeth . . .

With a growing feeling of dread, Logan picked up Geordie's as-yet-unread post mortem report.

The bit about the bite-marks was quite precise.

He closed his eyes and swore.

Five minutes later he was flying out of the door, dragging a bemused-looking WPC Watson with him.

The Turf 'n Track looked every bit as ratty and unwelcoming as it had the last time. Falling snow had not lent it a jolly, festive air; instead the squat concrete rectangle of shops looked more dismal than ever. WPC Watson slithered their pool car into the front car park, where they sat looking out at the howling wind and flying snow, waiting for confirmation that the patrol car – Quebec Three One – was in place around the back. It wasn't their normal beat, but they were free.

There was a knock at the passenger-side window and Logan jumped.

Standing in the snow was a nervous looking man wearing a heavily-padded leather arm protector. Logan wound down the window and the nervous man said, 'So . . . this Alsatian . . . big is it?' His face said he hoped the answer was no.

Logan held up the cast of teeth for the handler from the Dog Section to see. It didn't make the man any happier.

'I see . . . Big. With lots of teeth,' the handler sighed. 'Great.'

Logan thought about the grey muzzle. 'If it's any consolation: he's quite old.'

'Ahh . . .' said the handler, looking even more

depressed. 'Big, lots of teeth and experienced.'

He carried a long metal pole with a strong plastic loop hanging out of the end, and he banged his head on it gently, sending a flurry of water sprinkling in through the open passenger window.

The radio crackled into life: Quebec Three One was in position. Time to go.

Logan clambered out into the slippery car park. WPC Watson was first to complete the journey from the car to the Turf 'n Track, flattening herself beside the door, truncheon at the ready, just like they did in the movies. Hands deep in his pockets, shoulders hunched, ears going bright red in the freezing wind, Logan followed her, the two dog-handlers grumbling and slipping along behind him.

When they reached the bookies both the handlers copied Watson, standing flat against the wall, clutching their long metal poles.

Logan looked at the three of them and shook his head.

'It's not Starsky and Hutch, people,' he said, calmly opening the door, letting a deafening barrage of noise out.

The smell of wet dog and hand-rolled fags washed over him as Logan stepped over the threshold. It took his eyes a moment to adjust to the gloom. A pair of televisions flickered away, one in each corner of the room above the long wooden counter. Both showed the same dog race, the pictures jumping, the sound cranked up far too loud.

Four men sat on the edge of their cracked plastic seats, all staring and shouting at the television screen.

'Come on you lazy fucker! Run!!!'

Desperate Doug was nowhere to be seen. But his Alsatian was lying splayed out on the floor, next to the three-bar electric fire, tongue lolling out the side of its mouth, fur gently steaming in the heat.

A gust of wind barged past Logan into the dark, smoky room, bringing a flurry of snow with it, setting the posters on the wall fluttering. Without looking around, a large man dressed like a tramp on his day off shouted, 'Shut the bloody door!'

The wind ruffled the fur on the sleeping dog and its paws twitched as if it was chasing something. Something tasty. A rabbit; or a policeman.

Watson and the two dog-handlers slipped in after Logan, closing the door behind them. They eyed up the sleeping Alsatian as if it was an unexploded bomb. Licking his lips in nervous anticipation, one of the handlers lowered the loop on the end of his pole at the mass of steaming grey and tan fur, and crept forward. If they could get it while it was asleep then maybe no one would have to get bitten. With all the punters' attention firmly fixed on the race, he tiptoed closer and closer, until the noose was hanging inches from the dog's grey muzzle. On the television a greyhound in a yellow bib charged over the finishing line, just a hair's breadth in front of one in blue.

Two of the punters leapt to their feet and cheered. The other two swore.

The sleeping dog's ears twitched at the sudden noise and up snapped his old, wolf-like head. For a heartbeat the dog just looked at the handler, with his pole and dangling noose.

The handler went 'Eeek!' and lunged. But he wasn't fast enough. The old dog leapt to his feet and let out a volley of gunfire barks as the pole clattered against the three-bar fire, shattering one of the heating elements.

Every face in the room turned to stare at the dog. And then at the four policemen.

'Wharafuck?'

Now all the punters were on their feet. Clenched fists and tattoos. Bared teeth, snarling, just like Desperate Doug's Alsatian.

There was a crash at the far end of the shop and the door through to the back room burst open. Simon McLeod stood in the doorway, the annoyance on his face swiftly turning to anger.

'We don't want any trouble.' Logan had to shout to be heard over the barking dog. 'We just want to speak to Dougie MacDuff.'

Simon reached out a hand and switched off the lights. The room was plunged into darkness, the ghostly green-grey glow from the flickering television sets doing nothing more than highlighting shapes.

The first one to cry out in pain was the dog-handler. A crash, a snarl, the sound of someone hitting the deck. A fist whistled past Logan's head and he ducked, flailing out with a fist of his own. There was a brief, momentary feeling of skin and bone breaking under his knuckles, a muffled cry, a splash of something wet on his cheek, and another crash. He hoped to hell he hadn't just flattened WPC Watson!

The dog was still barking its head off, between snarling, biting noises. The televisions blared as the next race was announced and more greyhounds were loaded into the traps. A metal pole clattered into Logan's back and he stumbled forward, tripped over a supine body and fell headlong to the floor. A foot came down hard next to his head and then was gone again.

White light spilled over the scene and Logan twisted his head round to see a hunched figure, silhouetted against the snowstorm outside. The figure dropped the plastic bag it was carrying. Four tins of Export and a bottle of Grouse clattered against the tatty linoleum.

In that moment the room was revealed in the soft glow of winter daylight. One of the handlers was on the floor, his leather-padded arm being savaged by the snarling Alsatian. WPC Watson had blood streaming out of her nose and a large tattooed man in a headlock. The other handler was being punched in the guts while another punter held him down. And Logan was lying, half-sprawled, over someone in a boiler suit with a bloody gap where their front teeth used to be.

The figure in the door turned and ran.

Desperate Doug!

Swearing, Logan hauled himself off the floor and lurched towards the closing door. A hand clutched his ankle and he pitched forward again, hitting the floor hard, feeling the scars in his stomach scream. The grip on his ankle tightened and another hand clapped onto his leg.

Gasping in pain, Logan grabbed the fallen whisky bottle, gripped it like a club and swung. It battered his assailant's head with a dull clunk and the hands holding him went limp.

Logan back-pedalled, struggled to his feet again and staggered through the door. The pain in his stomach was like fire. Someone had injected him with petrol and set it alight. Hissing through clenched teeth, he dragged his mobile out and told Quebec Three One to get their arses into the betting shop, now! He leant heavily on the railing that separated the shops from the car park. Desperate Doug might have done a runner, but he was hardly a spring chicken any more. He couldn't have got far.

Left: nothing but empty road and parked cars, fading in and out of sight through the snow. Right: a grey wash of brick-and-concrete tenement blocks. More parked cars. Someone disappearing into one of the lifeless, gloomy buildings.

Logan pulled himself off the railing and lurched after the disappearing figure. Behind him, Quebec

Three One roared into the icy car park, lights and sirens going full blast.

The wind drove needles of ice into his face as Logan pushed himself on. The pavement beneath his feet was treacherous, threatening to send him sprawling every time his feet hit the slush. He scrabbled up the path to the building Doug had vanished into, leaping the small flight of steps and banging through the front door. It was quiet and cold in the entrance and his breath fogged the air. Dark stains around the concrete doorways – spreading tree shapes from groin height to the ground – marked where someone had repeatedly urinated against their neighbour's door. The smell hung sharp and rancid in the freezing hallway.

Logan screeched to a halt, breathing hard, eyes stinging in the urine reek. Doug could have gone to ground in any of these flats. Or he could be hiding just out of sight, behind the stairs. He inched forwards to look, but Desperate Doug wasn't there. The back door was ajar.

'Damn.' Logan took a deep breath and ran through it, back out into the snow.

The buildings were arranged so that between each row of three- and four-storey tenements there was a communal drying green. Not that it was particularly green, even at the best of times. Fresh footprints, slowly disappearing in the falling snow, heading for the tenement on the opposite side.

Logan followed them at a run straight through

the building opposite. Another street and another line of tenement buildings. A door slammed directly ahead and Logan slithered his way down the path, across the road, through the door, down the hallway, and out the other side again. Only this time there wasn't another row of bleak grey buildings: this time there was only a six-foot chainlink fence separating the drying green from a band of rough scrubland. An industrial estate was visible through the fence, and a couple of high-rise buildings behind that: Tillydrone.

Desperate Doug MacDuff was clambering his way over the top of the high fence.

'Hold it right there!' Logan legged it across the snow, slipping and sliding to a halt at the end of the drying green just in time to see Doug vanish from sight again. 'What are you, bloody Houdini?'

Clambering up the chainlink, Logan suddenly realized how Desperate Doug had managed to disappear so suddenly. The fence marked the dividing line between the Sandilands Estate and the railway track north out of the city. Hidden by the scrubland and bushes was a deep, wide, man-made ravine with railway lines at the bottom. Doug had slithered his way down one side of the steep siding.

The old man wasn't running very fast any more. He had slowed to a lurching jog, clutching one arm to his chest as he scuffed his way along the railway tracks.

Logan pitched himself over the top of the fence and hit the ground hard. Immediately his feet went out from under him. Gravity did the rest. He tumbled down the bank like a boulder, scraping through gorse and bracken, smacking into the hard gravel at the bottom of the ravine. He hit with a cry of pain. Blood was seeping from a gash on the back of his hand. His head rang from its sudden stop against the gravel. But worst of all was the pain exploding in his belly. One year on and Angus Robertson, the Mastrick Monster, was still hurting him.

The high banks of the railway siding sheltered the bottom of the ravine from the wind. Here the snow fell steadily from the sky, drifting down like a blanket in the still air.

Logan lay on his side, groaning, trying not to be sick, letting the snow settle on him. He couldn't even move. But he did have a perfect view of Desperate Doug as the old man risked a glance over his shoulder and saw the policeman who'd been chasing him lying, bleeding on the railway tracks. He stopped running and turned to watch Logan, his breath fogging the air in huge, ragged lungfuls.

And then he started back up the tracks towards Logan. He dug in one of his pockets and something shiny sparkled in his hand. Something sharp.

Ice water rushed through Logan's body. 'Oh God . . .'

He tried to roll over, get to his feet before

Desperate Doug reached him. But the pain in his stomach was too much, even with death walking slowly up the tracks towards him.

'You didn't have tae follow me.' Doug's voice came out in jagged puffs. 'You could've just minded yer own bloody business. Now I'm gonnae have to teach you a lesson, Mr Pig.' He held up the shiny thing: it was a Stanley knife, the blade fully extended.

'Oh God, no . . .' It was happening again!

'I'm real fond of bacon, me.' Doug's face was bright red, creased and florid with broken veins. His milky, dead eye, the same colour as the snow, his twisted smile nicotine-brown. 'Thing 'bout bacon is, you gotta slice it nice and thin.'

'Don't . . .' Logan desperately tried to roll over again.

'Aw, now you're no goin' tae cry are you, Mr Pig? Gonnae greet like a bairn? Hell, wouldn't blame you like. It's gonnae fuckin' hurt!'

'Don't . . . please! You don't have to do this . . .'

'No?' Doug laughed, the sound turning into a thick, rattling cough and a stream of black-and-red spit. 'What,' he asked when he finally got his breath back, 'what have I got to lose? Eh? I've got the cancer, Mr Pig. Nice wee man at the hospital says I've got me one, maybe two years, tops. And they're gonnae be shitty years. And you bastards are after me, aren't ye?'

Logan gritted his teeth and pushed against the ground, getting as far as his knees before Doug put a foot in the centre of his back and pushed. The ground slammed against Logan's chest. 'Aaaaaaaaaaaa . . .'

'See, youse bastards are gonnae lock me up again. I'm no comin' out alive. No with the cancer eatin' ma lungs and bones. So what can they do to me if I slice you up? I'm dead before my sentence is up anyway. What's one more dead body, eh?'

Logan groaned and rolled onto his back, feeling the snow falling cold against his face. *Keep him talking. Keep him talking and someone might come. One of the uniform. WPC Watson. Anyone. God, please let someone come!* 'Is that . . . is that why you killed Geordie Stephenson?'

Doug laughed. 'What's this? You think we're gonnae have us a nice wee chat and I'm gonnae 'fess up tae everything? Keep the old fart talking and he'll spill his guts?' He shook his head. 'You watch too much television, Mr Pig. Only guts I'm gonnae spill are yours.' He waggled the Stanley knife and grinned.

Logan kicked him in the knee. Hard. There was a loud pop and Doug collapsed, dropping the knife, clutching at his ruined kneecap. 'Ahyafucker!'

Hissing through his teeth, Logan rolled onto his side and lashed out with his foot again, catching the old man on the side of the head, opening up a three-inch gash.

Doug grunted, his hands covering his bleeding scalp as Logan aimed another blow at the old man's head. Two of his fingers snapped beneath Logan's boot. 'Fuckinbastard!'

He might have been old and riddled with cancer, but Doug MacDuff had earned his reputation as a hard man in the toughest prisons Scotland had to offer. Earned it the hard way. Snarling, he scrabbled backwards, getting out of range. And then he lunged, wrapped his nicotine-stained hands around Logan's throat and squeezed, his face creased and brutal as he strangled himself a detective sergeant.

Logan grabbed at the hands encircling his neck, trying to pull them away, but the man's grip was like iron. Already the world had started to take on a red tinge, his ears ringing with the pressure in his head. He let one hand go, curled it into a fist and smashed it off the side of Doug's face. The old man grunted, but didn't let go. Screwing his face up, Logan did it again and again, blood from Doug's wounds dripping down all around him, turning the snow pink. Fighting for his life, he slammed his fist into Doug's head, cracking the jaw, closing the milky, unseeing eye. Punching for all he was worth as the world started to go dark. Again and again and again . . . until at last the hands around Logan's throat went slack and the old man went limp, slumping over sideways to lie, bleeding in the falling snow.

29

They rushed Douglas MacDuff straight through Accident and Emergency and into a treatment room. He looked like death. His lined and wrinkled face was covered with a growing network of dark red bruises. His breathing was shallow and rattling. He hadn't regained consciousness in the ambulance on the way to Aberdeen Royal Infirmary, just lay there, oozing blood from his battered face.

The ambulance men hadn't spoken a word to Logan all the way over here. Not once they learned he was the one who'd beaten up the old age pensioner.

Standing in silence, shivering, Logan watched as a nurse wired Desperate Doug up to a bank of monitors, bleeps and pings marking time with the old man's heart.

She looked up to see Logan standing at the foot of the gurney. 'You're going to have to go,' she told him, unbuttoning the old man's shirt. 'He's been beaten up pretty badly.'

'I know,' Logan left off the fact that he was the one who'd done it. His voice was rough, painful.

'Are you a relative?' Her face was concerned and professional as she carefully peeled Doug's shirt open.

'No. A police officer: DS McRae.'

She stopped, her expression becoming cold. 'I hope you catch the bastard who did this and lock him away for life! Beating up an old man!'

And then the doctor arrived: a short, balding man with a clipboard and a stressed expression. He didn't care that Logan was an officer of the law. Everyone was to leave so that the patient could be diagnosed and treated.

'His name is Douglas MacDuff,' said Logan, trying to keep his gravelly voice level. 'He's the chief suspect in a murder investigation. He is to be considered extremely dangerous.'

The nurse backed away from the gurney, wiping her hands down the front of her blue smock, the latex of her surgical gloves making a dull, squeaking sound beneath the regular ping and beep.

Logan rubbed tenderly at his throat. 'I'll post a PC to watch him,' he said, swallowing painfully.

The nurse gave him an uncertain smile, but the doctor was already poking and prodding Dougie's battered body. With a deep breath she squared her shoulders and went to work.

Logan arranged for someone to stay by Desperate Doug's bedside and left them to it. Out in the hall he almost fell over a nurse pushing a trolley covered with bottles of pills. He turned to apologize and found himself looking into a familiar face. Only this time Lorna Henderson's mother was sporting a huge black eye. She'd tried to cover it up with six inches of make-up, but the bruising still shone through. 'Are you OK?' he asked.

A nervous hand fluttered up to the puffy eye and she forced a smile onto her face. 'Fine,' she said, her voice brittle round the edges. 'Never better. How are you?'

'Did someone hit you, Mrs Henderson?'

She smoothed down her blue nurse's uniform and said no. She had walked into a door. It was an accident. That was all.

Logan gave her one of DI Insch's patented silences.

Slowly the fake smile slid away, leaving her pale and jowly again. 'Kevin came round. He'd been drinking.' She picked at the name badge pinned to her chest, not looking Logan in the eye. 'I thought he'd come back to me. You know, dumped that flat-chested tart. But he said it was all my fault that Lorna was dead. That I should have never made her get out of the car. That I killed her . . .' She looked up, tears making her eyes sparkle in the fluorescent lighting. 'I tried to make him understand we could get through it together. Be there for each other. That I still loved him. That I knew he still loved me.' A single fat tear spilled over the edge and down her cheek. She wiped it away on the back of her hand. 'He got upset and shouted even louder. Then he . . . I deserved it! It was all my fault! He's never coming back . . .' Tears spilling down her face, she abandoned her trolley and ran.

Logan watched her disappear through a set of double doors and sighed.

WPC Watson was sitting in the waiting area, with her head back and a scrunched-up handful of toilet paper jammed against her face. It was bright red.

'How's the nose?' asked Logan, plonking himself down on the next plastic chair along. Trying to keep himself from trembling.

'Sore,' she said, peering at him from the corner of her eye, not moving her head. 'Ad leasd I don'd thing id's broken. How's the prisoner?'

Logan shrugged and instantly regretted it. 'How's everyone else?' he asked, his voice coming out as a painful croak.

WPC Watson pointed off down the corridor to the treatment rooms. 'One of the dog-handlers is gedding his ribs checked out. Everyone else is OK.' She smiled and winced. 'Oww . . . Someone from the bookies god their front teeth knocked out.' She peered at him again, watching as Logan rubbed a hand around his throat for the umpteenth time since sitting down. 'You OK?'

Logan pulled down the collar of his shirt, exposing his neck in all its strangled glory.

Watson winced again, but this time for him. Desperate Doug's finger marks stood out against the pale skin in red and purple. The two biggest bruises sitting on either side of the windpipe, where the old man's thumbs had tried to squeeze the life out of him.

'Jesus, whad happened?'

'I kind of fell down and couldn't get up.' Logan went back to rubbing his throat. 'Mr MacDuff wanted to make it permanent.' The knife blade flashing in the light. He shivered again.

'The old bastard!'

Logan almost smiled; it was nice to have someone on his side for a change.

DI Insch was not so understanding. When they got back to Force Headquarters, Logan with another pocket full of painkillers and WPC Watson with confirmation that her nose wasn't broken, the message was delivered by the desk sergeant: Logan was to report to the inspector's office. Now!

The inspector was standing with his back to the door, hands clasped behind his back, his bald head shining in the overhead lighting as Logan entered. Insch was staring out of the window at the steadily falling snow. 'What the hell did you think you were doing?' he asked.

Logan rubbed at his throat again and said he was trying to arrest George Stephenson's killer.

Insch sighed. 'Sergeant, you just beat an old man unconscious. The hospital say his condition is serious. What if he dies? Can you imagine how that's going to play in tomorrow's paper? "Policeman Beats Pensioner To Death!" What the hell were you thinking?'

Logan cleared his throat and wished he hadn't. It hurt. 'I . . . I was defending myself.'

Insch spun around, his face beetroot-red. 'Reasonable force does not include battering old . . .' He stopped when he saw Logan's bruise-ringed neck. 'What happened? Watson go into a love-bite feeding-frenzy?'

'Mr MacDuff tried to strangle me. Sir.'

'That why you hit him?'

Logan nodded, wincing. 'It was the only way to make him stop.' He dug a clear plastic wallet out of his pocket and clunked it down on DI Insch's desk with a trembling hand. There was a Stanley knife inside. 'He was going to carve me up with that.'

Insch picked up the knife, twisting it around, examining it through the plastic. 'Nice to see the old ways aren't dying out,' he said at last before looking Logan square in the eye. 'You're probably going to be suspended from duty while this is investigated. If Desperate Doug decides to press charges . . .' he shrugged. 'You know what it's like around here right now. We don't need any more bad PR.'

'He was going to kill me . . .'

'You beat an OAP unconscious, Logan. It doesn't matter why. That's all they're going to see. Police brutality of the worst kind.'

Logan couldn't believe his ears. 'So you're hanging me out to dry?'

'Sergeant, I'm not doing anything. Professional Standards won't let me. This is all out of my hands.'

The incident room was empty except for Logan and his paperwork. He sat in the semidarkness, a cup of cold coffee on the table next to a half-eaten packet of Maltesers. Trying not to shake.

The knife.

Logan ran a hand over his face. He'd not thought about that night for a long time. Lying on the tower block roof, half-unconscious, while Angus Robertson stabbed and stabbed and stabbed . . . Desperate Doug MacDuff had brought it all screaming back.

Logan had filled in all the forms, explaining why he'd put an old age pensioner in the hospital. Had spent a happy hour and a half while Inspector Napier scowled at him, asked leading questions and left him in no doubt about what was going to happen next. Now there was nothing left to do but sit back and wait to be told he was suspended. One week back on the job and already his career was down the tubes. And it wasn't even his fault!

Sighing, he looked up at Geordie Stephenson's dead face. Worst of all Desperate Doug was going to be that much harder to convict now. The jury would see a poor old man, beaten by the police, fitted up for the murder of an Edinburgh hoodlum. How could that old man murder anyone? He was so frail! The Procurator Fiscal wouldn't touch it with a bargepole.

Logan let his head sink forward until it clunked off the pile of papers. 'Shit.' He banged his forehead on the table, in time with the words: 'Shit, shit, shit, shit . . .'

He was interrupted by the blaring tune from his mobile phone. Sighing, he pulled the thing out, and stuck it to his ear. 'Logan,' he said, without enthusiasm.

'DS McRae? This is Alice Kelly, we met yesterday? At the safe house? We were looking after Mr Philips?'

Logan had the sudden image of a frumpy, plainclothes policewoman with too many rings. 'Hello . . .' He stopped and sat up. 'What do you mean: you "were" looking after him? Where is he?'

'Ah, yes. You see that's the thing.' Embarrassed pause. 'DC Harris went out to the shops for a pint of milk and some crisps while I was in the shower—'

'Don't tell me you've lost him!'

'We didn't really lose him. I'm sure he's just gone out for a walk. He'll be back as soon as it gets dark . . .'

Logan looked at his watch. It was three-thirty. It was already dark. 'Have you looked for him?'

'DC Harris's out there now. I'm staying here, in case he comes back.'

Logan banged his head off the table again.

'Hello? Hello? Is something wrong?'

'He's not coming back.' The words came out through gritted teeth. 'Have you told Control he's missing?'

Another embarrassed pause.

'Oh for God's sake,' said Logan. 'I'll let them know.'

'What do you want me to do?'

Logan was a gentleman and didn't tell her.

Ten minutes later every patrol car in Aberdeen knew to keep an eye out for Roadkill wandering the streets. Not that Logan needed psychic powers to know where he would be going. He'd be making for the farm and its buildings full of dead things.

It was a fair walk to Cults from Summerhill, especially in the driving snow, but Roadkill was used to long walks. Pushing his own portable morgue along the highways and byways of the city. Collecting dead animals along the way.

But Bernard Duncan Philips didn't get that far. He was found three and a half hours later, lying in a pool of slowly freezing blood, in Hazlehead Woods.

The woods were fairytale black and white, old twisted trees frosted with ice, blanketed in snow. A single-track road twisted its way through the centre of the park and Logan crept his pool car along it, keeping the speed down trying to keep the thing from sliding off the road and into a tree.

A mile and a half into the woods there was a rough car park, no tarmac, just dirt compacted over years and years of use, hidden beneath the snow. A single, large beech tree sat in the middle, bedecked in winter and surrounded by policemen milling about with no real obvious purpose, breath pluming out into the bitter air. Freezing their nuts off.

Logan pulled up next to the grubby IB van, killed the engine and clambered out into the slippery, hard-packed snow. The cold air was like a slap in the face. He shivered his way to the crime scene tent, hoping to God it would be warmer inside. It wasn't. Blood was spattered out from the middle of the tent, where a big pool of dark red was thickening with ice crystals, making the surface glitter. There were footprints everywhere and a man-shaped depression, straddling the pool of blood. Roadkill had been lying on his side. Bleeding his life out into the snow.

Logan grabbed the photographer. It was Billy: the balding AFC fan who'd taken photos at the tip. He was still wearing the same red-and-white bobble hat.

'Where's the body?'

'A&E.'

'What?'

'He's no dead.' The photographer looked down at the crimson stain and then at Logan. 'No yet anyway.'

Which was how Logan ended up back at

Aberdeen Royal Infirmary for the second time that day. Bernard Duncan Philips had been admitted with a fractured skull, broken ribs, broken arms, one broken leg, fractured fingers and internal injuries consistent with someone repeatedly stamping on his stomach. He'd been taken straight into surgery, but the mob had done a thorough job this time. Roadkill wasn't expected to survive.

Logan waited at the hospital, because there wasn't really anywhere else for him to go. He wasn't going to go back to FHQ and wait for his suspension to become official. At least if he was out here, with his phone switched off, he could pretend it wasn't going to happen.

Four hours later a serious-looking nurse appeared and escorted Logan through the maze of corridors to intensive care. The doctor who'd dealt with Desperate Doug was standing at Roadkill's bed, reading a chart.

'How is he?'

The doctor looked up from his clipboard. 'You back again?'

Logan looked at the battered, bandaged figure. 'Is it as bad as it looks?'

'Well . . .' There was a sigh. 'He's suffered some brain damage. We won't know how much for a while yet. He's stable for now.'

They stood watching Roadkill's shallow breaths.

'Is there any chance?'

The doctor shrugged. 'I think we caught the internal bleeding in time. I can tell you one thing for sure though: he's not going to have any more children. Both testicles ruptured. But he'll live.'

Logan winced. 'What about the man I came in with earlier? Mr MacDuff?'

'Not good.' He shook his head. 'Not good at all.'

'Is he going to be OK?'

'I'm afraid I can't discuss that. Patient confidentiality. You'd have to ask Mr MacDuff.'

'OK I'll do that.'

The doctor shook his head again. 'Not tonight. He's an old man; he's been through a lot today. It's nearly midnight. Let him sleep.' He raised sad eyes to Logan's face. 'Trust me: he's not going anywhere.'

Outside, the snow had stopped and the sky was clearing: a bowl of inky-black, the stars blurred by the city's lights. Logan walked out of A&E and into the icy night.

An ambulance carefully pulled up to the entrance, its lights flashing away.

Turning his back on the scene, Logan climbed into his pool car, his breath instantly fogging up the windscreen, dug out his mobile phone and switched it back on. Might as well face the music, now that it was too late for anyone to be calling him.

He had five messages. Four of them were from Colin Miller, desperate to know what had happened to Roadkill. But one was from WPC Jackie

Watson asking if he didn't have anything better to do that is, if he would, but it was OK if he didn't, like to maybe go see a film, or maybe not a film, maybe just have a drink, because it had been a rough day . . . And if he did want to, you know, do something, then he could maybe give her a call back? The message was left at eight. Right about when Logan was sitting down to wait for Roadkill to come out of surgery.

He stabbed her number into the phone. It was late: after midnight, but maybe not too late . . .

It rang and rang and rang. At last a tinny, metallic voice told him that the number he had called was not available, please try again later.

For the second time that day he punctuated a list of obscenities by banging his head on something. The steering wheel made little boinging noises as he bounced his forehead against the plastic.

It had not been a good day.

When the windscreen finally cleared Logan revved the engine, spinning the car out of the hospital car park in a foul mood. With his teeth gritted he slammed on the brakes as the car sailed up to the junction, taking grim pleasure as the car's back end decided it wanted to overtake the front. He floored the accelerator and steered into the skid, whipping the car back in line as it drifted round the corner and on to the main road. There was a truck stopped at the lights up ahead and Logan had the sudden desire to put his foot down and plough right into the back of it.

But he didn't. Instead he swore quietly to himself and slowed the car down to a crawl.

The sound of his mobile screeching in his jacket pocket made him jump. It was Jackie, WPC Watson calling back! Grinning, he scrabbled the phone out and up to his ear. 'Hello?' he said, sounding as upbeat as he could.

'Laz? That you?' It was Colin Miller. *'Laz, I've been trying to get hold of ye for hours, man!'*

Logan sat with the phone against his ear, watching the traffic lights change from red to amber. 'I know. I got your messages.'

'They beat the shit out of Roadkill. Did you hear? What happened? Spill the beans!'

Logan said no.

'What? Come on, Laz, I thought you and me was friends here?'

Logan scowled out at the cold, empty night. 'After what you did? You're no bloody friend of mine!'

There was a stunned silence.

'After what I did? What you talking about? I've no put the boot into your pantomime dame for ages! I did your damn puff-piece! What the hell more do you want?'

The light finally went green and the truck pulled away, leaving Logan and the pool car behind.

'You told everyone we'd found Peter Lumley's body.'

'So? You did find it, what—'

'He was going to come back. The killer. He was going to come back and we were going to catch him!'

'What?'

'He'd hidden the body. He was going to come back to it. But because you splurged your story all over the front bloody page he knows. He won't go back. He's still out there and you just screwed up the best chance we had of catching the bastard! The next kid that goes missing is your fault, understand? We could have caught him!'

Another silence. When Miller finally spoke his voice was low, barely audible over the car's blowers. *'Jesus, Laz, I didn't know. If I'd known I'd've never published a word! I'm sorry.'*

And the thing was he genuinely sounded sorry. Logan took a deep breath and slid the car into gear. 'You have to tell me who your source is—'

'You know I can't do that, Laz. I can't.'

Sighing, Logan pulled away from the lights, heading back into town.

'Listen, Laz, I'm about done here, you want to meet up for a drink? There's still places open down the docks . . . I'm buying?'

Logan said he didn't think so and hung up.

Traffic was light all the way across town. He abandoned his car outside his flat and slouched up the stairs. The place was cold, so he cranked up the heating and sat in the dark, watching the lights twinkling outside the windows, feeling sorry for himself. Trying not to think about the knife.

The little red light on his answering machine was flashing at him, but it was just more messages from Miller. Nothing from WPC Watson saying she was waiting up for him with a bottle of champagne and a negligee. And maybe some toast?

Logan's stomach gave a low growl. It was coming up for one o'clock in the morning and he'd not eaten a thing since breakfast except a handful of Maltesers and some painkillers.

There was a packet of biscuits and a bottle of red wine in the kitchen and Logan opened them both. He poured himself a big glass of shiraz and stuffed a chocolate Hob Nob into his mouth then went back to sulking and slouching in the lounge.

'Not to be taken with alcohol,' he said, toasting his reflection in the lounge window.

He was halfway through his second glass when the doorbell went. Swearing, he pulled himself out of his chair and over to the window, peering out to see a familiar flash motor squeezed in across the road.

Colin Miller.

The reporter was standing on the doorstep with a contrite expression and two large carrier bags.

'What do you want?' asked Logan.

'Aye, look, I know you're pissed off, OK? But I didn't do it on purpose. If I'd known I would've kept ma mouth shut. I'm really, really sorry . . .'

With an apologetic smile he hoisted the carrier bags. 'Peace offerin'?'

They settled into the kitchen, Logan's bottle of shiraz joined by Miller's chilled chardonnay and an array of plastic dishes, each one exuding the heady, spicy smell of Thai takeaway. 'I know the owner,' said Miller, spooning green-curried tiger prawns onto a plate. 'Did him some favours when he lived in Glasgow. And he's open hell of a late.'

Logan had to admit that the food was good. Much better than chocolate biscuits and red wine. 'So did you come all this way, in the snow, just to bring me takeaway?'

'Well, funny you should mention that.' Miller heaped fried noodles onto his plate. 'You see I've got this moral dilemma, kinda thing.'

Logan froze, fork halfway to his mouth, a glistening strip of chicken awaiting his attention. 'I knew it!'

'Whoa there, tiger,' Miller smiled. 'The moral dilemma is this: I've got this killer story, only it's a shoe-in to wreck someone's career.'

Logan raised an eyebrow. 'Considering what you did to DI Insch, I'm surprised you even paused for thought.'

'Aye, fair enough. Problem is, I kinda like the guy this'll ruin.'

Logan stuffed spicy chicken into his face mumbling, 'So? What's the story?' as he chewed.

'Local Police Hero Batters OAP To Death.'

30

Logan tried not to make eye contact with anyone as he went into work on Tuesday morning. No one said a word to him, but he could feel their eyes on his back, feel the gossip as it followed him through the building and into DI Insch's morning briefing. He'd slept badly, the dreams full of tower blocks, burning skies and flashing knives. Angus Robertson's face, twisted and grinning as he carved up Logan's stomach.

The inspector was in his customary place, leaning one round buttock on the edge of the desk, the strip lighting gleaming off his bald head. He didn't look at Logan, just kept his attention on a sherbet double dip. Eating with care, trying not to get red-and-orange powder all down the front of his black suit.

With his face slowly turning red, Logan took his usual place at the front of the room.

DI Insch made no mention at all of that morning's article in the P&J. The one spread all over the front page, with an extra-long editorial on page twelve. Instead he told everyone about Roadkill being attacked. And how the search teams had come up with nothing more than heavy colds. Then he handed out the day's duties and called the meeting to a close.

Logan was the first to his feet, ready to run for it, but Insch wasn't letting him get away that easily. 'Sergeant,' he said in a voice like treacle. 'A moment if you'd be so kind.'

So Logan had to stand there like an idiot as everyone filed past, looking anywhere but at him. Even WPC Watson wouldn't meet his eyes. It was probably just as well: he felt bad enough already.

When the last PC was gone, and the door to the briefing room closed, Insch produced a copy of that morning's paper and slapped it down on the table. 'Lazarus came back from the dead, didn't he?' asked the inspector. 'Well, I'm not a religious man, Sergeant, but your career seems to have performed the same trick.' He poked the headline: 'KILLER OAP ARRESTED: LOCAL POLICE HERO FIGHTS FOR HIS LIFE!' And below that a picture of Desperate Doug when he was being sent down for crippling a builder's merchant with a ratchet screwdriver. With the milky-white eye, the snarl and the flaming tattoos he didn't look like anyone's granddad.

Miller had called in every favour he had at the paper to get the new front page in place. Not that it wasn't a damn sight more newsworthy than

'Tillydrone Fundraiser Gets off to a Flying Start!'

'Inspector Napier is spitting nails.' A smile broke across Insch's face. 'So, as you're no longer going to be fired, DI Steel says you can get your arse over to the hospital and take Desperate Doug's statement.'

'Me? Doesn't she want to do it?' Detective sergeants didn't usually get to interview murder suspects without a DI there to hold their hand.

'No she does not. Something about "keeping a dog and barking yourself". Now hop it.'

Logan commandeered another in a long line of rusty Vauxhalls and WPC Watson. She didn't say anything to him as she pulled the car out of the car park. She waited until they were nowhere near Force Headquarters before bursting out laughing.

'It's not funny.'

The laughter subsided into a smirk. 'Sorry, sir.'

Silence.

Watson took them up through Rosemount. The break in the weather was holding, beautiful blue skies sailing above the sparkling grey granite.

'Sir,' she said, stopped, cleared her throat and started again. 'Sir, about that message I left on your phone last night.'

Logan's pulse began to quicken.

'Well,' said Watson, joining a queue of traffic behind a bus. 'It wasn't till later I thought about it. You know, about how it might have been misconstrued. I mean, when you didn't call back I thought I might have offended you. Or something.' It all came out in one breath.

The smile froze on Logan's face. She was backing out of it. Pretending it was all a big misunderstanding. 'I was in the hospital. They don't allow mobile phones. I didn't get your message until after midnight. I tried, but your mobile was off . . .'

'Oh,' she said.

'Yeah,' he said.

And then they both said nothing for a while.

The sun beat down through the windscreen, warming the inside of the car, turning it into a four-wheeled microwave. At the next junction the bus went left and Watson went right. The houses here were all done up for Christmas: trees in the windows, lights round the doors, wreaths and festive gnomes. One even had a plastic reindeer with an electric nose that blinked red. Very tasteful.

Logan sat, watching the snow-covered houses slip past, staring at the decorations, thinking of his own, bare apartment. There wasn't even a single card up. Maybe he should get a tree? Last year he hadn't needed one. He'd spent Christmas at Isobel's huge home, with its two real trees, both dripping with all the most fashionable trimmings. No family, just the two of them. Roast goose bought in from Marks and Spencer. Isobel didn't believe in all that peeling and chopping. They'd made love all morning.

And this year he was probably going to have to go to his parents for Christmas. Who'd have the whole family round. Arguments, bitterness, drinking, forced smiles, bloody Monopoly . . .

A figure up ahead broke his train of thought. It was a man, head down, trudging along through the snow. Jim Lumley: Peter's stepfather.

'Pull over a minute, OK?' said Logan and Watson drew up at the kerb.

He stepped out into the December air and crunched along after the trudging figure. 'Mr Lumley?' Logan reached out and tapped the man on the shoulder.

Lumley turned, his eyes as red as his nose. His chin was covered with grubby stubble, his hair unkempt and wild. For a moment he just stared at Logan and then something clicked inside him. 'He's dead,' he said. 'He's dead and it's my fault.'

'Mr Lumley, it's not your fault. Are you OK?' It was a stupid bloody question, but Logan couldn't help asking it. Of course the man wasn't OK: his child had been snatched, killed and raped by a paedophile. He was dying inside. 'Can we give you a lift home?'

Something that had once been a smile clambered across the man's unshaven face. 'I like to walk.' He raised a hand and swept it around him, indicating the snowy pavements and slushy roads. 'Looking for Peter.' Tears welled up in his eyes, spilling down red cheeks. 'You let him go!'

'Let who . . .' It took Logan a moment to realize

he was talking about Roadkill. 'Mr Lumley, he—'

'I have to go.' Lumley turned and ran, slipping and sliding on the icy snow.

Sighing, Logan watched him go, before clambering back into the car.

'Friend of yours?' asked Watson, pulling back into the traffic.

'The boy we found in the toilets. That was his father.'

'Jesus, poor sod.'

Logan didn't answer.

They abandoned the car in a space marked 'HOSPITAL STAFF ONLY' and went in to the main reception area. The lobby was wide, spacious and open plan, the hospital's coat of arms picked out on the floor. A huge, curved wooden reception desk sprawled in one corner. Logan asked politely where he could find Mr Douglas MacDuff and two minutes later they were clacking their way down a long, linoleum corridor.

Desperate Doug was in a private room, guarded by a young PC reading a book. With a guilty jump he stuffed the Ian Rankin under his seat.

'It's OK, Constable,' said Logan. 'I won't tell anyone. Get us three coffees and you can go back to your tales of police derring-do.'

Relieved, the PC scuttled off.

It was hot in Desperate Doug's room, sun streaming through the window, dust motes drifting lazily in the early December sun. A television, high up on the wall opposite the bed, flickering away soundlessly to itself. The room's occupant was propped up on the bed, looking dreadful. Bruises ran rampant all over the right hand side of his face and his milky white eye was swollen almost shut; but even with the swelling, Desperate Doug looked gaunt. It was hard to believe this was the man who had almost killed him yesterday with his bare hands.

'Morning, Dougie,' said Logan, dragging the visitor's chair out of the corner and plonking himself down at the end of the bed.

The patient didn't even acknowledge his presence. He just lay there staring up at the silent, iridescent screen. Logan glanced over his head and then at WPC Watson. She picked the remote off the bedside cabinet and clicked the telly off.

A slow, rattling sigh escaped the old man in the bed. 'I was watchin' that.' The words came out loose and sibilant and for the first time Logan noticed the set of teeth floating in a glass at the side of the bed.

'Urrgh, put your teeth in, Doug, for God's sake! You look like a turtle!'

'Fuck you,' said Doug, but his heart didn't seem to be in it.

Logan smiled. 'Well, now that we've got the pleasantries out of the way, why not get down to business? You killed George "Geordie" Stephenson.'

'Bollocks.'

'Come on, Doug. We've got all the forensic evidence we need! Your dog's teeth match the bite-marks on his legs. His kneecaps were hacked off with a machete! That's got Doug MacDuff written all over it. What happened? The McLeod boys hold him down while you hacked away?'

Doug snorted.

'Come on, Dougie, you're not telling me you could hold a great big bruiser like that down on your own? While you de-kneed him? You're what: ninety?' Logan settled into the seat, resting a foot on the end of the bed. 'Let me tell you how I think it went down, OK? Just jump in if I get anything wrong.'

Standing quietly in the corner WPC Watson was taking notes, keeping a low profile.

'Geordie Stephenson comes up from Edinburgh all full of himself, looking to do a bit of business. While he's up he fancies a bit of a flutter. So he does the rounds of the bookies, losing big time. Only he can't cover his debts. And they don't take kindly to that at the Turf 'n Track.' Logan paused. 'How much did they slip you to do him, Doug? More than a week's pension? Two weeks'? A month's? Hope it was a lot, Dougie, because Geordie Stephenson worked for Malk the Knife. And when he finds out that you've snuffed one of his men, he's going to skin you alive.'

A smile played round Doug's toothless mouth. 'You are so full of shite.'

'You think? Hell, Dougie, I've seen some of the things left behind after Malkie's boys have finished with somebody. Arms, legs, willies . . .

You don't stand a chance.' Logan gave a friendly wink. 'But tell you what: you tell us all about Simon and Colin McLeod and their debt collection methods, and I'll make sure you get locked away somewhere Malkie can't get at you.'

And at this Doug actually started laughing.

Logan frowned. 'What?'

'You haven't—' The word was interrupted by a cough, a dry wheeze that shook the old man's frame. 'Haven't got—' Another cough, this one deeper, working its way slowly into his chest. 'Got a—' Again. 'Got a fuckin' clue—' This time the whole bed rattled as Doug racked back and forth, a shaking, thin hand almost covering his mouth. Finally he slumped back into his pillows, wiping his hand down the front of his pyjamas. It left a black and red smear. 'Have you, Mr Pig?'

'Do you want me to get a doctor?' Logan asked.

The old man laughed bitterly, the laugh dissolving into yet more coughing. 'No point,' he wheezed, the breaths coming ragged and fast. 'Saw one of the buggers this mornin'. I told you Mr Pig: I got me the cancer. Only it's no a year or two any more. Doctor says now it's a month.' He thumped his chest with a bloodstained hand. 'One big tumour.'

Dust motes drifted by in the silence that followed, each one a spark of gold in the heady sunlight.

'Now fuck off and let me die in peace.'

*

Bernard Duncan Philips didn't have a private room. He had to share a double in intensive care. His narrow hospital bed was surrounded by equipment, monitors, ventilators; you name it they'd plugged it into Roadkill's battered body. Logan and Watson stood in the doorway, sipping the lukewarm, plastic-flavoured coffee the PC had finally delivered.

Desperate Doug had looked bad, but Roadkill looked worse. White bandages separated by bruises. They'd put both his arms and one of his legs in plaster since Logan had seen him last. As if he was in a Carry On film.

The oxygen mask was gone, replaced by a tube with a nosepiece in the middle, the clear plastic line looped over his ears and taped to his cheeks to stop it from falling out.

'Can I help you?'

It was a short woman, dressed in a nurse's uniform: sky-blue slacks and a short-sleeved top with an upside-down watch pinned over the left breast.

'How is he?'

The nurse examined Logan with a practised eye. 'You family?'

'No. Police.'

'You don't say.'

'How is he?'

She picked the chart off the end of Roadkill's bed, skimming it. 'Well, he's doing a lot better than we thought. Surgery went well. He actually came round for an hour this morning.' She smiled.

'Bit of a surprise that. I put money on "coma". Still: win some, lose some.'

It was the last time Logan saw Roadkill alive.

DI Steel wasn't surprised he'd got nothing out of Desperate Doug. Instead she just sat back in her chair, feet up on the desk, and puffed smoke rings at the ceiling.

'If you don't mind me asking, ma'am,' said Logan, fidgeting in the seat on the opposite side of her desk, 'how come you didn't go and inter-view him yourself?'

She smiled languidly at him through a haze of smoke. 'Dougie and me go way back. When I was first in uniform and he was in his prime . . .' Her smile became wry. 'Let's just say that we had a bit of a falling out.'

'What are we going to do about him?'

She sighed, sending cigarette smoke drifting across her desk like a wall of fog. 'We go to the Procurator Fiscal and we give him the forensic evidence. He reads it and he says, it's enough to go to court on, and we say great. And then Dougie's lawyer says my client is going to snuff it in under a month. And the PF says well in that case bugger it. Why waste the money?' She worked a chipped nail in between her teeth, dug something out and stared at it for a moment before flicking it away. 'He'll be dead before this thing comes to court. Let sleeping Dougs die, I suppose.' She stopped, as if something had suddenly occurred to her. 'You did check with his doctor, didn't you? He is dying, isn't he? Not just pulling your dick?'

'I checked. He's really dying.'

She nodded, the glowing tip of her fag bobbing up and down in the semidarkness. 'Poor old Doug.'

Somehow Logan found it difficult to feel a great deal of sympathy for the man, but he kept his mouth shut.

Back in the incident room Logan took down Geordie Stephenson's photograph. Both the one from Lothian and Borders Police and the one from the morgue. Now that Desperate Doug MacDuff was dying no one would ever be found guilty of Geordie's murder. But the man had no wife, no kids, no brothers or sisters. No one to claim his body. No one was going to miss Malk the Knife's enforcer. No one except Malk the Knife. And what was he going to do to Dougie? The old man would be dead in a month anyway. And it'd be painful: the doctor said so. All Malkie could do was put him out of his misery and Doug knew it. Maybe that was why he'd laughed when Logan had talked of retribution. Either way it didn't matter.

He stuffed everything relating to Geordie Stephenson's death into the file, including his report on yesterday's shenanigans. There would be some paperwork to tidy the thing off, but other than that the case was as dead as Geordie.

With that all packed away, the only thing left in Logan's little incident room was the unknown girl. Her dead face looked down at him with blank eyes.

One down, one to go.

Logan sat down and waded through the statements once more: everyone living within easy access of the communal bins. One of them had killed the girl, stripped her, tried to hack her up, wrapped her body in brown packing tape and stuffed it into the bin. And if it wasn't Norman Chalmers, who was it?

31

Sunset painted the sky above Rosemount in violent orange and scarlet flames. From street level, hemmed in on all sides by long lines of grey three-storey tenements, it was only visible as ribbons of iridescent colour. Here and there sulphurous-yellow streetlights flickered and hummed in the crisp December air, giving the buildings a jaundiced pallor. It wasn't even five o'clock yet.

Against all the odds WPC Watson had managed to find them a parking spot in front of the building Norman Chalmers lived in. The communal bin stood directly in front of the front door. It was a large black barrel, chest height, flattened at the sides and chained to a post. That was where the girl must have been dumped. Where the scaffies collected her from, taking her body to the council tip along with all the other garbage.

Forensics had been all over the bin and come up with nothing except the fact that someone in the building was into leather-fetish pornography.

'How many buildings we going to do?' asked Watson, balancing a pile of statements against the steering wheel.

'Start from the middle and work out. Three buildings each side: that's seven buildings. Six flats in each . . .'

'Forty-two flats? God, it'll take us for ever!'

'Then there's the other side of the road.'

Watson looked up at the building next to her, then back at Logan. 'Can we not get some uniforms in to do it?'

Logan smiled. 'You are uniform, remember?'

'Yeah, but I'm doing something: driving you about and all that. This'll take ages!'

'Longer we sit here, longer it'll take.'

They started with the building Chalmers lived in.

Ground floor left: an old lady with shifty eyes, urine-yellow hair and breath that stank of sherry. She refused to open the door until Logan had shoved his warrant card through the letterbox and she'd phoned the police station just to make sure he wasn't one of these paedophiles she'd heard about. Logan didn't point out she was about ninety years safe from people like that.

Ground floor right: four students, two of whom were still asleep. No one had seen or heard anything. Too busy studying. 'My arse,' said Watson. 'Fascist,' said the student.

First floor left: timid single woman with big glasses and bigger teeth. No she hadn't seen anyone or heard anything and wasn't it all simply dreadful?

First floor right: no answer.

Top floor left: unmarried mother and three-year-old child. Another case of see, hear and speak no evil. Logan got the feeling you could commit regicide in her bathroom while she was taking a bath, and she'd still swear she'd seen nothing.

Top floor right: Norman Chalmers. His story hadn't changed. They had no right to harass him like this. He was going to call his lawyer.

And back out onto the street again.

'Well,' said Logan, stuffing his hands into his pockets to keep out the chill. 'Six down, seventy-eight to go.'

Watson groaned.

'Never mind.' Logan gave her a smile. 'If you're very, very good I'll buy you a pint when we've finished.'

That seemed to cheer her up a bit and Logan was on the verge of adding an invitation to dinner when he caught sight of his reflection in the car windscreen. It was too dark to make out much detail on the building behind him, but the windows shone like cats' eyes in the dark mirror of glass. All of them.

He turned and stared up at the building. Every single window on the front of the building was ablaze. Even the supposedly empty first floor right flat. As he watched a face appeared at the window, staring down at the street. For a heartbeat their eyes met and then the face was gone, wearing a terrified expression. A very familiar face.

'Well, well, well . . .' Logan patted WPC Watson on the shoulder. 'Looks like we have ourselves a contender.'

Back inside, Watson pounded on the door of the offending flat. 'Come on: we know you're in there. We saw you!'

Logan leaned back against the banister and watched her bash at the black-painted door. He'd brought the pile of statements in with him and was flicking through them, looking for the one that fitted the address. First floor right, number seventeen . . . A Mr Cameron Anderson. Who came from Edinburgh and made ROVs.

WPC Watson mashed her thumb on the door-bell again, still hammering away with her other hand. 'If you don't open this door I'm going to break the damn thing down!'

All this racket out in the hall and not a single face peeked out from the other flats to see what was going on. So much for a sense of community.

Two minutes and still the door remained resolutely shut. Logan was beginning to get a bad feeling about this. 'Kick it in.'

'What?' Watson turned and whispered loudly at him, the words hissing out. 'We don't have a warrant! We can't just break down the door! I was only bluffing—'

'Kick it in. Now.'

WPC Watson took a step back and slammed her foot into the door, just below the lock. With an explosive bang the door flew open, slamming into the flat's hall and bouncing back, rattling photographs in their frames. They rushed in, Watson into the lounge, Logan taking the bedroom. No one.

Like Chalmers's flat, upstairs, there wasn't a door on the kitchen but it was empty anyway. That only left the bathroom and it was locked.

Logan rattled the door, banging the flat of his hand on the wooden door. 'Mr Anderson?'

From inside came the sound of sobbing and running water.

'Damn.' He gave the door one last try before asking Watson for a repeat performance.

She nearly kicked it off its hinges.

Clouds of steam billowed out into the tiny hallway. Inside, the small bathroom was clad in wood, like a sauna, partially concealing a nasty avocado suite. The room was just big enough for the bath to fit along the far wall, on the other side of the toilet, a shower rigged up over it, the curtain drawn.

Logan yanked the curtain open to reveal a fully-dressed man on his knees in the rising water, hacking away at his wrists with a broken disposable razor.

They took Mr Anderson directly to A&E, without waiting for an ambulance. The hospital was less than five minutes away. They wrapped his wrists in layers of fluffy towels before stuffing them into discarded plastic carrier bags from the kitchen so he wouldn't bleed all over the car.

Cameron Anderson hadn't done a very good job of killing himself. The cuts weren't deep enough to fully open the veins, and he'd gone across, rather than down their length. A few stitches and a night's observation was all he needed. Logan smiled as he was told the news and promised the nurse that Mr Anderson would get all the observation he needed in a cell back at Force Headquarters. She looked at him as if he should be scraped off her shoe.

'What the hell is wrong with you?' she demanded. 'That poor man has just tried to kill himself!'

'He's a suspect in a murder enquiry—' was as far as Logan got before she scowled in recognition at him.

'I know you! You're that one was here yesterday! The one beat up that old man!'

'I don't have time for this. Where is he?'

She crossed her arms and refocused her scowl.

'If you don't leave I'm calling security.'

'Good for you. Then we'll see how you get on with a charge of obstruction. OK?'

Logan brushed past her heading into the row of curtained-off cubicles. He identified the one Anderson was in by the sound of snivelling in an Edinburgh accent.

The man sat on the edge of the examination bed, rocking back and forth, crying to himself, snatches of words escaping through the tears. Logan pushed his way through the curtains and sat on a black plastic chair opposite the bed. Watson followed him in, taking up position in the corner, notebook at the ready.

'Hello again, Mr Anderson,' said Logan in his best friendly voice. 'Or can I call you Cameron?'

The man didn't look up. A small patch of red had seeped through the bandage on his left wrist. He couldn't take his eyes off it.

'Cameron, I've been wondering about something,' said Logan. 'You see, there was this bloke who came up from Edinburgh and ended up in the harbour. We put his picture in all the papers and stuck posters up all over the shop, but no one came forward. Seems they didn't like the way his kneecaps were hacked off with a machete.'

At the words 'hacked off' Mr Anderson flinched. 'Machete' elicited an anguished moan.

'Now the thing that confuses me, Cameron, is that you never gave us a call. I mean you must have seen the picture. It was on the news and everything.' Logan pulled a rectangle of paper from his pocket, unfolding it into a photograph of Geordie Stephenson from when he was alive. He'd been carrying it about since they'd done their tour of Aberdeen's seedier bookies. He held it up in front of the weeping man. 'You do recognize him, don't you?'

Anderson's eyes flashed up to the photograph then back to the stain on his bandage. In that swiftest of glimpses Logan knew he'd been right. Cameron Anderson and Geordie Stephenson. They didn't share the same surname, but they shared the same heavy features, the same bouffant hair. The only thing missing was the porn-star moustache.

Anderson said something, but it was too low and muffled to make out.

Logan laid the photograph on the floor, positioning it so Geordie's dead eyes stared up at the man on the bed. 'Why'd you try to kill yourself, Cameron?'

'Thought you were him.' The words were mumbled rather than spoken, but at least this time they were audible.

'Him who?'

Anderson shivered. 'Him. The old man.'

'Describe him.'

'Old. Grey.' He made scratchy, claw-like gestures at his throat. 'Tattoos. One eye all white. Like a poached egg.'

Logan settled back. 'Why him, Cameron? What does he want with you?'

'Geordie was my brother. The old man . . . he . . .' One hand went up to his mouth. He started methodically biting the nails on each finger down to the quick. 'He came to the flat. Told Geordie he had a message for him. From Mr McLennan.'

'Mr McLennan? Malk the Knife?' Logan

scooted forward in his chair. 'What was the message?'

'I let him in and he hit Geordie with something. And then he started kicking him when he was on the ground.' Red-rimmed eyes darted imploringly at Logan. Tears tumbled down the pasty cheeks. 'I tried to stop him, but he hit me . . .' That explained the bruise he'd been sporting the day he'd let them into the building.

'What was the message, Cameron?' The mysterious message that Simon McLeod said all of Aberdeen knew about. Everyone except the police.

'He spat on me . . .' A sob escaped, followed by a silvery trail that leaked out of Cameron's nose. 'He dragged Geordie out of the flat. He said he'd be back for me! I thought you were him!'

Logan examined the man sitting in front of him, rocking back and forward on the edge of the bed, eyes and nose running freely. He was lying. He'd looked out his front window and seen Logan and WPC Watson standing in the street. He knew it wasn't Desperate Doug back to finish him off. 'What was the message?'

Cameron waved a hand in random circles, the red smudge on his bandaged wrist growing ever larger. 'I don't know. He just said he was coming back!'

'What about the little girl?' Logan asked.

Anderson acted as if Logan had slapped him across the face. It took him a good ten seconds to recover enough to say, 'Girl?'

'The girl, Cameron. The one that ended up dead, wearing a bin-bag belonging to your upstairs neighbour. You remember her? A nice man from the police came round and took your statement.'

Anderson bit his lip and wouldn't meet Logan's eyes.

They couldn't get anything more out of him. Instead they all sat there in silence until a pair of uniformed constables arrived to take him away.

The PC guarding Desperate Doug MacDuff's room was halfway through his novel when Logan and WPC Watson turned up at the door. He'd had a boring day, except for flirting with a couple of the nurses. Logan sent him off to fetch coffees again.

Doug's room was buried in semidarkness, the flickering television screen casting its green-and-grey glow, making shadows writhe and jump. It was like being back in the Turf 'n Track again. Only this time no one was trying to kick the living hell out of them. The only sound came from the air conditioner, the humming machinery, and the pallid, wheezing old man lying on the hospital bed, gazing up at the silent TV. Logan sat himself down at the foot of the bed again. 'Evening, Dougie,' he said with a smile in his voice. 'We brought grapes.' He plonked a paper bag on the blankets by the old man's feet.

Doug sniffed and went on staring at the television screen.

'We've just had a very interesting chat with

someone, Dougie. About you.' Logan leaned forward and helped himself to a grape from the bag. In the light of the TV they looked like little gangrenous haemorrhoids. 'He's fingered you for assaulting and abducting the late Geordie Stephenson. He watched you do it! How about that, Dougie? First we get forensic evidence and now we've got a witness.'

No reaction.

Logan helped himself to another grape. 'Witness says you also killed that little girl.' It was a lie, but you never knew your luck. 'The one we found in a bin-bag.'

That took Doug's attention off the television set. He sat, propped up with half a dozen pillows, glaring at Logan with his one good eye. And then he went back to the television. 'Little fucker.'

The silence stretched out in the gloom. Lit by the TV's ghostly glow, Desperate Doug looked like a skeleton, all sunken cheeks and dark-ringed eye sockets. His teeth were still floating in a glass.

'Why'd you kill her, Dougie?'

'You know,' said the old man. His voice was low and gravelly, a whisper forced through broken glass. 'I was a fuckin' stallion when I was young. Aye, no that much younger mind. Women fallin' over themselves to get a bit of it Dougie-style. Women mind. Women. No like them sick fucks.'

Logan watched as Doug coughed: a wet, rattling sound that ended with a globule of dark phlegm being spat into a bedpan.

'I gets word Geordie's stayin' with his faggot half-brother in Rosemount. So I go round. Pay them a little visit. Geordie tries to come off all hard to start with, you know? He's the man. I'm just some old fuck. "Go home, granddad or I'll break your zimmer . . . "' A toothless smile turned into a laugh that turned into another fit of coughing. Doug lay back on the mound of crunchy hospital pillows, breathing hard. 'So I kicked the shit out of him. Right there in the lounge. Then his poof-bastard-brother comes bargin' in from the bedroom, all wrapped up in this pink dressin' gown. And I'm thinking nothin' of it. You know, figure he's going for a bubble bath or some shite like that. Only I can hear somethin', like a kid cryin'.' He shook his head at the memory. 'Fucker's standing there shouting at me: "You can't come in here! You can't do this!" Like I give a shit. And I can still hear the cryin'. So I go see what it is, only poof-boy's no gettin' out of the way: "You've got no right . . . "' He smacked a fist into his palm. 'Bang. There's this little girl in the bedroom. Wearin' nothin' but a fuckin' Mickey Mouse hat. You know, with the ears?' He looked at Logan for confirmation, but Logan was too shocked to answer. 'So I'm lookin' at this naked wee girl and that bastard's in there, barely dressed.' He grimaced. 'Went back in the lounge and kicked the shite out of him too. Sick bastard.'

Logan finally recovered enough to say, 'What happened to the girl?'

Desperate Doug MacDuff dropped his eyes to his hands. They lay curled in his lap like wizened talons. Arthritis, just beginning to turn the joints into swollen balls of pain. 'Aye. The girl . . .' He cleared his throat. 'She . . . came in as I'm givin' the sick bastard a goin' over. And she's foreign. You know, like German or fuckin' Norwegian. Somethin' like that. And she's lookin' up at me with these big brown eyes, an' she's cryin' and sayin' fuckin' filthy things: "I suck your dick." "Fuck me in the ass . . . " Over and over again.' The old man gave a shuddering breath and dissolved into a bed-shaking fit of coughing. He was white as milk when he finally stopped. 'She's . . . She's holding onto my leg, cryin' and snotterin' everywhere, bare naked, and tellin' me she wants me to fuck her in the arse. I . . . I pushed her away . . .' His voice dropped. 'Fell against the fireplace. Bang. Head into the brick.'

They sat in silence once more. Doug lost in thought, Logan and Watson trying to come to terms with what they'd just heard. It was Doug who spoke first.

'So I picked up Geordie, took him somewhere nice and quiet, and fucked him over. You should have heard him scream when I hacked off his fuckin' knees. Filthy bastard.'

Logan cleared his throat. 'How come you let his brother live?'

Doug looked at him with sadness written in the deep lines of his face. 'Had a job to do. Message to deliver. I was goin' to go back the next day. Show him what happened to sick bastards like him. You know, with a Stanley knife? Only when I went back there was all these pigs clamberin' all over the place. And the next day and the day after that . . .'

Logan nodded. The first lot of policemen must have been his team arresting Norman Chalmers. The rest doing door-to-doors, trying to find witnesses. While all the time Desperate Doug MacDuff was hovering in the shadows, watching them.

'Standin' like a fuckin' idiot in the snow and rain, gettin' myself some pneumonia to go with the cancer.' Doug lapsed back into silence, a faraway look in his good eye, the milky one shimmering in the television's glow.

Logan stood. 'Before we go there's one thing that's been bothering me: what was the message?'

'The message?' A smile spread across Desperate Doug's toothless face. 'You don't steal from your employer.'

32

The interview room was close and stuffy, the radiator in the far corner belching out heat, the opaque window resolutely refusing to let fresh air in. A smell of cheesy feet and nervous armpits filled the room as Cameron Anderson sat on the other side of the table and lied.

Logan and Insch sat opposite, listening with deadpan faces as Cameron Anderson once more placed the blame for everything on Desperate Doug MacDuff. The dead girl was nothing to do with him.

'So,' said Insch, his heavy arms crossed over his barrel-like chest. 'You're telling us that the old man brought the child with him.'

Cameron tried an ingratiating smile. 'That's right.'

'Desperate Doug MacDuff, a man who has killed dozens of people, a man who hurts people for a living, took a four-year-old girl with him when he turned up to drag your brother away and hack

469

his kneecaps off? What was it: Take Your Granddaughter To Work Week?'

Cameron licked his cracked lips and said, 'I can only tell you what happened,' for about the twentieth time. He was doing surprisingly well. Like this wasn't his first police interview. As if he'd been through it all before. Only there was no record of him ever having been arrested.

'That's funny,' said Insch, pulling out a packet of jelly babies. He offered one to Logan, took one himself and then stuffed the packet back in his pocket. 'You see, Doug says that you were in the bedroom with the girl when he arrived. He says that you were wearing nothing under your dressing gown. He says you were screwing her.'

'Douglas MacDuff is lying.'

'So if he's lying, how did the girl end up dead?'

'He pushed her and she fell against the fire-place.'

It was about the only bit of Cameron's story that matched what Desperate Doug had told Logan.

'And how did she end up in your neighbour's bin-bag?'

'The old man wrapped her in packing tape and hid her body in the bag.'

'He says you did it.'

'He's lying.'

'Really . . .' Insch sat back and sucked at his teeth, letting the silence grow. He'd tried it a couple of times already, but Cameron wasn't as stupid as he looked. He kept his mouth shut.

Insch leaned over the table, staring Cameron Anderson down. 'You really expect us to believe Desperate Doug got rid of the girl's body? A man who's quite happy to hack off your brother's kneecaps with a machete can't dismember a little girl's corpse?'

Cameron shuddered, but didn't say anything.

'You see, we know you tried to cut up the body, but you couldn't, could you? It made you sick. So you puked. Only you got some in the cut.' Insch smiled like a shark. 'Did you know we can get DNA from vomit, Mr Anderson? We've already had it analysed. All we need to do is match it to yours and you're screwed.'

Suddenly Cameron's composure cracked. 'I . . . I . . .' His eyes darted round the room, looking for a way out, looking for inspiration. And then calm returned. 'I . . . I was not completely honest with you earlier,' he said, under control once more.

'That's a shock.'

Cameron chose to ignore the sarcasm. 'I was trying to protect my brother's reputation.'

Insch smiled. 'His reputation? What as: a violent wee scumbag?'

Cameron carried on regardless. 'Geordie turned up at my door a fortnight ago. Said he was in town on business and needed a place to stay. He had a little girl with him, said she was his girl-friend's child. He was looking after the kid while

she was in Ibiza on holiday. I didn't know anything was going on, but the night Geordie was
killed I came home to find him and the girl naked
in bed together. We had a fight, I wanted him out
of my house. Told him I was going to call the
police.' Cameron glanced down at his hands, as
if seeing the story written there. 'But that was
when the old man came to the door. Said he had
a message for Geordie. I let him in and went to
check that the little girl was OK. That Geordie
hadn't hurt her . . . There's this big crash from
the lounge and I run through to see Geordie curled
up on the floor. And the old man's kicking him
and punching him and Geordie's crying and I try
to make him stop, but the old man's like an
animal! Then . . . then the little girl comes through
from the bedroom and grabs the old man. He . . .'
Cameron's voice caught in his throat. 'He pushed
her away and she fell against the fireplace. I went
to help, pick her up, but she was already dead.
The old man started in on me.' He shivered. 'He
. . . He had a knife. He wanted me to cut her up.
Said if I didn't he'd cut me up . . . I couldn't do
it. I tried, but I couldn't.' Cameron hung his head
before telling them how Dougie had beaten him
up again. Made him wrap the little girl's body up
in parcel tape and hide her in a bin-bag. Only
there were none in the flat. But it was bin-day
the next day and there was an almost-empty bin-
bag on the upstairs landing, outside Norman
Chalmers's flat. Anderson had taken it, put the

body inside and carried it down to the communal bin parked outside the front of the building. It was very late at night, dark, and there was no one about. He put the girl in the bin and covered it up with other bags. Then the old man told him he was an accessory now and that if he told anyone what had happened the police would lock him away.

'Fascinating,' said Insch dryly.

'He then threatened to kill me if I told anyone what had happened. And that was the last time I saw him, or my brother, or the little girl.'

When Cameron had finished they sat in silence, only the gentle whirring of the tape recorder intruding on the quiet.

'If you're Geordie's brother,' said Logan, 'how come you've got different last names?'

Cameron shifted uncomfortably in his seat. 'Different mothers. He was from my father's first marriage. They got divorced so Geordie was brought up with her maiden name, Stephenson. Dad got married again and I was born six years later.'

Silence fell. It was Logan who broke it. 'What if I told you we found seminal fluid in the girl's mouth?'

Cameron blanched.

'How much do you want to bet it matches the DNA sample we took from you? How are you going to pin that on Desperate Doug?'

Cameron looked as stunned as DI Insch. He sat

on the other side of the table, mouth working up and down like a dying fish. Silence.

'Sergeant,' said Insch at last, 'can I have a word with you outside, please?'

They suspended the interview and Logan joined Insch in the corridor, leaving Cameron under the watchful eye of the silent PC.

A frown creased Insch's face, turning the corners of his mouth into an ugly snarl. 'Why did no one tell me we'd found semen in the girl's mouth?' he asked, his voice dangerously neutral.

'Because we didn't.' Logan smiled. 'But he doesn't know that.'

'You're a dirty cheating bastard, DS McRae,' said Insch, the frown turning into a smile of paternal pride. 'Did you see his face when you said it? Looked like he'd shat himself.'

Logan was about to expand upon the theme when a worried-looking WPC trotted up the corridor and told them about Roadkill. A doctor at the hospital had made a 999 call. Someone had put Bernard Duncan Philips out of his misery.

Insch swore and ran a large hand over his face. 'He's supposed to be in protective custody! But he still manages to get himself beaten up, hospitalized and killed.' The inspector sagged against the wall. 'Give us five minutes,' he told the WPC before heading back into the interview room.

They took DI Insch's filthy Range Rover, the windows smudged and streaky where his spaniel had rubbed its nose against the glass. Insch drove them up through Rosemount's snow-lined streets.

Looking morosely out of the window, Logan watched the granite terraces drift by, his mind half on Roadkill and half on the strained conversation he'd had with WPC Jackie Watson as they drove along this very road.

As Insch pulled the car round the corner, making for the hospital, something tugged at Logan's mind. He stared out at the houses on this side of the road. A plastic reindeer, all lit up, complete with neon-red, flashing nose, jogged his memory. This was where they'd seen Peter Lumley's dad. Still wandering the streets looking for his missing child. Even though he knew his stepson was dead . . .

'You've got a face like a pig's arse,' Insch told him, indicating to turn up Westburn Road. 'What's up?'

Logan shrugged, still seeing that wretched figure, tromping through the snow with his head down, the legs of his overalls damp with snow and slush. 'Not sure . . . maybe nothing.'

Inside the hospital it was too hot, the heating cranked up to combat the winter's chill, leaving the whole place in a sub-tropical, antiseptic fug. The room Bernard Duncan Philips, AKA Roadkill, had shared was no different, only more crowded – Identification Bureau personnel, a photographer, DI Insch and Logan all dressed in identical white paper coveralls as if they were some sort of conceptual dance troupe.

The room's other bed was empty; a tearful nurse in her late forties told Logan the man sharing with Roadkill had died of liver failure that afternoon.

In between the high-pitched whine and clack of the photographer's flash, Logan was treated to the sight of Roadkill's battered body. He was sprawled across the bed, one plastered arm hanging out over the linoleum, blood drips slowly clotting on the tips of pale fingers. The bandages on his head were bright red around the eyes and mouth, the ones on his chest so saturated with blood they were almost black.

'What the hell happened to the PC watching him?' Insch was in a foul mood.

A sheepish-looking constable held up his hand and explained that there had been some trouble in A&E. Two drunks and a bouncer, trading blows. He'd been summoned by the nurses to help break it up.

Insch creased his face and counted to ten. 'I suppose death's been declared?' he asked when he got to the end.

A WPC said that it hadn't, eliciting a barrage of swearing from the inspector.

'It's a hospital! The place is filthy with bloody doctors! Go get one of the lazy bastards to officially declare death!'

While they waited, Insch and Logan examined

the body as best they could without actually touching it.

'Stabbed,' said Insch, peering closely at the small, rectangular puncture marks in the bandages. 'That look like a knife to you?'

'Something with a chisel point. Could be a screwdriver? Stiletto? Pair of scissors?'

Insch squatted down, searching under the bed for a discarded knife. All he found was more blood.

While the inspector was looking for a murder weapon, Logan worked his way carefully along the body. The stab-marks were all exactly the same, no more than fifteen millimetres long, two millimetres wide, all radiating out from the left side of the body. The killer had been frenzied, the stab wounds multiple and furious. He closed his eyes and pictured the scene: Roadkill unconscious, killer standing on the left side of the bed, the side furthest away from the door. Stabbing rapidly, again and again.

Logan opened his eyes and stepped back, feeling slightly nauseous. There was blood everywhere. Not only on the body and the bed, but up the wall too. He craned his neck back to see little red flecks splattered on the off-white ceiling tiles. Whoever did this would have looked like something from a horror film by the time they'd finished. Not someone you'd forget seeing in a hurry.

This wasn't random violence. Nor was it the violence of a self-righteous mob. This was revenge.

'What is the meaning of this? Why have I been dragged down here?'

The voice was stressed and irritable, just like its owner: a well-built female doctor in a white coat, complete with stethoscope around her neck.

Logan raised his hands in submission and backed away from the body. 'We need you to declare death before we can move the body.'

She scowled at him. 'Of course he's bloody dead. You see this?' She pointed at her name badge. 'It says "doctor". That means I know a dead body when I see one!'

Inspector Insch stood up on the other side of the bed and pulled out his warrant card. 'You see this?' he said, holding it under her nose. 'It says "Detective Inspector". That means I expect you to behave like a grown up and not take whatever your problem is out on my officers. OK?'

She glowered at him, but didn't say anything. Slowly her face softened. 'Sorry,' she said at last. 'It's been a long, shitty day.'

Insch nodded. 'If it's any consolation I know how you feel.' He stepped back and pointed at Roadkill's pincushion corpse. 'Care to hazard a guess at the time of death?'

'Easy: some time between quarter to nine and quarter past ten.'

Insch was impressed. 'Not often we get an estimated time of death within half an hour.'

The doctor actually smiled at him. 'That's when the last shift was through. The beds get checked regularly. He wasn't dead at quarter to nine. Quarter past ten, he was.'

DI Insch thanked her and she was about to say something else when the pager at her hip let out a series of bleeps. She grabbed it, read the message, cursed, apologized, and ran from the room.

Logan stared down at the bloody remains of Bernard Duncan Philips and tried to figure out what was nagging him about all this. And then it hit him. 'Lumley,' he said.

'What?' Insch looked at him as if he'd grown an extra head.

'Peter Lumley's stepdad. Remember him? He walks round this area of town the whole time. Last time I saw him he was walking away from the hospital. He blamed Roadkill for his son's death.'

'So?'

Logan gazed down at the blood-soaked body lying on the bed. 'Looks like he's got his own back.'

33

Hazlehead was dark and cold as midnight rolled in. The snow was lying thicker here than it had been in the middle of town, the trees standing out like Rorschach inkblot tests. Streetlights cast yellow pools of light, the flickering blue flash of patrol car lights making dark shadows dance. Most of the tower block was shrouded in darkness, but here and there a twitching curtain showed a neighbour peering out, trying to see what the police wanted.

The police wanted Jim Lumley.

The Lumley's flat looked nothing like it had the last time Logan had been here. It was a pigsty. Discarded carryout containers lay in piles on the carpet, joined by empty tins of Special and cheap lager. All the photos had been taken down from the rest of the flat and put back up again in the lounge: one big montage of Peter Lumley's life.

Jim Lumley hadn't put up any sort of struggle when Insch rang the doorbell and barged his way in, dragging Logan and a couple of uniformed PCs

with him. He'd just stood there in his filthy overalls, unshaven and rumpled, his hair sticking out
like an electrocuted hedgehog. 'If you're looking
for Sheila, she's not here,' he said and collapsed
onto the couch. 'Went two days ago. Staying with
her mother . . .' He pulled a tin of Special free of
its plastic handcuff and cracked it open.

'We're not here to see Sheila, Mr Lumley,' said
Insch. 'We're here for you.'

The ragged man nodded and took another swig.
'Roadkill.' He didn't bother to wipe away the beer
dripping down his stubbly chin.

'Yes, Roadkill.' Logan settled down on the other
end of the settee. 'He's dead.'

Jim Lumley nodded slowly and then stared hard
at his tin of beer.

'Want to tell us all about it, Mr Lumley?'

Lumley threw his head back and drained the
tin, froth spilling down the sides of his mouth
and onto the front of his grubby overalls. 'Not
much to tell . . .' he said, shrugging. 'I was walking
around, looking for Peter and there he was. Just
like his picture in the paper. Right there.' He pulled
another tin of Special free, but Insch liberated it
before he could pop the top.

The inspector told the two uniforms to search
the place for the murder weapon.

Lumley picked a cushion off the couch and
clutched it to his chest like a hot water bottle. 'So
I follows him. Into the woods.'

'Into the woods?' This wasn't quite what Logan

had been expecting, but Insch cast him a warning glance before he could say anything more.

'He was just walking along like nothing had happened. Like Peter wasn't dead!' Lumley's face flushed red, the crimson rising from the dirty neck of his overalls. 'I grabbed him . . . I . . . I was only going to talk to him. Tell him what I thought of him . . .' He bit his lip and stared down at the stitching holding his cushion together. 'He started to yell and I hit him. Just to shut him up. Make him stop. Only I couldn't. Stop. Just kept on hitting and hitting and hitting . . .'

Jesus, thought Logan, and we'd thought he'd been attacked by a mob. It was only one man!

'And then . . . then it started to snow again. It was cold. I washed the blood off my hands and face with handfuls of snow and then I went home.' He shrugged. 'Told Sheila what happened and she packed her bags and left.' A tear ran down his cheek, leaving a thin trail of clean skin behind. He sniffed and tried to take another drink out of his empty beer can. 'I'm a monster . . . just like him . . .' He looked into the empty tin and saw only darkness. 'So he's dead, eh?' Lumley crushed the can in his fist.

Insch and Logan shared a frown. 'Of course he's bloody dead,' said Insch. 'Someone turned him into a sieve.'

A bitter smile twisted Lumley's tear-streaked face. 'Good fuckin' riddance.'

*

Outside, tiny flakes of delicate white drifted out of the dark orange sky. Grey clouds lit from below by the city streetlights. Logan and Insch watched Jim Lumley being bundled into the back of a patrol car and driven away.

'Well,' said the inspector, his breath pluming out in great clouds of white. 'Wrong man, right reason. Fifty, fifty.' He pointed the open end of a packet of fizzy cola bottles at Logan. 'No? Ah well.' Insch helped himself to a handful, popping them into his mouth one at a time as they walked back to his mud-splattered Range Rover.

'You think they'll do him?' asked Logan as Insch started the car up and set the heaters going full pelt.

'Aye. Probably. Shame he didn't do the stabbing though. Would've been nice and neat.'

'Back to the hospital?' asked Logan.

'Hospital?' Insch checked the clock on the dashboard. 'It's nearly one in the morning! She'll string me up.' The inspector's wife was not known for her generous nature when it came to late nights. 'I've got uniforms taking statements. We'll go through them in the morning. Half the place is asleep anyway.'

Insch dropped him off at his flat, and Logan watched the car scrunch its way carefully down the street and away before letting himself in. The little red light was flashing away on his answering machine. For a brief second, Logan thought it might be WPC Jackie Watson, but when he pressed play it was Miller's voice that crackled out of the speakers. He'd heard about Roadkill being stabbed and wanted an exclusive update.

Grunting, Logan hit 'DELETE' and slumped off to bed.

Wednesday started as it meant to go on. Just out of the shower, Logan was too slow to get the phone before the answering machine kicked in. Another call from Miller wanting Logan to spill the beans. Logan didn't bother picking up; just let the reporter prattle away to himself as he went through to the kitchen to fix himself some tea and toast.

On the way out of the flat he paused for just long enough to delete Miller's message without listening to it. He doubted it would be the last call he'd get from the reporter today.

The morning briefing was a subdued affair, with DI Insch doing a lot of yawning as he took everyone through the events of last night, both at the hospital and in interview room number three. The order of the day was going to be door-to-door. Again.

Logan hung back at the end of the briefing, sharing a smile with WPC Watson as she filed out to start questioning doctors, nurses and patients. He still owed her a pint.

Insch was parked in his usual spot, on the edge of the desk, one haunch up on the wood while he rummaged through his suit pockets for something sweet. 'Sure I had some fruit pastilles . . .' he muttered as Logan came up and asked him what the plan was for the morning. Coming up empty on the confectionery front, he asked Logan to get Cameron Anderson into an interview room on his own. 'You know the drill,' he said. 'Nice burly PC standing in the corner glowering at him for a bit. That'll make his sphincter clench.'

By the time nine o'clock came around Cameron Anderson had been sitting in a baking-hot interview room, with a hostile-looking PC for nearly an hour and, as Inch had predicted, he was squirming.

'Mr Anderson,' said Insch with zero warmth as they finally sat down to begin the interview. 'How nice of you to take time out of your busy, busy schedule!' Cameron looked terrified and exhausted, as if he'd been up all night crying.

'I take it,' said Insch, helping himself to a fruit sherbet, 'that you've concocted some other miraculous interpretation for the evening's events? Perhaps aliens did it?'

Cameron's hands trembled on the tabletop. His voice was thin and quiet, shaking like his hands. 'Geordie and me never met until I was ten. His mum went down with breast cancer, so he came to live with us. He was bigger than me . . .' Cameron's voice dropped so low that Logan had to ask him to speak up for the tape. 'He did things. He . . .' A single tear ran down his cheek. Cameron bit his lip and told them about his brother.

Geordie had come up from Edinburgh three weeks earlier. He was doing some business for his boss. Something to do with getting planning permission. He was spending money like it was going out of fashion. Gambling mostly. Only he wasn't winning. Then the thing with the planner didn't work. He'd spent all the bribe money by then anyway. So he tried threats. And then he had to get out of town quick.

'He pushed the planner under a bus,' said Insch. 'He's in Aberdeen Royal Infirmary with a shattered skull and pelvis. He's going to die.'

Cameron didn't look up, just went on with his story. 'A week later Geordie comes back. Said his employer wanted to know what had happened to all the money. He didn't have it and there were people from the bookies coming round to my flat. They took Geordie away. When he came back the next day he was peeing blood.' He shuddered, his eyes glistening. 'But Geordie had a plan. He said someone was looking for something special. Something he could get his hands on.'

Logan scooted forward in his chair. That was what Miller had said. That someone was after 'livestock'.

'I didn't see him again for a couple of days. He had this big suitcase with him and there was this girl inside. She was drugged. He . . . he said she was the answer to all our troubles. He was going to sell her to this man and get enough to pay off the bookies and give his boss the bribe money back. No one was going to miss her.'

'What was her name?' asked Logan, his voice cold in the oppressive heat of the room.

Cameron shrugged, the tears beginning to well up over his bottom lid, a small sparkling drip forming at the end of his nose. 'I . . . I don't know. She was foreign. From somewhere Russian I think. Her mother was a tart in Edinburgh, brought over special. Only she died of an overdose. So the kid was, you know, going spare . . .' He sniffed. 'Geordie bagged her up before anyone else came to claim her.'

'So you and your brother were going to sell a four-year-old girl to some sick bastard?' The menace in Insch's voice wasn't very well concealed. Colour had risen up the fat man's cheeks and his eyes sparked like black diamonds.

'I had nothing to do with it! It was him! It was always him . . .'

Insch glowered, but said nothing more.

'She couldn't speak any English, so he taught her to say things. You know,' he buried his head in his trembling hands, 'dirty things. She didn't know what they meant.'

'And so you abused her. You taught her to say: "fuck me in the ass" and then you made her do it.'

'No! No! We couldn't . . .' A blush raced over his face. 'Geordie said she had to be, you know, still a virgin.'

Logan's face creased up in disgust. 'So you made her suck your dick?'

'It was Geordie's idea! He made me do it!' The tears spilled down Cameron's face. 'Only once. I only did it once. When the old man came round. He was beating up Geordie and I tried to stop him. Then the girl came in and she's saying these things Geordie taught her. And she grabs the old man and he pushes her away and she falls and hits her head and she's dead.' He looked imploringly into Insch's cold eyes. 'He told me he was going to kill Geordie, then he was coming back for me!' Cameron rubbed the back of his sleeve over his eyes, wiping away the tears. But more sprang up in their place. 'I had to get rid of her! She was lying on the fireplace and she was naked and dead. I tried to cut her up, but I couldn't. It was . . . it was . . .' he shuddered and wiped at his eyes again. 'So I wrapped her up in tape. I . . . poured bleach in her mouth to . . . you know . . . make it clean again.'

'Then you had to find a bin-bag to put her in.'

Cameron nodded and a sparkling drop fell from his nose, splashing onto the tabletop between his trembling hands.

'And then you threw her out with the trash.'

'Yes . . . I'm sorry. I'm so sorry . . .'

After his statement, after Cameron Anderson had admitted sexually abusing a four-year-old girl, they put him back into his cell and arranged for him to appear in the Sheriff Court the next day. There wasn't any celebration. Somehow, after Cameron's confession, no one was in the mood.

Back in the incident room Logan sighed and unpinned the little girl's photo from the wall, feeling hollow inside. Catching the man who had abused her and disposed of her body as if it was nothing more than household rubbish, had left him feeling dirty by association. Ashamed to be human.

Insch settled himself down on the edge of the table and helped Logan stack up the statements. 'Wonder if we'll ever know who she was?'

Logan scrubbed at his face with his hands, feeling the first rasp of stubble under his fingers. 'I doubt it,' he said.

'Anyway,' Insch dumped the statements into the case file and gave an expansive yawn, 'we've still got enough on our plate to worry about.'

Roadkill.

This time they took one of the pool cars to the hospital, WPC Watson driving.

Aberdeen Royal Infirmary was a lot busier than it had been the night before. They arrived just in time to see lunch getting served: something boiled with boiled potatoes and boiled cabbage.

'Remind me to go private,' said Insch as they passed a housekeeper trundling a steaming trolley that reeked of cabbage.

They gathered all the PCs who'd been questioning the patients and staff together in an empty day room to get their updates. There wasn't much worth listening to, but they went through them all anyway, thanking the uniformed officers for their work. No one had seen, or heard anything. They'd even been through the security tapes: no blood-soaked figures running off into the night.

The inspector gave something like a rousing speech, and sent them all back to work. That left only Logan and Watson. 'You two better go make yourselves useful too,' said Insch, beginning the familiar hunt through his suit. 'I'm off to speak to that doctor we saw last night.' He ambled off, still hunting for the elusive confectionery.

'So,' said WPC Watson, trying to sound efficient. 'Where do you want to start?'

Logan thought about her legs, poking out from beneath his T-shirt in the kitchen. 'Er . . .' he said, deciding that now was neither the time nor the place. 'How about we go take a look at those security tapes. See if there's anything that's been missed.'

'You're the boss,' she said and threw in a jaunty little salute.

Logan tried to keep his mind on work as they walked through the hospital, making for the security guard's station. But it wasn't working. 'You know,' he finally mustered the courage to say as they reached the lift. 'I still owe you a pint from last night.'

Watson nodded. 'I hadn't forgotten, sir.'

'Good.' He punched the lift button and tried

to look casual, resting against the railing that ran round the inside of the elevator. 'How about tonight?'

'Tonight?'

Logan felt the colour starting to rise into his cheeks. 'If you're busy it's OK. You know, some other night . . .' Idiot.

The lift shuddered to a halt and WPC Watson smiled at him. 'Tonight would be good.'

Logan was too happy to say anything else until they got to the security room. It was compact: a long black desk with a wall of little television screens above it. A bank of video recorders whirled away, taping everything that went on. And in the middle of all this sat a youngish man with bleached-blond hair and spots dressed in standard security-guard brown with yellow trimmings and a peaked cap. Looking like a jobbie in a hat.

He explained that there were no security cameras watching the room where the murder took place, but they did have them in all the main corridors, A&E, and all the exits. Some of the wards had them too, but there were 'issues' with videoing sick people getting medical attention. Privacy and stuff.

There was a pile of tapes from the previous night. The search team had already been through them, but if Logan wanted to have another pass it was OK by him.

That was when Logan's mobile phone went off, the sound loud and intrusive in the small room.

'You know,' said the guard sternly, 'mobile phones have to be switched off!'

Logan apologized, but this would only take a minute.

It was Miller again. *'Laz! Beginning to think you'd fallen off the arse of the earth, man.'*

'I'm kind of busy right now,' said Logan, turning his back on the spotty youth with the turd-brown uniform. 'Is it urgent?'

'Kinda depends on what your point of view is. You anywhere near a telly?'

'What?'

'Television. Moving pictures—'

'I know what television is.'

'Aye, well, if you're near one: turn it on. Grampian.'

'Can you get regular television on any of these things?' Logan asked the security jobbie.

The spotted youth said no, but Logan could try one of the rooms down the corridor.

Three minutes later they stood in front of a flickering television screen with an American soap opera dribbling away on it. Behind them, on the bed, an old woman with purple-rinsed hair was snoring it up, her teeth floating in a glass.

'Gee, Adelaide,' said a suntanned blond with perfect teeth and a washboard stomach. *'Are you saying that baby's mine?'*

Dramatic music, close-up of over-made-up brunette with pneumatic breasts; cut to commercial. Stair-lifts. Crisps. Washing powder. And then the face of Gerald Cleaver filled the screen. He was sitting in a wingback leather chair, wearing a cardigan, looking all avuncular and wholesome. *'They tried to make me look like a monster!'* he said and the camera cut to a shot of him walking a jolly labrador. *'They accused me of terrible crimes I didn't commit!'* Another camera jump, this time to Cleaver sitting on a low drystone dyke, looking earnest and pained. *'Read about my year of hell, only in this week's* News of the World*!'*

'Oh God,' said Logan as the paper's logo spun on the screen. 'That's all we need.'

34

Logan and Watson grumbled their way back to the security office. Berating the paper and its decision to give Gerald Cleaver money for his story. The spotty youth in the shitty-brown uniform was in the process of charging into action, straightening his peaked cap as he went.

'Trouble?' asked WPC Watson.

'Someone's stealing Mars Bars from the gift shop!' And off he ran.

They watched him disappear round the corner, feet and elbows flying in his haste to reach the scene of the crime. Watson gave a wry smile. 'How the other half live . . .'

A second security guard – a heavy-set man in his early fifties, with a comb-over and eyebrows like a terrier – was now manning the console. He was swigging from a bottle of Lucozade, his head buried in a copy of the morning's paper. 'KIDDIE-KILLER SUSPECT STABBED TO DEATH!' was splashed across the front page. When Logan told him why they were there, he grunted and waved at a pile of labelled video tapes.

Settling down at a console with a tape player, Logan and Watson started to wade their way through the videos. The search team that had been here before had made things a lot easier, winding the tapes forward to when Roadkill was murdered. Slowly, Logan and Watson worked their way through them all, the security guard slugging away at his Lucozade and sucking his teeth in the background.

Figures jumped and jerked across the screen, the camera only taking one frame every three or four seconds, making everything look like experimental Canadian animation. The faces were pretty blurred, but it was still possible to make people out when they got closer to the camera. Half an hour later Logan had recognized a handful of the hundreds of faces that had drifted through various parts of the hospital: the doctor who'd treated Desperate Doug; the nurse who thought he was a monster for beating up an old man; the PC who was supposed to be guarding the geriatric hitman; the doctor who'd declared death on Roadkill last night; the surgeon who'd spent seven hours stitching Logan's insides back together; and Nurse Henderson, her black eye clearly visible on the tape as she stomped along, dressed in her street clothes – rugby shirt, trainers and jeans, an overnight bag slung over her shoulder.

'How many more tapes have we got to go?'

asked Logan as Watson gave a huge yawn and stretch.

'Sorry, sir,' she said, composing herself. 'Two more exit tapes and that's the lot.'

Logan slipped the next one into the machine. A side entrance to the hospital. Faces flashed by, talking and laughing, or people with their heads down as they stepped into the biting wind. Nothing suspicious. The last one was the main A&E reception area. The tape here ran at normal speed, ready to capture the all too common flare-ups of antisocial behaviour that came with a hard night's drinking. Logan recognized more faces here: he'd arrested a lot of them. Peeing in doorways, petty larceny, vandalism. One bloke had been done for 'giving himself a treat' in Union Terrace gardens with a wine bottle. But again, there was nothing out of the ordinary here. Not if you didn't count the sudden explosion as two staggering drunks launched themselves at a huge bouncer who had his arm in a makeshift sling. Screams, overturned chairs, more blood. Nurses trying to pry them apart. And then, at last, a blurry police constable charged into the crowded room and put an end to the whole thing with three liberal doses of CS spray. After that it was mostly rolling about on the ground, screaming. But no sign of Roadkill's murderer.

Logan sat back in his seat and rubbed at his eyes. The time stamp on the video said ten-twenty. The PC with the CS spray stayed to make sure everyone was still alive. Ten twenty-five: PC hero accepts a cup of tea before returning to his vigil outside Roadkill's door. Ten-thirty . . . Logan was getting bored with this. They weren't going to find anything on the tapes.

And that was when Nurse Henderson came back into view, the black eye a lot more noticeable. Logan frowned and paused the tape.

'What?' Watson squinted at the tableau.

'Notice something?'

WPC Watson confessed that she didn't, so Logan tapped the screen, right on top of Nurse Henderson, still carrying the overnight bag. 'She's wearing her uniform.'

'So?'

'She was wearing her civilian clothes in the other tape.'

Watson shrugged. 'So she got changed.'

'She's still carrying the bag. If she got changed, why didn't she leave her bag in the lockers?'

'Maybe they don't have lockers?'

Logan asked the older security guard if the nurses' changing room had lockers in it.

'Aye,' he said. 'But if you think I'm showin' you a video tape of nurses gettin' changed: you've got another bloody think comin'!'

'This is a murder investigation!'

'I don't care. You're no seein' any tape of naked nurses.'

Logan bristled. 'Listen, sunshine—'

'We've no got cameras in there.' He grinned,

showing a perfect set of dentures. 'We tried, but the governors were havin' none of it. Didn't trust us to keep our minds on the job. Shame. I coulda made a fortune floggin' those tapes ...'

The administration centre of the hospital was nicer than the bit sick people occupied. Here the smell of antiseptic on squeaky linoleum was exchanged for carpet and fresh air. Logan found himself a helpful young woman with bleached-blonde hair and an Irish accent and sweet-talked her into going through last night's shift records.

'Here you go,' she said, pointing to a screenful of numbers and dates on her computer. 'Nurse Michelle Henderson ... Did a double shift last night. Got off at about half-nine.'

'Half-nine? Thanks: thanks a lot. You've been very helpful.'

She smiled back at him, pleased to have been of assistance. If there was anything else she could do for him, just give her a call. Anytime. She even gave him a business card. Luckily Logan didn't see the look on WPC Watson's face as he accepted it.

'Well?' she demanded as they rode the lift back to the ground floor.

'Henderson gets off shift at nine-thirty. Nine-fifty she's on camera, changed and ready to go home. Ten-thirty she's back in her uniform again, leaving the building.' Watson opened her mouth, but Logan carried on, grim triumph in his voice. 'We were looking for someone covered in blood.

Mrs Henderson just got changed and walked right out of there as if nothing ever happened.'

They grabbed a pair of uniformed officers from the search party and called back to base. DI Insch was not in the best of moods when the call was put through: he sounded as if someone had been massaging his backside with red-hot pokers. *'Where the hell have you been?'* he demanded, before Logan could get a word in. *'I've been trying to call you for the last hour!'*

'Still at the hospital, sir. All mobile phones have to be switched off . . .' But mostly he'd switched it off so Colin Miller couldn't call him back.

'Never mind that! Another kid's gone missing!'

Logan felt his heart sink. 'Oh no . . .'

'Aye. I want you to get your arse over here to Duthie Park: the Winter Gardens. I'm pulling in all the search teams. Bloody weather's getting worse, snow's going to make any evidence we've got disappear. This is now our number one priority!'

'Sir, I'm just on my way to arrest Nurse Michelle Henderson—'

'Who?'

'Lorna Henderson's mother. The kid we found in Roadkill's steading. She was at the hospital last night. She blames Roadkill for her daughter's death and the break-up of her marriage. Motive and opportunity. The Fiscal agrees: apprehension and search warrants.'

There was a moment's silence on the other end of the phone, then a muffled conversation as Insch gave someone else a hard time. And then the inspector was back. *'OK,'* he said, sounding as if he was about to clobber someone. *'Pick her up, chuck her in a cell and get your backside over here. Roadkill's not getting any more dead. This kid might still be alive.'*

They stood on the top step in the snow while Logan rang the doorbell again. 'Greensleeves' started up for the fourth time.

Watson asked Logan if he wanted her to kick it down, her breath fogging in the chilly air, nose and cheeks bright red. Behind them the two uniforms they'd liberated from the hospital search team expressed their agreement. Anything to get out of the freezing cold.

He was just about to give her the nod when the door opened a crack and Nurse Michelle Henderson's face appeared. Her hair looked like a chimpanzee had slept in it.

'Can I help you?' she asked, the chain still on the door. Her words reeked of stale gin.

'Open up, Mrs Henderson.' Logan held up his warrant card. 'You remember us. We need to talk to you about what happened last night.'

She bit her lip and looked at the four of them, standing there like carrion crows against the falling snow. 'No,' she said. 'I can't. I have to get ready for work.'

She went to close the door, but WPC Watson

already had her boot wedged into the thin gap. 'Open up or I'll break it down.'

Mrs Henderson looked alarmed. 'You can't do that!' she said, clutching the neck of her dressing gown closed.

Logan nodded and pulled a thin sheaf of paper from his inside pocket. 'We can. But we don't have to. Open up.'

She let them in.

It was like stepping into an oven. Michelle Henderson's little flat was a lot tidier than it had been the last time they were here. Everything was dusted, the carpet hoovered, even the *Cosmopolitan*s on the coffee table had been stacked in a neat pile. She sank into one of the lumpy brown armchairs, drawing her knees up under her chin, like a small child. It made her bathrobe fall open and when Logan sat on the sofa he took care not to avail himself of the view.

'You know why we're here, don't you, Michelle?' he said.

She wouldn't look him in the eye.

Logan let the silence grow.

'I . . . I have to get ready for work,' she said, but made no move to get up, just hugged her knees all the tighter.

'What did you do with the weapon, Mrs Henderson?'

'If I'm late then Margaret can't get away. She has a toddler to pick up from nursery. I can't be late . . .'

Logan gave the nod and the pair of PCs left the lounge to give the house a quick once-over.

'You got blood all over your clothes, didn't you?'

She flinched, but didn't say anything.

'Did you plan it?' Logan asked. 'Make him pay for what he did to your daughter?'

More silence.

'We've got you on tape, Mrs Henderson.'

She stared hard at a spot on the carpet that had somehow eluded the hoover.

'Sir?'

Logan looked up to see one of the PCs standing in the doorway clutching a mound of blanched clothes. There was a pair of jeans, a T-shirt, rugby shirt, two socks and a pair of trainers all bleached almost white.

'Found these hanging over a radiator in the kitchen. They're still damp.'

'Mrs Henderson?'

No response.

Logan sighed. 'Michelle Henderson, I'm arresting you for the murder of one Bernard Duncan Philips.'

Duthie Park was a well-manicured stretch of park-land on the banks of the River Dee, complete with duck pond, bandstand and fake Cleopatra's Needle. It was a favourite spot for families, its wide-open spaces and ranks of mature trees giving plenty of scope for children to play. Even buried under a foot of crisp white snow there were signs of life. Snowmen in various stages of construction punctuated the white plain like standing stones: silent watchmen, lords of all they surveyed.

Jamie McCreath – four in two weeks' time, the day before Christmas Eve – had disappeared. He'd been on a trip to the park with his mother, a distraught woman in her mid-twenties with long red hair the colour of autumn leaves escaping from under a knitted hat with a ridiculous gold tassel on top. She cried on a bench in the Winter Gardens while a flustered-looking woman with a small child in a pushchair did her best to comfort her.

The Winter Gardens – a large Victorian structure, white-painted steel holding up tons of glass, protecting the cactus and palm trees from the snow and ice outside – were a hive of activity, crawling with uniformed police officers.

Logan found DI Insch standing on an arched wooden bridge spanning a blue, dappled pool full of gold-and-copper fish. 'Sir?'

The inspector glanced over his shoulder, a frown sitting on his round features, making him look bullish and impotent. 'You took your bloody time.'

Logan tried not to rise to the bait. 'Mrs Henderson's keeping her mouth shut. But we found all the clothes she was wearing drying on the radiator. Every last one of them bleached within an inch of their lives.'

'IB?' asked Insch.

'I've got them going over the washing machine and the kitchen. Those clothes must have been saturated with blood. We'll find it.'

The inspector nodded, lost in thought. 'At least that's something,' he said at last. 'I've had a call from the Chief Constable: this is the last kid that goes missing. Four of Lothian and Borders finest are on their way up the road as we speak.'

Logan groaned. That was all they needed.

'Aye,' said Insch. 'Show the poor thick parochial bobbies how to do it properly.'

'What happened?'

The inspector shrugged. 'Too much publicity, too little progress.'

'No, here—' Logan indicated the verdant jungle sprawling under glass all around them. 'What happened with the kid?'

'Ah. Right.' He straightened up and pointed towards the entrance, hidden behind a large clump of tropical rainforest. 'Mother and child enter the Winter Gardens at eleven fifty-five. Jamie McCreath likes the fishies, but the birdies frighten him. Aye, and so does that bloody talking cactus. So they come in here and he sits on the edge of the bridge and watches the fishies swimming about. Mrs McCreath spots a friend and says hello. They talk for a while, about fifteen minutes she thinks, and next thing she knows Jamie is nowhere to be seen. So she starts looking for him.' He held out a large hand and traced it along the paths that crossed and bordered the pond. 'No sign. She's seen the papers and the telly, so she starts to panic. Screams the place down. Her friend calls 999 on her mobile, and here we are.' He let the hand fall back to his side. 'We've got four search teams going through the place: under every bush, bridge, into every storeroom. You name it. Another two teams are out in that—' Insch inclined his head towards the fogged up glass, indicating the park outside. 'We'll get more teams doing the park when they arrive.'

Logan nodded. 'What do you think?'

Insch slowly sank forward, his elbows on the railings that bordered the wooden bridge, his face closed, staring down at the fish swimming languidly below. 'I'd love to think he's just wandered off, bored. That he's outside building a snowman . . . But deep down? I think he's got him.' He sighed. 'And he's going to kill him.'

35

Insch ordered the mobile incident room brought down to Duthie Park. It was little more than a glorified caravan, a grubby white rectangular box with 'GRAMPIAN POLICE' written on the outside and a small, sectioned-off interview room inside. The rest of the space was taken up by a couple of desks, a microwave and a kettle. The latter was going full time, filling the claustrophobic room with belching clouds of white steam.

The search teams weren't having any success and the snow was hungrily eating up any evidence there was, the wind sweeping it across the park, filling every indentation, making everything uniformly white and rounded.

Logan sat at the desk nearest the door, getting a chill in his kidneys every time the thing was opened and another frozen body staggered in, stomped their feet clean of snow on the carpet and looked hungrily at the kettle. He was hammering away at a laptop, a list of all known sex offenders in the city scrolling past his eyes. If they were lucky they'd find someone living near enough to the park to make it an attractive hunting ground. It was a big 'if': the other two bodies had been found on the other side of the city. One on the banks of the Don, the other in Seaton Park. Both a stone's throw away from the river that cut through the northernmost third of the city.

'Maybe we're looking for a different man?' he said aloud, causing Insch to look up from his pile of reports.

'Don't even think about it! One sick bastard abducting children is enough!'

Logan shivered as the door banged open again and a red-nosed WPC stumbled in from the snow. While she begged a cup of Bovril, Logan went back to his list of perverts, rapists and paedophiles. There were two registered in Ferryhill, the area directly butting onto Duthie Park, but they were both down for raping women in their mid-twenties. They weren't likely to kidnap, kill and abuse four-year-old boys, but Logan sent a couple of patrol cars anyway. Just to be sure.

More and more negative reports were coming in from the search teams. Insch had abandoned any hope of finding Jamie McCreath in the Winter Gardens and had sent everyone off to comb the park instead.

Logan's eyes drifted across a familiar name and he stopped. Douglas MacDuff: Desperate Doug.

He wasn't a registered sex offender, but he was on the list as a suspect for some rapes twenty-odd years ago. The rest of the names were only recognizable because Logan had been through this exercise just last week, looking for suspects who might have taken little David Reid, or Peter Lumley.

A headache was beginning to nip him between the eyes. That was what he got for sitting here in a perpetual draught, hunched over this damn laptop. Achieving nothing. It was hard to believe this was only Wednesday. He'd been back on the job for eleven days now. Eleven days without a break. So much for the working time directive. Grunting, he rubbed the bridge of his nose, trying to get the growing pain to shift.

When he opened his eyes again he was staring at another familiar name: Martin Strichen, 25 Howesbank Avenue. The man who could fell slimy lawyer bastards with a single blow. And Slippery Sandy had the brass neck to say that Cleaver going free was the police's fault . . . A small smile flickered onto Logan's face as he played the moment of impact in his head. Bang. Right on the nose.

Insch looked up from the shivering WPC's report. 'What's so damn funny?' he asked Logan, his expression making it clear that there was nothing to laugh about.

'Sorry, sir, I was just remembering when Slippery Sandy got his nose broken.'

The annoyed look slid off Insch's face. Maybe there was something to smile at after all. 'Bang!' he said, slapping a fat fist into the other palm. 'I've got it on video now. Going to get someone to cut it to disk so I can use it as a screensaver on the computer. Bang . . .'

Logan grinned and looked back down at the laptop. There were plenty more names on the list to go through. Ten minutes later he was standing in front of the large-scale map of Aberdeen laminated and mounted on the mobile incident room's far wall. They'd marked it up in red and blue pen, just like the map back at Force HQ: red for where the kids had been abducted, blue for where the bodies had been found. Only now there was a red circle over Duthie Park as well.

'Well?' Insch demanded at last, when Logan had been standing there, motionless, for five minutes.

'Hmm? Oh, I was wondering about the parks connection. We found Peter Lumley in Seaton Park, Jamie McCreath was snatched from Duthie Park . . .' Logan picked up a blue marker pen and tapped it against his teeth.

'And?' There wasn't a lot of patience in Insch's voice.

'David Reid doesn't fit.'

With a growl of low menace, Insch asked Logan what the hell he was talking about.

'Well,' Logan prodded the map with the pen, 'David Reid was snatched from the amusement arcades down at the beach and dumped by the river in the Bridge of Don. No parks.'

'We've been through all this!' Insch glowered.

'Yes, but back then we only had the two disappearances. Maybe not enough to see a pattern.'

The door battered open, bringing with it a howling gale and WPC Watson. She clattered it shut again and banged her feet, making a miniature snowstorm on the linoleum. 'God, it's freezing out there!' she said, her nose like a cherry, her cheeks like apples, her lips like two thin strips of purple liver.

Insch let his glare leave Logan, roam towards Watson and return. Oblivious to the inspector's gaze, she wrapped her gloved hands around the kettle, stealing as much heat from it as she could.

'There has to be something,' said Logan, staring at the map, the blue marker pen clicking off his top teeth again, 'something we're not seeing. A reason this kid is different?' He stopped. 'Or maybe he isn't different at all . . . all these places have something in common . . .'

Hope shone in Insch's eyes. 'What?'

Logan shrugged. 'No idea. I know there's something, but I can't put my finger on it.'

And that was when Detective Inspector Insch finally lost his temper. He slammed his fist down on top of the desk, making the piles of paper dance and demanded to know what the blue fucking hell Logan thought he was playing at? There was a child missing out there and all he could do was play silly fucking games? His face was glowing beetroot-red, spittle arcing in the incident room's fluorescent lights as he tore a strip off of the first target to have presented itself since the McCreath child had gone missing.

'Er . . .' said Watson when Insch paused for breath.

The inspector snapped such a baleful look in her direction that she actually took a step backwards, holding the hot kettle to her chest like a shield. 'What?' he roared.

'They're all maintained by the council?' she said, getting the words out as quickly as possible.

Logan turned back to the map. She was right. Every single place he'd marked was maintained by the council's Parks Department. The Lumley's house had a chunk of ground right next door to it, and the beachfront where David Reid disappeared from was public property too. And so was the riverbank where he was found.

Something went click in Logan's head.

'Martin Strichen,' he said, pointing at the laptop's screen. 'He's on the sex offenders list. He always gets community service with the Parks Department.' He poked the map, smudging the blue circle he'd drawn over Seaton Park. 'That's how he knew those toilets weren't going to be used until spring!'

Watson shook her head. 'Sorry, sir, but Strichen was done for masturbating in a women's changing room, not fiddling with small boys.'

Insch agreed, but Logan wasn't going to be put off so easily. 'It's a swimming pool, right? So what do mothers take to the swimming pool? Children! The kids are too young to leave them on their own in the male changing rooms, so the mothers have them in with them! Little naked girls and—'

'—little naked boys,' Insch finished for him. 'Bastard. Get an APB out. I want Strichen and I want him now!'

They had the lights and sirens going all the way from Duthie Park to Middlefield, only switching them off as they got within earshot of Martin Strichen's house. They didn't want to scare him off.

25 Howesbank Avenue was a middle terrace house in a sweeping street on the north-west corner of Middlefield. There was nothing behind the row of white-harled buildings except a small belt of scrubby grassland and then the disused granite quarries. After that it was a steep climb down to Bucksburn with its paper mills and chicken factory.

The wind was howling along the back of the houses, kicking up a curtain of snow from the frozen ground to mix with the fresh, icy flakes falling from above. It clung to the building's walls as if someone had wrapped them in glittering cotton wool. Christmas trees sparkled and flashed in the darkened windows; jolly Santas stuck to the glass. And here and there someone had tried to recreate old-fashioned leaded windows with black electrical tape and spray-on snow. Classy.

Watson pulled the car up around the corner from the house, where it couldn't be seen.

Insch, Watson, Logan, and a uniformed PC Logan still thought of as the Bastard Simon Rennie, all clambered out into the snow. It had taken the Fiscal exactly three minutes to approve an apprehension warrant for Martin Strichen.

'Right,' said Insch, looking up at the house. It was the only one on the street that didn't have a Christmas tree merrily sparkling away in the front window. 'Watson, Rennie: you go round the back. No one in, no one out. Give us a bell when you get there.' He held up his mobile phone. 'We'll take the front.'

The uniformed contingent hunkered down into the ripping, ice-laden wind and disappeared around the back of the terraced row.

Insch looked at his DS with an appraising eye. 'You going to be up to this?' he asked Logan.

'Sir?'

'If this gets rough: are you up to it? I'm not having you drop down dead on me.'

Logan shook his head, feeling the tips of his ears burn in the bitter gale. 'Don't worry about me, sir,' he said, his breath whipped away by the wind before it could make a cloud of vapour. 'I'll hide behind you.'

'Aye,' said Insch with a smile. 'Just make sure I don't fall on you.'

The phone in the inspector's pocket buzzed discreetly. Watson and Rennie were in place.

Number 25 had a front door that hadn't seen a coat of paint in years. The peeling blue revealing bloated grey wood underneath, sparkling with frost. A pair of rippled glass panes were set into it, revealing a darkened hall.

Insch tried the doorbell. Thirty seconds later he tried the doorbell again. And a third time.

'All right! All right! Hold your bloody horses!' The voice came from deep within the small house, followed by blossoming light that oozed through the glass.

A shadow fell across the hall, bringing with it muttered swearing, not quite low enough to be inaudible.

'Who is it?' It was a woman, and her voice, rough from years of booze and fags, had all the welcome of a rabid Rottweiler.

'Police.'

There was a pause. 'What's the little bastard done now?' But the door remained shut.

'Open the door please.'

'The little bastard's not here.'

Colour was beginning to travel up DI Insch's neck. 'Open this damn door now!'

Click, clunk, clatter. The door opened a crack. The face that peered out at them was hard and lined, a cigarette dangling out of one corner of the twisted, thin mouth. 'I told you: he's no here. Come back later.'

Insch wasn't having any more of this. Pulling himself up to his full height, he leant his considerable weight on the door and shoved. The woman on the other side staggered back and he stepped over the threshold and into the small hallway.

'You can't come in here without a warrant! I have rights!'

Insch shook his head and marched past her, through a small kitchen, and opened the back door. Watson and Rennie staggered in out of the cold, snow whipping past them into the dingy room.

'Name?' demanded Insch, pointing a fat finger at the outraged woman. She was dressed for the next ice age: thick woollen jumper, thick woollen skirt, heavy woollen socks, big fleecy slippers and, over the top of it all, an extra large cardigan in dung-brown. Her hair looked as if it had been styled in the nineteen fifties and not touched since. It glistened in greasy-looking curls, held tight to her head with hairgrips and an off-brown net.

She crossed her arms, hitching up her sagging bosoms. 'You got a warrant, you tell me.'

'Everyone watches too much bloody television,' muttered Insch, pulling the apprehension warrant out and slapping it in her face. 'Where is he?'

'I don't know.' She scrabbled backwards towards the dingy lounge. 'I'm not his keeper!'

The inspector took a step forward, his face purple, veins standing out on his face and neck. The old woman flinched.

Logan's voice cut through the tension. 'When did you last see him?'

She swivelled her head. 'This morning. Went to do his bloody community service. Little bastard's always doing community service. Dirty little pervert. Can't get a bloody job, can he? To busy playing with himself in bloody changing rooms for that.'

'OK,' said Logan. 'Where was he working today?'

'I don't bloody know, do I? The little bastard calls them in the morning and they tell him where he's supposed to go.'

'Calls where?'

'The council!' She almost spat at him. 'Where else? Number's on the phone table.'

There was an occasional table, not much bigger than a postage stamp, with a grubby cordless phone on it and a small pad marked 'MESSAGES'. A letter was pinned to the mahogany-effect wood by the phone's base unit. It bore the crest of Aberdeen City Council: three towers, bordered by what looked like barbed wire, on a shield supported by a pair of rampant leopards. Very regal. It was Martin Strichen's community service notice from the Parks Department. Pulling out his mobile phone, Logan punched in the number and spoke to the man responsible for handing out Strichen's work details.

'Want to take a guess?' he said when the call was over.

'Duthie Park?' said Insch.

'Bingo.'

They dragged details of Martin's car out of his mother while PCs Rennie and Watson searched the house. Watson returned, grim-faced, holding a clear plastic evidence wallet containing a pair of secateurs.

Once Mrs Strichen heard what her little boy had done, she was more than happy to help the police lock him up for life. He deserved it, she said. He'd never been any good. She wished she'd strangled him at birth, or better yet stabbed him in the womb with a coat hanger. God knew she'd drunk enough gin and whisky to kill the little bastard off when she was carrying him.

'Right,' said Insch when she'd stomped off upstairs to the toilet. 'It's highly unlikely he's going to come back here to the loving arms of his delightful mother, not after we get his name and description out to the media. But you never know. Watson, Rennie, I want you to stay here with the Wicked Witch of Middlefield. Keep well clear of the windows: I don't want anyone knowing you're here. If her boy does come home: call for back-up. You only tackle him if it's safe.'

Watson looked at him incredulously. 'Come on, sir! He's not coming back! Don't leave me here. PC Rennie's enough to keep an eye on things!'

Rennie rolled his eyes and puffed. 'Thanks a bundle!'

She frowned at him. 'You know what I mean. Sir, I can help, I can—'

Insch cut her off. 'Listen up, Constable,' he said. 'You are one of the most valuable people I have on my team. I have the greatest respect for your professional skills. What I don't have is time to massage your bloody ego. You're staying here to take charge of things. If Strichen does come back I want someone here who can put his lights out.'

PC Rennie looked affronted again, but wisely kept his mouth shut.

The inspector buttoned his coat back up. 'Right, Logan, you're with me.' And with that they were gone.

WPC Watson watched the door close behind them with a scowl on her face.

The Bastard Simon Rennie sidled up beside her. 'Gee, Jackie,' he said in a whiny American accent. 'You're so big and special. Will you protect me if the nasty man comes back?' He even fluttered his eyelashes.

'You can be such a dick at times.' She stormed off to the kitchen to make a cup of tea.

PC Rennie, grinned to himself in the hallway then flounced after her, calling, 'Don't leave me! Don't leave me!'

Out in the patrol car Logan cranked up the heaters and waited for the windscreen to turn transparent again. 'You sure about this?' he asked the inspector, who had discovered an open packet of winegums in his overcoat and was busily picking off the little bits of fluff and pocket-grit.

'Hmmm?' Insch stuffed a red one in his mouth and offered the packet to Logan. The next one down was dark green and devoid of fuzz.

'I mean,' said Logan, plucking the sweet from the roll and popping it in his mouth. 'What if he comes back?'

Insch shrugged. 'They don't call her "Ball Breaker" for nothing. I put loads of uniforms out here and they're going to scare him away. This has to be low key. I'm going to put a couple of unmarked cars down the road. If he comes back: they'll see him. But my guess is he's going to one of his little council hideyholes. And even if he is stupid enough to go home, I doubt he'll give Watson any trouble. Strichen's not got form for violence, not real violence.'

'He decked Sandy the Snake!'

Insch nodded and smiled happily. 'Yeah, at least he did some good in his life. Anyway, you and I have plenty of other things to worry about. To the Bat Cave!' He pointed a fat hand in the direction of Force Headquarters.

Logan pulled the patrol car out into the blizzard, leaving 25 Howesbank Avenue, and WPC Watson, behind.

36

Every patrol car in the city was out looking for Martin Strichen, all of them armed with the details of his scabby Ford Fiesta. Forensics had found blood on the secateurs, wedged into the hinge; it was the same type as David Reid's. If Strichen was out there they were damned well going to find him.

Four and three-quarter hours, and counting.

Back at Force Headquarters, DI Insch and DS McRae were wasting time. The big boys from Edinburgh had arrived. Two detective sergeants, both dressed in smart dark blue suits, with toning shirts and ties, one detective inspector with a face like the underside of an ashtray, and a clinical psychologist who insisted that everyone call him 'Doctor' Bushel.

The DI had run two serial killer cases, both times getting his man. The first after six strangled students had been found on Carlton Hill, over-looking the east end of Princes Street. The second after a prolonged siege in the old town. No survivors. Three members of the public and one police officer had lost their lives that time. It was not, Logan thought, a great track record.

The new inspector listened with cold hard eyes as Insch took the visiting muscle through the case to date. The DI asked some pretty searching questions along the way. He wasn't an idiot: that was clear enough. And he was impressed that Insch and Logan had managed to identify their killer after only two bodies.

Dr Bushel was so smug it was unbearable. Martin Strichen fitted the profile he'd provided perfectly – the one which said their child killer would have 'mental health problems'. He didn't seem to grasp the fact that it had been bugger all use in identifying Strichen.

'And that's where we are now,' said Insch when he'd finished, making a 'ta-da!' gesture, indicating the contents of the incident room.

The DI nodded. 'Sounds like you don't need any help from us,' he said, the words coming out low and gravely, just laced with a hint of Southern Fife. 'You know your man, you've got the search teams out. All you've got to do now is wait. He'll turn up sooner or later.'

Sooner or later wasn't good enough for Insch. Sooner or later would mean Jamie McCreath had joined the ranks of the dead.

The doctor got to his hind legs and peered at the crime scene photographs, pinned to the wall, making cryptic 'Hmmm . . .' and 'I see . . .' noises.

'Doctor?' said the DI. 'You got any idea where he's going to turn up?'

The psychologist turned, the light flashing artfully off his round glasses. He flashed a smile to go along with it. 'Your man isn't going to rush this thing,' he said. 'He wants to take his time. After all, this is something that he's been planning for a long time.'

Logan shared an oh-my-God look with Insch. 'Er . . .' he said, treading carefully. 'Do you not think this is more of a knee-jerk reaction?'

Dr Bushel looked at Logan as if he was an errant child, but one he was willing to indulge. 'Explain?'

'He was abused by Gerald Cleaver when he was eleven. Cleaver was found not guilty on Saturday. On Sunday we found the Lumley child before Strichen could get back and mutilate him. Today there are adverts all over the telly: Cleaver's sold his story to the papers. Strichen can't cope with it all. It's sent him over the edge.'

The doctor smiled indulgently. 'An interesting theory,' he said. 'The layperson often confuses the signs. You see, there are patterns here that only a trained eye can discern. Strichen is a highly organized offender. He takes great care to make sure his victims' remains are not discovered. He has a highly ritualized fantasy world and those rituals mean he has to abide by his own internal set of rules. If he doesn't do that then he has become nothing more than a monster preying on

522

small children. You see, he's ashamed of what he does—' Dr Bushel pointed at a post mortem photograph of David Reid's groin. 'Pretending the child isn't male, by removing the genitalia. Telling himself his crime is less heinous, because it's not little boys he's violating.' He took off his glasses and polished them on the end of his tie. 'No, Martin Strichen must be able to justify his actions, if only to himself. He has his rituals. He will want to take his time.'

Logan didn't say another word until Insch had shown the visitors the canteen and they were alone, back in the incident room again. 'What a sack of shite!'

Insch nodded and rummaged through his pockets for the umpteenth time that afternoon. 'Aye. But that wee sack of shite has helped catch four repeat offenders, three of them murderers. He's got all the people skills of diphtheria, but he's experienced.'

Logan sighed. 'So what do we do now?'

Insch gave up on the sweetie hunt, sticking his large hands desolately into the trouser pockets of his suit. 'Now,' he said. 'Now we sit back and hope we get lucky.'

In summer the rear windows would look out across rolling tufts of scrub grass, gilded with golden sun, the view stretching out to the horizon. Bucksburn's grey sprawl would be hidden by the steep hill down from the quarries. On a good day, when the paper mills weren't belching out cumulus clouds of strange-smelling steam, the hillsides, farmland and woods on the other side of the River Don would shine like emeralds. A bucolic haven, insulated from the droning traffic on the dual carriageway below.

But none of it was visible now. The snowstorm had turned into a blizzard and, standing at the master bedroom window, WPC Jackie Watson couldn't make out much beyond the back garden's fence. Sighing, she turned her back on the grey, howling afternoon and stomped back downstairs.

Martin Strichen's mum was hunched in an overstuffed armchair gaily upholstered in roses and poppies. She had a fag dangling from the corner of her mouth, and a graveyard of them sitting in the ashtray beside her. The telly was on: a soap opera. Watson hated soap operas. But the Bastard Simon Rennie loved them. He sat on the floral couch and stared at the screen, slurping away at cup after cup of tea.

The remains of a packet of Jaffa Cakes sat on the coffee table and Watson grabbed the last two on her way past to stand directly in front of the two-bar electric heater, determined to get warm, even if she had to set fire to her trousers in the process. The whole house was freezing. As a special concession to her visitors Mrs Strichen had put the fire on, but not without a great deal of complaining. Electricity wasn't free, you know. And how was she supposed to cope when that little bastard brought no money in? Mrs Duncan down the road, her son was a drug dealer. He brought home lots of money and they went on two foreign holidays every year! Of course he was doing a three-year stretch in Craiginches for possession with intent, but at least he was bloody trying!

When the steam rising from the backs of her trousers became too hot to bear Watson slumped through to the kitchen to put the kettle on, yet again. Endless cups of tea were the only way to keep warm in this sodding fridge of a house.

The kitchen wasn't big, just a square of linoleum with a small table in the middle and work surfaces around the walls, all decorated in nicotine yellow. Watson clattered three mugs off the draining board and onto the worktop, not really caring if she chipped them. Three teabags. Sugar. Boiling water. But only enough milk for two. 'Arse.' There was no way she was going to stay here, in the cold, without even a cup of tea to sustain her. PC Rennie would have to take his black.

She took them through and dumped the two mugs on the coffee table. Mrs Strichen grabbed hers without even a word of thanks. PC Rennie got as far as, 'Ooh, smashing . . .' before he realized there was no milk in his. He gave Watson his best lost-puppy-dog look.

'Don't bother,' she told him. 'No more milk.'

He turned a disappointed look at the dark liquid in the cup. 'You sure?'

'Not a drop.'

Mrs Strichen scowled at them, sending a stream of smoke hissing between her teeth. 'Do you mind? I'm trying to watch this!'

On the screen a man with a fat head and patchy beard was watching TV and drinking tea. PC Rennie stared down into his tea again. 'I could go get some more milk,' he offered. 'Maybe some biscuits too?' Now that Watson had eaten all the Jaffa Cakes.

'Insch told us to wait here,' she said with a sigh.

'Yea, but we all know Strichen's not coming back here. It'll take me what? Five, ten minutes? There was a wee newsagents on the corner—'

Mrs Strichen even took the cigarette out of her mouth this time. 'Will you please shut up!'

They went out to the hall.

'Look, I'll only be a minute. And it's not like you couldn't kick the shit out of him if he comes back! And there's two cars out there watching the roads.'

'I know, I know.' She looked back through the door to the flickering television and Martin Strichen's venomous mother. 'I just don't like going against the inspector's orders.'

'I won't tell if you won't.' PC Rennie grabbed one of the thick overcoats hanging up in the hallway. It smelled a bit of stale chips, but it would keep the cold out. 'Wanna give me a kiss for luck?' He puckered up.

'Not if you were the last man on earth.' She pushed him towards the door. 'And get some crisps too. Salt and vinegar.'

'Yes, ma'am.' He executed a sloppy salute.

She watched the front door bang shut before heading back into the lounge to sit in front of mindless drivel and drink her tea.

It was hard to believe just how many buildings were either maintained or owned by Aberdeen City Council's Parks Department. The list had been faxed through by a grumpy-sounding man, not happy at being called back into the office at a quarter to seven. Each and every building would have to be visited and searched. Dr Bushel was adamant that Strichen would have taken the child to one of them.

Logan didn't bother to point out just how bloody obvious that was.

The chances of picking the correct building to search, from the extensive list, were slim. They weren't going to find him in time. Little Jamie McCreath wasn't going to live to see his fourth birthday.

Trying to whittle it down a bit, Logan had got the grumpy man at the Parks Department to search their records for every place where Strichen had done community service. That list was almost as long as the first. Martin Strichen had been in and out of trouble since he was eleven. Since Gerald Cleaver got his grubby hands on him.

Strichen had done his time raking up leaves, pruning bushes, spraying weeds and unblocking toilets in most of the city's parkland.

Working in reverse chronological order, Logan got the search teams going, starting with the places Strichen had worked in recently. After that they'd work their way backwards through the list. With any luck they'd find the kid before he was violated. But a sinking feeling told Logan that wasn't going to be the case. They'd pick Strichen up in a couple of days, somewhere like Stonehaven, or Dundee. There was no way he was going to hang around Aberdeen. Not with his face on the front page of all the papers, on the television, his name and description on the radio. They'd pick him up and he would, eventually, lead them to the murdered child's body.

'How's it going?'

Logan looked up to see Insch standing in the doorway of his little incident room. The main room had too many clinical psychologists in it for Logan's liking and the peace and quiet had helped him get the search teams organized.

'Search is underway.'

Insch nodded and handed Logan a chipped mug of strong coffee. 'You're not sounding hopeful,' he said, settling onto the edge of Logan's desk and examining the list of possible venues.

Logan admitted that he wasn't. 'There's nothing more to do: the search teams have their orders, everyone knows what buildings they're to do next. That's it. Now they either find him or they don't.'

'You want to be out there?'

'Don't you?'

The inspector gave him a sad smile. 'Aye. But I'm babysitting the big boys . . . One of those privileges of rank.' Insch pulled himself off the edge of the desk and patted Logan on the shoulder. 'But you're just a lowly DS.' He winked. 'Get your arse out there.'

Logan checked a rusty blue Vauxhall out of the car park. It was dark, going on for seven. The Wednesday night traffic was light, most people going straight home after work. The terrible weather had kept them there. Only the most foolhardy were bustling from pub to pub beneath the Christmas lights.

As the traffic grew scarcer the snow gained a hold on the roads. The black glistening tarmac of the city centre giving way to grey and finally white as Logan worked his way out from Force Headquarters. He didn't have any real destination in mind: he was driving for the sake of doing something. Just another pair of eyes looking for Martin Strichen's car.

He drove up Rosemount and did a tour of Victoria Park and the surrounding streets, never once getting out of the vehicle. With the snow driving in at ninety miles an hour and the temperature sub-zero, there was no way Martin Strichen was going to park miles from where he was going. Not when he had a kidnapped child in tow.

There was no sign of Martin's leprous Ford Fiesta anywhere near Victoria Park, so Logan tried Westburn Park, across the road. It was much bigger, crisscrossed with snow-covered, single-track roads. Logan slowly crunched his car through the blizzard, looking for any nook or cranny Strichen might have hidden his vehicle.

Nothing.

It was going to be a long night.

WPC Watson stared out of the kitchen window, watching the snow whip back and forth on the furious wind. PC Rennie had been gone for fifteen minutes and since then her bored resentment had changed to nervous anticipation. It wasn't that she was worried about Martin Strichen coming back – after all, as the Bastard Simon Rennie had said, she could easily kick the shit out of him. All modesty aside, she could kick the shit out of most people. Her nickname had been hard won. No, what worried her was . . . To be honest: she wasn't sure what was worrying her.

Maybe it was being taken out of the investigation to sit on a long shot? She should have been out there. Doing something. Not stuck here, watching soap operas and drinking tea. Sighing, she clicked off the kitchen light and watched the snow.

The sound, when it came, made her jump. A clicking at the front door.

All the hairs on the back of her head leapt up. He'd come back! The silly bugger had come back home like nothing had happened! A grim smile pulled at her face as she crept out of the kitchen and into the darkened hall.

The door handle creaked down and she tensed. It swung open and she grabbed the figure, pulling him off balance, throwing him down against the plastic carpet protector. Leaping on top of him, her right hand balled into a fist.

The figure screamed and threw his hands over his face. 'Aaaaaaaaaaaaaa!'

It was the Bastard Simon Rennie.

'Oh,' she said, dropping the fist and settling back on her haunches. 'Sorry about that.'

'Jesus, Jackie!' He peered out at her from between his fingers. 'If you wanted to jump my bones you only had to ask!'

'Thought you were someone else.' She climbed off Rennie and helped him to his feet. 'You OK?'

'Might have to see if there's a clean pair of boxer shorts upstairs, but other than that I'm fine.'

She apologized again and helped him through into the kitchen with the shopping.

'Got some Pot Noodles as well,' he said, emptying the bags onto the counter top. 'You want chicken and mushroom, beef and tomato, or spicy curry?'

Watson grabbed the chicken, Rennie the curry:

the sour-faced Mrs Strichen could have what was left. While the noodles were soaking up a kettle of hot water, PC Rennie filled her in on his trip to the shops. One of Insch's cars was parked down at the entrance to the street opposite the shops and he'd spent a couple of minutes speaking to the occupants. They were from Bucksburn, just down the road and didn't think much of their assignment. It was a complete waste of time! Strichen wasn't coming back. But if he did, they were going to kick seven bells out of him for making them sit out there in the freezing cold.

'Did they say how the search was going?' she asked, stirring absently at the rehydrating noodles.

'Bugger all. Lots of buildings and no idea which one he's going to be in.'

Watson sighed, staring out the back window again, watching the snow. 'It's going to be a long night.'

'Never mind,' Rennie grinned, 'she's got EastEnders on tape.'

Watson groaned. As if the day could get any worse!

There was no sign of Martin Strichen's Ford Fiesta in Westburn Park. Not for the first time Logan wondered if Strichen wouldn't just hit the main road out of Aberdeen. He had to know they were after him by now. Since leaving the station Logan had heard at least a dozen appeals for information on local radio. If he was Martin Strichen he'd be halfway to Dundee by now. Gradually he let the car drift further out.

Now and then a patrol car would pass in the opposite direction, trawling the streets, just as he was. Maybe Hazlehead would be worth a try? Or Mastrick? In the end he knew it didn't really matter where he went. Little Jamie McCreath was surely already dead. Sighing, he turned the car onto North Anderson Drive.

His mobile phone blared out its offensive ring tone and Logan pulled into the side of the road, the car bumping up onto a ridge of icy snow that hid the kerb.

'Logan.'

'*Laz, my man! How's it going?*'

Bloody Colin Miller.

'What can I do for you, Colin?' he said with a weary sigh.

'*Been listenin' to the news, been readin' the press releases. What's goin' on?*'

An articulated lorry thundered past, sending a three-foot wave of slush spattering against the side of the car. Logan watched the tail-lights, twin eyes of red, disappear around the roundabout.

'You know bloody well what's going on! You published your bloody story and cost us our best chance at catching this bastard.' Logan knew he was being unfair, that Miller hadn't meant for it to turn out like this, but right now he didn't care. He was tired, frustrated and wanted someone to shout at. 'He's snatched another kid because you had to tell the world we'd found a poor wee dead . . .' He trailed off into silence as he finally saw what had been staring him in the face all along. 'Fuck!' He slammed his hand on the steering wheel. 'Fuck, fuck, fuck, fuck!'

'Jesus, man, calm down! What's wrong?'

Logan gritted his teeth and hammered the steering wheel again.

'You havin' a seizure or something?'

'You always know when someone's dead, don't you? You always fucking know when we find a dead body.' Logan scowled out of the car window as another lorry roared past, buffeting the car with its wake.

'Laz?'

'Isobel.'

There was silence on the other end of the phone.

'She's your mole, isn't she? Ferreting about, bringing you titbits. Helping you sell bloody papers!' He was shouting now. 'How much you paying her? How much was Jamie McCreath's life worth?'

'It's no like that! It . . . I . . .' There was a pause. And then Miller's voice returned, sounding very small. *'She comes home and tells me about her day sometimes.'*

Logan looked at the phone as if it had just farted in his face. 'What?'

A sigh. *'We're . . . She does a hard shitty job.*

She needs someone to share stuff with. We didn't know it would end up like this . . . I swear! We—'

Logan snapped the phone shut without another word. He should have spotted it a mile off. The opera, the flash car, the clothes, the fancy food, the mouth like a sewer. It was Miller. He was Isobel's 'bit of rough'. Sitting on his own, in the car, in the snow, in the dark, Logan closed his eyes and swore.

If WPC Watson had to watch one more bloody soap opera she was going to scream. Now Mrs Strichen had started in on the videoed episodes. Miserable people with miserable lives, buggering about in a miserable, pointless parade of misery. God, she was bored. And there wasn't a book in the house either. So all they had was the television and its endless barrage of bloody soap operas.

She stomped back into the kitchen and stuffed her empty pot noodle carton into the bin, without bothering to turn on the light. This was such a waste of time!

'Jackie? Put the kettle on while you're in there!'

Watson sighed. 'What did your last slave die of?'

'Milk and two sugars, eh?'

Grumbling, she filled the kettle back up again and stuck it on to boil. 'I made it last time,' she said, back in the lounge. 'Your turn to make the tea.'

PC Rennie, looked at her aghast. 'But I'll miss the start of Emmerdale!'

'It's on video! How can you miss the start of Emmerdale if it's on video? Pause the damn thing!'

Sitting in her overstuffed armchair, Mrs Strichen ground another dead cigarette into the pile. 'Do you two ever stop bloody fighting?' she said, pulling out her lighter and her fags. 'Like bloody children.'

Watson gritted her teeth. 'You want tea? You make tea.' She turned to head upstairs.

'Where you going?'

'I'm going for a pee. That OK with you?'

PC Rennie held up his hands in self defence. 'OK, OK. I'll make the tea. Sheesh, if it's that big a deal . . .' He pulled himself out of the sofa and collected the empty mugs.

With a small smile of satisfaction WPC Watson went upstairs.

She didn't hear the back door opening.

37

The toilet had one of 'those' flushes. No matter how hard or how often she forced down the handle, it just wouldn't make things disappear. WPC Jackie Watson sat on the edge of the bath and pumped the handle again before peering under the lid. At least all the toilet paper was gone now. Anything left was dilute enough to be unnoticeable.

Like the rest of the house, the bathroom was an icebox. Suppressing a shiver, she washed her hands, took one look at the off-grey towel hanging on the back of the door, and dried her hands on her trousers.

Someone was standing right outside the bathroom door when she opened it. She jumped, her breath catching in her throat. Strichen was back!

She snarled and launched a fist at his face without thinking, only swerving at the last moment when her brain caught up with her vision. Not Martin Strichen. His mother, her eyes wide with shock. They stood looking at each other, blood thudding in their ears.

'Don't do that!' Watson said, dropping the fist back to her side.

'Shift over,' said Martin's mum, her voice shaking slightly, eyeing Watson as if she was an escaped loony, 'my bladder's killing me.' She shuffled past, clutching her cardigan shut with one hand and an *Evening Express* with the other. 'Your boyfriend's taking his own sweet time making that bloody tea.' She slammed the door, leaving WPC Watson standing alone, at the top of the stairs, in the dark.

'Lovely woman,' she muttered. 'No wonder her kid's a monster.'

She went downstairs thinking about the pint that DS McRae owed her. Much better than yet another cup of tea. Grumbling away to herself, she slumped onto the settee. The opening titles of Emmerdale were flickering on the television screen, paused in the middle of flying over some fields. How nice of them not to start until she'd finished her wee. 'Come on, Rennie!' she called through from the lounge. 'What's taking so damn long? Teabag, water, milk. It's not hard.' She slumped back into the couch and scowled at the telly. 'Oh for God's sake!' She dragged herself up and barged into the kitchen. 'Can you not even make the bloody . . .'

There was a body lying full length on the linoleum floor.

It was PC Rennie.

'Shite!' She grabbed the radio off her shoulder. And the world exploded in a barrage of yellow and black fireworks.

She couldn't have been unconscious for long. She knew that from the clock on the cooker. Only five minutes. Groaning, she tried to sit up, but something was wrong with her arms and legs. The kitchen spun around her head as she slumped back to the floor.

Closing her eyes only made it worse. There was a coppery, metallic taste in her mouth, but she couldn't spit it out. Someone had tied a rag into a knot and stuffed it into her mouth. And the same someone had tied her hands behind her back and bound her ankles together.

She rolled onto her back, sending the room spinning again. She let it settle for a moment, before continuing all the way over so that she was facing away from the lounge towards the back door.

PC Rennie lay flat on his face, his features slack and pale. He was trussed up just like she was, a slick of blood making his dark hair shiny and crimson under the kitchen lights.

From upstairs came the sound of the toilet repeatedly flushing.

She flipped over again. This time the world took less time to stop screwing the top of her head off.

Flush, flush, flush.

There was a holdall lying next to the bin. A big one. Lumps of snow clung to the stitching.

WPC Jackie Watson tried to press the transmit button on her radio with her chin. It was still strapped to her shoulder but no matter how hard she tried she couldn't get purchase on it.

And then a pair of legs came into the kitchen. They were clad in thick stockings and a heavy woollen skirt, the dark hallway framed behind them. Watson looked up into the face of Mrs Strichen. The woman's eyes were round and white, the flaccid circle of her lips working wordlessly as she stared at the trussed-up figures on her kitchen floor. She spun around, hands flying to her hips. 'Martin! Martin!' Her voice was that of a murderous rhinoceros. 'What the hell do you think you're doing, you dirty little bastard?'

A shadow fell across her.

Lying on the floor Watson could just make out the edge of a large-boned man, his hands huge and fluttering. Like a bird caught in a net.

'Mum—'

'Don't you "Mum" me, you little bastard! What the hell is this?' She pointed at the restrained figures.

'I don't—'

'You've been fiddling with little boys again. Haven't you?' She poked him hard in the chest with a bony finger. 'Bringing the police to my house! You make me sick! If your father was alive he'd beat the shit out of you, you snivelling little bastard pervert!'

'Mum, I—'

'You have never been anything but a leech! You were a maggot wriggling at my breast!'

He took a step backwards. 'Mum, don't—'

'I never wanted you! You were a mistake! You hear me? You were a nasty, rotten, fucking awful mistake!'

Watson could see the legs shift as Martin Strichen turned his back on his mother. Running away, making for the lounge. But Mrs Strichen wanted her pound of flesh. She stormed after him, her voice rising like a rusty chainsaw. 'Don't you turn your back on me, you little bastard! Two years! You hear me? Two years your father was inside when I had you! You ruined everything! You were always useless!'

'Don't . . .' The word was quiet, but Watson could hear the threat in it.

Mrs Strichen couldn't. 'You make me sick!' she screeched. 'Fiddling with little boys! You filthy, dirty bastard. If your father was alive—'

'What? What? If my father was alive: what?' Martin's voice was thunderous, shaking with rage.

'He'd beat you to a pulp! That's what!'

Something smashed in the lounge. A vase or a jug.

Taking advantage of the noise, Watson curled her legs beneath her and pushed, inching her way along the floor like a caterpillar. Making for the hall and the telephone.

'This is all his fault!'

'Don't you blame your father for what you are, you filthy bastard!'

The hall carpet was rough under her cheek as Watson wriggled out of the kitchen and into the hall. In the living room something else crashed against the wall.

'He did this to me! Him!' There were tears in Martin's voice, but they couldn't cover the rage underneath. 'He put me in hospital! He gave me to that . . . that . . . Cleaver! Every night! Every bloody night!'

'Don't you talk about your father like that!'

'Every night! Gerald Cleaver used me every fucking night! I was eleven!'

Watson had reached the phone table, the hall carpet giving way to the cold plastic mat.

'You miserable, whining little bastard!'

A slap rang out, flesh against flesh, and there was a moment's silence.

WPC Watson risked a glance into the lounge, but all she could see were shadows on the wallpaper. Martin Strichen was crouched with one hand on his face, his mother towering above him.

Watson wriggled forward, level with the phone table. Now she could see right into the living room and the small dining room beyond. A pile of clothes sat next to an ironing board. And right in front of them Mrs Strichen aimed another stinging hand at her son.

'You filthy, filthy little bastard!' She punctuated each word with a vicious slap to Martin's head.

Watson gave the phone table a shove with her shoulder, the noise hidden by all the shouting and yelling. The phone rocked in its cradle, once, twice, then pirouetted silently to the floor. No one heard it clunk against the plastic matting.

'I should have strangled you at birth!'

Watson fumbled the phone into her hands, twisting her head over her shoulder to see the buttons, punching 999 in with her thumb. She cast a frantic glance back at the lounge. No one was looking in her direction. She couldn't hear the phone ringing over the racket of Mrs Strichen attacking her son, but she scooted down anyway, pinning the phone to the floor with her ear, her gagged mouth over the mouthpiece.

'Emergency Services. Which service do you require?'

She did her best to answer, but all that came out was a series of muffled grunts.

'I'm sorry, can you repeat that?'

Sweating, Jackie Watson tried again.

'This is an emergency number.' Friendliness had vanished from the voice on the other end of the phone. *'It is an offence to make prank phone calls!'*

All Jackie could do was grunt again.

'That's it. I'm going to report this!'

No! No! They had to trace the number and send help!

The line went dead.

Furious, she dropped the phone and wriggled forward once more, grabbing the handset to dial 999 again.

The thud, when it came, was soft and wet.

She snatched her eyes away from the phone and into the lounge. Mrs Strichen was staggering toward the couch, her face white as the snow outside. Behind her stood Martin, the iron in his hand, his expression strangely calm and serene. His mother stumbled, grabbing onto the overstuffed cushions for support and Martin stepped up behind her and brought the iron down in a sweeping arc. It connected with the back of her skull and she went down like a sack of potatoes.

Watson felt her gorge rise. Shivering, she mashed her thumb on the keys again.

Mrs Strichen's quivering hand flailed at the back of the couch. Her son held the iron at chest height, his other hand stretching out the electrical cord. Something like a smile twisted the corners of his mouth as he bent down and wrapped the cable around his mother's neck. Her foot thumped against the carpet as he squeezed the life out of her.

Gritting her teeth, WPC Watson grabbed the phone and wriggled back towards the kitchen. She was crying openly now, impotence and self-pity mingling with the terror of seeing another human being murdered. And knowing that she was going to be next.

Taking a deep, shuddering breath, she closed her eyes and tried to remember DS McRae's mobile number. Behind her, through the open kitchen door, she could hear Mrs Strichen's foot ever more faintly pounding against the floor.

Jackie's thumbs traced Logan's number on the phone's keypad and she did the same drop-and-wriggle routine she'd tried on the Emergency Services. Come on, come on! Pick up!

Click.

'Logan.'

She screamed, the rag in her mouth smothering the noise until all that came out was a squeak.

'Hello? Who is this?'

No! Not again! He had to hear her!

'Miller? Is that you?'

She screamed again, obscenities this time, cursing him for being so bloody stupid.

Martin Strichen's shadow fell across the kitchen. He still had the iron in one hand, thick red splashes coating the polished metal surface. Greasy, curled hairs stuck to the clots.

Her eyes darted from the iron to Martin's face. Scarlet freckles covered the right-hand side of his broad, pockmarked features. He looked down at her with sorrow, then picked up the phone, held it to his ear and listened for a second to Logan demanding to know who was calling his mobile. Then, calmly, he pressed the red button and ended the call.

The scissors came from the top drawer, under the kettle, their blades glinting in the cold overhead light. He smiled down at Jackie.

Snip, snip, snip.

'Time to do it properly . . .'

Logan stared at the phone in his hand and cursed. As if he didn't have enough to worry about without prank phone calls! He punched the button that brought up the last number that had called. It was local, but he didn't recognize it. Scowling, he hit 'call back' and listened as the phone automatically bleeped and beeped its way through the number that had called him, returning the favour.

It rang and rang and rang. No answer. Right, he decided, there were two ways to skin a cat. He scribbled the number down and called Control, asking them to put an address to the telephone number. It took the man on the other end of the phone almost five minutes, but he finally came back with: '*Mrs Agnes Strichen, 25 Howesbank Avenue, Aberdeen* . . .'

Logan didn't wait for the postcode, just shouted, 'Fuck!' and floored the accelerator. The car slithered snakelike out onto the road. 'Listen to me,' he told Control, whipping the rusty Vauxhall through the snow and ice, 'DI Insch has two cars in Middlefield. I want them at that address now!'

By the time Logan got there, the two cars were already slewed across the road outside the front of number 25. The wind was dying away and fat flakes drifted down from the dirty orange sky. The air tasted of pepper.

Logan slammed on the brakes and the car skidded on the snow-covered tarmac and only came to a halt when it bounced off the kerb. He scrambled out of the car, slipping and sliding his way up the stairs and into the house Martin Strichen shared with his mother.

Mrs Strichen was in the lounge, lying on her front, the back of her head caved in, thick red lines circling her throat. The sound of angry voices came from the small kitchen and Logan burst through to see two uniformed policemen, one bending over a crumpled figure on the floor, the other on his radio: 'Repeat we have an officer down!'

Logan's eyes darted around the cramped room, coming to rest on a pile of fabric in the corner next to the bin.

A third uniform exploded into the room, breathing hard. 'We've been all over the house: no sign of anyone.'

Logan prodded the pile of cloth. It had been a pair of black trousers at one time. And there, underneath it were the remains of a black jumper and a white blouse. The kind with loops on the shoulders, specially designed to incorporate police epaulettes. He looked over his shoulder as the fourth of DI Insch's watchdogs screeched to a halt in the hall, behind his partner. 'Where is she?'

'There's no one in the house, sir.'

'Damn it!' Logan jumped to his feet. 'You and you—' he pointed at the two latecomers, who'd been searching the house, '—out front! He's got WPC Watson. Search every street, every open door, everything you can find!'

They stood for a moment, looking down at the crumpled figure of PC Simon Rennie on the kitchen floor.

'Move it!' Logan yelled.

They scrambled away.

'How is he?' he asked, stepping over the body and opening the back door, letting a wall of cold air collapse into the room.

'Taken a nasty blow to the back of the head. He's breathin' but he's no lookin' too good.'

Logan nodded. 'Stay with him.' He jabbed a finger at the last PC. 'You, come with me!'

In the back garden the snow was up to their knees. It had drifted against the walls of the building, ramping up to just under the windows, but there was an easily discernible path leading away into the darkness.

'Damn it.'

Gritting his teeth, Logan waded into the snow.

38

It wasn't much more than a shack. A concrete lean-to off the quarry road. This was where he had played as a child. No, not played. Hidden. Hidden from his father. Hidden from the world.

The granite-grey bowl of the quarry wall was only visible as a shadow through the drifting snow. They had cut straight into the rock, making a cliff, then turned their attention on the deposit underground, leaving behind a deep, treacherous lake. Even in the height of summer the water was cold and dark, its depths snarled with binding forests of weed and shopping trolleys near the shore, dropping off to a bottomless pit further in. No one swam in the quarry lake. Not since two boys had disappeared in the late fifties.

This was a haunted place. A place for the dead. It suited him just fine.

The police weren't supposed to be at the house! That wasn't right. They shouldn't have been there . . . He crunched his way through the ankle-deep snow towards the quarry cabin, breathing hard. They were heavy, making his shoulders ache. But it was all going to be worth it. *She was a good girl. Didn't struggle.* Martin had only kicked her in the head once, and after that she was good as gold. All quiet and peaceful as he snipped off her clothes.

His hands had trembled at the feel of her skin: cool to the touch and soft as he cut away, leaving just the bra and pants. What they hid scared him. Made him ache . . .

And then the phone went. Ringing and ringing and ringing as he hefted her over his shoulder, picked up the big holdall, and staggered out of the back door. They were coming for him.

A big brass padlock held the cabin door shut, next to a sign saying 'WARNING: DANGER OF COL-LAPSE. ACCESS PROHIBITED.'

Grunting, he took a step back and slammed his foot into the wood, next to the lock. The old door boomed, bouncing under his attack, but the pad-lock stayed firm. He kicked it again, and once more for luck. The third boom echoed off the quarry walls, covering the sound of cracking wood as the padlock's fixings gave way.

Inside, it was freezing and dark, the smell of rats and mice fading away under years of dust. Grinning nervously, he slid the woman off his shoulder onto the concrete floor. Her pale skin shone against the dark grey and he shivered, trying to pretend it was the cold. But he knew it was her.

The large holdall went next to her. Afterwards, he knew, it would make him sick to his stomach. Make him sick until there was nothing left but bile and shame. But that was for later. For now his blood roared in his ears.

With numb fingers he tugged down the zip.

'Hello?' he said.

Inside the bag, little Jamie McCreath opened his eyes and began to scream.

The footprints were disappearing fast, thick white flakes of snow filling them up, making everything smooth and featureless. Logan slithered to a halt, his eyes scanning the landscape. The trail had led directly away from the house, right out into the darkness. And now the trail was gone.

He swore bitterly.

The PC he'd dragged along puffed to a halt behind him. 'What now, sir?' he asked, panting for breath.

Logan looked about him, trying to guess which way Martin Strichen had gone, taking WPC Watson with him. Damn it! He'd told Insch it was a bad idea to leave just two of them at the house! 'Split up,' he said at last. 'We need to cover as much ground as we can.'

'Which way do you want me to—'

'I don't care! Just find her!'

He pulled his mobile out of his pocket as the PC, looking hurt, stomped off at a forty-five degree angle into the snow.

'DS McRae,' he told the woman who answered. 'Where are my reinforcements?'

'*One moment . . .*'

Logan swept his eyes across the featureless landscape again. It was as if someone had erased the world, leaving nothing behind but a plain of white under a yellowed-slate sky.

'*Hello, DS McRae? DI Insch says they're on their way. And PCs from Bucksburn should be with you in two minutes.*'

He could already hear the faint wail of sirens, the sound deadened by the falling snow.

Logan forged on through the drifts, icy water slowly seeping into his trousers, making his legs heavy. He was breathing like a train, his breath coming out in thick clouds of vapour, hanging around his head in the still night, his own personal fog bank.

A sinking feeling was forming in his chest. There was little chance of finding Martin Strichen in the dark and snow. Not without dogs. Maybe he should have waited for the dogs? But he knew there was no way he could just sit there and not do something. Anything.

There was a slight rise in the ground and he laboured up it, the snow coming to his knees. And then he was at the top, feeling his heart leap into his throat, his bowels clench. The ground had disappeared! He stood on the lip of the precipice, arms pinwheeling to keep his balance, one foot hanging in space.

Logan staggered back onto firm land, then inched forward until he was standing on the edge of the cliff again.

It was one of the quarries. A wide, three-quarter circle of sheer walls with a dark lake at the bottom. The falling snow, drifting down below him only made the feeling of vertigo worse. It had to be fifty, sixty foot straight down to the cold, black water.

His heartbeat was still furious, pounding through his veins, making his ears buzz.

There was a boxy concrete cabin at the foot of the cliffs not far from the water's edge. A thin, yellow light blossomed in a cracked window before sweeping away.

Turning, Logan began to run.

The torch didn't exactly give the cabin a cosy feel. The torch's beam was a cone of jaundiced, washed-out light, making the shadows inside the cabin seem even thicker than before.

Groaning, WPC Watson flickered an eye open. Her head was stuffed full of burning cotton wool. All she could smell was copper, and her face was sticky and cold. Her whole body was cold, deep frozen. A shiver grabbed her, rattling her bones, making her head throb.

Everything was blurred, swimming in and out of focus as she struggled back to the surface. She'd been doing something. Something important . . .

Why was she so cold?

'Are you awake?'

It was a man's voice, nervous, almost shy. Trembling.

Everything snapped back into place.

WPC Watson tried to jump to her feet, but she was still tied hand and foot. Her lurch of intent made the room whirl around her head, the edges rushing in and out like some demonic hokey-kokey. She squeezed her eyes hard shut and hissed breath through her teeth. Gradually the pounding stopped. When she opened her eyes again she was looking straight into Martin Strichen's worried face.

'I'm sorry,' he said, one trembling hand coming up to brush the hair from her face. 'I didn't want to hit you. But I had no choice. I didn't mean to hurt you . . . Are you feeling OK?'

All she could do was mumble through the gag.

'Good,' said Martin, not understanding the barrage of abuse she'd just thrown at him. 'Good.'

He stood and turned his back to her, bending over the large holdall she'd seen in the kitchen, and in a light, whispering voice began to sing the 'Teddy Bears' Picnic'. Stroking something inside the bag.

Watson's eyes darted around the small room, looking for a weapon. The place had been an office of some sort once. A metal rack for timecards was still screwed to the wall by the door and a bloated, mildewed calendar of naked women was nailed to another. The furniture was gone, leaving nothing behind but the graffiti-covered walls and the cold concrete floor.

Another shiver grabbed her. How could it be so damned cold? She looked down, alarmed to find that she'd been stripped.

'You don't have to worry, little one,' said Martin, gently.

A low moaning sob came from inside the bag and Jackie's blood froze. Jamie McCreath was still alive. She was going to have to watch the sick bastard kill a child!

Bunching all her muscles, she strained against her bonds. There wasn't an inch of give in her restraints. Arms and legs trembling with effort, all she managed to do was make the ropes cut deeper into her skin.

'It won't be like it was for me.' He went on stroking the child softly, making soothing noises. 'I've had to live with what Gerald Cleaver did to me for my whole life . . . You'll be free. You won't feel anything.' Watson could hear the tears in his voice. 'You'll be safe.'

She wriggled over onto her back, gasping as bare flesh came into contact with freezing concrete.

Martin picked the child out of the bag and sat him down on the floor next to Watson.

Jamie was still dressed in his snowsuit – orange and blue, with a double-bobbled hat. His eyes were huge and full of tears, his nose streaming twin silver trails into his twisted mouth. Low sobs made him shake all over.

Martin bent over the bag again and his hand emerged with a length of electrical cable. With practised ease he made double knots at each end, pulling them tight. He put one knot in the palm of his left hand, winding the cable twice through his clenched fist. He did the same with the right, pulling it tight and nodded in satisfaction at a job well done.

With sad eyes he looked up at WPC Watson, struggling against her bonds. 'It'll be OK after this,' he told her. 'I just need to . . .' He blushed. 'You know . . . Get going. Then it'll all be OK. We'll do it and it'll be OK. I won't need this any more.' He bit his lip and flexed the cable again. 'I'll be normal and it'll all be OK.'

Taking a deep breath, he made a loop out of the cable strung between his fists. Just big enough to fit over Jamie McCreath's head.

The little boy moaned in terror, his eyes fixed on Jackie as she bucked and writhed.

'If you go down to the woods today . . .'

With a snarl WPC Watson kicked her legs into the air, rocking back on her arms, arching her back so she was nearly upside-down.

Martin's face came up, the song dying on his lips as she pushed her knees as far apart as she could and lunged for his head. He didn't have time to move before she'd wrapped her legs around his neck and was squeezing for all she was worth.

Terror stretched Martin Strichen's face wide,

making his eyes bulge with horror. Watson struggled to get her ankles locked – left over right – to get more leverage so that she could crush his windpipe.

Strichen's hands were all tangled up in his makeshift garrotte. His hands battered ineffectually at her thighs.

With a triumphant grunt, Watson managed to get her ankles into position. Now she could throw her full weight into it, watching with grim satisfaction as Martin's face started to go purple. She wasn't going to stop until the sick bastard was dead.

Panicking now, Martin flapped his hands free of the electrical cable, punching and scratching at anything he could reach. Pounding his fists into her abdomen.

Pain exploding through her stomach, Watson closed her eyes and kept on squeezing.

Martin sank his teeth into her thigh, just above the knee. He bit down with all his might, tasting blood, shaking his head, trying to tear off a chunk of flesh.

She screamed behind her gag, and Martin bit down again, still punching and scratching. A fist slammed into her kidneys, and Jackie went limp.

Martin was out of the leg-lock in seconds, scrabbling backwards, only stopping when he banged into the far corner of the cabin. Blood was trickling down his chin, his hands massaging his throat, fighting for breath. 'You're . . . You're just like all the rest!' he shouted, his voice hoarse and raw.

Jamie McCreath started to bawl, a high-pitched, screeching sound that echoed off the bare concrete walls.

'Shut up!' Martin staggered to his feet and grabbed the boy by the upper arms, hauling him off the floor. 'Shut up! Shut up! Shut up!'

But this only made the child scream louder.

Snarling, Martin backhanded him, the slap hard and stinging, splitting the child's lip and bloodying his nose.

Silence followed.

'Oh God . . . Oh God, no . . .' Martin dropped the child to the floor, his face horrified.

He stared at the sniffing, terrified little boy, working his hands round and round, trying to wring the sting of the slap away.

'I'm sorry! I didn't mean to—' He reached forward but Jamie McCreath, eyes like dinner plates, flinched back, covering his face with his mittened hands.

Strichen glowered at WPC Watson in the weak torchlight. She lay on her side, panting through the gag, blood running scarlet from the bites in her legs.

'This is all your fault!' He spat the taste of her blood out onto the concrete floor. 'You made me hurt him!'

A boot slammed into Jackie's stomach, lifting her off the floor. She choked back a scream as fire lanced through her belly.

'You're just like all the rest!'

Another boot, this time to the ribs.

Martin was screaming now. 'It was all going to be OK! You ruined it!'

The door exploded open.

Logan charged into the gloomy cabin. In the pale light of a dropped torch he saw everything: WPC Watson half-naked, lying on her side, eyes closed in pain; Jamie McCreath scrabbling backwards, blood on his face; Martin Strichen pulling back his boot for another kick.

Strichen froze, turning just as Logan smashed into him, sending them both crashing into the far wall. A fist glanced off the side of Logan's head, a high-pitched whine rattling his ears. Not interested in a fair fight, Logan went straight for the groin: hammering his fist into Martin Strichen's crotch.

The large-boned man gasped and staggered back, one hand grabbing his genitals, his face going ashen-grey. Lurching, he vomited all over himself.

Logan didn't wait for him to stop, just grabbed the hair on the back of Strichen's head and ran him into the concrete wall. Martin's head hit with a dull clunk, the impact hard enough to make the mildewed girlie calendar bounce off its nail. He staggered back, blood streaming down his face and Logan made a grab for his arm, twisting it up behind his back.

A huge, bony elbow lashed out, catching Logan just under the ribs, sending pain scouring through his scarred stomach. Hissing in agony, he crumpled to the floor.

Strichen wobbled in the middle of the cabin floor. Grunting, he wiped the blood from his face. Then, with a lunge he grabbed up Jamie McCreath by the front of his snowsuit with one hand, the holdall with the other, and ran out into the snow.

Logan pulled himself to his knees. He stayed there for a moment, panting, trying to keep his insides from falling out. At last he managed to get to his feet and lurch for the door.

He stopped at the threshold. There was no way he could leave Watson like that. He stumbled back to where she lay, spotlighted by the fallen torch. Angry red weals were blossoming on her stomach and upper legs and a pair of bite-marks bleeding freely onto the concrete floor. He could feel ribs shifting beneath the skin as he untied her hands and helped her to sit up.

'Are you OK?' he asked, removing the gag. It left angry, deep, scarlet marks around her mouth.

She spat a wad of wet rag onto the floor and coughed, causing her face to crease up in pain . She clasped at her broken ribs. 'Go!' she hissed. 'Get the bastard . . .'

Logan draped his overcoat across her naked shoulders and staggered out the cabin door into the snow.

Torches were bobbing all around the quarry's rim and the sound of dogs barking echoed against the manmade cliffs. More torches to the south were closing in, their beams making the falling snow glow as if it was on fire.

A silhouette slid to a halt, less than two hundred feet away.

Strichen.

He twisted round, fumbling with the wriggling child, as he looked for somewhere to run, his face illuminated by the weaving torchlight.

'Come on, Martin,' said Logan, limping through the snow towards him, one hand clutched over his burning innards. 'It's over. You've got nowhere to run. Your picture's everywhere, everyone knows your name. It's finished.'

The figure spun around again, face wide with fear. 'No!' he wailed, desperately seeking a way out. 'No! They'll send me to prison!'

Logan thought that was pretty bloody obvious and he said so. 'You killed children, Martin. You killed them and you abused them. You mutilated their bodies. Where did you think you were going to go? Holiday camp?'

'They'll hurt me!' Strichen was crying now, his sobs puffs of white cloud in the darkness. 'Like he did. Like Cleaver!'

'Come on, Martin, it's over . . .'

Little Jamie McCreath squirmed and kicked, screaming at the top of his lungs. Strichen dropped the holdall to get a better grip on him, but Jamie

McCreath slipped out of his hands, falling to the snow.

Logan lurched forward.

Strichen pulled a knife.

Logan staggered to a halt. The blade sparkled in the dark night, and something constricted around Logan's bowels.

'I won't go to prison!' Martin was screaming now, eyes flickering between Logan and the approaching cordon of police.

Unnoticed, Jamie McCreath crept to his feet and ran.

'NO!' Martin swung around to see the toddler charge off through the snow as fast as his little legs would go. Only Jamie wasn't running towards the police flashlights. The sound of barking dogs. He was heading straight for the quarry.

Martin leapt after him, the blade flashing in his hand, shouting, 'Come back! It's not safe!'

Jaw clenched against the pain, Logan followed, but he had a lot of ground to make up.

A hidden dip in the ground swallowed Strichen's foot and he went down, sprawling on his face in the snow. He was up again in an instant, but Jamie was well ahead, running deeper into the granite bowl of the quarry. Towards the black lake. Suddenly the little boy slithered to a halt. He'd gone as far as he could. There was nothing but cold, dark water ahead. He turned back, his face terrified.

'It's not safe!' Martin ran after him.

But Martin Strichen weighed a lot more than a small child. The ice that supported Jamie's weight wasn't up to Strichen's fifteen stone. A gunshot crack boomed out into the quarry. The larger man slid to a halt, arms spread wide, not moving. Another crack, louder this time, and he shrieked.

Twelve feet away, Jamie watched him with frightened eyes.

The ice gave way with a roar, a hole the size of a transit van opening up beneath his feet, and Martin Strichen was gone. Straight down. The black water swallowing his scream.

On the other side of the hole, Jamie crept forward and peered down into the inky darkness.

Martin didn't come up again.

39

Logan stood in the softly falling snow, watching the ambulance's lights flickering away into the distance. They'd taken Watson away: concussion, hypothermia, some nasty bruises and a couple of cracked ribs. She'd get a tetanus jab for the bites. Nothing to worry about, said the paramedic. Not when you thought about what could have happened . . .

Logan clambered into the pool car he'd liberated from the FHQ car park, turned the engine over and the heaters up full pelt. He let his head sink forward onto the steering wheel and groaned. WPC Jackie Watson and Jamie McCreath were on their way to hospital and the Bastard Simon Rennie was already there. But Martin Strichen was dead and so was his mother

He looked up just in time to see an expensive car pull in. Two long, elegantly-clad legs swung out of the driver's seat and into the snow. The pathologist was here. Logan felt his heart sink even further.

Isobel MacAlister was dressed in some sort of Bond-Girl winter outfit, all camelskin and fur. And the worst thing was, it suited her.

Working a stray hair back under her fur hat she popped the boot and pulled out her medical bag.

Isobel and Miller
Up a tree
K.I.S.S.I.N.G . . .

If he went to Professional Standards first thing tomorrow morning, the ginger-haired, sour-faced Inspector Napier would have her frogmarched out of the building quicker than you could say 'gross misconduct'. At least it would get Napier off *his* back.

Logan stared morosely at the Strichen house. She'd be ruined. No police force in the country would touch Isobel with a bargepole. Unemployable. What was it Miller had said? She just needed someone to share her day with . . . Someone to be there for her . . . Just as Logan had been there for her. Once upon a time, in the bad old days.

And now the only way Logan would ever feel the touch of her cool hands again would be when he was lying on his back in the morgue. With a tag on his toe.

'Great,' he told himself as the windscreen finally cleared. 'Good image. Very healthy . . .' Sighing, he pulled the car away from the kerb.

The city was quiet as he slid the vehicle across

North Anderson Drive. Only taxis and eighteen-wheelers were out, cutting parallel black ribbons in the snow-covered roads. The wake from their wheels – arcing sprays of slush and melt-water – were turned into golden fireworks by Logan's headlights.

The car's police radio crackled and bawled almost continuously: news was travelling fast. Strichen was dead! The kid was alive! Watson had been in her bra and pants!

Snarling, he twisted it off. Only the silence was worse than the noise. Silence encouraged the 'what-ifs' to rattle around his head.

What if he'd gone left instead of right? What if he'd turned up five minutes later? What if he hadn't frozen when Martin Strichen pulled out the knife? What if he'd got to him in time . . . Determined not to think about it, Logan clicked on the other radio, spinning the dial until the dulcet tones of a Northsound DJ boomed out of the speakers. It was a small sign that the world was still where it should be.

Tapping his fingers to the music, he felt some of the tension go out of his shoulders. Maybe things had turned out OK. Maybe Martin was better off dead. It was probably better than being banged up in Peterhead Prison, where every third inmate was another Gerald Cleaver.

But Logan knew he was going to have nightmares.

He slipped the car off the drive and cut through

the north side of town, where there was nothing on the roads but him, the snow, and globes of streetlight. The music on the radio drifted off into silence. After a pause of about ten seconds, followed by a giggling apology, came the news. They were still putting out Martin Strichen's description, still telling everyone to be on the lookout. Even though he was dead.

By the time Logan got back to Queen Street the clock was wending its merry way towards half-past ten. He abandoned the car around the back and slouched his way into Force Headquarters, wondering where everyone had got to. The building was as silent as the grave. Very appropriate.

Give it a half hour. Then he'd call the hospital and find out how WPC Watson was getting on. First he'd get some coffee. Tea. Anything, just as long as it was warm. He was halfway across main reception when someone shouted at him.

'Lazarus!'

It was Big Gary, spraying little bits of Tunnocks Tasty Caramel Wafer over the front desk. His grin was wide enough to fit a coat hanger sideways.

His companion's head snapped up, the telephone pressed to his ear. He grinned too, giving Logan an enthusiastic thumbs-up through the glass. Big Gary barged through the side door and embraced Logan in a bear hug. 'You wee darling!'

Nice though a bit of recognition was, it made

Logan's heavily-scarred stomach scream. 'Enough! Enough!'

Big Gary released him and stepped back with a paternal smile of pride. It disappeared when he saw the pain on Logan's face. 'God, I'm sorry! Are you OK?'

Logan waved him away, gritting his teeth, trying to breathe slowly, just as they'd taught him at the Pain Clinic. In and out. In and out . . .

'You're a bloody hero, Lazarus,' said Gary. 'Isn't he, Eric?'

The desk sergeant, now free of the phone, agreed that yes, Logan was indeed a hero.

'Where is everyone?' asked Logan, changing the subject as quickly as he could.

'Next door.' Meaning the pub. 'Chief Constable's buying. We've been trying to get you on the radio for ages!'

'Oh . . .' He smiled rather than tell him he'd switched the damn thing off.

'Better get over there, Lazarus, my man,' said Big Gary, once more looking as if he might engulf Logan in another rib-cracking, stomach-tearing hug.

Backing away, Logan agreed that he would.

Archibald Simpson's was noisy for a Wednesday night. Everywhere Logan looked there were police men and women drinking their own bodyweight in alcohol. The mood was festive, like New Year's Eve, except that no one was fighting.

As soon as someone recognized Logan the shout went up and rapidly turned into a football-terrace version of 'For He's A Jolly Good Fellow'. Endless hands slapped him on the back, drinks were pressed on him, people shook his hand, or kissed him, depending on how they were feeling at the time.

Finally Logan worked his way through the crowd to a relative haven of calm. He located the expansive bulk of Detective Inspector Insch and plonked himself down on an empty stool next to him. Insch looked up, a broad smile split his face and he slapped Logan on the back with a huge hand. On the other side of the table Logan saw the Edinburgh contingent. The DI and his sergeants looking rosy and pleased, calling out congratulations, but the clinical psychologist looked as if the smile he was wearing might cause him permanent damage.

'The CC said tonight's on him!' beamed Insch, pounding Logan on the back again. 'Flash your warrant card at the bar and it's free!' He leaned back and downed half a pint of dark beer in one go.

Logan looked round at the assembled horde: Grampian's finest. Tonight was going to cost the Chief Constable a fortune.

40

Thursday morning at Grampian Police Force Headquarters was a sombre affair. Largely because ninety-five percent of the staff were heavily hungover. No one knew what the final tab for last night's revelry had been, but it had to be huge. After the beers, lagers, vodka and red bulls, the whole place descended into tequila shooters. The bar should, technically, have closed three hours before the last partygoer staggered off into the snow. But who was going to do the pub for breaching their liquor licence? Three-quarters of Aberdeen's police force were in there screaming for more limes and salt.

Logan winced his way into work, having breakfasted on Irn-Bru and painkillers. He couldn't face solids. The morning had brought blue skies and a crisp wind that coated the previous night's snow with frosted ice.

There was a press conference at half-nine and Logan was dreading it. Someone had climbed inside his head and was trying to push the contents out of his ears. His eyes, normally a reasonable crystal blue, looked like something out of *The Brides of Dracula*.

When he entered the briefing room there was another rather quiet round of applause, accompanied by a lot of wincing from the participants. He waved them a greeting and slumped down into his usual seat.

DI Insch shushed everyone into silence and then launched into the briefing. Flying in the face of nature, the inspector was remarkably chirpy. Even though he'd been the one calling for flaming Drambuies at two o'clock in the morning. There was no justice.

Insch worked his way through the events of the previous night, eliciting more applause at the appropriate moment. And then it was business as usual: search teams, research, door-to-doors . . .

When everyone else had filtered out Logan was left alone with DI Insch.

'So,' said the fat man, settling back on the desk and pulling out a pristine packet of fruit pastilles. 'How you feeling?'

'Other than the brass band kicking seven shades of shite out of my brain? Not bad.'

'Good.' Insch paused and picked at the wrapping. 'Divers found Martin Strichen's body at six-fifteen this morning. Caught in the weeds under the ice.'

Logan didn't even bother trying to smile. 'Right.'

'Just so you know, you're going to get a commendation for last night.'

He couldn't meet the inspector's eyes. 'But Strichen died.'

Insch sighed. 'Aye, he did. And so did his mum. But Jamie McCreath didn't, and neither did WPC Watson. And no other kid's going to either.' He laid a bear-like hand on Logan's shoulder. 'You did good.'

The press conference was a cattle market: journalists shouting, cameras flashing, television pundits grinning . . . Logan bore it with the best grace he could.

Colin Miller was waiting for him when the conference was over, hanging around at the back of the room looking uncomfortable. He told Logan what a great job he'd done in finding the kid. How everyone was proud of him. He handed him a copy of that morning's paper with the headline: 'POLICE HERO FOILS CHILD KILLER!!! JAMIE RETURNED SAFE TO HIS MOTHER! PICTURES PAGES 3 TO 6 . . . '. He bit his lip, took a deep breath and said, 'Now what?'

Logan knew Miller wasn't talking about the case. He'd been asking himself the same question all morning. Ever since he'd walked into Force Headquarters and didn't go straight to see Inspector Napier and the rest of his Professional Standards goons. If he turned Isobel in she was ruined. But if he kept his mouth shut it could happen again: another investigation could be compromised, another chance wasted to catch a killer before he killed again. Logan sighed. There was only really one thing he could do. 'You clear everything she tells you through me. Before you print it. If you don't: I go straight to the Procurator Fiscal and she gets dragged through the mud. Criminal prosecution. Jail time. The whole thing. OK?'

Miller's face went blank, his eyes locked on Logan's. 'OK,' he said at last. 'OK. It's a deal.' He shrugged. 'From what she said, I kinda thought you'd throw the book at her if you found out. Said you'd jump at the chance to get rid of her.'

Logan's smile was as forced as his words. 'Yeah, well she was wrong. I hope you guys are going to be happy.' He couldn't look Miller in the eyes.

When the reporter had gone Logan wandered down to the reception area, staring out of the large glass doors at the gently falling snow. Thankful of the respite, he sank down on one of the uncomfortable purple seats and leaned his head back against the glass.

Jackie was going to be OK. And he was going to see her this afternoon, armed with a mound of grapes, a box of chocolates, and an invitation to dinner. Who knew, maybe this would be the start of something good?

Smiling, he stretched in his seat, yawning happily, as a heavy-set man pushed through the front doors, brushing the snow off his coat. The man was in his mid-fifties, with a carefully-sculpted beard which was now more salt than pepper. He marched purposefully towards the reception desk. 'Hello,' he said, twitching as if he had fleas. 'I need to speak to the detective with the biblical name.'

The desk sergeant pointed at Logan. 'Biblical hero, right over there.'

The man walked resolutely across the linoleum floor, his step only slightly loosened by however many whiskies he'd had to get his courage up this far. 'Are you the Biblical Detective?' he asked, his voice reedy and a little slurred.

Against his better judgment, Logan admitted that he was.

The man stood up straight as a stair rod, chest out, chin in the air. 'I killed her,' he said, the words coming out as if they were fired from a machinegun. 'I killed her and I'm here to take the consequences . . .'

Logan rubbed a hand over his forehead. The last thing he needed was another case to worry about. 'Who?' he said, trying to keep the impatience out of his voice. And failing.

'The girl. The one they found in the steading . . .' His voice cracked and for the first time Logan saw that his eyes were cherry-red, his cheeks and nose scarlet from crying. 'I'd been drinking.' He shivered, locked in the past. 'I didn't see her . . . I thought . . . all that time . . . When you arrested that man, I thought it would all go away. But he was killed, wasn't he? He was killed because of me . . .' He wiped the back of an arm over his eyes and dissolved into tears.

So this was the man who'd killed Lorna Henderson. The man Bernard Duncan Philips had died for. The man Nurse Henderson had killed for.

Sighing, Logan pulled himself out of his seat. Another case solved. Another life ruined.

LOGAN MCRAE RETURNS IN

Dying Light

due for publication in May 2006

1

They will scream … they will burn … and they will die …

He stood in the shadows, on the opposite side of the dark street, watching as they entered the boarded-up building: scruffy wee shites in their tatty jeans and hooded tops. Three men and two women, nearly identical with their long hair, pierced ears, pierced noses and pierced God knew what else. Everything about them screamed 'Kill Me!'

He smiled. They would be screaming soon enough.

The squat was halfway down a terrace of abandoned two-storey buildings – dirty granite walls barely lit by the dull streetlights, windows covered with thick plywood. Except for one on the upper floor, where a thin, sick-looking light oozed out through dirty glass. The street was deserted, abandoned, condemned like its inhabitants, not a soul to be seen. No one about to watch him work.

Half past eleven and the music got even louder; a pounding rhythm that would easily cover any noise he made. He worked his way round the doorframe, twisting the screwdriver in time with the beat, then stepped back to admire his handiwork – six-inch galvanised woodscrews all the way round the door, holding it solid against the frame, making sure it stayed irrevocably shut. A grin split his face. This would be good. This would be the best one yet.

He slipped the screwdriver back into his pocket, pausing for a moment to stroke the cold, hard shaft. He was hard too, the front of his trousers bulging with barely concealed joy. He always loved this bit, just before the fire started, when everything was in place, when there was no way for them to escape. When death was on its way.

Quietly he pulled three glass bottles and a green plastic petrol can from the holdall at his feet, leaving all the things he'd stolen from the scruffy shites' hiding place nestling at the bottom of the bag. He spent a happy minute unscrewing the bottle caps, filling them with petrol and popping the torn rag fuses in place. Then it was back to the screwed-shut front door. Lever open the letter box. Empty the petrol can through the slot, listening to the liquid splashing on the bare, wooden floorboards, just audible under the pounding music. A trickle seeped out under the door, dribbling down the front step to form a little pool of hydrocarbons. Perfection.

He closed his eyes, said a little prayer, and dropped a lit match into the puddle at his feet. *Whooooomp*. Blue flame fringed with yellow raced under the door, into the house. Pause, two, three, four: just long enough for the blaze to get going. Throw a half brick in through the upstairs window, shattering the glass, letting the throbbing music out. Startled swearing from inside. And then the first petrol bomb went in. It hit the floor and exploded, showering the room with burning fuel. The swearing became screaming. He grinned and hurled the remaining bottles into the blaze.

Then it was back to the other side of the road, to lurk in the shadows and watch them burn. Biting his lip, he pulled his erection free. If he was quick he could come and go before anyone arrived.

He needn't have hurried. It was fifteen minutes before anyone raised the alarm and another twelve before the fire brigade turned up. By then everyone was dead.

Blind to the Bones

Stephen Booth

Withens is a small village in the Peak District, but it's no idyll. Dark and dour, it's troubled by theft and vandalism, mostly generated by local family-from-hell, the Oxleys. Now it is the main focus of a murder investigation – a young man's body has been found on the desolate moors nearby, and the man is an Oxley.

DC Ben Cooper is trying to crack the case and to do that he must crack this clannish family. On top of that, his difficult boss, Detective Diane Fry, is also in Withens on business – one Emma Renshaw, a student who vanished two years ago. Some ominous new evidence relating to Emma has turned up, but her parents are convinced she is still alive and act accordingly – and very strangely.

So, with one murder and one as yet unsolved disappearance, Withens's reputation for grimness is growing. And it looks like things are only going to get darker …

'Another very fine book, masterfully plotted'

Daily Telegraph

'Excellent'

Country Life

'A darkly terrifying tale that carries a chill of forbidden things into the cosiest living room'   *Northern Echo*

The Blind Man of Seville

Robert Wilson

The man is bound, gagged and dead in front of his television. The terrible self-inflicted wounds tell of his violent struggle to avoid some unseen horror. On the screen? In his head? What could make a man do that to himself?

It's Easter week in Seville, a time of passion and processions. But detective Javier Falcón is not celebrating. Appalled by the victim's staring eyes he is inexorably drawn into this disturbing, mystifying case. And when the investigation into the dead man's life sends Javier trawling though his own past and into the shocking journals of his late father, a famous artist, his unreliable memory begins to churn. Then there are more killings and Falcón finds himself pushed to the edge of a terrifying truth . . .

'Gripping and exhilarating . . . A potent blend of beauty and terror'   HARLAN COBEN

'An ingenious and compelling thriller'   *Daily Telegraph*

0-00-711781-7